WHY MUMMY DRINKS ON HOLIDAY

Why Mummy Drinks
Why Mummy Swears
Why Mummy Doesn't Give a ****
Why Mummy's Sloshed
The Saturday Night Sauvignon Sisterhood
Why Mummy Drinks at Christmas

WHY MUMMY DRINKS ON HOLIDAY

Gill Sims

HarperCollins*Publishers*

HarperCollins*Publishers*
1 London Bridge Street
London SE1 9GF

www.harpercollins.co.uk

HarperCollins*Publishers*
Macken House, 39/40 Mayor Street Upper
Dublin 1, D01 C9W8, Ireland

First published by HarperCollins*Publishers* 2024

1 3 5 7 9 10 8 6 4 2

A catalogue record of this book is
available from the British Library

HB ISBN: 978-0-00-859198-4
PB ISBN 978-0-00-861251-1

Printed and bound in the UK using 100%
renewable electricity at CPI Group (UK) Ltd

MIX
Paper | Supporting
responsible forestry
FSC™ C007454

This book contains FSC™ certified paper and other controlled
sources to ensure responsible forest management.

For more information visit: www.harpercollins.co.uk/green

To Katie.
You will always be my best friend.

Thursday 21 July

'Muuuuuum! MUUUUUM! MUMMUMUMUMUMUMUMUM! MUUUUUUUM!'

I was in the attic rooting around for Summer Essentials, such as adorable wicker picnic hampers containing such redundant items as cutlery and plates that my children would inevitably reject, and slightly less Essential items like sunhats, shorts and the sandals that I'd so hopefully put away last year in the futile hope that they might fit the children again this year. My pleasant rummagings were disrupted by increasingly hysterical screams from Jane, my ten-year-old. Bitter experience has taught me that if Jane is capable of screaming 'MUM' over and over again then nothing very terrible has happened and I need not dash too quickly to respond. The screaming was fairly relentless, though, so I put down my grandfather's fly-fishing rod that I'd had a glorious Vision of the children delightfully romping in a salmon river with (despite the fact we have no salmon rivers nearby, and although I know almost nothing about fishing, I'm fairly sure 'romping' is frowned upon), and shuffled across to the top of the ladder leading downstairs to respond.

'WHAT?' I bellowed through the aperture, as Jane's howls of 'MUUUUUUM' showed no signs of stopping.

'Peter called me a poo head and said I love Freddie Dawkins and Freddie Dawkins is a speccy ginger four eyes TWAT and I am NOT a poo head!' shrieked Jane from two floors below me.

I sighed.

'Jane, we've talked about this. You are not to call people speccy four eyes, that's very unkind, Freddie can't help his glasses. And you are not to call people twats, that's very bad language. And you are not to call people ginger as an insult, that's … gingerist?' I finished rather feebly. I rallied and yelled again. 'And Peter, don't call your sister a poo head, and don't wind her up.'

'He smells of old broccoli, though,' Jane bellowed. 'Am I even allowed to say that?'

'Who? Freddie or Peter?'

'Freddie. Peter just smells of POOOOOO!'

'I DO NOT!' came a robust and indignant shout from Peter, followed by a dull thud that I assumed was some kind of physical violence being inflicted by one of my children upon the other. There was a brief silence. Maybe they'd even made up and were playing nicely? No, what a stupid idea. What ten-year-old girl plays nicely with her eight-year-old brother, outside the fever-ish imaginations of Mumsnet, whose contributors like to claim that along with making a chicken last for a whole week's worth of hearty meals, their children never have a cross word and enjoy nothing more than eating a massive salad while playing wholesome boardgames together. Sure enough, the screams soon began again, accompanied by more accusations shouted up the stairs about 'looking at me', 'not fair', 'SHE STARTED IT' and, in a new low for Jane, 'JANE SAYS I'M ADOPTED AND YOU'RE GOING TO SEND ME BACK BUT I'M NOT, AM I MUMMY?!'

'Jane,' I yelled sternly in my best authoritative parenting voice. 'That's not a kind thing to say to your brother. No, Peter, of course you're not adopted, not that there's anything wrong with that anyway, and if you were we'd love you just the same and would never send you back,' and Oh, CHRIST, why is parenting so complicated nowadays?

I do not, of course, condone being physically violent to children, but given the way they batter the everlasting fuck out of each other, seemingly with no dire consequences, would it have been so terrible to pursue a more Victorian method of parenting where I demanded they were seen and not heard and rapped them over the knuckles if they questioned my authority? I mean, probably, yes, that's why people don't do that anymore, but sometimes I did have a pang of envy for the sort of Victorian mothers who lived in houses large enough to have a separate wing for the children and only have the nanny bring them for a viewing once a week or so. I even sometimes longed for a slightly more chavvy version of parenting where one did not feel racked with guilt for plugging little Peroni and Kopparberg into the electronic babysitter. Just imagine the joy of feeding them beige food without attempting to make a middle-class joke about it being 'freezer tapas' and then attempting to force-feed them Fairtrade dried mango from the Oxfam shop to offset the chicken nuggets and the guilt?

And despite my best efforts to counter my poor parenting with some pathetically middle-class crafts and quinoa, I then feel so judged for it by society every time I venture out of the house, and by Mumsnet every time I venture onto the internet. And, of course, there's a lot of judging by the perfect Yummy Mummies in the school playground when the children make some helpfully loud announcement about 'Can we just watch *SpongeBob* for six hours again tonight, Mummy?' in front of them (not that I have ever actually let my little cherubs watch six hours of *SpongeBob*, obviously. Their grasp of time is as hazy as their desire to embarrass me is strong).

Most of all, though, I feel judged by myself, like I'm failing the children by not providing some sort of magical *Mary Poppins/ Sound of Music* (without the Nazis, of course) and *Famous Five*-style childhood for them. Though on reflection, Enid Blyton parents left a great deal to be desired in the safeguarding stakes, with their dubious habit of simply turning primary-school-age children loose for the holidays with nothing more than their bicycles, a packet of sandwiches and a somewhat class-based and superior sense of social justice that led them to suspect all commoners and foreigners to be in the grip of criminal habits. Lucky bastards, those parents were. I bet no one ever looked at Dick and Julian tying up a kidnapper in a dungeon and asked their mama and papa if they had considered trying 'gentle parenting'.

Oh dear, the children were still fighting.

'I HATE him, though,' Jane was bellowing up the stairs, as I wondered who would crack first over this conversation shouted between attic and ground floor, and whether I'd descend or the children would ascend (I knew the answer really, of course).

'Mum, why can't we send him to boarding school?'

'Too expensive,' I snapped without thinking. 'And anyway, he'd still come home for the holidays.'

'How do you KNOW it's too expensive, though?' Jane demanded. 'Have you checked?'

'Yes.'

'Why are you checking how much boarding school is?' Peter chuntered in outrage. 'Why do I have to go to boarding school? Why can't SHE go?'

'I checked for both of you,' I groaned, in a last-ditch attempt to keep the peace. I decided it was probably best not to tell them I'd discovered how extortionate boarding school was when I'd been having a Very Bad Day with them as toddlers and had googled – in hope, more than anything – to see if there were such things as boarding nursery schools (there weren't), as I could already see how this conversation was going to sound when they related it to their father over dinner. I could almost hear Simon saying, 'But why on earth would you say such a thing to them, Ellen?' as I attempted to explain that sometimes, when you spend a lot of time with small children, things just get *said* without thinking. Like the time Peter spent a year with a phobia of getting in the car, because while at the end of my tether I'd shouted that if he kept undoing his allegedly child-proof seat buckle and I had to brake suddenly, he'd *fly through the window and I'd run him over.*

Clearly that wasn't a fine moment for me, but in my defence, after that, although I had to wrestle him into the car every time, as he screamed he didn't want to die – DON'T KILL ME, MUMMY – and the neighbours looked on aghast, he didn't undo his seat buckle anymore.

I gave in, obviously, and clambered down the ladder to go and start peace negotiations between my children using the medium of Fab ice lollies and threats to change the Wi-Fi password and keep it to myself.

Blissful quiet restored, I returned to the attic to continue looking for fishing nets, and buckets and spades, and other marvellously wholesome things to facilitate japes and frolics, ready for the Best Summer Ever.

I am very excited about this summer. I just *know* it is going to be the best summer ever for Hannah and me, because for the first time in years, in fact, since we left school, we are going to have time to spend the holiday together. After much deliberation and discussion with my beloved husband Simon, we have decided that I should take a two-month sabbatical instead of the usual mad juggle of summer clubs and childminders and sports camps to cover two months' worth of childcare, resulting in me ending the summer burnt out, frazzled and virtually sobbing at the school gate as I thrust my precious moppets on the mercy of full-time education for another blissful term.

Simon did try to claim the summer holidays were difficult for 'both of us', but I shirtily pointed out that the entire burden of arranging the children to be looked after for the summer – not to mention most of the actual dropping off/picking up and taking time off – fell on *me*. He still tried to insist that his great Busy and Importantness was too much to allow him to actually be of any use to me and his children. That is, apart from the two weeks he nobly takes off to pack a pair of swimming trunks and ask me why I'm not ready, as I pack up everything the children could possibly need on holiday from thermal underwear to treatments for heat-stroke, and at the last minute fling some flip-flops, a too-small swimming costume and a crumpled dress in a case for me, which is *not* what I think the magazines mean by 'holiday capsule ward-robe'.

We are lucky enough to be able to afford this extraordinary luxury of me taking two months off work unpaid because last year I was very clever indeed and came up with a game app called *Why*

Mummy Drinks, in which you had to negotiate all sorts of obstacles in a parent's day, like the lurking Yummy Mummies, the festering lunchboxes at the bottom of school bags coming to life and the avalanches of letters from the school about nothing at all actually. If you missed anything you'd have to start all over again, but your reward for completing each level was an increasingly large glass of virtual wine.

Curiously, this game had proved enormously popular – including with the terrifyingly perfect mothers at my own little darlings' school – and enough people had bought it to put Simon and me on a fairly sound financial footing for the first time ever in our marriage, enabling us to pay off our mortgage, which frankly wasn't something I'd ever envisaged happening. Sadly, I didn't realise that in the complex ecosystem of app-based games, today's *Angry Birds* is tomorrow's roadkill, and despite the unbelievable and almost overnight success of my game, a few short, if heady months later it had been replaced by the new hip 'n' cool must-have game, and people simply stopped buying it.

However, my game had provided more financial security than I could ever have dreamed of in the overdrawn months and years of hiding from the credit card bills that preceded it, and I'd be eternally grateful for it, along with the knowledge that whatever else happened we had a home and that many people would never find themselves in this position. I tried repeatedly to remind myself how very, very lucky I was to be here and that I shouldn't feel bitter that despite the success of my game, I had to keep working.

This was because the rest of the delicious little nest egg *Why Mummy Drinks* had provided had been spent on buying a house for my batshit-crazy sister-in-law Louisa and her many, many children after she abandoned her vile husband – we think he was her husband anyway, they were both vague on the legalities of their 'union'. Louisa, being nothing if not feckless, had appeared on our doorstep with six kids and no plan as to how to support them and where they were to live. Then someone came up with the bright idea that she could move into the dilapidated bungalow next door to her parents, if only the money could be found to buy it, and in theory she could then rent it back from us at an affordable rate, a theory that somehow never quite materialised in practice.

In vain did Simon point out what a Good Thing I had done. Also in vain did he point out that I'd wished to spend said nest egg on a holiday home in Wells-next-the-Sea, even though I'd never actually been there and just liked the name. In fact, he suggested, wouldn't buying Louisa a house to give her some security or buying us a house in Wells-next-the-Sea so I could live out some sort of 1930s coastal-murder-solving fantasy just have left me in exactly the same position re the whole working-for-a-living thing? I try to console myself with the thought that perhaps one day Louisa will take some responsibility for herself, get a job and find a house of her own. I'm nothing if not an eternal optimist. I think I'd probably be less bitter about the whole thing if Louisa was at least a little bit grateful for everything that has been done for her.

I suspect that, feckless though Louisa is, I also have some envy for her sheer *uselessness*, that she just assumes someone will rescue her, or bail her out, and thus there is no need for her to sully her ideals by 'working for The Man'. Although deep down I know I could never stand living with that level of insecurity, I must confess that I don't really like working, and I certainly don't work for the love of it, or for the 'camaraderie' or because I 'need something to do'. I'm fairly sure that I could very happily do nothing at all, all day long, should the opportunity ever arise.

I'm always astounded when I see people who win about eleventy fucking billion pounds on the lottery and who insist they'll continue to work at their back-breaking, minimum-wage job, because they 'need something to do'. I wonder how many of them *actually* do that once the cameras have stopped rolling. No, I work for the money, plain and simple. That sounds dreadful, of course, but it's true. I like having *my own* money. We agreed when both the children were born that I'd take their first year off to be at home with them. And one of the worst, most terrifying parts of that year, was not having *my own* money. I had my maternity pay – pittance as it was – for part of the time, of course. And Simon was always very good about the money, insisting his salary was *our* money, not *his* money, which was perfectly true, and it all went into the joint account, so it wasn't like I ever had to ask him for money, like some bastards you hear of.

But I felt trapped. I love that knowledge that I've got something of my own, that I've earned something, that I can pay for things with money that's mine. And I know lots of people don't feel like that at all, and I know bringing up children is very much valid 'work', but call me shallow, I like *my own* money. So until I manage to think up some other fabulous game or I win squillions on the lottery or turn out to have a secret fairy godmother, I've simply got to keep working. I once tried explaining this to Simon, but it didn't go very well. Apparently saying things like 'It's not that I *want* to leave you, I just want to know I *could* leave you if I *did* want to …' wasn't the mark of a good and loving wife.

Despite all that, after the small success of *Why Mummy Drinks*, I did feel like I could take Simon up on his suggestion and take the summer holidays off, and we'd manage on his salary for a couple of months, because after all, I'd paid for the bloody house, hadn't I? And I couldn't deny that it would also make life a lot easier, not least because Simon possesses an extraordinary knack of every Very Important Project at work suddenly coming to fruition over the weeks of the summer holidays, meaning that apart from the fortnight I forced him to take off for us to go away, it was simply *impossible* for him to take any more time off to help with the childcare. I had my suspicions about the truth of this, but despite being fairly sure he only came up with this idea to avoid having to spend the summer with the children himself, I was thrilled at the thought that I'd finally have the japes-and-frolics-filled summer of my dreams I had envisaged when Jane was born.

These japes and frolics had never materialised in previous years, as until *Why Mummy Drinks* had eased our financial situation, continuing to earn my living over the holidays had taken priority, even if my salary mainly went on holiday clubs and childminders, due the fact that as we weren't living in an Enid Blyton novel, I couldn't simply bid the children farewell and leave them on an island deserted but for desperate thieves, smugglers and kidnappers for the entire break. I'd been initially unsure we could really afford this even now, but as Simon pointed out, by the time you took off childcare costs, it didn't really make an enormous amount of difference.

And, if I was perfectly honest, the thought of two months without the crushing, misery-making drudgery of my tedious and dull IT job, a job that helped to pay the bills but at the cost of sucking my very soul out of me, was bliss. I knew I was lucky to have a job at all, let alone one that was reasonably flexible about childcare, and let me work from home for a couple of days a week, but despite the money and the all-important financial independence it brought me, I hated my colleagues, I hated my boss – and I was bored. So terribly, terribly bored.

It had been wonderful to have the brief, creative outlet of the game, of using my brain to do something other than prop up the ailing IT systems of the Cunningham United Nautical Trust and explain once again to Lisa from Accounts how to use a bastarding spreadsheet. I hadn't even finished up for the summer before I was dreading going back, and secretly I wondered if I couldn't use all this glorious time, these two whole empty months stretching ahead of me, to find something else to do. To reinvent myself, to actually have time to create another game or to write a book (after all, if people could write a novel in a month in the bizarrely named NaNoWriMo – who came up with *that* catchy acronym? – then surely I could knock something out with eight weeks on my hands). Or perhaps I could take up pottery or discover some other hitherto hidden but nonetheless virtuoso talent, then I'd never have to darken the dated 1970s doors of the Cunningham United Nautical Trust again, nor tread those distressingly sticky beige carpets on the way to my Cubicle of Doom, my heart sinking a little further with each slight tug to release my shoe.

To add to the Summer Joy, instead of our usual summer holiday staying with Simon's parents, who lived in France, Sylvia and Michael had announced that although they were flying to the States, hiring an RV and driving down Route 66 for the summer, they'd still love us to come and use the house. Simon had fretted that they were having some kind of post-midlife crisis, but I didn't give two hoots. The thought of a couple of happy weeks in France, in Sylvia and Michael's frankly rather gorgeous not-quite-a-chateau-but-nearly house (Sylvia's mouth had gone very cat's bummy when she was merrily trilling to someone that it 'wasn't really *quite* big enough to call a chateau, darling', and I'd helpfully suggested that maybe it was more of a chatette), but without the in-laws to contend with, was wonderful.

I couldn't wait for those long, blissful hours by the pool with chilled white wine and leisurely barbecues, instead of Sylvia hanging on Simon's every word and sighing to me regularly about how tired he looked and criticising my parenting (Simon's parenting was obviously above reproach. The only comments to be made about that were to simultaneously coo over what a good father he was while looking shocked if he attempted to lift a finger with the children and ordering me to do it instead as 'Simon needed a break'.)

Oh, it was going to be perfect.

And quite apart from all that, there were adventures to be had closer to home with Jane and Peter. My head was filled with visions of wicker picnic hampers, me in a white dress and a shady hat reclining elegantly on some sort of faded ancient silk carpet, handing out slices of homemade cake to my cherubs and dispensing cloudy lemonade from stone bottles into quirky vintage glass goblets for us (with perhaps a small nip of gin in mine), before we picked gooseberries, or ran free as the wind, our hair blowing Instagrammably behind us along a golden, sun-drenched beach. We'd bicycle home on delightful old-fashioned bikes, such as one would definitely use to foil horrid gangs of lower-class criminals, wild flowers in their baskets, my trusty terrier Judgy Dog, who would have behaved beautifully all day and not run away or killed any ducks or tried to hump anything, running alongside, or perhaps even sitting in the basket of my bicycle with the wild flowers without biting me when I tried to put him in it, and as my cherubs tumbled into their beds, cheeks all rosy with the fresh air and plump with good country milk, they would laugh merrily and say, 'Oh Mamma! This is the best summer ever. What happy, happy memories we're making, and how we shall treasure them forever.'

And then the icing on the (homemade, wholesome, probably with cherries in it) cake happened. My very best friend Hannah announced she was changing jobs and had carefully timed her leaving strategy so that her gardening leave coincided with the holidays, so that she too didn't have to pay a fortune in childcare for her kids, Emily and Lucas, over the summer. So, there it was – everything had fallen into place for the most perfect summer ever, with Hannah and me both not working, and our darling children available for adventures and cavorting gloriously through cornfields and romping in sun-dappled glades. The only thing that could have made it even more perfect was our dear friend Sam getting the summer off as well to join us, but that was really too much to hope for, and in a way I was glad it was just going to be Hannah and me (and the children, of course). We'd been friends for so long, and who knew when we'd ever have a chance to spend so much time together again? Sam's wonderful, and all the children adored each other, but despite Hannah and me liking him a lot, he's very much a New Friend, and this was going to be *our* summer. The young things could have their Hot Girl Summers – this was going to be our Best and Oldest Friends Summer.

Even more importantly, though, it would be the Summer of Happy Memories, because surely that's what summer holidays are for. All right, maybe originally they were so the children could be put to work in the fields to glean the barley or whatever the fuck it is you do in fields, but given that child labour is now so very frowned upon, the holidays are for creating those magical moments that will warm the cockles of our hearts when we're old and grey, and look back and remember those golden sun-drenched days, filled with laughter. As the most annoying meme in the world never fails to remind us each year, we only have #18PreciousSummers with our children, and every summer I'm racked with guilt that I'm working and the children are sitting in summer clubs being taught to play basketball by a bored spotty youth who did not see this as the end goal for his Sports Science degree, and making random craft objects out of unsustainable plastic products. And then, in previous summers, I've felt so exhausted with juggling so many things – and under so much pressure to ensure that what little time I did have with the children was perfect – that I ended up snapping with frustration when things don't go according to plan.

Surely, though, I only needed one summer to make those perfect memories, and that was what I was determined to do. Happy memories for all of us – for Hannah and me, for the children and me, and maybe even for Simon and me. Slow, lazy mornings, packing delicious picnics of homemade cakes and thickly stuffed sandwiches (on homemade bread? Too far? Oooh, maybe we'd make sourdough – the children and I could make a starter, and we'd keep it alive and it would be science *and* Happy Memories, and maybe one day they'd make sourdough in the summer holidays with their own children from the very starter we made all those years ago, in that happy summer they remembered so well). There would be no rushing about, no shouting, no stress. Just the enjoyment of each other's company.

Before any of that could happen, though, I first needed to find all the necessary accoutrements, such as the shady hat I bought three years ago and never used, and the little fishing nets I picked up two years back in a quaint little Cornish village for the children to explore rock pools with, and which they used to try to poke each other's eyes out, hence the nets' relegation to the attic. But they're older now, and I was sure they'd do no such thing this year. Not in the Summer of Happy Memories.

Friday 22 July

Hannah and I decided the Summer Fun really should start as we meant to go on, and so, despite protestations about treating children cruelly and many wails of 'unfairness', for our first delightful adventure we'd hit upon the excellent plan of a trip to a forest park.

'Just think,' I enthused to Hannah as we sweated our tits off packing the cars, 'so much potential for smugglers.'

'Smugglers live in caves, not forests,' Hannah objected, and I was forced to concede this point and admit that maybe I'd meant bandits or outlaws.

'I don't think that's a very good idea either,' said Hannah doubtfully. 'Bandits and outlaws don't sound very much fun. Besides, I'm fairly sure there aren't any in Massingdon Woods, as they're owned by the National Trust. The Trust frowns upon bandits and outlaws.'

I airily pooh-poohed Hannah's doubts and pointed out that in a National Trust forest one would only encounter very middle-class and tasteful bandits and outlaws.

'Sort of like *The Children of the New Forest*,' I said vaguely.

'If we encounter the descendants of children who've been living feral in the woods since the Civil War, we'll be beyond the help of the National Trust,' said Hannah in alarm.

'The Children of the New Forest were not *feral*,' I countered. 'Jane, tell Hannah about the Children of the New Forest.'

'The what?' Jane looked at me blankly.

'Darling, you remember, you read it with Mummy. That very good book about the children orphaned in the English Civil War who go and live a noble and simple life in the woods.'

'I don't remember,' Jane insisted. 'You made me read so many boring books with you, Mum, and they were always about miserable orphaned children somewhere, who you always said were not miserable, but leading noble and simple lives. Often the children are crippled as well as noble and simple and orphaned. I've probably got a complex from that, you know.'

'You've got no soul,' I grumbled. 'I take it by the crippled child you mean the noble Katy Carr in *What Katy Did*?'

'I dunno,' said Jane. 'Like I said, there were so many. Like that one where the boy is totally ableist and takes the disabled girl's wheelchair, and she magically learns to walk again and everyone said he'd done a good thing by taking her wheelchair. That's a very problematic book, Mother, you probably shouldn't have exposed me to it at such a young age.'

'That's *Heidi* you're talking about,' I spluttered in outrage. 'It's a *classic*!'

'Everything's a classic according to you,' Jane snorted. 'Anyway, why do we have to come with you today? Why can't me and Emily go to the cinema by ourselves? We're definitely old enough. You can just pick us up afterwards, but don't talk to us, yeah?'

'If they're going to the cinema, me an' Lucas want to go to Laser Quest,' chimed in Peter, never one to miss a trick. 'It's not fair if we've to go to the stupid woods when they get to go to the cinema, and it's *too hot*!'

'It's not too hot,' I insisted. 'And anyway, it would be even hotter inside Laser Quest. We're all going to go out and have a lovely day. Together. Having japes and frolics.'

'I hate japes and frolics,' muttered Peter.

'Ellen, what is all this?' Hannah demanded, peering into my car. 'Why are we taking fishing nets? And butterfly nets? What are they for?'

'Well, we might find a pond for the children to look for interesting things. Or a sunny meadow for them to run free chasing butterflies.' I explained.

'I don't think you're allowed to catch butterflies. Or fish things out of ponds on National Trust properties. They're all endangered newts and things, aren't they? And do we really need the wicker picnic hampers?'

'Yes.'

'But hampers plural, Ellen? Why do you have so many?'

'Because TKMaxx keeps selling different sizes and configurations for ludicrously cheap prices, and every time I see one I realise a new and important scenario that I need it for,' I huffed. 'So yes, I do need them all, actually. Because I'm trying to make HAPPY MEMORIES!'

'All of them? Today? Peter's right, it's bloody hot and we're going to have to carry all this. Can't you make happy memories without them?'

'No.'

'All four of your floral picnic blankets too, though? I'm already on the verge of heatstroke just loading all this up, Ellen. It's 25 degrees and it's only 10 a.m.'

'Climate change isn't an excuse to let standards slip,' I insisted. 'All the more reason to make Happy Memories while we can.'

Hannah muttered something under her breath that sounded suspiciously like 'Happy memories, MY ARSE.'

Eventually, after some argument between Hannah and me about an acceptable number of picnic hampers and rugs, and considerable argument between us and our precious moppets about who went in which car, we set off, Hannah with the girls in hers, and me, drawing the short straw with Farticus One and Two in the back, who quickly turned my car into an even more fetid cesspit than usual.

'There,' I said with satisfaction as we drew up in the car park. 'Look at all that glorious nature.'

'What if we get sunstroke? Can't we just go home and play *GTA*?' asked Peter.

'Look, a squirrel,' I cried, declining to even answer the question after spending three hours last night listening to Peter's lengthy explanations about why, despite the 18+ certificate, he should be allowed a go of Simon's *GTA*, because *everyone else, literally everyone else, in his class played it.*

Obviously, I'd refused to give in and was frankly considering shoving the whole bloody PlayStation up Simon's arse, as it was entirely his fault for buying the damn game in the first place. I'd also spent the whole journey listening to emotive arguments about how they should have been allowed to bring their Nintendos, and why did Judgy get to sit in the front, so I wasn't really in the frame of mind for another of Peter's 'debates'. Judgy, meanwhile, was just giving me reproachful stares. I couldn't blame him. The broccoli I'd insisted Peter ate last night seemed not to have agreed with him, and if I was finding it that pungent, God knows what it was doing to Judgy's sensitive canine nose.

I unloaded the boys as Hannah pulled in behind me and got out the car.

'How were they?' I asked.

'No idea,' said Hannah. 'I just turned up the radio and let them get on with it.'

We set off, all of us laden with various bags and cool boxes and rugs and the bastarding butterfly nets, which I'd refused to leave behind on point of principle.

'Isn't this fun!' I exclaimed. 'Look, a stream. Maybe we'll find some frog spawn, and you can fish it out with your nets and put it in a jam jar to take home.'

'Not in July,' said Jane crushingly.

'Oh yes. Well, we could follow it to its source. Maybe there'll be treasure.'

'Hot,' groaned Peter. 'It's so hot. Can I have a Coke?'

'WILL YOU JUST HAVE SOME SOUL AND MAKE SOME HAPPY MEMORIES!' I shouted.

'How can we make happy memories when we've only been here five minutes and you're SHOUTING AT US about HAPPY MEMORIES!' yelled Jane crossly.

'Because you're not even trying,' I snapped. 'How can you make happy memories if you don't try to make happy memories?'

'AARRRRRGH!' howled Peter, tripping over a butterfly net and falling some distance down a slope, as I flung hampers and rugs aside to hurtle after him.

'I think I've broken my leg,' Peter groaned bravely as I reached him near the bottom. 'Am I going to die, Mummy?'

'You're fine,' I said after a brief inspection, 'nothing's broken. Get up.'

Peter sat up, looking rather disappointed, as a trip to A&E was in his opinion always the highlight of a day out, but he immediately collapsed again, screaming hysterically.

'What now?' I said in exasperation.

It turned out the issue was BLOOD. Peter isn't good with blood, and on sitting up he'd spied a tiny cut on his knee oozing a very small amount of blood, so he was now doing a passable impression of a rather OTT Lady Macbeth. Fortunately, he was magically cured with a plaster and a biscuit, but of course that meant that everyone else had to have a biscuit, and then Lucas suggested that we could save ourselves a lot of effort if we just ate the picnic *now*, so we didn't have to carry it.

'No,' I said firmly. 'I can still *see* the car park. We're not having a picnic when we're less than a hundred yards from the car park. And what if we get lost in the woods and we've no supplies because we've eaten them all already? We'll look pretty silly then, won't we?'

'*You'll* look pretty silly,' muttered Jane. '*You're* the adult that *made* us come here and *you're* the one who is responsible for us, so if we get lost and we've no food and are found starving and turning into cannibals, actually it will be *your* fault for getting us lost.'

'*If* we got lost, which we aren't going to do, we wouldn't starve anyway,' I insisted. 'We'd live off the land, like the Children of the New Forest.'

'How?' asked Peter.

'What would we eat?' asked Lucas.

'Berries,' I said.

'We can't just live on berries,' Lucas pointed out.

'Rabbits!' I invented wildly. 'I'm sure they eat rabbits in *The Children of the New Forest*.'

'How would we catch them?'

That stumped me. I was fairly sure Edward just shot the rabbits in the New Forest, but obviously we were not fiendish gun-toting Americans and so we'd not come to the woods all tooled up. I wondered if we could fashion some sort of snare from a Laura Ashley floral picnic blanket? Lure the bunnikins into a hamper and then ... But oh! I wasn't sure I could bring myself to dispatch a bunny, even to bring succour to my starvlings. *Peter Rabbit* had made a profound impact on me at a formative age and I'd never been able to eat rabbit since. My father had once ordered it in a restaurant when I was about Jane's age and I'd spent the whole meal weeping piteously about the poor thing, so a collective decision had been made by the family that perhaps rabbit was best off the menu in front of me. When a similar thing happened with poor dear Jemina Puddleduck, my parents started to lose sympathy with me and curse the very name of Beatrix Potter.

As I pondered this open-mouthed, before five expectant faces (thanks Hannah, I thought, thanks for helping me out), my trusty hound Judgy appeared out of the undergrowth, having taken off for some japes and frolics of his own, as soon as I'd let him off the lead. I always greet Judgy with relief, as it's generally touch and go whether he'll return at all, and if he does deign to rejoin us there's always the very real risk that it will be after he has rolled in something unspeakable or done something unmentionable to some highly strung pedigree princess dog.

'Ha!' I said triumphantly. 'Judgy would catch rabbits for us.'

Six faces now looked at me in astonishment, none more astonished than Judgy's at the thought of him doing anything so altruistic as to provide us with *his* rabbits, were we starving in the woods. Judgy has many fine attributes, but compassion isn't one of them. He'd doubtless happily feast like a king upon the rabbits until we all starved to death, then eat us too.

'Oh, come on,' I said crossly. 'Let's go on a bit further and find a nice spot for lunch. Or at least somewhere where we can't see the car park.'

On we trudged for another mile or so, by which point I was very much wishing I'd listened to Hannah's wise words about 'Did I really need all this crap?' My Lovely Things were proving very heavy, and it was indeed *very* hot. I could tell it was very hot by the unpleasant way I could feel the sweat trickling down my cleavage, but never fear, in the unlikely event of me failing to notice the heat, my children were on hand to tell me every thirty seconds that it was VERY HOT!

I was starting to think to myself that perhaps it wasn't strictly necessary to decorate the perfect picnic site – when I found it – with bunting, and maybe I could live without rendering the forest Instagram-ready if the trade-off was an end to my sweat-chafed tits and chiropractor-ready back. But then we turned a corner, and there before us appeared a glorious, sparkling waterfall. We all stopped in wonder and stared at the water thundering down, silver and blue, with rainbows darting off on either side in the sunshine.

'Oh …,' I said.

'This is wonderful, Ellen,' said Hannah in admiration.

'OMG, if you would let me have Insta, this would make such a good photo,' said Jane, duck-facing in front of it.

'Yay! So hot! Let's paddle!' cried Peter and took off towards the water. All the children seemed to think this was a splendid idea and flew off after him, the girls at least pausing on the bank to remove their shoes.

'Oh, this is lovely,' said Emily.

'The water is sooo nice and cool, you should come in too, Mum,' yelled Jane, splashing happily, Insta demands and duck faces forgotten.

'Look,' I said happily to Hannah. 'They're definitely frolicking. It's an omen.'

'An omen for what?' Hannah asked doubtfully.

'For our Perfect Summer, *obviously*.'

'I'm going to go in deeper!' yelled Peter, and he plunged towards the centre of the river.

'Nooooo!' I cried a moment too late. I'd been so transfixed by all the frolicking that I'd forgotten Peter's near-fatal attraction to water and mud, or his favourite, muddy water.

It was no good, though. I dashed after him to retrieve him but he was already wading knee deep towards the waterfall, followed by Lucas a beat behind him. Maybe this time it would be all right, I thought, watching him clambering over an inconvenient rock instead of going around it. Maybe he's finally developed some co-ordination and he won't –

'MUUUUUUUM!!!!!'

Just as I was sending up prayers to the Gods of Dry Pants and Small Boys, Peter slipped and fell headfirst into the river.

'Don't worry, Peter, I'll save you!' yelled Lucas, and immediately jumped in after him. Their heads popped up briefly and then vanished again under the water. Oh fuckety, fuckety, buggering bollocks – they were actually drowning. I suppressed the thought about how INCONSIDERATE they were to drown at the start of my Perfect Summer after only approximately twenty-seven seconds of frolicking, and attempted to go to the rescue.

'Just, I dunno, tread water or something,' I shouted as we dashed down the bank. 'Remember your swimming lessons. Mummy's coming!'

Hannah and I scuttled to the edge of the river, and I tentatively stepped out onto a protruding rock to get closer to the drowning cherubs. Looking down, I realised that the river was barely a foot deep, and the boys could get out perfectly easily if they tried to, instead of giving me palpitations about drowning. Peter chose that moment to pop his head up again and announce that he was all wet.

'Of course you're wet,' I said furiously. 'You've fallen in a bloody river. And the longer you sit there, the wetter you'll get.'

'You need to help us, Mum,' implored Peter. 'We can't get up, we're all wet!'

'Yes. Because you're SITTING IN A FUCKING – I MEAN A SODDING – I MEAN A DAMN RIVER. That's how rivers work. They're WATER, and if you sit in them you GET WET!'

Nonetheless, my maternal instincts were lurking somewhere under the rage, the thoughts of the laundry and the WHY THE FUCK DOES THIS HAVE TO HAPPEN EVERY BASTARDING TIME WE GO OUT?, and I leant out from my rock to attempt to proffer a helping hand. I leant too far, though, and began to over-balance perilously myself. However nice the thought of washing the sweat off was, I had no desire to spend the rest of the day squelching around and then wringing out my knickers at home, so I windmilled furiously in an attempt to regain my balance. This tactic worked, but I windmilled so furiously that the hamper I'd slung so jauntily over my shoulder flew off and went sailing through the air, to land with a splash in the middle of the river.

'Fuck,' I said.

'Ellen,' wailed Hannah, 'that had all the food! Mine has the drinks.'

'Oh no, Mummy, are we going to starve?' shrieked Peter.

'It's all your fault, Peter, if we starve,' howled Jane.

Ten minutes of directing rescue operations via the already sodden boys later ('Why do I have to go and get it?' 'Because you're already wet and in the river. Go!' 'Why can't we just leave it there?' 'Because there might be something salvageable from the picnic and also it cost £19.99, so I'm not just leaving it!'), and I was very much regretting my pretentious notion of wrapping the sandwiches in greaseproof paper and string à la Enid Blyton instead of just using Tupperware like anyone who wasn't a COMPLETE TWAT would have done. The cheese and pickle might've stood a chance in Tupperware, but my entire lovingly made picnic was a soggy disintegrating mess. I'd held out some hope for the Victoria sponge, safely ensconced in a (fuckety heavy) Emma Bridgewater tin, but alas the lid had been slightly dislodged on impact and it was distinctly damp and, as the children complained when I tried to make them eat it anyway, 'tasted like frogs'. I decided it was best not to ask Peter how he knew what a frog tasted like.

'Never mind.' Hannah tried to offer succour through the medium of warm, weak lemon squash, with the promise of Capri Suns on the way home if everyone 'was good'. There seemed about as much chance of that happening as there was of us becoming self-sufficient and living off rabbits caught by Judgy, who had regarded the whole river affair with disgust, as he's a Proud and Noble Border terrier and does not do water.

Nonetheless, we insisted the children plodded on, and 'enjoyed the walk', even the wet ones, who had been highly resistant to my suggestion they took off their wet clothes and fashioned a sort of toga from the floral picnic rugs, so I'd told them to get on with it.

'ISN'T THIS FUN?!' I shouted slightly passive–aggressively every few minutes, just in case there was any doubt about the matter.

'Ellen, I need to talk to you,' said Hannah, as we trailed behind the children. 'I've got something to tell you.'

'Oh my God, are you OK? Oh! OH! Has Charlie proposed? Are you getting married?'

'No!' said Hannah. 'Nothing like that. It's –' Before she could say any more, though, there were shouts to 'COME AND SEE' from further along the track, and we set off at a run, in alarm.

'Oh God, what are they doing now?'

'I think they've found something dead. Oh my God, what if it's a murder scene? What if they've found a body, and we're the first to find it and we investigate and solve it? Oh. My. God. Solving a murder would SO be the perfect summer, Hannah!'

'Unless you're the poor sod who got murdered. And I don't think desperate murderous sorts fall sufficiently into your middle-class criminal categories, do they?'

'They do in Agatha Christie,' I retorted. 'It's never someone common who does the murder.'

'What about the whole "the butler did it" thing?'

'Not in Agatha Christie,' I said firmly. 'Murdering vicars, yes. Butlers? Definitely not. Come on, we'd better catch them up in case they really have found a body and are traumatised for life.'

Alas, the deceased proved only to be an unfortunate squirrel, and the culprit probably a fox or one of Judgy's kin, so we trudged on, the children complaining once more of starvation. As the path looped back down towards the river, I let out a whoop of joy. All along the river bank were small bushes, with dark smudges hanging from their branches.

'We're saved,' I cried. 'We shall not starve. I told you if we lost all the food we could live off the land, and behold, we SHALL! Look, darlings – wild blueberries. What could be more divine? We shall FEAST!'

The children looked mutinous and Hannah doubtful.

'Ellen, are you sure they're blueberries?'

'Yes,' I insisted. 'Quite sure. Dad had a dalliance with a Danish woman one summer and she was mad on the whole foraging thing long before Instagram. I've forgotten most of what she tried to teach us, but I *do* remember what the blueberries look like. See? Yum.' I crammed a handful into my mouth.

'Maybe we should wait five minutes and see if you die?' Hannah suggested.

'I won't die,' I said scornfully. 'Here, I'll feed Judgy some. Would I feed them to him if they were poisonous?'

'Are you trying to say you value his life more than ours?' demanded Jane.

'Nooooo,' I said guiltily. 'Not *more* than … um … look, see, he's *yumming* them down. Come on, try some.'

After a few more minutes of prevarication, when neither Judgy nor I fell to the ground in our death throes, hunger got the better of everyone else and they consented to try the blueberries.

'They're nice,' declared Peter in surprise.

'And look.' I triumphantly produced a fistful of (clean) poo bags from my pocket. 'We shall pick lots to take home, and when we get back we can make jam, and then on our next picnic we can take cake and scones with home-made jam made from the wild blueberries we picked in the woods.'

My God, I could see the Instagram caption already: #Foraging #Wholesome #LookAtHowFuckingFabulousIAm

#IAmSummeringBetterYouThanYou   #BestSummerEver
#HappyMemories #EllenIsTheBestAtSummer. Yay fucking
me! Maybe I could make the Vision of our Perfect Summer so
enviable that even the likes of Perfect Lucy Atkinson's Perfect
Mummy and her sidekick Fiona Montague – the Yummiest
Mummies in the playground – would be jealous about just how
damned *good* I was at summer. They might even *comment* on one
of my posts.

Picking wild blueberries, though, was quite labour intensive,
and they were not as filling as one might have hoped, and so after
about half an hour we finally gave in and headed back to the car,
agreeing that yes, we could get an ice cream from the van in the
car park, and yes, raspberry sauce is probably one of your five a
day. As we trudged into the car park, a charming group of German
tourists was heading out for a brisk hike and they stopped in
horror to gaze at our bedraggled band. I glared back crossly. So
perhaps the children were not immaculate, or rather, in the case of
Peter and Lucas, looked like sodden urchins. And maybe they
were all smeared with purple and looking like grubby Smurfs.
What did they expect? Children were *meant* to get dirty when
they played in the woods. Maybe *German* children were perfect
and didn't get dirty, but there wasn't anything wrong with a bit of
good, clean dirt. It stimulated their immune systems.

Too late, I realised why the nice Germans were casting such
appalled glances at the children. They were all still clutching their
poo bags filled with blueberries for jam-making fun and, evidently
feeling peckish as we approached the car park, had decided to start
snacking out of them. I, too, looked on in horror and understood
why everyone was looking so disgusted, as it appeared our filthy
children were happily cramming handfuls of dog shit into their

mouths, while their mothers paid no heed. I decided my very limited German was entirely inadequate to explaining that despite the unfortunate result of the Brexit vote, Britain had not yet sunk to such depths that the country's youth was now being fed on dog poo, and I gave my best middle-class 'nothing to see here, we're quite respectable, thank you' high-beam smile to the tourists as we hustled the children past.

We were sitting on the 'rustic bench' (a log) in the 'rustic park' (splintery-looking play equipment built from fallen logs) beside the ice cream van, when Hannah reminded me again that she had something to tell me.

'Sorry, yes, we'd better try to actually converse quickly before some other disaster kicks off,' I said cheerily.

'Well … the thing is … you know Dan split up with Michelle?'

'No, I didn't. Ha ha ha, good. What happened? Did she dump him?' I demanded gleefully. Hannah's ex-husband was a no-good, cheating, useless streak of weasel piss, in my humble opinion, and I could take nothing but delight in any misfortune that might befall him.

'Yes, she met a BODYPUMP instructor called Carl and buggered off with him. *And* Dan's been made redundant.'

'Oh dear, what a shame,' I sniggered. I nobly refrained from adding that I wouldn't be at all surprised if he'd been made redundant because 'unemployable' was now added to his list of faults.

'Oh God, does that mean he's going to be even more hopeless over your child support?' I added with a sudden pang of conscience, remembering that this wasn't in fact about my views on Dan, but rather how it impacted on Hannah. 'Are you OK for money? Can I do anything? Obviously I'm not working right now, but we could probably do something –'

'No, it's OK, I'm not tapping you up for a loan, though I appreciate the offer. No, it's … his best friend Tim lives in Cape Town. But Tim's spending three weeks in the UK with his mum and dad over the summer, and he's asked Dan to house-sit for him, because he doesn't want to leave it empty. Apparently it's really nice. There's a pool and a vineyard and everything.'

'Dan has a best friend?' I asked incredulously.

'Ellen!'

'Sorry. Lucky Dan, with a best friend who just gives him an amazing house in Cape Town for a month when he's just been dumped and made redundant. Wish I had a best friend like that.'

'Instead of me?'

'No, of course not. You know what I mean. Anyway, what has any of this got to do with us? Unless Dan's invited us all to go and stay with him for the month, ha ha ha!'

'Well, that's just it. He has. He rang last night to ask if we wanted to go. And it's only three weeks, not a month.'

'Three weeks, a month, close enough. Ooooh. I mean, on the one hand, it's Dan. On the other hand … a month in Cape Town, maybe I could be persuaded …'

'No, Ellen. Not you. When I said *us*, I meant me and the kids.'

'Oh. Oh, I see. But what about me?'

'What about you?'

'You're not going to go, are you? What about our Best Summer Ever? What about the Happy Memories? What about US? Who will I have japes and frolics with? You can't go, it'll ruin *everything*!' I wailed dramatically.

'Of course it won't,' Hannah said soothingly. 'Think about it, Ellen, from my point of view. When am I ever going to be able to afford to do something like this for the kids? A month in South

Africa! We could go on safari. Even a few weeks on the other side of the world, experiencing a totally new culture, it'll be the most amazing experience for them.'

'When would you be leaving?'

'Monday. I booked the flights last night. Got a good deal too, which surprised me. I'm going to tell the kids tonight. I've got so much to do to get ready, though.'

'Monday! But what about *me*?'

'What about you?'

'We had this all planned. Our summer. Our first summer together since we were kids. I bought these hampers especially. And now you're abandoning me!'

'You're being a bit childish. And selfish. Come on, Ellen, try to be happy for me about this?'

I tried. I really, really tried to be happy for Hannah. And I wanted to be happy for her. Of course it was an amazing opportunity, of course she'd be mad not to grab it with both hands. But a small, nasty voice inside me said, 'Why doesn't anything this lucky happen to *me*?' Which was obviously a shitty thing to think, because loads of very lucky things had happened to me and hadn't happened to Hannah, whose husband had left her for an over-botoxed, body-pumped bint because she'd promised him a blow-job round the back of Boots (he'd been crass enough to tell Hannah about the Boots' blowjob – apparently the 'illicitness' of it had made him 'feel alive'), so how could I possibly feel sorry for myself and jealous of Hannah? But I did.

Clearly this was because I was a terrible person. And also because it was *South Africa*! For *three weeks*! Who wouldn't be jealous? But worse, Hannah had just blithely made these plans without even thinking about all the plans *we'd* already made. She hadn't even considered me in any of this. I'd never have done that to her. And now she wanted me to be *happy* for her.

I swallowed hard and tried to be a better person than the nasty goblin on my shoulder wailing, 'But what about *meeee*?' and 'It's not *faaaiiir!*'

'Of course I'm happy for you,' I ground out with considerable effort. 'Thrilled, in fact.'

'I knew you'd understand,' Hannah beamed.

'Mmmm.' I tried to smile too. And then it was no good, I had to say something. 'I just wonder if you've really thought this through properly? I mean, Dan? For a month?'

'Don't start, Ellen, please,' begged Hannah.

'I'm not starting,' I said indignantly. 'I'm just *saying*, are you sure this is a good idea?'

I was just being a *good friend*, I reasoned to myself. Looking out for Hannah. Nothing to do with *me* and what *I* wanted. Just concerned for Hannah's well-being, like any *good friend* would be.

'It's just South Africa is such a long way away,' I pointed out in my most reasonable tones.

'I know that,' Hannah pointed out right back, also in her most reasonable tones.

'And you'll be all on your own,' I tried. 'Without *me*,' the goblin hissed in my ear. 'With the kids,' I added out loud.

'I won't be on my own, Dan will be there,' Hannah reminded me, still in her reasonable tones.

'Yes, but he's Dan. He's not *reliable*, is he?' NOT LIKE ME! 'What if he meets someone else out there? What if he *brings* someone else?'

'He won't. We've discussed this. We're having a nice family holiday together for the sake of the children.'

'But he's useless with the children,' I burst out, as the goblin decided I'd ignored its clamourings long enough. 'He's useless at everything. He's just *useless*! Why are you doing this?'

'Why are *you* doing this? I thought you were happy for me?'

'*Happy* for you?' I spat. The goblin had free rein now, and I was apparently just its mouthpiece. '*Happy*? Happy that you're ABANDONING me for fucking *Weasel Piss Dan*, Weasel Piss Dan, moreover, who left you for another woman. And who was there for you when that happened? Me! I was! And now you're dumping me for him. You know what, this is *just like* when we were fifteen and Christopher Bennett asked you out, and you said yes, and you spent *all summer* with him – *and* his horrible sister Popular Lisa, and her horrible friends Lindsey and Karen – until he chucked you because you wouldn't give him a handjob and Horrible Popular Lisa and Lindsey and Karen told everyone you were frigid. And who was there for you then? ME! EVEN THOUGH you'd left me on my own ALL SUMMER! I was still there for you.'

'It was two weeks,' said Hannah indignantly. 'I went out with Christopher Bennett for *two weeks*.'

'That's not the point,' I said, summoning up as much dignity as was possible at this stage. 'The point is, you're choosing a man over me. Again! And talking of men – what will Charlie think about this?'

HA! I thought. You can't have your (probably delicious and exotic) South African cake *and* eat it, Hannah. What does your lovely new boyfriend Charlie think of you swanning off to South Africa with your wanker ex, eh?

'Charlie thinks I should go for it. He agrees it's an amazing opportunity for the kids. And that it will do them good to get a chance to spend a chunk of time with their father.'

'You talked to Charlie about this before me?' I spluttered in outrage. 'How? How could you?'

'He rang right after Dan. I needed to talk it over with someone. Someone impartial.'

'I'M impartial!'

'No, you're not. You hate Dan. And all you've talked about for weeks is your bloody perfect summer. Why can't you just try to be happy for me, instead of just thinking about yourself and your bloody never-ending wittering about *fucking* japes and *bastarding* frolics?'

'Don't take the hallowed name of japes and frolics in vain,' I hissed. 'I'd be happy for you if you weren't just pissing off on a whim with that useless fucker and spoiling all our plans.'

'You're going on holiday,' Hannah protested. 'How is this any different?'

'That was planned. It was accounted for when we planned the summer. It's totally different. And two weeks at my in-laws isn't quite the same as a month in sodding Africa. And I'm not going with bloody Dan. And if I was, I'd have consulted you first, not just presented you with a *fait accompli* that ruins ALL OUR PLANS.'

'We hadn't actually *made* any plans. You just keep shouting "Happy Memories" and "Best Summer Ever" at everyone. And anyway, your in-laws live in the south of France. It's hardly a wet weekend in a caravan in Skegness,' Hannah pointed out. 'Are you jealous of my trip?'

'No!' I snapped. 'Why would I be jealous? You're the one who's got to spend a month with Weasel Piss Dan. *I* can't think of anything worse.'

'It's three weeks. And this is exactly why I discussed it with Charlie, not you,' said Hannah furiously. 'This could be really good for me and Dan and the kids. Really positive for us to spend time together as a family and for the kids to see us getting on. It would be good for me to build a better relationship with him and for the children to see us behaving like civilised adults. If you and Simon divorced, that's what I'd want for you. But you never have a good word to say about him, and you seem to overlook the fact that he's still my children's father and always will be, and so whether I like it or not, I do need to get on with him. And if we can find a way to be friends, I'd rather do that than spend the rest of my life at loggerheads with him. So if he's trying to offer an olive branch in the form of this trip, well, I'm going to take it, whatever nasty names you might call him.'

'Well! Excuse *me* for trying to be a supportive friend. Jane. Peter. Come on, it's time to go home.'

'Why does everything have to be about YOU?' snarled Hannah as I marched away to gather up the children. 'All the good things happen to you. You made that game and all that money, you've got the happy marriage and the loving husband. You've got everything, and I'm always happy for you. And yet you can't even do the same for me. Maybe I'm sick of being happy for you and want something nice for myself. Maybe I'm sick of you.'

'What?'

I turned back to her. I'd heard people talk about 'feeling the blood drain out your face', and I suddenly realised what it meant. That cold, sick, shaky feeling that suddenly hit me, my face chilled and clammy despite the heat. All the most terrible, mean-spirited things I'd just thought about myself, had worried about being, had told myself I wasn't. To have Hannah – of all people – tell me that I *was* all those things was the worst feeling in the world. It couldn't be happening. I was imagining it. I'd misheard her.

'You don't mean that?'

'We always do what *you* want. You're always telling me what to do. You're the confident one, the outgoing one, and sometimes I feel like I'm just your sidekick. And when I do finally get something for myself, like Christopher Bennett, which admit it, you were jealous as hell about – and still are, it seems – or this trip … you can't even be happy for me then. So yes. Maybe I've had enough. Maybe after thirty years of *you*, I need some time for *me*! Maybe it's time for us both to find some new friends.'

And with that, she stormed off, grabbing Emily and Lucas, as I stood rooted to the spot, lost for words.

After the children had gone to bed, I filled Simon in on Hannah's great and immense perfidy. He seemed rather more unmoved and less outraged on my behalf than I'd hoped.

'I don't think this is the end of the world that you seem to think it is,' he shrugged.

'My best friend doesn't want to be friends with me anymore, and you don't think it's the end of the world?' I was incredulous.

'Well, you didn't behave terribly well, did you, darling? She tells you about the opportunity of a trip of a lifetime, and you just bang on about those fucking picnic hampers and this wretched summer of fun you'd planned.'

'You're supposed to be on my side.'

'I am on your side. But you and Hannah have lived in each other's pockets since you were ten or eleven, so I don't think it would do either of you any harm to broaden your horizons and make some new friends.'

'I don't *want* new friends. I want *Hannah*.'

'Hannah will come round. And in the meantime, look on it as an opportunity.'

'An opportunity for what?'

'Like I said. New friends. Look how much fun you've had since you met Sam. He's a new, well, newish friend now, isn't he?'

I grudgingly conceded this.

'Right. Well, just think. If you make new friends, you can have a lovely time introducing them all to the ways of your infernal japes and frolics, and educating them in the true path of eleventy fucking billion wicker picnic hampers.'

'I suppose so. Do you really think Hannah will come around?'

'Of course.'

'I'm not apologising, though. *She* can apologise.'

Simon sighed. 'Ellen, must you always be so bull-headed about everything? You're not always right, and sometimes you just need to admit that.'

Monday 25 July

Hannah buggered off to South Africa today, but I consoled myself with the fact that while she was on an eleven-and-a-half-hour flight with two small children, I myself had come up with the genius idea of suggesting to our friend Sam that since he was off today, we should go to the pub next to the park for the afternoon.

The management of the pub realised fairly early on that they were onto a winner here with a captive audience of stressed-out parents unable to face another overpriced latte from a man with dodgy facial hair and too-short trousers in a converted vintage camper van in the park. So they provided for us by building a delightful outdoor deck overlooking the play area, complete with a gate straight into the park. This meant that we could watch the children, and they could come and go at will without worrying about ROADS and STRANGER DANGER and all the other potential hazards threatening our moppets at every turn, and instead we could just sit and drink wine and also feel virtuous because our darlings were indulging in creative play in the fresh air, thereby creating the perfect setting for Happy Memories!

We arrived at the pub, and shoved Peter and Jane and Sam's children Sophie and Toby out towards the park with wild promises of chicken nuggets and chips and yes, even *Coke* if they were good, because it's the holidays.

Sam and I were delighted to bagsy the prime position within sight of both the play area and the pub toilets. After the usual debate that ended in us concluding a bottle was just much better value, we poured ourselves large glasses of white and settled down to have a good bitch about the last-day-of-term-one-upmanship-of-every-one by Perfect Lucy Atkinson's Perfect Mummy and her sidekick Fiona Montague, the Yummiest Mummies in the playground ('Oh … Capri … no, I'm sure *you'll* have a wonderful time there, it's just we found it dreadfully over-commercialised. Oh, the Maldives! Yah, we went there last year. Where are you staying? Oh dear. Of course, *we* didn't have to worry about the environmental impact on a fragile eco system, because *we* stayed in a totally carbon neutral eco lodge. Yah, the aircon was actually powered by these adorable local children on static bikes. No, it's not child labour, they're having fun. NO, they are. You can see them smiling in the videos. How are you off-setting the flights? We did it by buying another Tesla').

In fairness, Perfect Lucy Atkinson's Perfect Mummy and Fiona and the rest of the Yummy Mummies have been much nicer to me since they found out I was the genius creator behind their favour-ite game *Why Mummy Drinks*, and they also seemed far more human for revealing that they too sometimes long for their precious moppets' bedtime and a vat of Sauvignon Blanc. But they're never going to be Kindred Spirits.

I was longing to snipe about Hannah to Sam, but felt guilty, as she was his friend too, and I was afraid he might take her side, which I still rather felt Simon had done.

'Anyway, what are your plans for the summer, now Hannah's off on safari?' Sam asked.

'I don't know,' I said sadly. 'I wish you were off for the summer. *We* could have lovely fun!'

'I wish I was too,' grumbled Sam. '*Some* of us have to work, you know.'

'Oh God, I know. Poor you. I'm dreading going back already. But I'll help out with the kids, and you must be able to take a few more days off, and come and join us for japes and frolics?' I said hopefully.

'Not really,' sighed Sam. 'Apart from today, because they had the dentist this morning. I don't know why I'm bothering, when it's so hot here at the moment, but I'm using most of my annual leave when I take the kids to Greece, and most of my annual bloody salary paying for holiday clubs for the rest of the time. Apart from the days you've kindly offered to have them. Thank you.'

'So you can't take *any* more time off?' I asked plaintively, as I saw my Best Summer Ever dissolving into an endless round of breaking up fights, providing snacks and fending off the constant demands about 'What are we going to do *today*?' I took a large slug of wine and tried to remember I did at least have my lovely in-law-less holiday in France to look forward to, before I flung myself upon Sam and wailed 'But what about meeeeeee?!' at him too. When I'd done this to Simon yesterday he'd told me I should 'cultivate inner resources, like I was always telling the children to do'. Seriously, why does no one feel my pain?

Luckily the much-anticipated nuggets and chips arrived at that moment, and the children had to be retrieved from the park, where, *of course*, Perfect Lucy Atkinson's Perfect Mummy and Fiona Montague were perched on a bench with their oat milk frappés from the man with a moustache that ten years ago would have had us wondering if he was on some kind of sex offenders' register, but who nowadays is considered simply hip and quirky.

Obviously, I'm happy that men can now express themselves so freely, but I can't help but wonder about the hygiene aspects, given that it seems to be some sort of law these days that all men in the hospitality industry must resemble a cross between an impoverished lumberjack wearing his baby brother's trousers and Hercule Poirot after a particularly heavy night on the crème de menthe.

'Ellen,' trilled Lucy Atkinson's Perfect Mummy. 'You're here! I was going to ring you; we thought the children were abandoned. Is Sam here too?'

'Errr, yes, we're just over there,' I muttered, gesturing vaguely in the direction of the pub, while hopefully not pointing directly at it. After all, I reasoned, we weren't actually doing anything dreadfully wrong, we were just as close to our children as Lucy's Mummy and Fiona were to their children, and probably paying more attention to what they were doing than the pair of them, who until I came over had been engrossed in a conversation about whether Pilates or yoga was more effective for the perfect core.

'But that's the *pub*,' gasped Fiona in horror. 'And … good lord, isn't it a *Wetherspoons*?' she added, looking genuinely traumatised.

'No, no!' I said brightly, attempting to round up all the children without letting on to Lucy's Mummy and Fiona about the dreaded nuggets and hoping that afternoon drinking would be deemed more acceptable if one wasn't getting 'like, totally *SPOONSED!*' as I'd heard some youths on the train recently describing their exploits in that delightful chain of cut-price pubs.

'Are you having wine?' asking Lucy's Mummy curiously.

'Oh, you know,' I said airily. 'Just being … err … continental. It's so hot, you know!'

'And can you see the children all right?'

'Yes, clear as day. We're just through that gate.'

'Oh Fiona!' said Lucy's Mummy in excitement. 'Shall we go and have a glass of wine?'

Fiona spluttered in horror. 'Wine! In the afternoon? When we're in charge of the children? What if there's a medical emergency? What would we say in A&E?'

'Fiona, we've sat on this bench at least three times a week for the last ten years and there's never been a medical emergency,' said Lucy's Mummy impatiently. 'Come on, live a little. What's the worst that can happen? No, no, don't answer that, I don't need a list of all the medical emergencies that could take place. One glass of wine. To be continental, like Ellen says.'

'I don't think French mothers sit in a pub garden drinking while Héloïse and Pierre fall off the slide and *concuss* themselves,' sniffed Fiona. 'Really, I don't know what's got into you. What if you need to drive Lucy to hospital, and you've been drinking? *How would you live with yourself?*' she hissed.

'You're right,' said Lucy's Mummy sadly. 'I know. It's just it did sound such a nice idea, a lovely chilled glass of something delicious in the sunshine – get us in the spirit for Italy. And it's so hot, this frappé latte's just not cutting it. Maybe I should go and see if he has any acai smoothies left?'

Perfect Lucy Atkinson, however, had other ideas, and begged and cajoled her darling mama to be allowed to go and sample the forbidden delights of the pub garden with Jane and Sophie.

'Please, Mummy,' pleaded Lucy. 'Jane says they've got a swing.'

'There's swings here,' attempted Lucy's Mummy. 'And you've got a swing at home.'

'No,' insisted Lucy. All these swings were rubbish. The only swing that she could countenance was the mythical pub swing Jane had spoken of. Lucy's Mummy wasn't very good at saying no to Lucy, and Fiona was eventually persuaded that the world wouldn't end if she set her perfectly pedicured foot in a beer garden, so we all trooped off back to the pub.

'Chips, Mummy,' said Lucy wide-eyed, as they came through the gate into the pub garden. 'And fizzy drinks …' Her Mummy blanched slightly, realising that she'd unwittingly entered a temple not only of Lovely Booze, but also of saturated fat and doubtful protein sources and tartrazine and sugar. But on the other hand, Sam was there, and Lucy's Mummy and Fiona were both still hopeful of luring Sam from the dark side that was his association with the likes of myself, and turning him into their handsome gay best friend, to advise on fashion and relationships and shout 'You GO, girl' at them sassily. This was never ever going to happen, partly because Sam regards them both with mortal fear, and partly because Sam knows nothing about fashion, either male or female, and his idea of relationship advice when Hannah was single was to suggest she just got a bit pissed and tried to get off with someone who didn't look too dodgy, which wasn't entirely helpful for her.

There was a slight contretemps in the pub garden when Lucy's Mummy and Fiona had asked for a wine list from the frazzled barman collecting glasses and been told the choice was red or white, and they had to order at the bar, he didn't do table service, and Lucy's Mummy looked like she might have to breathe into a paper bag at the news.

The situation was saved, though, when Lucy expressed vocal delight about how much better the pub swing was than any other swing she'd ever seen, although Fiona insisted on inspecting both the swing and the other play equipment to make sure it was safe for The Montagues, as she disconcertingly referred to her offspring.

Eventually we were all sitting down at the table together again, Lucy's Mummy and Fiona having plumped bravely for sparkling water instead of wine, and the conversation turned, inevitably, to the holidays.

'So, Ellen, what are your plans for the summer?' enquired Lucy's Mummy.

'Oh, we're going to France for a couple of weeks,' I said blithely.

'How nice. Do you have a place there?'

I shot Sam A Look, crossed my fingers and said, 'Yes, yes, we do actually.' After all, it wasn't *strictly* a lie; there *was* Louisa's house, which we owned, even though we were almost certainly never going to benefit from it in any way. And Simon's parents' chatette, well, technically this was a 'family place'. And one day it would be ours. Well, Simon's. Half Simon's. That wasn't the point, though.

'You're brave,' said Lucy's Mummy. 'We got rid of our place in France, so impossible to get staff to look after it. Terribly Bolshevik, the French, don't you find? Also, I got frightfully bored with France, because mostly it was full of Brits. So now we go to Italy.'

'We find it *much* more *authentic*,' beamed Fiona. I wasn't sure quite how one compared how authentically Italian Italy was, as opposed to how French France was, but I wasn't going to be crushed by their aspersions, because I was certain that everything would be different in France, and the entire fortnight would consist of sunbathing, in between tripping to the boulangerie in a floaty skirt and ballet flats to purchase baguettes and croissants for *le petit dejeuner*, and then repairing to the quaint bistros in the town square for all other meals. Wait, was the *boulangerie* the bakery? Or was it the butcher's? My recollection of school French was somewhat hazy, and needless to say, despite having started this year like I started every year, determined that this year I'd definitely learn French, I had not yet managed to do so. But never mind. We had ages before we went away – definitely more than enough time to get on Duolingo and be able to converse charmingly with the jolly *boulangerie monsieur*. Well, assuming he wasn't the butcher. I didn't wish to converse with the butcher, which suggested alarming amounts of cooking in Sylvia's terrifyingly immaculate kitchen.

I had so many glorious notions about how this holiday would unfold, chief among which was a delightful vision of me bartering merrily in the market for a kilo of cherries to put in my wicker basket, and perhaps some dark and wicked Frenchman would fall in love with me and gaze at me longingly across the trestle tables. By a lucky coincidence he'd own several hundred acres of vineyards, producing delicious wine, and he'd somehow persuade me to come with him one day in his open-top vintage sports car to visit said vineyard in a very safe and totally not weird kidnapper way.

As well as the vineyard, he (I thought it likely he'd be called Jean-Pierre – names are so much sexier in French; one couldn't imagine breathing 'Oh, John-Peter' romantically) would have a crumbling chateau and call me *Cherie*, and try to persuade me to run away with him and live in the chateau and wear shady hats and floaty dresses for always, but I'd reproach Jean-Pierre for trying to seduce me by telling him I was a virtuous married woman, at which point he'd regretfully renounce me, telling me he'd never love another and … I suddenly realised Lucy's Mummy and Fiona were looking at me expectantly, waiting for me to ask what they were doing.

'And what are your plans?' I muttered feebly, and much too late.

'Well, we've booked this wonderful little castle in Umbria for six weeks, and Fiona and Hugo are coming out with the kids too. We've only got a week at home now before we leave, and a week at the end to get the children settled back into a routine before they go back to school. It's going to be *such* fun. Are you in France all summer?'

'Er, no, just two weeks,' I mumbled. How did they always make me feel so inferior? I thought I'd nailed it with my claims of our 'little place in France' and once again, they'd Top Trumped me.

'But why only two weeks,' cooed Fiona, 'if it's your own place? Oh!' She stopped and looked embarrassed. 'I'm so sorry. Is it … is it a *timeshare*?'

'No, no!' I attempted a tinkly laugh. 'No, it's more a family property. So we like to let the rest of the family use it.'

Fiona and Gemma looked unconvinced and began to interrogate Sam about his holiday plans.

Lucy's Mummy was just looking far more enthusiastic about Sam's planned fortnight in Rhodes than my own delightful *vacances françaises* when she had to interrupt him with an 'Ooh, sorry, that's my phone, I must take it. It's Giles.'

Lucy's Mummy answered the phone to what sounded like some furious shouting down the line, and suddenly turned ashen. She leapt up and scurried away, hissing, 'Giles, Giles, *calm down*, you're not making any sense.'

While she standing in the corner of the pub garden, having what looked like a very intense and serious conversation with her husband Giles, Fiona attempted to helpfully suggest some potential summer plans 'if you're at a loose end, Ellen', including an intensive reading programme – 'Ottilie's reading age had gone up *two* years after the summer she took part in it.' I didn't know how to tell Fiona that Peter had once eaten our copy of *The Tiger Who Came to Tea*, and I still wasn't totally sure if he could read, but I *did* know a summer reading programme wouldn't suffuse him or Jane with the same joy it had apparently brought 'The Montagues'.

Lucy's Mummy staggered back to the table and grabbed the nearest wine glass, downing it in one.

'Are you all right?' I asked in genuine concern. 'Has something happened?'

'Yes,' gulped Lucy's Mummy, collapsing into a seat and pouring herself another glass. 'Something terrible has happened.'

'Has someone died?' Sam enquired, as I kicked him under the table and Fiona made chuntering noises about the wine downing.

'Worse,' whimpered Lucy's Mummy. 'Giles has had an email from the Contessa we were renting the castle from, and they've cancelled our fucking booking!'

'Language,' said Fiona automatically, the full portent of what Lucy's Mummy was saying not yet registering with her.

'*Fiona*,' gasped Lucy's Mummy. 'Did you hear what I said? They've cancelled the castle! Giles is LIVID, he's threatening to sue, but that doesn't really help with what on earth we're going to do this summer, does it?'

Fiona also reached for a wine glass as she went pale and stared slack-jawed at Lucy's Mummy. 'No,' she whispered. 'No, this can't be happening. WHY have they cancelled?'

Lucy's Mummy blinked for a second and glanced at me, before saying firmly, 'It's double booked.'

'Double booked?' said Fiona in outrage. 'Double booked? Well, why should the other booking get to go over *us*? The Montagues will be *devastated*. Call Giles and get me the number of the Contessa, I'll sort this out. We'll see about double booked!'

'No!' yelped Lucy's Mummy. 'Giles already tried, they said … they said the other booking is being prioritised.'

Fiona turned puce with fury. Other people being prioritised over The Montagues was simply *not acceptable*. Surely this was why Strongly Worded Letters had been invented.

'I shall write to my MP,' Fiona declared. 'And go to the media if necessary.'

Sam and I exchanged looks at the thought of Fiona and the little Montagues sadfacing in the *Daily Mail*, perhaps posing complete with their suitcases, and a suitably heart-tugging headline about 'Tots' heartbreak at castle cock-up'. I couldn't see it somehow. I would, however, pay good money to see our MP's face upon opening a missive from Fiona, doubtless co-signed by the rest of The Montagues to make the true gravitas of the situation clear, berating him for wasting his time on potholes and funding cuts for schools and the elderly and vulnerable, when the true problems of Broken Britain were staring him in the face – namely nice middle-class ladies having their nice middle-class holiday plans mildly inconvenienced.

'Oh no, Fiona,' Lucy's Mummy said quickly. 'Don't do that. What would Hugo say if you ended up in some ghastly tabloid?'

'True. I just don't understand it. Who would they rather have than *us*? Oh! Oh, maybe it's the Clooneys? I'm sure I read in *Hello!*. I mean, err, I was just flicking through it at the dentist, obviously, I don't *buy* it every week, ha ha ha, they're having the house on Lake Como renovated this summer. I bet that's it, isn't it?' Fiona looked round, wild-eyed. 'I've had an idea. We can ask the Clooneys if we can share.'

'I don't think we can share a castle with the *Clooneys*, Fiona.'
Even Lucy's Mummy sounded doubtful about the likelihood of
this happening.

'Yes,' insisted Fiona. 'Why not? I'll find his agent's number, or
better yet, you get onto the Contessa and tell her to ask the
Clooneys if we can just share. They have children, don't they?
Think how much the Clooney children could learn from The
Montagues. And Lucy, of course,' she added hastily.

'Why not?' I put in helpfully. 'It happens all the time in films, it's
like a perfect plot from a jolly summer rom-com – double booking, everyone is cross, there's a series of hilarious mishaps, and
everyone ends up getting on splendidly and living happily ever
after.'

Fiona's hope visibly deflated before my eyes.

'Ellen's right. It's a stupid idea,' sighed Fiona. 'I'll see what else
we can find.'

'Well,' I said, attempting to offer comfort, 'for that scenario to
properly happen like in the pictures, there has to have been an
awkward romantic encounter between two of you in the past, and
secret lingering hopes of rekindling the flames, so unless either of
you have shagged George Clooney and forgotten to mention it, or
Hugo or Giles had a dalliance with Amal, it would never have
worked out.'

'Please don't mock our pain, Ellen,' said Fiona. 'We'd better take
the children home and break the news to them, while I get online
and see if I can't find something else suitable, though the chances
of that are now slim.'

'They're non-existent,' sighed Lucy's Mummy. 'Giles' PA has
been looking all day, and there's nothing.'

'Nothing? There must be something,' Fiona insisted. 'I'm going on Cottages to Castles now. God, I'll look at booking.com if I've got to.'

Half an hour later, after both of them had been fully engrossed in their phones, with occasional cries of 'What about … oh no,' 'Ooooh, we could go to … no,' they looked up and admitted defeat.

'What shall we do?' whispered Lucy's Mummy.

'I don't know,' Fiona whimpered. 'Ellen, what do you do for the rest of the summer when you're not on holiday?'

'Um, we, err, have japes and frolics?' I offered feebly.

Fiona sat up a little straighter 'Japes and frolics?' she demanded. 'What sort of thing do you mean?'

'Well, you know. Days out. Picnics. That sort of thing.'

Fiona considered. 'We could do that,' she said thoughtfully. 'We could have the best japes and frolics ever.'

'Could we?' said Lucy's Mummy sadly, shaking the last drops of the bottle Sam had kindly gone to the bar and fetched for us, since they'd polished off our first bottle in their extremis, into her glass.

'Yes!' Fiona was rallying. 'The Montagues will not be defeated by the likes of George Clooney. We'll have the best japes and frolics, and the best summer ever!'

Hang on, I thought crossly. That's my line! I'm having the best japes and frolics – and the best summer ever. What the fuck does Fiona fucking Montague know about it?

'Are you in, Ellen?' slurred Lucy's Mummy. 'Let's make this the best summer ever.'

'Yes, come on, Ellen,' insisted Fiona bossily. 'We'll show them how it's done! I'm going to tag George Clooney on Instagram so he knows what he's missing in his *stupid* castle. Stupid Clooneys.'

'Yes,' I said. 'Yes, I'm in!'

Ha ha! I thought. Finally, finally this was my chance to impress and show off to Fiona Montague and Perfect Lucy Atkinson's Perfect Mummy, for surely who knew more about japes and frolics and Happy Memories and Best Summers Ever than ME? And while they were tagging George Clooney (was he even on Instagram?) about what he was missing, maybe *I'd* tag Hannah in some amazing photos of me and Fiona and Lucy's Mummy all looking super-glam and cool and fabulous and having the best summer ever WITHOUT HER, because I don't need her!

Tuesday 26 July

Lucy's Mummy and Fiona had departed shortly after they declared the Best Summer Ever to be GO, and Sam brought Sophie and Toby back to my house for a sleepover and we had another bottle of wine, as Simon had gone out for a drink with a client after work.

I tottered downstairs this morning to clamours for some viral YouTube waffle recipe to be made, and tried not to snarl as I dumped Weetabix in bowls to the dismay of the children, since all the nice cereal had been eaten and apparently this was a *terrible* start to the day. I sliced some bananas on top of the Weetabix in an attempt to cancel out yesterday's junk food and snapped at them that it was a good, wholesome, hearty breakfast to start a delightfully wholesome, blissful summer, so they could all just eat it or go hungry.

'But HOW is it going to be fun?' Jane demanded. 'You keep saying it's going to be the best summer ever and we're going to have so much fun, but HOW? What are we actually going to *do*?'

'Ah ha!' I said smugly, holding aloft my floral-patterned notebook especially purchased from TKMaxx for this purpose, 'that's what we were planning last night. While you were all rotting your brains with electronics, WE were coming up with lots of amazing ideas to create really, really #HappyMemories this summer. Honestly, kids, this is going to change your lives! When you're grown up and have children of your own, this summer will be the template for how you bring them up! You'll look back on this and realise it was what childhood is truly about!'

'MUUUUUM,' said Jane in horror, 'it's, like, mega CRINGE when you actually SAY "hashtag" something. Like, it's only sad people and old people who say that, so can you just, like, *not*?'

'Yeah, and I'm never having children,' shuddered Sophie. 'It's gross!'

'I know how babies are made!' announced Peter proudly. 'The man gets his willie out and he does a wee in the lady's china, and then I suppose she must drink it and that's how a baby gets in you, when you drink the wee the man did in your china!'

'Oh my God, Peter,' Jane howled in disgust. 'That isn't how it happens. You haven't even done that bit in Living and Growing yet, have you? You're so stupid, no one wees in anyone! Sophie, come on, let's go upstairs.'

'Yes, they do,' said Peter stubbornly, as the girls trooped out, and he continued to insist that was indeed what happened, Freddie Dawkins had informed them of these facts, and Freddie HAD done how babies are made in Living and Growing.

'It's called a sex wee,' added Peter helpfully. Toby, who had apparently been off sick on the day of Freddie Dawkins's impromptu biology lectures, was listening agog.

'So that's how it happens!' he breathed in wonder. 'But what about the cuddle?'

'What cuddle?' asked Peter.

'I heard you got a baby when a mummy and a daddy had a special cuddle!' said Toby.

'Well, he must give her a cuddle while she drinks the wee, obviously,' said Peter crushingly. 'And you haven't even got a mummy, you've got two daddies,' Peter pointed out.

'Look!' I wailed, trying to sound enthusiastic enough to distract the boys from the notion of their creation being some sort of perverted Mad Hatter's Tea Party and waving the notebook full of Summer Plans at them again. 'Look! We've made some wonderful plans for the summer. Do you want to see what they are?'

'I got borned from a mummy, though,' Toby said. 'But she couldn't look after me, so my daddies adopted me instead, silly! Don't you even know *that*?'

'Ah, I see,' said Peter, with the cheerful acceptance typical of children. I breathed a sigh of relief for Sam's excellent policy of honesty with the kids, and decided to shut down the conversation before it went any further.

'SUMMER PLANS!' I shrieked, slapping the notebook down among the remnants of Weetabix hardening on the table. 'Come on, look what fun we're going to have,' and I dramatically flung the book open.

'SUMMER' was scrawled across the first page. After that it descended into an illegible mess, rather as if a very drunk spider had fallen in an inkpot, climbed out and then lurched all around the page, which in truth wasn't a million miles from what had happened. It appeared I'd not been as clever or as organised as I thought I'd been last night.

'So what did Daddy's wee taste like?' demanded Peter, just as Simon came into the kitchen and turned puce.

'WHAT DID YOU SAY, PETER?' he bellowed. 'What the hell has been going on?' Simon turned to me in despair. 'Why would he ask that?'

'It's nothing to do with me,' I said indignantly. 'This is all the doing of Freddie bloody Dawkins!'

'Who's Freddie Dawkins? Is he some bizarre relation of Richard Dawkins?'

'No, but he might have a better grasp of basic biology if he was,' I yelped as my phone began to light up with a series of WhatsApps. Oh God, Lucy's Perfect Mummy appeared to have created a group called 'Super Summer Fun'.

Friday 29 July

'Why are we here?' I muttered to myself. 'What are we doing? How did this happen?'

Fiona Montague had come up with the hideous idea of a Public Transport Day for us. Apparently, she'd read about it in the PTA magazine, where else (I'd not even known such a publication existed)? The PTA had suggested it as a 'sponsored activity', but to my immense relief Fiona had decreed we could do it 'just for fun'. The idea was that we picked a location, and then had to work out how to travel there by public transport. This would, Fiona insisted, be super-fun. There had, however, been some argument about what constituted 'Public Transport'.

'Taking your car to the station does *not* count as Public Transport,' Fiona insisted. 'We're not using any private vehicles from the moment we set foot out of the house. If it's a Public Transport Day, we're only using Public Transport.'

'What about bikes?' Lucy's Mummy tried. 'Could we cycle to the station? Instead of getting the b … b … b … BUS,' she pleaded, her voice quivering.

'No,' said Fiona sternly. 'No bikes. Quite apart from the fact that there's two miles of dual carriageway between your house and the station, which I'm not convinced is safe for children, a bicycle is a means of private transport.'

'Except those ones in London and places you hire them,' put in Lucy's Mummy eagerly. 'So not all bikes are private. So it could count as public transport?'

'*If* we get lost and end up in London, we can hire bikes. But no, you can't take your *own* bike,' Fiona countered.

'An Uber Share?' I suggested hopefully. 'That's not a private means of transportation.'

'No, absolutely not! Now, we need to decide where we're going,' Fiona said, in a tone that brooked no argument.

'We could go to the beach,' I said swottily. 'That would be nice.' (See, Fiona? You're not the only one who can organise a 'super-fun' day out.)

'Good idea, Ellen,' Fiona said heartily. 'Which beach did you have in mind?'

'Er, the nearest one on a trainline?' I said equally heartily. I can do this. I can be just as good as you, Fiona!

But no. Fiona shook her head crushingly. 'That's not very sporting, is it, Ellen?' she chided. 'I know, why don't we stick a pin in a map, and then plan a route there?'

'What if we end up having to go hundreds of miles?' whimpered Lucy's Mummy. 'We might then have to go somewhere … *northern*! Or … or … to *Wales*!'

'Nothing wrong with Wales,' I said crossly. 'My grandmother was Welsh. Nothing wrong with the north either.'

'I do take your point that they're both a bit far for a day trip, though,' Fiona soothed. 'Why don't we print out a map of say, a fifty-mile radius, and stick a pin in that?'

'But what if we end up picking somewhere with no station?' said Lucy's Mummy in alarm.

Fiona sighed. 'Then we'd get the bus. Obviously.'

I nodded smugly, now blatantly sucking up to Fiona in order to show off my Summer Fun credentials, despite deep down agreeing with Lucy's Mummy, whom I should probably now stop referring to as Lucy's Mummy in my head all the time and try to think of by her actual name, Gemma, although the habit of calling her Perfect Lucy Atkinson's Perfect Mummy was a long-engrained one that I feared would be hard to break.

In the interest of fairness and 'involving them', it was decided that one of the children should do the pin-sticking. I hastily suggested that Lucy should be the sticker, as Jane had been reading about Matthew Hopkins, the Witchfinder General, and his habit of sticking pins in innocent women to determine if they were in league with the devil, and I had a nasty feeling that if given access to a pin, and a woman or two, she might take it upon herself to test Lucy and The Montagues for witchcraft.

Lucy, obviously, took her duty very seriously and carried it out beautifully. So beautifully that she managed to pick a delightful little seaside town that to her Mummy's chagrin didn't have a station, and so would definitely need to be accessed by bus.

And so here we were, standing in a bus stop at 7.30 a.m. on a slightly drizzly but muggy summer morning. I'd realised too late that I'd not factored in the effect my darling children had had on my bladder when I'd agreed to a lengthy bus journey to show off to Fiona Montague, and so I'd arrived at the bus stop extra-grumpy because I'd not even dared have a cup of tea first.

I'm not at my best without a cup of tea in the morning, but I was feeling quite smug that surely for once I'd *nailed* the right outfit, and was feeling rather natty in the acceptable Yummy Mummy uniform of a floral dress, Veja trainers and a denim jacket. It was far too hot for the other acceptable outfits of jeans and a Breton top – ideally Boden – and a 'jaunty' scarf, or some form of over-priced 'athleisure' leggings, an equally overpriced long padded coat and bright, chunky neon trainers.

Recently I'd noticed a new addition to the uniform creeping in, as more and more of the Mummies were showing up in the play-ground wearing some sort of fleece-lined tent affair called a 'dryrobe', so we all knew they were either on their way to or from 'wild swimming'. It's a well-known fact that it's simply not possible to go 'wild swimming' unless you make quite, *quite* sure everyone *knows* you've been wild swimming. It's actually very dangerous to go wild swimming without telling every single person you've ever met that you're going wild swimming, and posting it on every social media channel, and ideally writing an article for the *Guardian* about the benefits of wild swimming as well. I wasn't sure I could ever quite bring myself to publicly wear such a garment though, however smug-making its credentials might be.

I was therefore somewhat taken aback when Fiona and Lucy's Mummy (there I go again!) arrived in little linen White Company playsuits and Seasalt sandals. Although I secretly thought they looked like a pair of overgrown toddlers, I realised that once again I was behind the curve. I suddenly felt a longing – quite overriding my anger with her – for Hannah to be here so we could take the piss out of the romper suits, instead of feeling all wrong and overdressed.

Fiona rummaged in some sort of canvas knapsack affair and produced … a clipboard.

'Here we are,' she said briskly. 'I've got it all planned. The bus will arrive in exactly seven minutes and twenty-three seconds, it will take fifteen minutes till our first change, and then we've a five-minute wait for the next bus. Then, after a thirty-two-minute journey, we change again and wait six minutes for a Number 72, and then it's seventeen minutes PRECISELY to our destination.'

'Gosh,' I said admiringly. 'And to come home?'

'We do it all in reverse, obviously,' Fiona informed me, crushingly. 'Now have we got everything?'

'Yes.' I waved my adorable fishing nets jauntily and pointed to the now dried-out picnic hamper.

'What are they?' demanded Fiona.

'Fishing nets. For exploring the rock pools,' I beamed smugly.

'Ellen, you can't catch things from rock pools. It's ecologically damaging,' Fiona sniffed.

'Errr, obviously we weren't going to take anything out!' I said hastily.

'And have you got buckets and spades?' Fiona smirked, brandishing frankly fucking adorable tin buckets and spades at me. I looked sullenly at our faded and slightly cracked plastic buckets and spades, and felt a distinct pang of sandcastle envy. Why hadn't I thought of that?

'Where *is* the bus?' fretted Fiona. 'It should have been here forty-two seconds ago.'

'I think that's the trouble with public transport,' I tried to explain. 'It's not always terribly reliable. That's why people who have no choice but to use it find it a pain in the arse, not a novelty.'

'There's simply no excuse for it,' chuntered Fiona. 'Really, it's not hard to make things run on time. On the PTA everything runs like clockwork!'

I decided against explaining to Fiona that there might be a few small differences between running a tombola in the school hall, and running a fleet of elderly buses staffed by underpaid and demoralised drivers who just wanted to get to the end of their shift without being stabbed.

Fortunately, the bus arrived before Fiona became any more distressed at the vagaries of Public Transport and felt the need to lecture the bus driver on how The Montagues would run things, were they in charge, and we leapt merrily aboard, hampers and fishing nets ahoy, dragging the children after us clutching buckets and spades, to the mild alarm of the bus driver, as at that point we were nowhere near the seaside or any other large bodies of water.

'We're going on a Public Transport Day,' Lucy's Mummy explained brightly to the driver, as he muttered darkly at us and denied all knowledge of the day ticket Fiona insisted we could buy, finally charging us approximately the GDP of Luxembourg for all of us to go five miles down the road very slowly.

By the time we'd all piled on, every single commuter on the bus hated us with a passion. I couldn't blame them, as I rather hated us too, especially when Lucy Atkinson burst into loud tears about how much she hated the scary bus, Mummy, and why did people get buses, she thought buses were just for at the airport to take people flying with budget airlines to the aeroplane.

'Oh dear, poppet, come on now, it's FUN! Look, look out the window and let's see what we can see. Why, there's a man in a shell suit. I haven't seen one of those in years – I didn't even know you could still get them.'

Lucy continued to sniff loudly about how she just wanted to be in the Range Rover watching Netflix on the in-car entertainment system, so her Mummy had a bright idea to cheer her up, as the shell suit man and the possible re-emergence of the worse of eighties fashion had not done the trick.

'We could have a sing-song?' she suggested.

'No,' I hissed.

'Why not? It would be fun. We could get everyone to join in and I could video it, and we could put it on Instagram and it would probably go viral and everyone would love us and we'd be famous! It would be like a sort of singing flashmob thing. We'd probably be asked to be interviewed on the news.'

I hesitated for a moment. Awful though the idea of a bus sing-along undoubtedly was, I was quite impressed by this flight of fancy on the part of Lucy's Mummy, and deep down I was rather tempted by the idea of the viral video and becoming famous for being the women who brought some joy and cheer into this grey and soulless world. We'd practically be Pollyannas! We might get asked to be on *Loose Women*, and I'd be so witty and brilliant that I'd be offered a job as a television presenter on the spot, and then I'd be famous and fabulous and wouldn't ever have to go back to my shitty job at the Cunningham United Nautical Trust, except maybe when I'd be asked to come and open a new building, like the Queen! What would I present? Not a sick animal programme – it would be too sad; and not the news – boring! Oooh! Maybe they would give me my own chat show and I'd interview celebrities, and Rick Astley would come on and fall in love with me and marry me. From the faraway look in Lucy's Mummy's eyes, I suspected her thoughts were running along similar lines.

'What could we sing?'

'I don't know. Something jolly, like we used to sing at Guides. Not everyone might know them, though. Oooh, I know, what about something from *The Sound of Music*? Everybody knows those songs!'

'Absolutely not,' said Fiona, instantly crushing our dreams. 'That's a terrible idea. Filming us? Singing on a *bus*? With *bus people*? And you'd want people to see it? To be famous for *being on a bus*? What would Giles and Hugo say? And, just think, you might end up on one of those ghastly daytime television programmes like *Jeremy Vine* with all the fat people who marry their cousins and have to take lie detector tests because they've slept with their other cousins!'

'That's *Jeremy Kyle*,' I put in helpfully.

'What?'

'*Jeremy Kyle* was the one with the lie detectors and the cheating partners. *Jeremy Vine* is the one where people ring up and say they want the government to bring back National Service to sort out the youth of today,' I explained.

'Well, either way, it's not happening. What *would* your husbands say?' Fiona demanded.

'It's nothing to do with him,' I muttered.

Lucy had stopped crying, at least, even if she appeared to be playing a game with Jane that consisted of trying to make rude words as Fiona's daughter Ottilie ('*not* Tilly, we don't believe in nicknames, do we?') clutched her pearls and threatened to tell on them, and Peter and Fiona's twin boys Cosmo and Miles (they weren't identical but were so interchangeably insipid I could never tell which one was which) were … not there. Where were they? How had we lost the boys on a moving bus?

Fiona was consulting her clipboard, and Lucy's Mummy (Gemma! GEMMA!) was gazing out of the window, no doubt mourning her lost career as the next Cat Deeley, and I seemed to be the only one who had noticed they were gone. A rumpus at the back of the bus revealed the boys, whom an indignant woman was accusing of upskirting her.

'We were just looking for Miles's marble that he'd dropped and had rolled along the floor,' protested Peter, the picture of innocence, if innocence were covered in matter from the bus floor and some unidentified sticky substance. I'd long since given up trying to work out what was making Peter sticky – he simply *was* sticky. Sometimes I wondered if he just secreted stickiness, like a snail. It seemed the only explanation as to how, no matter how much I scrubbed him, within seconds, even when sitting in a clean bed, in clean pyjamas, still glowing from his bath, he was sticky!

Despite my profuse apologies, the indignant lady did not seem placated by the story of the marble, but Fiona was outraged, OUTRAGED, that anyone could accuse her cherub of wrongdoing.

'I shall be taking this to Mumsnet,' she declared. 'And I think you'll find that they'll all agree that I'm NBU and you're in fact BVU.'

'What on earth are you talking about?' the bus lady asked in confusion.

'NBU – not being unreasonable; BVU – being very unreasonable. How can you not know that? Are you on glue?' Fiona demanded. Oh God. Although 'Are you on glue?' seems to be considered a reasonable, nay hilarious, question to ask on Mumsnet, something told me it wouldn't be received in quite the same spirit on a packed commuter bus at 8 a.m. when our feral children had just committed some sort of assault in pursuit of a marble.

'Oh look, it's our stop,' I squeaked, and hustled everyone off the bus before the cross lady could make good on her threats to 'report us'.

I breathed a sigh of relief as we all assembled at the bus stop, and after a quick head count realised too late that although we had all the children and the bastarding fishing nets and hampers and … oh holy fuck, what did Peter have? Oh God, he had a shoe. He had someone's shoe.

'Where did you get that?' I demanded.

'I found it on the bus,' said Peter with satisfaction.

'You … found … a shoe?'

'Yes.'

'And you decided the best thing to do with that shoe you found was to bring it with you?'

'Yes.'

'What if someone's looking for it? Actually, that's the least of my problems. Leave the shoe, put the shoe down, does anyone have any baby wipes? So, I've got a random shoe, and I've left the bloody buckets and spades on the bus!'

'Language, Ellen,' reproached Fiona. 'Oh dear, what a shame. I suppose you'll have to buy more, although that's not very green.'

I longed very much to pick up one of Fiona's adorable vintage-style tin spades and smack her very hard in the face with it, given that I'd only gone and forgotten the bastarding buckets and spades due to trying to get everybody off the bus before Fiona got decked and our sons all ended up on the sex offenders' register.

Finally, another two buses later, we arrived at our destination. It was still only just 9 a.m., as Fiona had insisted we must leave at a ridiculous hour to 'make the most of the day' and to ensure we 'got a good spot on the beach'. There was no danger of us missing a prime beach spot, though, as the beach was deserted, everyone else having had the good sense to stay inside in the hope things would warm up and the sun would come out.

'There's a café,' I said hopefully. 'Maybe we could get a cup of tea?'

'Nonsense,' said Fiona, striding onwards to the beach. 'Don't be so wet, Ellen.'

'Being wet is exactly what I'm afraid of,' I whimpered, as large drops of rain began to fall. 'Please, Fiona, it's raining. Don't you think we should take shelter?'

Fiona cast a contemptuous glance up at the sullen grey sky and announced it was obviously just a 'clearing-up shower' and the sun would be out in just a moment.

'A clearing-up shower?' asked Lucy's Mummy. 'What is that?'

'Oh really, Gemma,' Fiona snapped in exasperation. 'It's a rain shower that you have just before the weather clears up – it clears the air and then the sun comes out. My granny told me about them. Everyone knows clearing-up showers are a thing.'

'It doesn't *feel* like a clearing-up shower,' shivered Gemma. 'It feels like it's going to rain for ages. *My* granny always said that if there was enough blue sky to make a sailor a pair of trousers, then the sun would stay; but there's no blue sky at all, the sailor's going commando.'

'What a ridiculous notion,' snorted Fiona. 'It's very unscientific. How big is the sailor? If he was a very small sailor, only a very little bit of sky would be enough. It makes no sense whatsoever.'

'It makes as much sense as a clearing-up shower,' muttered Gemma mutinously. 'What did your granny say, Ellen?'

'Um, well, one granny mostly said unrepeatably racist things, and the other one mainly said, "Get me another martini and a ciggy, darling." I know which one I hope I take after.'

'There!' Fiona was triumphant. 'The rain's going off. I *told* you it was a clearing-up shower. The Montagues are never defeated by the weather. We stay on the beach.'

An hour later there did seem to be a hint of my Vision coming true. Fiona had decided to organise the children in a game of French cricket and had tolerated no refusals, and now they were all romping around so delightfully I was almost ready to forgive her for the scene on the bus. I did an anxious head count every couple of minutes to make sure we hadn't lost anyone – so far so good – then stretched back on the sand and tried to enjoy the sensation of someone else being in charge for once.

Usually, I was the one bossing everyone around and making all the plans and trying to execute them, but my organisational skills were no match for Fiona's clipboard and spreadsheets, and I didn't really know what to do with myself. I was also regretting my trainers and long, wafty dress, as I had to arrange myself awkwardly to avoid flashing my knickers, and my trainers were now full of sand. I was starting to see the wisdom of the romper suits and the sandals. Somehow, as well as threatening to indecently expose me to the world, the dress was also very bloody hot, and I could feel my thighs starting to chafe – again, not a problem for people in playsuits or with thighs as waiflike as Fiona and Gemma's.

'Can I have an ice cream? Can I have an ice cream? Can I have an ice cream?'

Peter was breathing heavily in my face and repeating this mantra, clearly working on the principle that although I was probably going to initially say 'No', one of us would eventually break, and it wouldn't be him.

I sat up, feeling thrilled that at last I had something to do.

'Can I have an ice cream?'

'Yes! Come on then. We need to go and buy buckets and spades anyway. Jane! JANE! Is anyone else coming to the shop?'

It immediately transpired that everyone wanted to come to the shop, and Fiona nobly jumped in to volunteer to stay on the beach, 'to look after everyone's stuff'.

'Shall we bring you back an ice cream?' I offered, but Fiona looked faint at the very idea. 'Well, I'll get your kids one, since I think all the others will be getting them.'

Fiona was now ashen under the perfectly applied St Tropez.

'The Montagues have very delicate stomachs. Do you suppose they have organic ice cream?' she quavered. 'And Cosmo is dairy-intolerant, Miles is gluten-free and Ottilie is vegan.'

'I'll do my best,' I promised.

The village shop, needless to say, did not have any organic ice cream, whether vegan, non-dairy or gluten-free. I bought The Montagues a Calippo each, as it ticked three out of four of the criteria, though I told the children to dispose of the packaging before Fiona saw it, as I feared the list of colourings, including copper complexes of chlorophyllins, would fall foul of her ban on processed food. Still, I reasoned, copper was a natural substance and chlorophyllins must be something to do with chlorophyll, which came from plants, so they were *practically* organic!

Lucy's Mummy had vanished to the back of the shop, and Lucy was also clamouring for an ice cream, so I bought Feasts for her and my own fiends, deciding that I'd deal with her mother's objections later. These couldn't, after all, be any more painful than being fleeced £9.99 per bucket and spade kit for replacements for the ones I'd left on the bus.

Gemma, it turned out, had been searching the shop in vain for suitable suntan lotion, as she'd only brought one bottle along with her and was afraid of running out.

'There wasn't a thing!' she said despairingly to Fiona. 'Nothing at all!'

'There was some Ambre Solaire,' I put in helpfully. Their heads swivelled towards me as one, and stared at me aghast.

'But that's *chemicals*,' whispered Gemma, her big blue eyes brimming with fear. 'I only use organic, sulphate-free, paraben-free natural products on Lucy. Chemicals cause *cancer*, Ellen!'

I opened my mouth to point out that everything is chemicals. The beach was chemicals. The sea was chemicals. *WE* were chemicals, but I was slightly afraid they might waterboard me with their stainless-steel BPA-free water bottles containing only pure, filtered, natural mountain spring water until I repented of the error of my ways. Also, the conversation had reminded me that I'd not, in fact, put any sunscreen on my own little darlings, which was very remiss, given how hot it now was, so hot that poor Lucy's Feast had practically melted off the stick before Gemma had even noticed she was eating it.

Unsuncreened moppets is a failing of middle-class parenting so severe as to be punishable by having your MyWaitrose card and your National Trust memberships revoked. Truly it's a miracle how we all survived our own sunscreenless childhoods, as it's drummed into us now that TERRIBLE THINGS will happen should the children suffer any exposure to the SKY DEATH RAYS without liberal applications of Factor 50. We even had a letter from the school last January reminding us that despite there only being approximately five hours of daylight in the entire month, and a high likelihood it would be pissing down anyway, we must be sure to apply sunscreen each morning to our offspring in case there were a few dry moments and they ventured out into the playground. Quite where the sun was supposed to scorch them through the coats, hats, gloves and scarves the school also mandated they must be wearing wasn't made clear. I know it's not impossible to get hypothermia at the same time as getting sunburnt, but it does seem unlikely to happen in a British playground in January.

I made vague noises about 'reapplying sun cream', and responded to Fiona's astonished questions about 'But don't you use the twelve-hour waterproof one, Ellen?' by muttering it was better to be safe than sorry, and hastily summonsed the children, who objected violently to being dragged away from re-enacting a beach scene from *iCarly* (Jane) and investigating the innards of a dead seagull (Peter).

Despite my best attempts to discreetly apply my shameful Ambre Solaire, Jane insisted she could do it herself and needed no assistance, and proceeded to dab a small amount on her nose and a speck on each cheek, then declared herself 'done'.

'You're not done,' I snapped, as I attempted to wrestle Peter to a standstill to apply cream over him. 'No, you're not going yet. Wait till I've done your brother and then I'll do you, just hang on, Jane, WAIT.'

Meanwhile, Peter was still doing his best greased-piglet impression and now began screaming like a stuck one because I was attempting to rub sunscreen over him and he was sandy and the whole effect was ever so slightly abrasive. While I agreed that the experience mustn't have been pleasant for him, I didn't think it was in any way the 'AGONY' he insisted it was as he howled 'Owwww, Mummy, that hurts so much, why are you hurting me? Stop it Mum, stop HURTING ME'. Nonetheless, I could sense that people were watching us.

When I at last looked up I found the same German tourists who had witnessed me apparently feeding my children dogshit staring at me once again.

Seriously? I groaned to myself. What were the chances of them surfacing here? Why couldn't I speak German so I could go and explain to them that I did not torture my children nor make them eat faeces, but was trying my best to give them a MAGICAL SUMMER full of HAPPY MEMORIES? In fairness, they probably spoke impeccable English, but I felt the optics would be better if I told them all this in their own language, thereby demonstrating that I was a multicultural, well-rounded person. Not for the first time I cursed my mother for forcing me to do Latin at school instead of German. What use was it that I could merrily inform them that Caecilius was in the forum, the dog was in the street and that Quintus was doing whatever it was that Quintus did (actually, Quintus was a bit dodgy, as I recalled)?

Fiona, however, whether she couldn't bear the noise Peter was making or the shame of the Germanic judging, intervened and said sternly, 'Peter! Mummy is *helping* you. They're not kind things to be saying to Mummy! Why not just let Mummy help?'

To my astonishment, Peter calmed down, meekly stood still and let me smear him in sunscreen.

'How did you *do* that?' I gasped in admiration. Fiona looked surprised and said, 'Do what? Jane, wait, I can do you too. No, you're not finished. Ellen, throw the bottle over here and I'll finish Jane for you.'

'Um … oh dear, I think it's run out, actually. I'm sure Jane will be fine,' I prevaricated wildly, lest Fiona faint on the beach when she clocked my cheap sun lotion and we couldn't even revive her with *sal volatile* because *chemicals*.

'Oh don't worry, I've got three bottles, I'll use some of mine. It's on offer at the moment, by the way, it's a great deal. Only £32.99 a bottle if you buy three bottles!'

It was my turn to almost faint on the spot.

To my alarm, once my cherubs were suitably greased, Fiona brought out the clipboard.

'Now,' she said firmly. 'Let's do some planning. Since we're all at home for the holidays – well, except for lucky you going to France, Ellen – but as we're stuck here because of the *bloody* Clooneys, we need to really maximise our time. It's unfortunate all the classes are booked, but we can compensate for that ourselves, I feel. The first thing is identify our *key objectives* these holidays. Ellen, what are you hoping to achieve?'

'Well, just Happy Memories,' I said vaguely.

'Yes, but how exactly do you intend to achieve that?' insisted Fiona.

'Well, just … I suppose with –'

'Don't say "japes and frolics", please,' put in Fiona in a vaguely threatening way. 'Come on, concentrate. How are you going to optimise your goal-based learning for the children?'

'It's the holidays. Do they need to learn anything?' I tried feebly.

'Yes!' Fiona was horrified. 'Every moment with your children is a teachable moment, it's vital we don't waste them. Have a think, Ellen, and I'll come back to you. Gemma, I know Giles said he was very keen Lucy improves her languages this summer. And I, obviously, am always trying to broaden The Montagues' perspectives, so how do you suggest we go about this?'

'We could do language days,' suggested Gemma, 'where we only speak the chosen language of the day?'

'Like in the *Chalet School* books?' I asked eagerly.

They both looked at me blankly.

'What's the Chalet School?' demanded Fiona. 'Is it a new educational concept? Why haven't I heard of it?'

'Um, no, they're books,' I said feebly. 'School stories, you know?'

'School stories?' said Fiona in disgust. 'Aren't we a bit old for things like that?'

'Never,' I muttered rebelliously to myself, glaring at Fiona and Gemma, and wondering how I could ever turn them into kindred spirits if they didn't understand about school stories, and also wondering how Joey Bettany would have won them round? Apart from rescuing them from some sort of precipice peril or a spot of mild kidnapping before she fell into unconsciousness and lay at death's door for several days until Fiona and Gemma repented of their wicked ways and declared the Chalet School to be the totes best ever. There was a dearth of precipices on the beach, though. I looked hopefully at the other beach inhabitants on the off chance one of them should appear sufficiently common and foreign enough to attempt a kidnapping for me to foil. Perhaps the Germans? No, they were far too wholesome-looking to kidnap anyone.

Fiona was still on about Gemma's language days idea, though, and was now trying to decide which language we were going to speak, which was where the plan rather fell down, as it turned out Gemma's claims she could 'get by' in French, Italian and Spanish only extended to ordering drinks on holiday.

'Well, I've got GCSE French,' sighed Fiona. 'But there's the rest of the week, and I was hoping someone would be more fluent, so the children could really *immerse* themselves. Ellen, what about you? Someone must have at least an A-level language?'

'No, sorry, only GCSE here too.'

'In what, though? Maybe German? Russian?' Fiona pleaded hopefully. Russian? What sort of school did Fiona think I went to that taught Russian?

'French as well, I'm afraid.'

Fiona was crestfallen, so I attempted to cheer her up by adding, 'And Latin.'

'Latin. Well, that's practically Italian, isn't it?' Fiona was excited now. 'And also, Latin could be very useful for The Montagues when we do our museum projects.'

'We can't really spend a whole day just speaking Latin?' I objected.

'Why not?'

'Well, no one just *speaks* Latin all day, do they?'

'The Romans did,' Fiona pointed out.

'I can't remember enough to speak it all day. I don't think I ever knew enough to speak it at all.'

'Nonsense.' Fiona was now at her briskest. 'It'll soon come back to you. Just try and say something.'

'Errr … *Quanti canicula ille in fenestra*?' I dredged up from some forgotten corner of my mind.

'Splendid, see? I knew you could do it,' Fiona beamed. 'Now, what does it mean?'

Fiona's disappointment when I admitted it meant 'How much is that doggie in the window' was so immense that she abandoned the language day project altogether.

*　　*　　*

The beach got busier and busier, and I had to admit that Fiona had had a point about arriving early. Fiona and Gemma were now deep into an intense conversation about people from their Pilates class that I didn't know, one of whom they suspected of lying about a gastric band, and I didn't really have much to contribute to this. I gazed along the beach and saw a couple of women with kids about the same age as ours. They were sitting chatting, but unlike Fiona and Gemma, who were now hissing that the poor gastric-band woman should be forced to confess her pie-eating crimes to the class (well, words to that effect), they were laughing and sharing what looked suspiciously like a delicious bottle of pink sunshine wine.

The bucket and spade shop had sold wine. It had sold everything, actually, including the death sunscreen, but also wine. A big, lovely chiller cabinet full of cold, lovely wine. I'd stood longingly in front of it for some time, but had been unsure how to introduce the subject to Fiona and Gemma. Now I had the perfect excuse. They ran out of steam for Pilates Lady and there was a brief lull in their chuntering while they cast around for the next person to judge.

'Look,' I jumped in quickly, nodding in the general direction of the two happy women further down the beach. 'Look, they've got wine …?'

'WINE?' Fiona was like a meerkat, gazing round avidly. 'Wine? On the beach?'

'Yes, doesn't it look nice? Maybe we could …?'

Fiona wasn't listening, though.

'Wine on a day out with the children? And how will they drive home?'

'Maybe they came by bus as well?' I said, but Fiona merely sniffed at that.

I was still looking longingly at the two jolly women and their wine, and tried my final trump card. 'French women often have a glass of wine at lunch, though, and the entire population of French children haven't been taken off them, have they?'

Fiona looked confused, as the one thing the whole of Mumsnet is in agreement about is that anything French women do is desirable, classy and aspirational, in curious defiance of the fact that as well as their style and slenderness, French women are largely famed for drinking, smoking and adultery. Wine on the beach was bad … but was it also *French*? This didn't compute.

'I think it's time to paddle,' she finally said, glaring at me. 'You can't go in the sea if you've been drinking, can you? It would be *unsafe.*'

Alas, once again, the romper suits won out against my floaty floral dress. In my head, the dress had been perfect to paddle in while looking like something from a Merchant Ivory film, and perhaps a handsome man in a cream suit and a Panama hat, maybe a boater, would appear from nowhere and kiss me (no, not a boater, actually; with a cream suit this would be a bit too much like Dick Van Dyke in *Mary Poppins*, rather than George Emerson sweeping Lucy Honeychurch off her feet). In reality, however, I had to basically bunch it up rather unattractively round my bum, stopping just short of tucking it into my knickers, while Fiona and Gemma simply romped around in precisely the manner romper suits were designed for. There would be no doubt which of us a dashing Panama'd man would choose to kiss, should he appear. Actually, if he had any sense, he'd kiss one of the jolly wine women, who had now chucked a packet of sausage rolls at their little darlings and were both reading copies of the new Jilly Cooper.

Making new friends was proving harder than I'd initially imagined. When Fiona and Gemma had invited me along today, I thought I would slot in seamlessly, that I'd have arrived, at one with the popular girls at last. 'Take that, Hannah!' I'd sniffed to myself, 'I don't need you. I've got new friends. *Better* friends.' But gazing at the two women – now nudging each other and laughing over one of Jilly's marvellous puns, or maybe a particularly saucy bit – I missed Hannah. I wondered what time it was in South Africa, and if I could text her. But no. No. I hadn't done anything wrong. Hannah was the one who had abandoned me. I wasn't giving in first. *She* could apologise to *me*, and then – and only then – we could move on.

The rest of the afternoon passed without incident, apart from Peter trying to entice the junior Montagues into a competition to see who could wee the furthest, which I don't think was the sort of learning through play or teachable moment Fiona had quite had in mind. Other than the sunscreen episode, though, I was congratulating myself that surely this must count as a successful day of #HappyMemories. How could it not, when with Fiona in charge, no one had dared injure themselves, no picnics had been submerged and no dubious shrubberies consumed? I didn't know why Fiona was so obsessed with the potential Medical Emergencies she was always going on about; The Montagues were simply far too well trained to deviate even slightly from their mother's iron-clad plans.

'Well, that was fun,' said Lucy's Mummy as we got off the final bus (I'd counselled leaving early so we didn't meet the commuters returning home, lest we encountered the poor upskirted lady again). 'I don't want it to end. Why don't you all come back to mine, and I'll open some wine and give the kids dinner? I've lots of batch-cooked things in the freezer I can defrost. Oooh, there's a lovely quinoa, tofu and kale bake I made last week!'

'I can't possibly,' said Fiona in scandalised tones. 'The Montagues are having a Games Night. I set up the *Boggle* before I left. The children have been looking forward to it all week and would be devastated to miss it, wouldn't you, darlings?'

'Yes, Mummy,' Ottilie obediently replied. 'I love *Boggle*, but I do also enjoy *Trivial Pursuit*. You can learn a lot of useful general knowledge that way.'

'See?' smirked Fiona. 'Cosmo, Miles, you love *Boggle* too, don't you?'

Cosmo and Miles made slightly less enthusiastic noises than Ottilie had, and Cosmo muttered something that sounded suspiciously like '*Boggle* is bullshit.' I feared Peter had not been a good influence.

'Ellen?' Lucy's Mummy looked at me pleadingly. 'Go on. It'll be fun. Please, it's just Lucy and me this weekend. Giles is at some financial conference in Stockholm.'

I remained to be convinced that eating tofu and kale bake with Perfect Lucy Atkinson and her Perfect Mummy would be as much fun as was being promised, but Jane piped up with, 'Oh yes please, Mum. Lucy has a mini satin rabbit that she has promised to show me. You *know* I've always wanted a mini satin rabbit!'

'You've literally never mentioned this before now,' I pointed out. But Jane looked so eager, Peter seemed amenable when he was promised access to the PlayStation, and even Lucy herself was looking more like a normal child (i.e. slightly grubby with a hint of stickiness) than usual after her day at the beach, unlike The Montagues, who still gave the impression that they'd just stepped out of the pages of a Boden catalogue. Gemma seemed so keen too, and because I knew from Simon's work trips how long the days, let alone the weeks, could seem when you were on your own with the kids while everyone else was playing Happy Families, I gave in.

Also, I reminded myself firmly – new friends. What was the point of feeling a bit sorry for myself all afternoon, with the sense that I'd been left out by Fiona and Gemma because they knew each other so well, if I then turned down the chance to get to know one of them better myself?

Also, if I was perfectly honest, I was keen to have a proper nosy at Lucy Atkinson's house, as I'd only ever passed it on the outside, and I was dying to know if it was as perfect and tasteful as Lucy and her Mummy were. It did not disappoint. There was a 'mud room', though I couldn't believe any of the Atkinsons had ever been near mud, where gleaming wellies were lined up in order of size, and there were wicker baskets containing colour-coded sunhats and umbrellas and other outdoor paraphernalia, and there was a utility room as well, with giant washing machines and tumble dryers, even though there were only three people living there. The kitchen was a dream – the vast island alone was about the size of my entire kitchen – and there was a huge magic fridge, as Jane had once christened the swanky American-style fridges that make ice, and when Gemma opened it to get the bottle of Whispering Angel (what else?) out, everything was in nice containers and there was no suspicious lurking matter, or a Gü pot of ground coffee to attempt to get rid of the funny smell caused by the suspicious lurking matter. It was quite the nicest fridge I'd ever seen, apart from when I saw Nigel Slater's on TV, but I suspected he'd just pimped it up for the cameras and his *real* fridge didn't contain double cream decanted into Kilner jars (though deep down inside I hoped it did).

There was a walk-in larder as well. Oh, I've always longed and longed for a walk-in larder. The estate agent blurb for our house claimed it had one, but what it really has is a dark hole that should be the cupboard under the stairs that someone once knocked through from the kitchen. Technically you *can* walk into it, if you class a sort of sideways crab-like shuffle as walking, but it's not even comparable to the airy, light *room* that was Gemma's larder. I think it might be bigger than Peter's bedroom, though he'd probably be quite happy to sleep in a larder, with snacks constantly to hand. Maybe not Gemma's larder, though, as lentils and obscure grains featured heavily (decanted into glass jars, OBVIOUSLY), with not so much as a hint of Monster Munch or Coco Pops.

Off the hall I caught a glimpse of a perfectly white-on-white sitting room, and even the downstairs bog smelled delightful and had posh soap in it, despite the fact that Gemma hadn't been expecting visitors. I wage a constant war against Simon and the children about our downstairs loo, which I've designated the Non-Shitting Toilet, but no one listens. In fact, they seem to positively take glee in crapping in there to spite me, and of course, we also have the Phantom Shitter to contend with, who likes to go in and leave a huge floating turd bobbing round just before guests arrive. Everyone strenuously denies it was them, to the point that I'm torn between suspecting my entire family of gaslighting me, and wondering if *I'm* the Phantom Shitter and googling to see if 'Poo Amnesia' is A Thing (it's not, or at least it has not thus far been documented, although I did discover that a woman once apparently strained so hard on the loo she lost her short-term memory, so I suppose it is theoretically possible that I'm the Phantom Shitter).

If Hannah had been here, we'd secretly have whispered to each other that it was all 'a bit vulgar, really', before laughing and admitting that actually we were just ragingly envious that we couldn't afford a lifestyle or house even close to this. In fact, it wasn't the same at all, knowing there was no one to exclaim later to about 'Oh my GOD, and did you see the …?' Even if Hannah hadn't actually been there, I'd have taken sneaky photos in the loo to show her, to give her an idea of the place, and then we could have made ourselves feel better by saying we wouldn't really want a handwoven willow trug of quilted loo rolls with pot pourri sprinkled artfully over them *anyway* (although I very much *did* want such a thing, on reflection I imagined that pot pourri-ing the bog roll would probably give you a nasty rash on your unmentionables …).

I sternly forbade Peter to touch anything, *anything* at all, and Jane was borne off by Lucy to find the mini satin rabbit. Lucy's Mummy waved Peter through to Lucy's playroom off the kitchen, and he plonked himself happily down in front of the promised PlayStation, then almost immediately appeared again, complaining loudly that all Lucy's games were 'educational' and that there was no *GTA*. Lucy's Mummy looked shocked at this, as I hastily assured her that Peter was *joking* and *of course* I don't let him play *GTA*. I handed Peter my phone, with the express instruction that he wasn't to watch anything except YouTube Kids, or all screen time would banned for the foreseeable future, and he disappeared back into the playroom, looking distinctly unimpressed by the 'snack plate' of carrots, peppers and hummous that had been handed to him.

Lucy and Jane rushed back into the kitchen, Jane clutching a tiny and admittedly adorable rabbit. When she'd been wittering at me about mini satin rabbits, I'd envisaged some sort of cuddly toy, not a *real* rabbit.

'Look, Mum,' she squealed. 'Isn't he lovely? Can we get one, Mum, *pleeeease*! I'll look after it, I promise, you won't have to do anything. And look, Mum, he's house-trained, he hops round Lucy's room and he only poops in his litter box in his crate. I want a house-trained rabbit, Mummy. Please say we can get one, please, I'll be so good and I won't call Peter an arseface or tell him to die in a hole, if I can only have a little rabbit like this one Mum, can I, can I, can I –?'

I interrupted Jane to remind her of the practicalities of our life.

'Jane, what about Judgy?' I asked in my most reasonable tone.

'What about him?'

'He's a terrier, darling. What is he going to do with a house-trained rabbit?'

'Be friends?' Jane tried hopefully.

'No, darling. He'll eat it.'

Lucy burst into noisy tears. 'I don't want the dogs to eat the rabbits,' she wailed. 'That's not nice!'

'They won't,' I assured her, as Gemma rushed out from the giant larder, tofu and kale bakes in each hand, to see what was happening.

'Don't cry, Lucy. Judgy won't eat a rabbit, because we won't get one, because we can't get one, because we already have him.'

I decided not to tell Lucy he had, in fact, already eaten many wild rabbits, as I didn't feel it would help the situation. Jane was less tactful.

'He does eat rabbits. He ripped the head off one once, Lucy.'

Lucy's wails increased.

'Jane,' I hissed. 'Please do shut up.'

'Could we train him out of killing things?' Jane suggested, as Lucy's Mummy attempted to console Lucy as she wept hysterically about not wanting any bunnies to ever die, especially not with their heads ripped off. Jane, realising too late that she hadn't helped the situation, also attempted to console Lucy by pointing out that at least having your head ripped off by a murderous terrier was a *quick* way to die. 'Not like when a cat tortures a mouse for hours,' she added with relish. Oh God. Gemma was now administering tincture of valerian to Lucy to calm her down, and I was fighting the urge to slap Jane quite hard if she didn't keep her mouth shut.

In the end, Gemma had to break out the emergency ice cream to stop Lucy crying. 'Just this once, poppet,' she said in desperation, as Lucy finally hiccupped herself into silence.

I could see that Jane was about to say something again. 'Jane!' I said quickly. 'Now Lucy's cheered up, I think you should take Mr Waffles back to his crate. He looks tired. And *don't mention death or killing things or anything other than happy, fun things,*' I muttered threateningly as I passed her Mr Waffles.

'I'm afraid Lucy is very sensitive,' said Gemma, pouring another glass of wine. 'It's often the case with gifted and talented children.'

I immediately wondered if perhaps every time I'd thought my children were simply being arseholes was actually them being sensitive because they were so gifted and talented and I hadn't even noticed because I was such a bad mother. Sometimes it seemed like however hard one tried at parenting, it was still never good enough. There was always something you were missing, something more you should have done. Though in my defence, if

I'd missed the signs that my children were latent geniuses, so too – up to this point – had all their teachers, so perhaps I couldn't be held entirely to blame for this one.

'Anyway,' Gemma continued, 'what shall we have for dinner? I took the tofu and kale bakes out of the freezer. Or if you don't fancy that, I could make a nice seabass ceviche for us all, with a carrot slaw. That would be fun – sort of like fish and chips, since we've been at the beach!'

I gulped. The chip shop at the beach didn't open till 5 p.m., so we'd missed out on the fish and chips I'd promised the children (and also on the arguments with Fiona and Gemma about the carbs and the fat), but there was no way my precious moppets were going to eat either the famous tofu and kale bake, or Gemma's weird idea of fish and chips.

'Look, don't worry,' I said. 'I'll just make something for my two when we get home' (by which I meant go by the chippy on the way back).

'No, no, I promised you all dinner,' insisted Gemma. 'I must make them something to eat.'

'Really, it's fine. I don't mean to be rude, but I don't think they'll eat either of those dishes.'

'Oh.' Gemma suddenly looked deflated. 'Oh, I see. Well, let's see what we have got that they will eat,' and she dragged me to the larder and began to rifle through the shelves in a slightly despairing way. Finally she turned to me with a conspiratorial look on her face. 'I've had a very wicked idea,' she whispered. 'Giles would be appalled, but I'll bribe Lucy to keep quiet, so he'll never know. Would you be very shocked, Ellen, if we *ordered pizza*?'

To be honest, from the way Gemma had been whispering about secrets and wickedness, I'd thought she was going to suggest something really awful, like taking crack, so I was quite relieved that her idea of something shocking was a large stuffed-crust pepperoni.

'I think I could live with myself,' I said. 'And after all, it's FIAF!'

'What's FIAF?' asked Gemma, looking confused.

'FIAF? Why, FIAF is Fuck It All Friday. We've made it through the week, so we can reward ourselves for our maternal devotion and successfully keeping the children alive by feeding them pizza without guilt and drinking wine without guilt. It's the best day of the week, because it's the only guilt-free day. By Saturday morning you're rushing to swimming lessons and wondering if you've inveigled them into the right sorts of extra-curricular activities to enhance their futures, and by Sunday you're doing the laundry and thinking about the week ahead, but on Friday, that's all to come, and there's just junk food and wine and NO GUILT for a few blessed hours!'

'Oh, I *see*,' said Gemma. 'Yes, Fiona and I sometimes treat ourselves on Fridays too. We open a bottle of champagne and get a masseuse or a facialist or someone over. It's brilliant fun, isn't it.'

'Brilliant,' I agreed weakly, while still thinking what am I doing here.

'So that's a yes to pizza, then?' she said excitedly.

'Yes, why not? And I think I've got a Domino's coupon on my phone we can use.'

Gemma gasped in horror. '*Dominos*? I meant we should order one from that new artisan sourdough vegan place on the high street.'

Oh. Gemma may have made concessions, but it was clear we were still approaching FIAF from very different places. I suddenly felt utterly exhausted.

'Actually, Gemma,' I said, draining my glass, 'I think I need to go. I've remembered I need to do a … a … thing.'

'But we haven't ordered the pizza yet! There's still lots of wine left!'

'I know, sorry. Maybe another time?'

Back at home, the sandy, sticky, exhausted children had baths then collapsed into their beds. Simon and I sat out in the garden with a bottle of wine. It was still terribly hot, and I was slightly regretting leaving the cool, air-conditioned, marbled halls of Gemma's house so soon. I tried to explain to Simon about Gemma and Fiona's version of FIAF, and how alien it was to me.

'So you wouldn't want someone to come round on a Friday night to your big, clean, tidy house and give you a massage?' he said, slightly bemused.

'No, I would – obviously that would be amazing. Like … once or something? Not every week. Well, I would like it every week. But *as well* as proper FIAFing, you know?'

'By proper FIAFing, do you mean the bit where you and Hannah and Sam get shitfaced and sing *Wuthering Heights* very badly and do the special dance routine you made up, and then you text me from swimming lessons the next morning, threatening to vomit in the pool because you're so hungover?'

'YES! That's exactly what I mean. I just can't ever see myself doing that with Fiona and Gemma. Or being able to afford to FIAF their way. I just don't think they're My People, you know? I've not found my village in them.'

'Well, maybe you need to find a different village then,' Simon said quite reasonably.

'But how?' I wailed in despair. '*How* do I find a new village?'

'Well, try a bit harder with Gemma and Fiona?'

'But they're already their own little village. I'm just the … the …

leper at the gates. They toss me crusts but I'll never really be allowed in, and I'll just be left to sit and fester and die alone, reading *The Head-Girl of the Chalet School* in rags, starving and abandoned!'

'Ellen, you're overreacting and being melodramatic,' said Simon in exasperation. 'If you don't want to find new friends, and if you really don't want to persevere with Fiona and Gemma, then there's a perfectly simple solution to this whole thing, you know!'

'What?'

'Just message Hannah and make up with her. She's only gone for a month, you'll cope without her for a few weeks till she's back, and then you can just pick up where you left off.'

'No. No, I won't. If Hannah wants to apologise to me, then fine. But I'm not backing down. She left me, remember.'

'Right. Well, if you're going to be like that about it –'

'Like what?'

'Childish! If you're going to be so childish about a silly row with Hannah, then you'd better learn to like fucking quinoa and clean living and get yourself on Mumsnet, hadn't you? I'm going to bed!

Saturday 30 July

I woke up this morning with a dry mouth and a headache, both of which I firmly attributed to not drinking enough water yesterday and definitely had nothing to do with my enthusiastic consumption of pink sunshine wine. On the other hand, as I reasoned to myself, if one cannot drink pink sunshine wine on a sunny summer's day, then really what point is there in living in this cold, dark, cruel world?

I got up and tottered downstairs. The sun was already blazing outside and it felt scorching when I let Judgy out for a wee. Despite the heat, I put the kettle on to make some tea. There are few problems in the world unsolved by tea. Alas, I was quickly to realise that although this is true and tea solves *most* problems, there are some problems that remain intractable in the face of even a large pot of strong builder's, the most tea-resistant issue being that of my mother.

The doorbell rang as I was thickly buttering a lovely slice of toast to go with my steaming mug of healing tea (milk and two sugars, since this was a semi-medicinal situation, as I possibly had sunstroke), while at the same time trying to tune out Jane wittering on at me about the solutions she'd come up with overnight that would enable her to keep a mini satin rabbit in her bedroom with-out Judgy turning it into a tasty snack.

She had her arm around Judgy, who was doing his best inno-cent face and agreeing with Jane that he definitely wouldn't eat any rabbits that came into the house, but I've fallen for his innocent face too many times before – 'Look at me,' he says. 'Look at my little face. Am I not adorable? How could anything as cute as me try to savage next door's cat? Or shit in your favourite shoes? Or run away for hours on end until you're on the verge of a nervous breakdown? Not me. Never me ...' I didn't for one second believe him when he said he wouldn't eat the rabbit, and I could just see his evil mind working as he decided whether a small rabbit would constitute a full meal or simply a little snack.

'Jane,' I said firmly. 'Shush. I need to go and answer the door.'

'Maybe it's someone who's found a stray rabbit and they're look-ing for someone to take it in and we could adopt it and then I'd have a rabbit of my own?'

'I think that's very unlikely, darling.'

'It might be,' she insisted, 'but it's not impossible. If it's not a stray-rabbit man, can I go and wake up Dad and ask *him* if I can get a rabbit?'

'Yes,' I agreed. 'What a good idea. Go and make it your father's problem.'

I went through to the hall and opened the door, and found, to my complete surprise, my mother on the doorstep.

'Mum! What are you doing here?'

'I've left Geoffrey, darling, and have come to stay. Isn't that nice?'

You've *what*?' I reeled at this unexpected news. Mum stuck by her awful second husband Geoffrey through thick and thin due to

his Queen Anne rectory, and his gold-plated and extremely generous pension plan.

'It's all too sordid, darling. I don't want to talk about it. Are you
going to let me in, or are you going to keep your own mother
standing on the doorstep in the cold?'

'But Mum, it's only 9 a.m. Did you drive down from Yorkshire
overnight?'

'Don't be silly, darling, what a ghastly idea. Like some sort of
lorry driver? Why would I drive all that way? Geoffrey does the
driving on long journeys. No, I got the train down yesterday and I
stayed with Judith Frobisher last night – she and Malcolm only
live about half an hour away. Malcolm dropped me off, and here I
am. Now, why are you still in your pyjamas at this time, really?!
And on such a lovely day. You're *wasting* it.'

'Granny's here,' I announced feebly to Jane as Mum barrelled
through into the kitchen, crying, 'Oh good Lord, you're still in
your pyjamas *too*. And where is my grandson? And my son-in-
law?'

'Peter's in the sitting room,' I ventured. 'I'll go get him,' I
added quickly, before Mum found Peter in his usual Saturday-
morning state, slumped glassy-eyed on the floor with a bowl of
Coco Pops in front of *SpongeBob*. At least he's not in his pyjamas,
I thought, if only because he liked to sit in his pants for this weekend ritual.

'And Simon? Isn't he coming to say hello? Oh, silly me. It's
Saturday morning, isn't it? He'll be playing golf!'

Simon has never played golf in his life, but Mum is firmly
convinced that every middle-class man is as obsessed with golf as
Geoffrey is, and indeed looks on non-golfers as having some sort
of failing of moral fibre.

'I'll get him too,' I sighed.

'And get dressed, Ellen,' Mum called after me. 'For goodness' sake, you really need to buck up your standards and have some self-respect, darling!'

Jane, meanwhile, took a deep breath and started to tap up her grandmother to buy her a mini satin rabbit.

Simon took the news of my mother's arrival quite well, all considering.

'What the fuck do you mean, your mother's left Geoffrey and come to stay? For how long?'

'I don't know.'

'Why can't she stay with Jessica?'

In fairness to Simon, that was an excellent question. Why couldn't Mum stay with my perfect sister, whom she blatantly preferred to me? I wished I'd thought to ask her that.

'I don't know,' I admitted.

'Well, why has she left Geoffrey?'

'Because it's all too sordid.'

'What's too sordid?'

'I DON'T KNOW. She just said it was all too sordid.'

'Oh my God, do you think he wanted to try pegging?'

'SIMON! This is my mother and step-father we're talking about. Don't say things like that.'

Further questioning of Mum revealed that Geoffrey had been abandoned due to finding him kissing Bunty Barnsworth behind the scenes at the village am-dram summer performance of *Anything Goes*. Geoffrey and Bunty, it seemed, had taken the title rather too literally, so Mum had departed in High Dudgeon.

'He has to learn, darling, that he simply can't treat me like that.'

'So, is it over with Geoffrey, Mum?'

'Good Lord, no. Why ever would you say that? No, I just need to teach him a lesson.'

I took a deep breath. 'And how long do you think this lesson might take?'

'Oh,' Mum said airily, 'I don't know. A few weeks. He'll soon realise he and the cats can't do without me, and what he'd be throwing away by messing round with an old tart like Bunty. Apparently she's had,' Mum lowered her voice to a conspiratorial whisper, '*rejuvenation surgery, down there*! Can you imagine the state of her, if she's needed that? No, Geoffrey won't enjoy that sort of thing at all. He has quite specific tastes, Geoffrey.'

'MUM!'

'I'm just saying, darling. Clearly it was all Bunty's fault, and she seduced poor Geoffrey. But he must learn, and I'm not going back till he's apologised. Properly.'

'The thing is, Mum, you say a few weeks, but it's not as easy as that. It's the summer holidays. We've got a lot planned. Not least, we're going to France next week.'

'France!' Mum suddenly perked up. 'Whereabouts? Don't worry about me, I'm more than happy to come. Have you got a villa? South, I assume. Oh, a nice tan would be just the job to make Geoffrey jealous. Especially if I had *une petite liaison dangereuse* with some charming French fellow in Nice. This is perfect, darling. Clever old you! Or, if it's not a villa, I don't mind a hotel – I'm sure they'll squeeze me in.'

'No, no, it's a villa. Well, house, chateau almost, but …'

'But what?' demanded Mum.

'Well, it's Sylvia and Michael's place. They're away for a couple of weeks and they said we could use the house. I'd need to ask them, but I'm sure they won't mind and there's plenty of room.'

'Sylvia's house! I'm not staying in Sylvia Russell's house. That woman is nothing more than a jumped-up tart. I'm not going cap in hand to that dreadful woman like some poor relation, begging to stay so she can lord it over me for the rest of our lives.'

'That's my mother you're talking about, Yvonne, steady on,' Simon put in.

Mum now proceeded to have a fit of the vapours. I'd apparently just promised her a holiday in the south of France, to recuperate from the stress of Geoffrey and Bunty's illicit snog, and now I'd ruined it all!

'This,' said Mum dramatically, 'is typical of you, Ellen. You make everything about yourself, just like you did with your wedding!'

'I don't,' I said, stung by the same words Hannah had thrown at me. 'I don't make everything about me.'

'You made me book my own accommodation for your wedding, and now you're doing the same here. Selfish, Ellen. You've always been selfish. I bet Jessica wouldn't behave like this.'

How did my mother always do this? Ten minutes in her company and I felt like a child again. The endless comparisons with Jessica, who was always 'better' than me – Jessica, the 'good' one. The rational, adult part of me knew I hadn't done anything to wrong my mother, but another part of me still felt the need to apologise, to try harder, to promise to be better. And yet another part of me wanted to burst into tears and simply wail that it wasn't FAIR, I hadn't even DONE ANYTHING. Fortunately, Simon intervened.

'Maybe you should go and stay with Jessica then?' he said firmly. 'After all, Yvonne, we didn't exactly arrange this with you in mind. Five minutes ago you weren't going to France at all, so it's hardly fair to claim Ellen promised you a holiday and then snatched it away from you.'

Mum huffed. She couldn't stay with Jessica because Jessica was in Capri for three weeks, and somehow *this* was my fault as well.

'Maybe you could go to Capri,' I ventured. 'Meet a nice millionaire with a yacht.'

'Oh really, Ellen,' Mum snorted. 'Don't be facetious. I'm in *pain* here, and all I asked for was a little time to lick my wounds in the sun!'

'You could come, though,' I said, now on the verge of tears. 'There's a swimming pool, and a tennis court! You like tennis!'

I wasn't sure why I was now trying to talk my mother round to coming on holiday with us, when I couldn't think of anything worse, except she'd once again made me somehow feel so guilty that I felt I had to placate her and offer something. I knew Simon would tell me afterwards that there was no reason for me to feel guilty for arranging a holiday six months ago that my mother had decided today didn't meet her exacting specifications, one which she'd had no idea about until five minutes ago, since apart from birthday, Easter and Christmas cards, I'd barely heard from her all year.

But Simon had never been that little girl longing for her mother's love and approval, desperate to please, and still desperate – after more than forty years of disappointing her mother – to finally get something right. This was why I was scrabbling around trying to sell Sylvia and Michael's house to her, despite Simon's frantic head-shakings and Jane's horrified looks. Peter remained oblivious in front of the TV and didn't appear to have even noticed that his grandmother had arrived.

'Who,' said my mother in her most scathing tones, 'am I supposed to play tennis with?'

'Me?' I tried hopefully.

'You? *You*? After all the money I wasted on those tennis lessons for you, when you still can't even serve properly? You're not even close to my standard. *I* could have been a professional tennis player, you know, if I hadn't had you. Anyway,' Mum sniffed, 'I'd hoped I could have counted on some support from my family in my hour of need, but I see it's too much to ask for. Nonetheless, I take it you're not so very ungrateful that you'll deny me a roof over my head? After all, I did give you –'

'Life,' I sighed. 'I know. Of course you can stay, Mum, if you need to. But wouldn't it be better if you went back and sorted things out with Geoffrey?'

'I'll go back in my own time,' she declared. 'Now, is the spare room ready for me?'

'Well, no, because you didn't tell us you were coming,' I protested, as Mum put on her best martyred face and said she'd have another cup of coffee while she waited for me to sort it out. No, *not* instant, Simon, proper coffee please.

Later, I was up in the attic once again, as Mum has decreed her bedside lamp not to be up to her exacting standards and demanded another. I'd obediently been reaching for my phone to order her a new one from John Lewis, when Simon gave me A Look, and loudly said he was sure there was something in the attic that would be more to Mum's taste. I think it would be safe to say that Simon wasn't best pleased by Mum's arrival, or her comments about his mother, and he disappeared into his shed following Lampgate, stomping out with a brief aside to me to 'Just bloody stand up to her, why don't you?'

I longed for Hannah. Hannah was the only person who under-stood about Mum and me. Hannah had been there all through my teenage years, when nothing I did was right for Mum, when I tried and tried to please her, and she'd just dismiss my achievements and make 'helpful' suggestions about how I could have done better. Hannah had been there the night we'd been going off to our first grown-up dance, a flammable melée of jewel-coloured taffeta, Elnett and Excla'Mation perfume. We'd been so thrilled with ourselves, so delighted in our first ballgowns, taffeta bumbows and all, and Anne of Green Gables herself couldn't have been more pleased than we were with our puffed sleeves.

We'd jostled out into the hall, giggling and over-excited, to twirl and show ourselves off to Mum, and Hannah's mum, who'd come over for a drink with Mum to see us all dressed up and ready to go.

'Oh gorgeous,' cried Hannah's mum. 'Yvonne, don't they look wonderful? They're proper young ladies! Oh, I'm so proud of you both.'

'Mmmm,' said Mum, looking us up and down. 'You look very nice, Hannah, dear. Ellen, darling … well, I did tell you green wasn't your colour, didn't I, but of course you wouldn't listen. Still, too late now, so don't worry about it, poppet. The important thing to remember is that looks aren't everything, are they?'

'Looks aren't everything.' We'd spent hours getting ready, I'd never been so pleased with my own reflection and I looked – by the standards of the early nineties – bloody amazing. And then my mother, my *mother*, the one person who should think I was beautiful no matter what, let alone when I'd pulled out every last stop there was, told me that I wasn't to worry, because looks aren't everything.

Hannah was the only person who could understand how excited we were that night, and how my mother's words shattered that excitement, no matter the kind things Hannah's mother had said.

And when we got to the dance, and Lisa Bennett said she liked my dress and Lindsey said my make-up was cool, it made not the slightest difference. All I could hear was Mum's voice, tinged with that ever-present tone of disappointment when she spoke to – or of – me. 'Looks aren't everything.'

Bugger. Maybe Simon was right, much as it pained me to say so. Maybe I should just get in touch with Hannah and get this whole stupid row over with. I sat down heavily on an old three-legged ottoman that had been Simon's grandmother's, and which I kept up in the attic as a 'project' that I never quite got around to. Obviously, the ottoman collapsed, I fell off and knocked over a pile of boxes. A load of battered notebooks and folders of photographs spilled out. Oh God – my old teenage diaries and photos. I picked up a photo and looked at a young Hannah and myself, smiling, with terrible hair and the finest fashion Miss Selfridge could provide. I opened one of the diaries at random and hastily closed it again. It was clearly from that brief and embarrassing period when I'd taken up writing poetry. I put it to one side for burning, if it didn't first catch fire from the flames of mortification consuming my soul. I opened another diary – the summer of 1991, when Hannah had been going out with Christopher Bennett. I flicked through it and my eyes alighted on the following:

Dear diary, this is it. This is going to be the best summer
ever for me and Hannah. We've got it all planned, and this is
the summer we're going to Meet Boys. Actual, real, live
boys, not just being hopelessly in love with Rick Astley, who
is a ginger sex god no matter what anyone else says.
Everyone else can be as in love with Take That as they want

(except Fat Gary, yuck, imagine fancying Gary Barlow, ewwwww, gross!!!!!) but I'm faithful to my Rick. And Hannah's heart of course belongs to Keanu Reeves, who seems very nice, but isn't Rick Astley either. I've been in love with Rick Astley for years now, ever since 'Never Gonna Give You Up', and I'm sure that one day I'll marry him, when he hears how I continued to be in love with him even when he wasn't cool and it was sad to fancy him before he grew his hair long and everybody liked him again. I wonder what has happened to him though? He hasn't been in *Smash Hits* or had a single out for ages? Hannah is more fickle than me and so far has been in love with River Phoenix until he died (he was very handsome but always looked like he needed a bit of a wash), Vanilla Ice (????), all the Coreys, and Johnny Depp for a bit after he broke up with Winona Ryder. I'm not sure Hannah has the best taste in men. I wish I looked like Winona Ryder, though, she's literally the coolest girl in the world. I tried wearing baggy black clothes and having my hair cut like Winona's and making myself look pale and interesting and Daddy just asked me if I was practising my disguise for the Zombie Apocalypse. It's so unfair, no one understands me. I bet no one ever asked Winona that.

Well, that aged well, didn't it? Who could have ever predicted that while everyone was swooning over Mark Owen and Robbie Williams, it would turn out that Gary Barlow, as well as being the insanely talented one who wrote all the songs, twenty years later would end up being the Hot One, and everyone now pretended he'd always been the one they fancied. Except me, of course, because Ginger Sex God, etc, etc. What other past musings had been proved wrong?

> Christopher Bennett is at our tennis classes. Literally the only person cooler than Popular Lisa is her big brother Christopher. I've put extra Sun In in my hair and went to Boots for a waterproof mascara so it doesn't sweat off when I'm playing tennis. I told Hannah I really fancy him and she said the Sun In and mascara look really good and he'll definitely fancy me back.

Sun In! Does that stuff even still exist? Surely it was the biggest scam of the eighties and nineties, the hours we spent carefully applying it to our hair and basking in the sun, expecting to go inside to tumbling golden blonde tresses thanks to the magic of Sun In, only to find it had made … precisely no difference whatsoever and was about as effective as the lemon juice we'd also used when we couldn't stretch to Sun In, having spent all our pocket money on Rimmel Heather Shimmer lipstick and Body Shop Dewberry shower gel and Polo mints.

> Chris Bennett asked Hannah out and she said yes, even though she KNEW I fancied him! How could she do this to me? I asked her what she thought she was doing and she said she fancied him too, and was going to tell me but I got in first, and when I said that meant I'd bagsied him, she said you couldn't bagsy a person, and anyway, he'd asked HER out, not me, so it wasn't like he was going to go out with me even if she'd said no!

Bastard! And that was mean of Hannah. I was right, she was totally in the wrong there.

I hate Hannah. I asked her if she wanted to go to the cinema tonight, but she's going with STUPID CHRISTOPHER AND HIS STUPID SISTER STUPID LISA BENNETT. I HATE THEM ALL. I HOPE THEY GET HERPES!

I'd almost torn the paper with the pen here, so vehement were my rage and disappointment. Given that I'd ended up tagging along with Jessica and her friends to see *Death Becomes Her* – to their immense disgust – Hannah, Chris and Lisa were quite lucky I'd only wished herpes on them. *Just Seventeen* was mildly obsessed with herpes, though, and constantly warned against it; their campaign must have worked, because I've never had so much as a cold sore. But sitting in the cinema with Jessica and her friends Phillipa and Naomi, I'd felt so much the outsider, much like I had yesterday with Gemma and Fiona. Ellen: eternally the outsider, pressing my nose against the window of the cool gang.

Did nothing. Hannah busy. Hannah is always busy.

Was this going to be my summer again? No, I was going to be fabulous, remember? Wasn't I?

Tennis class. Saw Hannah, but she was partnered with Lisa, not me. I had to partner Chloe Watkins, who breathes too loudly and eats crisps with her mouth open. Chloe said she got fingered by a boy in Lanzarote on holiday. Why does everyone have a boyfriend except me?

Good God, why did Chloe tell people things like that? Were they even true? What ever happened to Chloe? I should google her.

Went into town on my own. Bought a new top in Jeffrey Rogers. Saw STUPID Hannah in McDonald's with her STUPID boyfriend. Met Chloe Watkins outside WHSmith. She said last weekend she got off with the cute boy who works in HMV. She asked me to her party next week and said there will be loads of boys there. Maybe there's hope for me after all.

Chris and Lisa are having a party. I saw Hannah in the paper shop when I was buying Polos and I thought she'd ask me to go to the party with her, but she didn't, so I asked her what she was doing on Saturday and she just looked at me and said 'Going to Chris's party' and I thought surely then she'd say 'Why don't you come?' but she didn't and she said 'Are you doing anything?' and so I thought 'FINALLY, she'll ask me' so I just said 'Oh, I dunno' and she said 'Oh well, have fun whatever you do' so clearly I'm NFI! I didn't want Hannah to think I was a total Billy No Mates, so I went to Chloe Watkins' party. Wasted wearing my new top, because I was the only one there apart from her sweaty cousin Nigel who has dog breath and BO and only talks about Dungeons & Dragons. He stared at my boobs for about an hour then asked me if I wanted to join his D&D game. I think that might have been him asking me out. This is what my life has become. On the way home, I saw Hannah snogging Chris Bennett in the bus stop. I hate my life. I'm going to be alone forever. All by myself.

I slammed the diary shut and my resolve against Hannah's perfidy hardened again. Reading the diary had brought back all the loneliness, shame and humiliation of that summer. And now Hannah had ruined another chance at the Best Summer Ever by going off with a boy again. Well, screw you, Hannah, I thought. I don't need you. I'm in with the popular people now, not sitting in Chloe Watkins's front room fending off Stinky Nige. Now I've got Fiona and Gemma, and fuck me if I'm not going to make the most of it and become FABULOUS! You won't recognise me when you finally return from sodding South Africa, and hell mend you! I shall, in fact, become SO cool, and SO fabulous and SO popular that even MUM will approve of me. HA!

Monday 1 August

Today was hotter than ever, and as is the law in Britain in a heat-wave, people are starting to tut about the heat and declare it to be Too Hot, and also that it is Unnatural.

Fiona had designated today's Summer Fun to be going to the local museum, as she was concerned we were not providing enough 'teachable moments' for our precious moppets. And instead of grumbling to myself about it, I was jolly well going to go along and teach those teachable moments and properly get into the spirit of it. Not only was I going to be a new and improved version of myself when Hannah got back, but Jane and Peter would be too!

The museum wasn't actually the worst idea Fiona had ever had for such a sweltering day, as it's one of those splendid institutions built by a Victorian industrialist back in an era when people who'd made a lot of money spent it on the Betterment of the Poor, rather than on space rockets that everyone assumed were simply compensation for a small penis.

I had Sam's children for the day too, and was rather hoping – thanks to the sunshine – that the museum would be quiet and we could just let them run amok for a couple of hours round the dinosaurs and the Egyptians, while we looked at some paintings and came home feeling rather more highbrow than we did after our usual days out with the kids.

Fiona, however, had other ideas and arrived armed with the dreaded clipboard.

'Which artefacts have you picked out for your Museum Project?' demanded Fiona bossily.

'What do you mean?'

'The Museum Project, Ellen, I detailed it all quite clearly in the message. Didn't you read it properly? Surely you've chosen some artefacts? We picked ours online while we were waiting for the cleaner to arrive, as I can't leave her a note telling her what needs doing because she's dyslexic. I tried writing in bigger letters but she claims that doesn't help, so I have to tell her in person.'

'What?' I said, even more confused.

'Marta, my cleaner. She's dyslexic, that's why we couldn't meet earlier. Gemma, have you chosen an artefact?'

'We thought we'd do something Egyptian,' Gemma said smugly.

'What? You need to be much more specific than that, ancient Egypt's a 3,000-year period! What have you been doing with your morning, when you were supposed to be researching artefacts for our Museum Project? And you, Ellen!'

I made non-committal noises, as my own morning had consisted of scrolling though Instagram DIY accounts trying to find cheap ways of making my house look like Gemma's; googling Chloe Watkins, who now appeared to be living in Ibiza and was posting a distressing number of photos captioned #LivingMyBestLife, which I vehemently hope is just Chloe still being as much of a fantasist as she was at school; shouting at Peter to just put some bloody trousers on already; and trying to tune out my mother, who was having a lovely time finding fault with everything in my house and my life and complaining because I, very unreasonably, would neither lend her my car nor chauffeur her around, since she had a perfectly good car sitting in Yorkshire that she'd chosen to leave behind.

She'd also spent some time trying to persuade me to consider Botox and fillers 'because those lines are so unflattering, Ellen, you don't want Simon going off with some young thing'. I had, however, in an attempt at having that backbone, lied to her and said we were going to the park when she demanded a lift into town, explaining regretfully that I'd not be able to drop her off as it was in the opposite direction to where we were going.

Had I told her that we were all heading to the museum, not only would I have had to endure her backseat driving, but probably also a lot of sighing about how unfortunate it was that I'd never made use of that Latin GCSE, nor indeed the rest of that expensive education she'd bestowed upon me. I was very well aware my career was almost as much of a disappointment to my mother as it was to me. Even when I gleefully told her about my clever game that had done so well, she'd just asked what it was called. When I told her it was 'Why Mummy Drinks', she'd simply sniffed and said, 'Oh no, I can't tell my friends about *that*. What on earth did you call it that for? Can you change it?'

Fiona was still talking about her plans for the day. Oh dear. I'd meant to do so well today, to be a proper Yummy Mummy, and I'd fallen at the first hurdle.

'Well, if you've not read the instructions I sent, let's get some lunch and then I'll explain it all', Fiona huffed.

I obediently went up to the counter to get the extortionately priced 'lunch boxes' for the children to pick over, as well as something for ourselves, then made my way back to the tables Fiona and Gemma had bagsied for us all. There were now so many in our group that we had to put the girls on one table, the boys on another, with a third table for the adults. I was just shouting across to Peter NOT to squeeze his juice box, as Peter squeezed his juice box and it erupted all over him, like every fucking juice box he has managed to get his hands on from birth, when my mother walked in with one of her cronies.

I swear that when she spotted us, she was going to try to blank us, but Peter was having none of it.

'GRANNY!' he bellowed 'HI, GRANNY! OVER HERE! GRAAAAAAAAAAAAAAAAAAAAAANY!' and he hurtled over to her, narrowly avoiding crashing into a woman carrying a tray of the museum's 'Cream Tea Special', consisting of an enormous but totally dry scone, a small pat of butter, a tiny pot of jam, and a rather mean-sized pot of tepid and weak tea, all for the princely sum of £9.99. The woman glared, as well she might when risking the loss of such costly bounty, and Peter, and the contents of his juice box, flung themselves onto my mother, who was unfortunately wearing a cream cashmere sweater.

'Hello, Granny,' beamed Peter, 'Are you coming to have lunch with us? You can have my apple, I only licked it a bit.'

Mum shuddered, but her friend seemed highly amused by Peter. Mum put on her bravest face and the two of them made their way over to us.

'Goodness, Ellen, what a surprise,' she trilled, giving me a look of pure malice. 'I thought you said you were going to the park and couldn't give me a lift into town.'

'Last-minute change of plan,' I said brightly.

Mummy narrowed her eyes in an 'I'm not making a scene here but I'll make you very aware of my views on this later' way that I remembered all too well.

'You remember my friend Vanessa, don't you?' Mum gestured vaguely to her companion. 'Of course you do. Vanessa Morris, she's married to Bill, they have two boys, Matthew and David. I did once hope you and David … but of course, that was too much to hope for from you. Vanessa, it's Ellen, my daughter. Not the thin one, that's Jessica.'

I made suitably 'Nice to see you again' noises at Vanessa, though I hadn't a clue who she, nor her son David – of whom Mum had once harboured hopes – were. Mum is one of those people who simply knows people wherever she goes. She might not like them, nor them her, but she'll nonetheless claim them as great chums should the need arise.

Mum suddenly perked up on seeing who I was with.

'And who are *your* friends, darling?' cooed Mum, suddenly all sweetness and light now she'd clocked Gemma's Chloé bag and Fiona's Mulberry, and thus deemed them suitable.

'Um, this is Fiona, and this is Gemma. This is my mother.'

'Yvonne, please call me Yvonne,' cooed Mum.

'But why is it so busy?' complained Mum, looking round. 'There are *children* everywhere. Why?'

'Well, it's the school holidays,' I explained. 'And the museum is free. That's what people do.'

'*I* didn't,' said Mum. 'What a ghastly idea, bringing all these children here to run about and scream and shout. I expected you to have inner resources.'

Which was why I spent most of my time in the school holidays at Hannah's house, I thought furiously. And which was why that summer she went off with Chris Bennett was quite so bloody awful for me, because I was stuck with you.

'I quite agree, Yvonne,' said Fiona smugly. 'It's dreadful the way people bring their children here to use it as some sort of free indoor playground. Children should be learning, and experiencing art and history when they're here. That's why I'm *trying* to explain about our Museum Project.' Fiona gestured over towards the children's tables, where it was easy to see whose children were whose. Miles and Cosmo had finished their lunch and were quietly drawing pictures of Roman amphorae, Ottilie was busily writing something, while Lucy was just sitting there, looking anguished.

Poor Lucy was torn between Ottilie – who was hissing at her to help with writing a sonnet in the style of Wordsworth that Fiona had set Ottilie as part of their Museum Project research on some papers once belonging to the poet that the museum apparently held – and Jane and Sophie. When these two had discovered that Ottilie was writing a poem, they had decided to loudly make up a poem of their own, with the word 'bum' featuring heavily. To be honest, I was relieved it was as mild as that. Meanwhile, Peter and Toby had also got on board with the making-art vibe and were apparently creating a re-enactment of a zombie apocalypse by wrapping the crusts of their sandwiches tightly in clingfilm and squeezing them until they exploded. 'POW! There goes another zombie brain!' yelled Peter as mashed-up Dairylea and ham splattered across Cosmo's drawing and he began to weep.

'Well done, Fiona,' said Mum. 'Really Ellen, why can't your children be more like this?'

Fiona beamed. 'Would you like to join us, Yvonne?' she offered graciously.

'Well,' said Mum. 'What do you think, Vanessa? They do have wine here, don't they?'

'Oh yes, Yvonne,' Fiona said warmly. Apparently, pensioners drinking Chardonnay in a museum café on a Monday afternoon was a totally different prospect to *mothers* drinking it on a beach on a Friday afternoon.

'Are you going on holiday?' Mum demanded of Gemma and Fiona, once everyone was settled again and she'd secured her mini bottle of wine, which she remarked was really *very* small. I braced myself for the inevitable tale of woe about her cruel daughter ruining her holiday plans.

Gemma sighed and shook her head, and Fiona quickly explained about the castle and the Clooneys. 'So we're really terribly envious of Ellen, having that lovely little family holiday house in France, aren't we?' she finished.

I froze, waiting for Mum to explain that I didn't in fact have a charming little chateau to call my own and kindly lend out to family members due to my exceptionally generous and giving nature, but that I was basically house-sitting for my in-laws for a fortnight. For once though, Mum's snobbishness and desire to keep up appearances came in handy.

'Oh yes,' she tinkled. 'It's marvellous. I always think there's something a little *seedy* about simply renting a villa somewhere – you've no idea what the previous occupants might have been up to, do you? Even the high-end ones, well, you can never be sure, can you?'

Gemma and Fiona looked a little nonplussed at the thought of the ways in which previous holiday houses could have been desecrated, and possibly not even by Hollywood A-listers, but Fiona rallied and enquired, 'And are you joining Ellen and Simon in France, Yvonne?'

'Me? Oh no, not this time. My summer is very full, and I prefer to travel outside of the tourist season. It's so commercialised at that time of year.'

'Well, your mother seems *charming*,' twittered Fiona, after Mum and Vanessa had tottered off. 'What a nice lady, and such sense she talked. It's ludicrous that people only come here for something to do in the holidays. I don't think you should be allowed in unless you buy a year's pass.'

'But it's free,' I pointed out.

'Well, quite,' sniffed Fiona. 'That's why it's full of riff raff. Not you two, of course,' she hastened to assure Gemma and me. 'Now, has everyone finished? Shall we get on with our Museum Project?'

Sam burst out laughing when I brought Toby and Sophie back to their home at the end of the day.

'What are you wearing?' he demanded, surveying the perfect outfit I'd changed into after he'd dropped the kids off this morning. 'Is … is that a Boden Breton top? You hate Boden. You hate Boden with a passion. And … on your feet? Tell me you're not wearing a snazzy loafer? You are! Oh my God, you are! You're now officially part of THEM. I don't know if I can be friends with you anymore. Tell me truthfully – you've thought about buying one of those yellow Joules waterproofs, haven't you? AHA! You have, Ellen, I can see you're blushing.'

'I have not,' I said sulkily. 'They're just very jolly on a rainy day, that's all.'

'There's no hope for you,' said Sam. 'I take my eye off the ball for one minute, one lousy minute while I try to earn an honest crust to feed my poor starveling babes, and you're off to the Boden sale.

What next? I suggest shots and you declare you'd just like a nice glass of homemade kombucha?'

'No,' I protested. 'Never. We're shots buddies for life!'

'Are we?' sighed Sam. 'Well, come and have a drink, and you can tell me if anything interesting's been happening for you while I've been slaving away over my computer.'

'My mother's come to stay,' I said gloomily.

'Yvonne? But why?'

'An excellent question. Can I have a bigger glass of wine, Sam?'

'Of course, of course. You poor thing. Now tell me exactly what's happened?'

'Oh dear,' said Sam, after I'd relayed the Sordid Tale of Geoffrey and Bunty's Bunk-Up. 'Maybe we need to come up with a plan to get rid of her and send her back to Geoffrey. Like … like *The Parent Trap*.'

'I don't think that after over forty years of my existence, given the fact that she gave birth to me – as she never ceases to remind to me – I'm going to manage to convince her that I'm an identical twin,' I said.

'All right, not *The Parent Trap*. Um. *Mrs Doubtfire* then?'

'Wouldn't that involve Geoffrey dressing up as a woman and coming to be a nanny to my children?' I asked in horror.

'Yes … maybe not that.'

'Apart from anything else, I've a horrible feeling he might enjoy prancing round in ladies' knickers just a bit too much.' I shuddered.

'TOO FAR, ELLEN!' shouted Sam. 'Jesus, I'm trying to *help* here, and you put images like that in my mind. Have you heard from Hannah?'

'No. Have you?'

'No, I hope she's all right, poor darling.'

Poor darling, my arse, I thought, as I buried my face in my wine glass and made a non-committal noise.

Mum was twittering round the kitchen in great delight when I got home, going on and on about 'your lovely new friends, darling. Such sweet girls. I do like them very much. And how *clever* of you to pretend you've got a holiday house, instead of admitting you're just basically *squatting* in Sylvia and Michael's. Don't worry, I won't give the game away!'

It seemed I'd *finally* done something to please my mother. I almost, *almost* felt a bonding moment, until of course she spoiled it by saying, 'If only you could have married someone like their husbands, Ellen darling, and then you wouldn't have to have that dreary computer job. Lucky Gemma and Fiona, eh?'

I was opening my mouth to attempt a spirited feminist defence of why it's important for women to maintain the option of working if they want to (which was quite hard to do when my gainful employment was indeed a 'dreary computer job', and, seeing Gemma and Fiona's lifestyles, I was starting to question the need for my own financial independence and wondering if indeed I could cope with a SAHM life like Gemma and Fiona, flitting from Pilates to aerial yoga via matcha lattes and gluten-free poke bowls, before remembering that I couldn't afford their lifestyle even when I'm working), when Mum added, 'You won't do anything to ruin it, will you?'

'Like what?' I demanded indignantly.

'Well.' Mum looked me up and down thoughtfully for a moment. 'Like being yourself.'

Wednesday 3 August

Fiona came up with a new idea for us today, and sent a message informing us that the day's activity and teachable moments would involve a 'No Spend Challenge'.

'Jolly good idea,' Simon said approvingly when I told him. 'I do see that it will be challenging for you, darling, although calling it a "challenge" makes it sound like you're climbing Mount Everest or something.'

'Oh, you can call anything a "challenge" now and make it sound important,' I said airily. 'It's the blessing and the curse of social media and reality TV. Haven't you seen all those influencers' posts about their "challenges" which are just blatant adverts? You know the ones – "A supermarket has challenged me to make dinner for my family tonight ONLY USING things I bought in their enormous bloody megastore." Oooh, what a CHALLENGE! Or, "Andrex have challenged me to wipe my arse with bog roll today!" You know the sort of thing.'

'Actually, that would be a great challenge for Peter,' Simon remarked. 'He seems deeply opposed to wiping his arse. And flushing.'

'Better for the planet, I suppose. Though not better for us when we all get cholera.'

'You're obsessed with cholera. Anyway, what are you doing for this "No Spend Challenge"?'

'Well, apparently we're all going over to Gemma's house. She has a hot tub, and a giant paddling pool she's putting up for the kids.'

'Ah, of course. A hot tub. A famously frugal way to spend the day. Well, have fun!'

'Did I hear you say we're going to Gemma's to use her hot tub?' demanded Mum, popping up from the sofa where she'd been lurking unseen. 'Lovely, I do adore a hot tub.'

'Mum, you're not invited.'

'Nonsense. Gemma is a dear girl, of course she meant me too in the invitation.'

'I really don't think she did. And there will be a lot of children there.'

'Splendid. I love children.'

'No, you don't.'

'Ellen, why must you always be difficult?'

'I'm not being difficult, it's just …' I cast around wildly for an excuse. 'Gemma's mum's just died and she finds it hard being round other people's mothers at the moment!' I crossed my fingers and hoped I hadn't just jinxed Gemma's mother, who as far as I could gather from Gemma was hale and hearty, and currently living her best life in the Algarve.

'Oh that poor girl. Perhaps I could comfort her. Be a second mother to her,' Mum mused.

'Yes. Maybe. But, um, not today. She needs prior warning to see people's mothers.'

'She was fine when I saw her at the museum.'

'No, she really wasn't. She was just being brave for you.'

'Of course,' murmured Mum. 'What a trooper.'

'So not today. But you can use the car?' I offered, to soften the blow.

'Oh, all right,' Mum grumbled. 'I suppose I could pop over to the Frobishers, see what they're up to.'

Gemma's 'paddling pool' turned out to be a vast ocean of a beast, more akin to an above-ground swimming pool than the inflatable puddles I was accustomed to purchasing every year from Asda that invariably were punctured by the following summer, leading to tears and devastation on the first hot day when I agreed to put it up.

It was so hot that Gemma didn't need to heat the hot tub. She just turned the thing on, and even Fiona gave up on her attempts to use the bubbles to demonstrate convection currents to The Montagues, just letting the children run amok as she settled back against a jet, muttering 'learning by play' to herself.

I'd cobbled together some rather bleak muffins from what I could find in the cupboard and fridge as my contribution to the 'No Spend Challenge', and Fiona had produced 'just a few little quinoa and courgette cupcakes'. Gemma, meanwhile, had created a 'summer drink' for everyone from the vastness of her larder fridge – 'Oh it's just pomegranate, acai, freshly squeezed OJ, and a little swirl of spirulina on top to zhoush it up!'

I took a gulp and said, 'God, that's delicious,' and before I could stop myself I added, 'All it needs is a dash of vodka.'

Gemma and Fiona stared at me.

'Ha ha,' I said quickly. 'Joking, obviously!'

'Oh, why not?' said Gemma. 'You both walked here, after all.' (Fiona had decided that using petrol to get somewhere counted as 'spending'). 'And we're celebrating, aren't we, Fiona? Let's do make it into a cocktail. I'll get the bottle, then we'll tell you our news, Ellen.'

Five minutes later, as we sat in the 'cool tub' sipping our now considerably zhoushed drinky-poo-poo, Gemma and Fiona dropped their bombshell.

'We've booked a holiday!' they squealed in excitement.

'What?' I looked at them blankly.

'Yes! We found something! Well, Giles's PA found it, really, a lovely villa in Sardinia. They had a cancellation – someone got divorced or died or something. Anyway, it doesn't matter, the point is we *snapped* it up.'

'Wow. I mean, that's great. Um, great.' I took a hefty slug of my drink and thought, You're leaving me too! First Hannah abandoned me, and now you're abandoning me, and I can't even say anything because all I can think of is my mother saying, 'Don't ruin it with them by being yourself,' and, oh FUCK, why is everyone leaving me? Why?

'When do you go?' I tried to say brightly.

'The week after you. So we'll be back the week after you get back. You don't look very excited? Aren't you *thrilled* for us? It's all right for you with your lovely place in France, but we thought we were going to be stuck here *all summer* and it was simply too depressing!'

It was essential I didn't show how upset I was. It would, after all, only be a week by myself until they were back. But I knew that when they did return, after two weeks away together, there would be more in-jokes, more stories that ended in 'You had to be there, really', more small and subtle ways in which they'd become closer and I was more the outsider than ever. All of this made it so important that I styled it out now, put a brave face on it and pretended I couldn't care less, because I was cool and edgy and had a holiday house in France instead of being needy and lonely, with, apparently, a personality that repelled people.

'Yes, oh God, yes! I'm so, so thrilled for you! Thank goodness you told me, though, ha ha ha, because actually my cousin Albertina' (Cousin Albertina? Cousin ALBERTINA? Where had *that* name come from?) 'yes, she'd asked to use the French house the week after we were there, but she just told me this morning that she can't come because they've got … um … cholera … and so I was going to ask if you guys would like to use it, but you've got something else lined up so I can ask, errr, Great Aunt Susan if she wants it. Yay! Yay, Sardinia. And yay, Great Aunt Susan. She's only got one leg, so she'll be over the moon.' I ran out of steam and realising they were both staring at me aghast.

'Cholera? Good lord! Where on earth does Cousin Albertina *live*?' said Fiona in dismay, edging away from me slightly.

My mouth was dry and my mind blank. 'Switzerland?' I offered.

'How do you get *cholera* in Switzerland?' said Gemma.

'Um, well, she didn't actually get it in Switzerland. She'd been … travelling. All over the place. She's a lady explorer, you see. Could have picked it up anywhere.'

'A lady explorer?'

'I mean a travel Instagrammer?'

'That sounds interesting. What's her account called?' demanded Fiona.

'She's closed it,' I croaked. 'Because of the cholera.'

'Well, it was terribly sweet of you to think of us, Ellen,' said Gemma kindly. 'Though thank goodness we found Sardinia, because I'd feel wretched if I thought we'd deprived poor Great Aunt Susan of a holiday. Was she travelling with Cousin Albertina?

'No, she's … she's an aunt by marriage, actually.'

'Gosh. What a complicated family you have.'

'Yes. So …' – I hastily attempted to change the subject before I invented any more dying Victorian relatives to demonstrate that I was a good and generous person with a house in France. In fact, why had I gone on like that? What was I supposed to do next year, if Fiona or Gemma asked to borrow it? I'd have to keep on inventing relations, each with more contagious diseases than the last. And what if they mentioned it to Simon? He definitely wouldn't go along with the lie. Why hadn't I just been honest in the first place? Why did I try to show off and impress them? 'Don't ruin it,' said my mother, 'by being yourself.' Well, who was I bloody trying to be then? – '… so, you must have loads to do to get ready?'

'GOD, yes,' Gemma groaned. 'I need *everything* done! Look at me, I'm a total mess. I've let myself go to rack and ruin, thinking we weren't going away.'

I gazed across at Gemma, who looked as immaculate as ever, with not a single hair out of place, the hair on her head in an artfully tousled beachy bun, her eyebrows perfectly groomed, laminated and microbladed, her lashes tinted and lifted. I, meanwhile, had only noticed while getting into the hot tub that I'd entirely neglected to shave all down the side of one leg, and changing into my bikini had involved a lot of careful tugging and stretching of fabric and tucking in of errant pubes.

'Again, so lucky, Ellen. You must have made all your appointments months ago,' Fiona sighed. 'End of the week, is it, you're getting it all done? I hate that week just before the big holiday overhaul when you feel like everything has just got out of hand. I don't know how you find the time, Ellen, when you're working.

Sometimes I think it's practically a full-time job in itself, keeping on top of everything!'

'Oh, you know …' I said vaguely, trying not to go off into any more vodka-fuelled flights of fancy, whereby I claimed to be the CEO of IBM or something. I wondered what it must be like to live this leisured life full-time, though, and if there was ever any chance of it happening for me. Perhaps if I invented another game. An even better one that made about eleventy billion pounds, and I'd never need to work again and could lie around in hot tubs drinking vodka all day talking about getting my unspeakables depilated. Would I get bored? Maybe. It would certainly be nice to get the chance to find out. What about Simon? Would he annoy me if he gave up work too and was at home all the time? Would he just sit in his shed?

'Do you *enjoy* working?' asked Gemma. 'Sometimes I think about getting a job, but Giles tells me I'd hate it. All the juggling. Lucy in after-school care. Always rushing around, missing things at school, being at someone else's beck and call.'

'Sounds like the bloody PTA,' snorted Fiona.

'I don't really enjoy it,' I admitted.

'Then why do it,' Gemma asked, 'if you don't like it?'

The most honest answer, obviously, was 'because we need the money', but again the vodka and the need to be seen as their equal – not to be looked down upon, not to be my sad little self – took over, and I said, 'Oh, you know. Independence and the patriarchy and all that. I'm thinking of giving it up for good, actually, and becoming a full-time game developer.'

Luckily, before I could say any more, or they could ask any further questions, Jane dashed up and grabbed my drink. 'I'm so thirsty,' she panted. 'I'm going to have some of your drink, Mum!'

'No!' I yelped, grabbing it off her, but not before she'd taken a sip and wrinkled her nose in disgust.

'Yours tastes funny. Why does yours taste funny? Have you got alcohol in it? What about your units, Mum? How many are in that? You're only supposed to have fourteen a week, and you had wine last night and I heard you telling Daddy that you were looking forward to lots of cheap wine in France – and that will all be more units. I hope you're not exceeding yours, because that's bad, Mum, because –'

To my immense relief – and before Fiona had a coronary – Peter, God bless him, cut short his sister's latest lecture on the evils of alcohol and her current fixation on units by hurling a bucket of water at her. Encouraged by this, Cosmo and Miles did the same to Ottilie and Lucy, and five minutes later a battle royale was raging round the garden in the form of an epic water fight.

'What *is* happening?' wailed Fiona.

'They're having a water fight,' I explained.

'Is it safe?' quavered Gemma. 'What if Lucy gets hurt?'

'Oh God, oh God, medical emergency and I've been drinking. Hugo will never let me hear the end of it if anything happens to The Montagues.' Fiona was inconsolable.

'They'll be fine,' I soothed. 'Don't worry. Mine do it all the time and they've never hurt themselves.' I crossed my fingers yet again.

'Is it a teachable moment?' Fiona asked plaintively.

'Oh yes,' I assured her. 'They're learning strategy!'

Thursday 4 August

Inspired by the hot tub chat, I'd had a good long look at myself in the mirror when I got home. Not in a metaphorical 'I shall become a better person' way, but in a literal 'My minge is out of control' way.

I'd told myself it didn't matter, that no one was going to see me at Sylvia and Michael's, and as long as I had a rough prune before I went and hacked at my legs with a Bic every couple of days, I'd be fine. But Gemma and Fiona were so *glossy*. Maybe that was where being as perfect as them started. Maybe it wasn't about the big houses and luxury SUVs and magic ice-dispensing fridges, maybe it was really all in the microscopic attention to detail, and thus, if I could start to look after myself as well as they did, I'd feel more in control of my life. Maybe if I dealt with my eyebrows, exfoliated properly, hydrated my skin and didn't have to play some sort of Whac-A-Mole with my pubes to get them into my swimming costume, it would constitute a significant step towards being the sort of person I wanted to be. And wouldn't Hannah get a shock the next time she saw me, when not only was I besties with Gemma and Fiona, but I was also poised, elegant and sophisticated?

With this in mind, I dashed to Superdrug this morning and spent an obscene amount of money. At least, I chuckled to myself, I could lie to Simon that it was for sunscreen when he saw the credit card bill and roared how did I manage to spend that much on fucking shampoo? When I got back, I decided I needed to treat myself. Pamper myself. I was going to be packing all day, so I'd have a little spa night before the packing was quite finished and the insanity of going on holiday began properly tomorrow.

Once the children were in bed, I shut myself away in the bathroom and began. First up was the exfoliation. I scrubbed and scrubbed until I looked like a lobster, but my skin felt amazing. I also did the same to my feet, and I swear so much dead skin came off them they were a full size smaller. It was disgusting, but also quite enjoyable – in a gross sort of a way. I plucked my eyebrows rather tentatively, as they're still recovering from the nineties, and then I just had to do the waxing and paint my toenails, and I could lie down and relax with a hydrating, nourishing, plumping, magic-fucking-bean-growing and God knows what else face mask on. It had cost £11.99, so it had better bloody well do *something*. And then I just needed to whack the fake tan on, and I'd emerge, a glowing, gleaming, polished *goddess*, and if Simon didn't notice my transformation, I'd wait till he was snoring and give him a back, sack and crack wax, so help me God!

So, to my own wax. I'd purchased a 'hot wax kit' involving strips you heated yourself in the microwave and then applied, which seemed a lot less mess than fannying around – if you'll pardon the pun – with bowls of wax and spatulas, and was likely to be more effective than the cold wax strips I remembered from my youth, which were about as much use as a marzipan dildo.

I popped on my dressing gown and shimmied downstairs to heat the strips. But after carefully following the instructions they were not very hot, and the wax was decidedly unmelted. Also, I still had to get up the stairs and stick them on before they cooled. Really, now I came to think of it, this was a poor system, because who has a microwave in their bedroom, but equally what sort of animal would wax their bikini line in the kitchen? It was simply not hygienic. I looked around and pondered what to do. I could put them in the toaster? No, I chided myself, don't be silly, Ellen. If the wax melts in the toaster, you'll never get it out – and I think even John Lewis will insist that toasted wax invalidates the warranty. Ah ha! Of course! The grill! It was a little bit bacony, but I gave it a quick wipe and popped the strips under on the highest setting for a couple of minutes. That was more like it! They were nice and hot now, and the wax was perfectly soft and melty.

I belted up the stairs and got to work. It did, I cannot lie, smart a bit. But it was very effective! Within ten minutes I was sporting a lady-garden lawn worthy of Centre Court at Wimbledon, so neat were the borders. I sniggered to myself and contemplated adding an up-and-down striped effect for that perfect tennis court illusion. I may have had some wine while I'd been about the whole lengthy beautifying process. Quite a lot of wine. I admired my handiwork in the mirror, then sat down heavily while reaching for my glass and taking another swig of wine. Too late, I felt an unexpected warmth between my buttocks as I collapsed on the bed.

My first panicked thought was that I'd somehow soiled myself. When I realised what had actually happened, I decided that would probably have been the better option.

Unsure how many of the hot wax strips it would take to deal with matters, I'd peeled the covers off all of them and spread them on the bed ready for use. Not even *my* shrubbery required that much attention, though, so there were a few strips left, one of which was now firmly stuck *right up my arse crack*, extending over and onto my poor battered perineum, which had never quite recovered from childbirth. I don't, of course, being a lady, have a hairy arsehole, but there may have been one or two strays lurking around there. And of course, it's quite a tender area. I reached around and gave an experimental tug. It was extremely painful. I tried again and decided that I didn't think I could do this.

I opened the bedroom and called softly for Simon. There was no response, of course.

'SIMON!' I eventually bellowed, and was finally rewarded by a faint 'What?' from downstairs, where he was no doubt getting his fix of *Wheeler Dealers* before two weeks of French TV.

'Can you come up here, please?' I asked, trying to sound less anxious than I was.

Simon marched upstairs, grumbling all the way, only for his face to light up when he came into the bedroom to find me naked, glowing, etc, etc.

'I say!' he growled. 'You should have said that was why you wanted me to come upstairs. As the actress said to the bishop!'

'No!' I snapped. 'That's not why I called you up here. Look!' and I turned around and bent over to demonstrate the nature of my problem.

'Ellen, you've always made your views on backdoor love very clear,' Simon said, confused. 'I know that no means no, so you really didn't have to go to these lengths.'

'For fuck's sake, Simon, just pull it off,' I cried.

'Why can't you pull it off?'

'It hurts too much. I can't bring myself to do it. You need to do it.'

'And they say romance is dead,' Simon muttered.

'And you said, "For better, for worse." And yes, I agree, this is definitely a "for worse" moment, but please will you just pull this wax strip off my arsehole? NOW!'

'What's the urgency? Do you need to fart?'

'No!' I insisted, though obviously as soon as I said that, I did need to fart.

'Why are you waxing your arsehole anyway? Is that a thing now?'

'I didn't mean to. I sat on the strip. Please, Simon, just stop talking and DO IT!'

'God, I remember when it meant something else entirely when you'd say that to me,' he sighed, as he bent over and prepared to perform his marital duty.

'Why does your arse smell like bacon?' he asked suddenly, 'JUST PULL THE DAMN STRIP OFF, SIMON! AAARRRRRRGHGGHHGGGGGHHHHHHHHHHHH!'

'There. Don't say I never do anything for you,' Simon smirked as he stood up, strip in hand. 'God, there's a lot of hair on here. You do have quite a hairy arsehole. What's that noise?'

'I don't know, go downstairs and find out. And bring me up some ice.'

The noise was Mr Dickson next door. As it was still swelteringly hot, even at 10 p.m., the windows were all open, he'd heard my anguished screams and had kindly come round to make sure Simon wasn't murdering me. Or more likely, if he'd heard some of our rows, that I wasn't murdering Simon. He was finally placated when I hobbled to the window, leaned out and waved merrily.

When the stinging had eventually subsided and I could walk again without wincing, and after I'd threatened Simon once again with a delightful hot-waxing experience of his own if he didn't stop going on about how much hair had been on the strip, I saw the funny side of it. It was too funny, in fact, not to share. I couldn't tell Sam, of course, as he claimed to be allergic to the word 'vagina', so 'perineum' might just tip him over the edge. But Fiona and Gemma were fellow women – they'd see the funny side, surely? I quickly messaged them about it, certain that they would find my mishap as amusing as I did. They both replied almost immediately.

Gemma: OMG, Ellen, you poor thing, did they cancel your waxing appointment at short notice? You should've let me know, my waxing lady might have been able to squeeze you in as a favour to me!

Fiona: Ellen, that sounds serious. You might need medical attention. You're really not meant to wax there, it's a very delicate area. Have you contacted NHS 111 for advice?

I reassured them both that I was fine, that I definitely wasn't calling NHS 111 to tell them I'd waxed my arsehole, and that it was *funny*. They seemed confused by this. For a moment I did actually consider calling NHS 111 about it, if only because I bet a nurse would find it funny too. Hannah would definitely have found it hilarious, I thought crossly, if she'd not been *so selfish*.

Saturday 6 August

And we're off to France, hurrah! Mum has been left to house-sit despite the many protests from her that she was being abandoned in her hour of need, and how could I do this to her (even though I've hardly bloody seen her since she arrived), and what was she supposed to do ALL BY HERSELF (Simon strongly advised me to lock up the gin before we left)? I thought it best that Judgy went to the dog-sitter as I didn't trust Mum with him – she's never forgiven him for attempting to snack on one of her Siamese cats.

We loaded everything but the kitchen sink into Simon's Volvo – I relented and said Mum could borrow my car while we were away – and set off on our quest for Wholesome Fun and also Many Baguettes. Of course, Simon and I were not speaking by the time we left, due to the fact that apparently it's all MY job to assemble and pack everything, as well as buying all the sunscreen, antihistamines and extra bottles of TCP that are necessary for a trip into the wilds of Abroad. I'm also responsible for making sure everyone's clothes are washed and ready to go (not ironed, bugger that, life's too short), that chargers and adaptors are located and packed, once I've ensured that all the devices have been full charged, and that we've got all the requisite passports, euros and other assorted paperwork, including printing off the tickets for the Channel crossing.

Naturally, I'm not actually allowed to be in *charge* of the passports and tickets, for that's a Manly Man's job. Simon's other jobs, as well as taking all essential documents and money in his Special British Man Abroad's horrible rucksack, are to ask why I'm getting so stressed and do I know where his bastarding sunhat is – hence, why we were not speaking. I'd found and brought everything that both his children might need on holiday and some things they probably won't need but that I'm taking JUST IN CASE, and I'd spent two days packing, and I really didn't think it was asking a lot to expect him to locate his own possessions, what with him being a WHOLE GROWN-ASS MAN and that. Simon then made the fatal error of uttering that ever-helpful phrase: 'There's no need to be like that.'

He'd also tried to be 'helpful' by suggesting the night before departure, since I 'seemed to be a little stressed', that I shouldn't go to too much trouble over dinner, and why didn't I just make a nice, simple lasagne? I spent some time explaining, for the eleventy fucking billionth time, how many pots lasagne uses, how it's *not* nice and simple, and how if he ever, ever, EVER says 'a nice, simple lasagne' to me EVER AGAIN, he'll be removing every single one of the pots required for that 'nice, simple lasagne' from various orifices about his person. I think, quite frankly, he was relieved when I stopped talking to him, instead of shrieking 'AND ANOTHER THING!' at him every ten seconds, as I recalled yet further unforgivable transgressions he was guilty of.

I'd naively thought it might be less stressful to drive to Sylvia and Michael's, rather than flying there and hiring a car on arrival, given that Simon goes into some sort of sergeant-major mode at the airport, marching us along furiously, shouting that we need to find the gate, find the gate, while I trail in his wake, clutching children and Trunkis and massive duty-free Toblerones. It's possible I was wrong about this, and it's just travelling with Simon full-stop that's stressful.

We finally arrived after approximately eleventy fucking billion hours of driving, if you factor in the many stops for wees, snacks, more wees, feeling sick, needing a poo, the poo not being ready, definitely needing a poo now, no, sorry false alarm, pull over Daddy before I poo my pants, the POO IS READY NOW, one flat tyre, which involved Simon shouting furiously at everyone to prove he was Manly enough to change a tyre and didn't in fact need to wait for the French AA, and a short delay at the Channel Tunnel on account of being pulled in for a random check and Peter deciding to tell the nice man that we were not his family and he'd never seen us before.

I also had a small panic attack at the wine warehouse in Calais, where I insisted we stock up on emergency supplies 'just in case' ('Just in case of WHAT, Ellen?' Simon demanded. 'In case France runs out of wine? I think that's LITERALLY forbidden in their Constitution or something. And anyway, Mum and Dad always have masses of wine in'), and then realised there was no room in the car for the two cases of wine I'd panic-bought ('Seriously, Ellen? I was thinking a couple of bottles, where did you *think* it was going to go?'), until I triumphantly solved the problem by forcing them into the footwell in the back of the car, under the children's feet. Obviously, this led to almost incessant complaining from them all the rest of way, so it was *just as well*, I'd pointed out to Simon, that we had extra wine, simply to numb the pain of a whole fortnight of uninterrupted japes and frolics with *les moppetes précieuses*.

Simon grumbled about the weather most of the way to his parents' house as well, having taken umbrage at the fact he'd been made to come all the way to Abroad and the weather was exactly the same as at home.

'I'm just saying,' he kept muttering, 'why are we going to all this trouble when it's perfectly sunny at home? Why do we bother going away, if not for better weather? But the weather back there's glorious, we could have stayed just where we were and I've got loads of things I could be getting on with, that's all.'

'For one,' I'd snapped (because obviously when I said I wasn't talking to Simon, I didn't meant I wasn't talking to him if he was wrong and needed correcting on something), 'the weather at home is far from guaranteed. Yes, there may currently be a heatwave, and yes, that's jolly nice, but it could equally well have pissed down all summer, so we've come away.'

'I'm just saying –'

'Well, stop just saying.'

'– I've a lot I could be getting on with.'

'And all those things you could be getting on with, do they involve power tools?' I asked sweetly.

'Yes,' said Simon, blundering straight into my trap.

'AHA. So in fact, if we hadn't come away, but I'd managed to persuade you to take some time off, you'd have spent it in your shed. And that's exactly why we're here, so we can spend time together and bond as a family!'

'We could have done that at home.'

'But we don't! That's the whole point. There's always something else going on. You're busy, I'm busy, the laundry needs doing, the kids want a friend over. We're here to have a nice time as a *family*.'

Simon made unconvinced noises, and said something that sounded suspiciously like 'I could have had a nice time in my shed.'

Late though it was when we finally reached Sylvia and Michael's, there were lights on and it all looked very welcoming. I always forgot just how glorious this house was – for all my unkind jokes about it being a chatette, it was actually a perfect miniature chateau, and not even that miniature, with the five bedrooms and the Grand Salon and the pool and tennis court. I suspected even Fiona and Gemma would be slightly impressed by it, and I was determined to spam Instagram with as many enviable #FrenchStyle photos as possible. Though should I? Wouldn't it just lead to more questions about my supposed ownership of the house? Fuck it, I'd cross that *pont* when I came to it.

'Look, darlings, we're here!' I cried cheerily to the children. 'Doesn't it look lovely?'

'Yay, can we go in the pool?' the children demanded, oblivious of the time and the darkness.

'Mum and Dad must have left the lights on a timer,' Simon grunted.

But as Simon parked and we stiffly stumbled from the car, I saw figures moving behind the lighted curtains. My first thought was BURGLARS, but there seemed to be no furtiveness about the movements. My second thought was that we had indeed found ourselves in some sort of hilarious double-booking scenario, similar to the one I'd sketched for Gemma and Fiona with the Clooneys, where Sylvia had got the dates wrong and another family were also staying here.

I wasn't too dismayed, to be honest, for in the books, the husband of the other family was always rather dishy and fell for the heroine, who would of course be me. After the best part of fourteen hours in the car with Simon, I was totally ready for someone, anyone, other than him to fall in love with me. Naturally, I'd be virtuous, and content myself with longing glances and perhaps the touch of a hand here and there, and when he finally declared himself, I'd regretfully decline. But still, it would be a jolly nice ego boost and make all the waxing, even of my arsehole, worth the pain.

The door was flung open and a voice cried, 'Welcome, Brother, welcome. And Ellen, my sister, my spiritual sister, welcome. Welcome all. We're here to bid you *bienvenue en France!*'

My heart sank. Simon's sister Louisa was the last person I wanted to see tonight. In fact, I'd rather hoped never to see her again after we'd waved her off in the clapped-out campervan to her new life in France, to the house I'd been manoeuvred into buying for her with the last of my game money. I was slightly put out to be so graciously welcomed to France by the wretched woman, when the only reason she was here at all was because of me.

I also thought rather it hard that Fate had ordained that not only did I have to finance Louisa's new life, but I had to put up with her company too. Surely it was only fair that I should at least be rewarded by not actually having to endure her anymore, or listen to her utterly batshit outlook on life, which was a sort of New Age hodgepodge pic'n'mix of astrology, Wicca, homeopathy, conspiracy theories and a whole lot of other random bollocks that she appeared to make up on the spot as and when it suited her.

I'd also hoped it would mean I no longer had to put up with her feral children. I did try not to judge the children, telling myself that anyone would be strange if they were brought up by Louisa, but it was quite hard, especially as Coventina, the middle child, had managed to turn out perfectly pleasant and normal, despite her mother's best attempts to raise her as another 'Child of the Moon Goddess'. Coventina had once confided in me that all she really wanted was 'loads of money. I don't know why everyone tells us capitalism is so terrible, I think it sounds great! And when I've got loads of money from capitalism, I'm going to buy a HUNDRED iPads and have TVs in every room as well, and only eat microwave dinners.' In fairness, I rather liked Coventina's Vision, and wouldn't have at all minded doing the same when I grew up.

The other children, though, were definitely as much a product of their natures as Louisa's nurturing. Cedric, the firstborn, had inherited all of her sense of entitlement, which he tended to express via stealing anything that took his fancy, while loftily proclaiming it wasn't stealing, because all property was theft. He had, at least, stopped nicking stuff from my kids after Jane twatted the everlasting fuck out of him and threatened to cut him if he ever touched any of her or Peter's belongings again.

Idalisa, the eldest girl, was one of those unfortunate children who just sort of fade into the background and no one ever notices, which in Louisa's household might have been more of a blessing than a curse, and the younger three – Nissien, Oilell and Boreas – while too young last time I saw them to have formed sufficiently distinct personalities to make an impression on any but their nearest and dearest, were mostly memorable for Louisa encouraging them to practise what she coyly referred to as their 'elimination communication' whenever – and wherever – it took their fancy. In other words, they liked to shit on the floor.

'Hello, Louisa,' I said warily.

'Lou, if you've come to welcome us, can you at least give us a hand with the luggage instead of prancing about?' asked Simon wearily, as Louisa now appeared to be dancing round the car, chanting something.

'I'm saluting the moon, my mistress,' said Louisa slightly shirtily. 'And for the last time, it's AMARIS. Anyway, I'm so glad you're here.' She enveloped me in a rather hairy embrace and looked at me fondly. 'We're going to have the Best Summer Ever!'

Sunday 7 August

Everyone was tired and scratchy this morning, as Louisa and her 'brood', as she called them (which was almost as annoying as Fiona's references to The Montagues), had hung around for over two hours after we arrived, her children obviously not having anything as bourgeois as bedtimes or routines. 'It's important they feel free. It's not for me to set their boundaries, they must find their own lines,' Louisa had trilled at me when I'd made vague noises about 'not wanting to keep her back' and insisting she 'mustn't keep the children up on our account'.

Louisa's gatecrashing of our arrival meant that Simon and I at least agreed on one thing, namely that we must attempt to avoid her at all costs. Our eyes had met across the room as Louisa emptied another bottle of Michael's wine into her glass and suggested we join her on some of the 'workshops' she was running at the 'poetry retreats' she now apparently held at her 'little abode', as she insisted on referring to what was, after all, MY house, I mean Simon's and my house. I wondered what Sylvia made of these events. Simon had discreetly shaken his head at me as I gazed at him in horror while Louisa was waxing lyrical about how 'empowering' we'd find her

'Couples Connections' poetry classes, and I'd nodded back at him in relief.

Today, however, that brief harmony found itself in jeopardy again, as Simon's devotion to his weather apps continued unabated. The first thing he did this morning, even before his coffee and his essential morning poo (he informed me solemnly it was a relief to find himself 'back on schedule after the travelling'), was check the weather back home. Weather checked, he then felt the need to find me to point out that it was touching 24 degrees at home, and just think of the money we could have saved by not coming on holiday.

'It only really costs petrol money,' I protested. 'And what would we be doing at home? At least we've got a pool here, and lots of new places to explore and things to do. It's a change, Simon. How many times do I have to tell you that a holiday is about more than the bloody weather?'

Simon muttered to himself. I swear I heard him say something along the lines of 'We're British, weather is life.'

Nothing daunted, I wore my brightest and best 'We're having fun on holiday' smile as I dished out croissants and cherry jam to the children (Sylvia, for all her faults, had left her chest freezer and larder well stocked for us, God bless her, with instructions to use whatever we wanted, so we had a couple of days' grace before I'd have to drag Simon out to brave a French supermarket), then beamed, 'What do we fancy doing today then, darlings?'

'It's too hot,' whined Peter. 'I don't want to do anything. Can't I just play Minecraft?'

'No,' I snapped. 'You've got all year to play Minecraft at home. Now you have two weeks in France to enjoy the food, the culture and the weather, and swim in that beautiful pool and play tennis.

So I'll ask again, what shall we do today? There's lots to do here, but would we all just like to chill out by the pool for the day? Simon, any ideas?'

'What? I dunno? Right, if you'll excuse me, it's that time …' and Simon wandered off, gathering up his iPad as he went for another lengthy morning contemplation.

By the time Simon came back down, I'd cleared away breakfast, sent Peter to get changed for the pool, banged several times on Jane's door and told her to get changed because we were going to the pool, and packed one of Sylvia's big wicker baskets with drinks, sunscreen and snacks so we didn't have to trail back and forth to the house every five minutes.

Peter had come down three times to inform me he couldn't find his swimming trunks, his UV top or his flip-flops, and I'd gone upstairs each time to find the missing article hiding in plain sight, i.e. on the chair in his room where I'd put them and where I'd told him they were. I'd then repeated roughly the same procedure with Jane, only with twice as many protestations about the deep unfairness of being forced to go and enjoy a swimming pool in glorious weather, which had caused me to embark on something of a rant about how children were starving and Jane should be grateful for her first world problems. This had, needless to say, fallen on entirely deaf ears.

When Simon finally reappeared I was doing a fair impression of wrestling with a greased weasel, as I attempted to get the sunscreen onto Peter. Jane had been so thoroughly vile about the whole thing that I'd flung a bottle of Ambre Solaire at her and snapped, 'Fine, do it yourself, get sunburnt, see if I care.' I wondered if it was true that a Mumsnetter died every time a mother lost her shit with a child.

'Could I get some help here?' I panted, as Simon nodded approvingly at proceedings and settled himself on the sofa, iPad still firmly in hand.

'Simon?' I tried again. 'Are you ready for the pool?'

'Hmmm? What? Oh no, sweetheart, it's a bit hot for me. I'm just going to stay here for a while and I'll maybe join you later when it's cooler. Also, I don't think my coffee has taken full effect yet, if you know what I mean. Best not go out till I'm sure.'

Simon looked back down at his iPad, as it started playing a familiar theme tune. Was that …? No, surely not … we were on holiday, he wouldn't. Would he?

'Simon,' I said in my calmest and most reasonable voice, 'are you watching *Wheeler Fucking Dealers*?'

'Eh?'

'*Wheeler Fucking Dealers*. Are you watching *Wheeler Fucking Dealers*?'

Simon beamed at me. 'Yes,' he said happily. 'I've just discovered there's a new "Best of" video someone has made on YouTube.'

'So you're not even watching an actual episode of *Wheeler Dealers*, you're watching clips of it on YouTube?'

'I can't get it here, so yes.' Simon still didn't appear to see the problem. Jane and Peter, however, on hearing the magic word 'YouTube' had immediately started shrieking like electrocuted cats that it wasn't fair. If Daddy could stay indoors and watch YouTube on *his* iPad, why couldn't they? They didn't want to go to the pool, they were also too hot, etc.

I finally got everyone to the pool and collapsed on a sun lounger. Oh God. What bliss. The baking heat was soaking into my very bones, and I could feel my spirits rising like a phone battery recharging. I had a book in my bag, which I'd read in a moment, but for now I'd just close my eyes. Just briefly.

'Mummy, watch me! WATCH ME!' There was a blood-curdling scream from Peter. Oh fuckety fuck, I'd taken my eyes off the children around a body of water and they must be drowning, and couldn't Simon watch them, and what would Fiona Montague and Mumsnet say? Fiona would never allow The Montagues to drown on the first day of their holiday.

Luckily, it turned out Peter wasn't drowning, he just wanted me to watch him doing his 'trick'. I couldn't *quite* grasp where the 'trick' aspect came in as he repeatedly jumped in and out the pool, but I watched dutifully, as any doting mama would.

'Jane, why don't you go in the pool?' I called across to her.

'Boring' was the sullen response. I sighed, and fished in the basket and produced two giant inflatable rings, and chucked one at each of my precious moppets.

'You can have a race blowing them up, and then you can use them to have races across the pool,' I cried brightly. 'Won't that be fun?'

Obviously blowing up the rings was both 'too hard' and 'unfair', but having woken up Simon, already snoring gently on a sun lounger oblivious to his children's mortal aquatic danger, to blow up one while I did the other ('No, it doesn't still count as a race if Daddy and I are blowing them up for you, no, that doesn't mean you've won'), the children eventually settled down happily to racing each other across the pool, shrieking and laughing as they did so. I lay back again and closed my eyes. Now the children were making an unholy racket, it was actually easier to relax, because as long as I could hear them both, I didn't need to be actually watching them. Mmmm, the only thing that could make this better would be a tiny glass of wine. I glanced at my phone. 10.47 a.m. Was that too early? Was breakfast wine a thing? We *were* in France, after all? Maybe before 11 a.m. was just a touch over-eager, I decided regretfully. Soon, though, my precious. Soon.

'Excuse me. I'm *so* sorry to bother you. Do you speak English? Um, *pardonez, excusez-moi*?'

Oh FUCKING HELL! What now? I sat up abruptly, to see a neat blonde head over the fence into the neighbouring property. Sylvia and Michael's had once been a small country estate that had been subdivided after the Second World War. Sylvia and Michael had the main house, and most of the grounds, Louisa lived in a 1960s bungalow at the end of the driveway ('It's perfect for popping in!' she'd threatened last night, to Simon's and my dismay), and on the other side another house had been built in the 1980s, which was occupied by a nice retired stockbroker from Weybridge called Mr Carruthers. This wasn't Mr Carruthers. Had he got himself a Lady Companion? Mr Carruthers, you old dog! Because the woman looking over the fence was only about my age, and Mr Carruthers was pushing ninety. Oh God, had she come to complain about the noise the children were making? That was all we needed – some officious golddigger telling us to keep it down. Mr Carruthers was deaf as a post and often remarked how delightfully quiet it always was, once when he'd dropped round for a drink and Peter and Jane were actively screaming almost right in his ear.

I sat up straight and channelled Fiona. What would she do if someone had the *nerve* to complain about The Montagues? Why, she'd Not Stand For It. And so neither would I.

'Yes?' I said coldly.

'Oh, thank goodness, you do speak English. I mean, I know it's terribly rude of me to say that in France. It's just my French isn't very good, and I wasn't sure how I'd explain things.'

I gave her a long, hard stare. I wasn't going to help her in her grousings in any language. Not that my French was all that either. Bloody Latin.

She stumbled on. 'It's just that I heard the children playing –'

I narrowed my eyes. I *was* Fiona Montague now. The honour of The Montagues, no, sorry, The Russells, was being challenged, and I'd do Battle Royale if need be.

'– and I was so glad to hear there was someone here, because we popped up to the house yesterday but no one was in, and so I thought if I just looked over the fence maybe I could catch you and have a word. It's the pool, you see?'

'What about it?' I snapped, wishing Simon would wake up and proffer some assistance in the defence of the Familial Honour of The Russells. I mean, I bet Hugo Montague wouldn't leave Fiona to do it all on her own. On the other hand, Hugo seemed to leave Fiona to do everything else with The Montagues, so maybe he would. Hugo Montague and Giles Atkinson were shadowy, almost mythical figures in the world of the school gates, mentioned only in hushed tones and rarely seen, and to go by the way their wives spoke of them, to be treated with awe and wonder when they deigned to appear, much like unicorns or white stags. As Simon showed no signs of regaining consciousness, though, it seemed my inner Fiona would have to suffice.

'Well, it's not working,' the blonde woman offered.

'It looks fine to me.' I haughtily gestured at the sparkling blue water, quite a lot of which was now slopped over Sylvia's rustic limestone paving due to the enthusiasm of the children's romping.

'Oh no, not your pool. Your pool looks lovely. I mean our pool. It's all sort of green and slimy.'

'I don't really follow.'

'Well, we're staying next door – you see, we've rented it for a couple of weeks – and there's something wrong with the pool.'

Now she mentioned it, I did have a very dim recollection of Sylvia saying something about poor old Mr Carruthers dying, and his son inheriting the house and putting it on Airbnb. Sylvia had been having a fit of the vapours about 'riff raff' and 'drugs parties', but Sylvia has a fit of the vapours if the postman is three minutes late and declares 'Standards to be slipping' and 'What is the world coming to?' so I hadn't paid very much attention apart from a passing moment of sadness for poor Mr Carruthers, who was a nice old duck. This must be one of the Airbnb'ers, though she looked perfectly respectable and not the drugs parties sort at all. Sylvia, no doubt, would say darkly that 'You never can tell, though'.

'I'm not quite sure what that's got to do with us?' I said, unFiona-ing a fraction now it appeared she wasn't here to complain about the noise.

'Well, there's a folder in the house with useful information, and we tried calling the maintenance number but there was no answer.'

'There wouldn't be on a Sunday in France,' I pointed out.

'As I say, the pool's all sort of green and slimy and the children are *so* disappointed, and it said in the folder as well that if there were any problems we should ask the couple next door, that they were very helpful and could probably sort out any issues if we couldn't get hold of the maintenance man.'

Oh, did the folder say that now? I thought crossly. How nice of Young Mr Carruthers to nobly volunteer us – well, probably Michael and Sylvia – to fix things.

I sighed. 'Simon,' I bellowed. 'Simon, wake up!'

'Eh?' Simon started to life. 'Wha's happening? Wha's going on? Where's am I?' He sat up and looked around blearily. 'Ugh, s'very bright.' He blinked owlishly at us. I felt he wasn't making a terribly Hugo Montague-esque impression.

'Simon, this lady, sorry, I didn't catch your name?'

'Angie.'

'Angie is staying next door in Mr Carruthers' house, and the pool is broken and apparently we've been volunteered to fix it.'

'What? Why?' Simon rubbed his eyes and shook his head. 'Ah. You need Mum and Dad, sorry. This is my parents' house. We're just staying here for a couple of weeks while they're on holiday themselves.'

Angie's face fell. 'Oh dear. So you don't know what's wrong with the pool? We were counting on you to fix it.'

Simon bristled. It was an affront to his masculinity to suggest something needed fixing and was beyond his capabilities, despite the fact that in all the many years I'd known him he had sworn a lot, spent a great deal of money on tools and untold hours browsing B&Q, not to mention lurking in his shed engaged in mysterious 'projects', but he'd never once successfully fixed a single thing.

'I mean, it's not really my area of expertise, but I suppose I could take a look,' he offered.

'Would you? Would you really? That would be so kind!' Angie said happily.

'There's a gate through at the bottom of the garden,' Simon sighed.

Of course, Peter immediately wanted to go too, and Jane's FOMO kicked in, and *she* wanted to go, and I thought I might as well go and have a nosy at the house, so we all went.

Poor Angie. The Carruthers' pool was indeed a stagnant, stinking swamp. She wrung her hands as she said, 'Airbnb say to take it up with the owner, but there's no answer there either. Oh, please say you can fix it.'

Simon poked around the pool with Angie's husband Steve and made manly noises, before investigating the pump room and making more manly noises, and nodding his head and sucking his teeth in a doom-laden way I knew for a fact he was copying off an electrician we'd had round a few months ago. Finally he made his pronouncement.

'I think the pump has gone,' he said importantly.

'Yeah, that's what I thought,' agreed Steve.

'But can you fix it?' Angie wanted to know. I was pleased to note she was wearing a floral maxi dress and Veja trainers. I *knew* they were still in style.

Simon shook his head sorrowfully and announced it would Need Parts and probably take a while to get them, and he was worried about invalidating the warranty, and so maybe it was best left to the maintenance man to get a pool engineer out, which sounded very manly and wise, unless you knew Simon as well as I did, in which case it would be immediately apparent that all that was bullshit for 'I've got no idea what's wrong here nor have I the first clue how to fix it, but I refuse to admit that.'

Angie and their three children – Imogen, fourteen, Ben, twelve, and Alex, nine – looked deeply mournful at this news, while Steve remained manly, shook his head and muttered about refunds from Airbnb.

'That's all very well,' hissed Angie. 'But we're now stuck here for two weeks in the blistering heat with no pool because you insisted on doing this on the cheap. I said if it looks too good to be true, it will be, and now here we are!'

I felt for poor Angie. If we hadn't had Michael and Sylvia's house to come to, I could see Simon doing exactly the same thing to me, in the interest of saving a couple of quid. I also felt bad thinking about our own beautiful, limpid pool just a few metres away, and found myself saying, 'Look, do feel free to come over and use our pool sometimes.'

I could sense Simon glaring at me furiously as we did the Proper British Thing, with Angie demurring, saying that was very sweet but they couldn't possibly, and me saying no, no, we *insisted*, and her saying well, maybe just for an hour sometimes, if we were really, *really* sure, and me going, oh yes, so sure, sure as a sure thing, even as I was thinking to myself, why on earth do I say these things? Why don't I stop and pause and take ten minutes to consider the offer I'm making, maybe even talk it over with Simon, and then if we were both in agreement, we could go back later and offer occasional pool use on quite restrictive terms. Or not, because this was *our* holiday, and Angie and Steve and their children's problems and pools, or lack of, were nothing to do with us.

But it was too late, the genie was out of the bottle, and however awful Steve and Angie might turn out to be, we'd have to spend the next two weeks pretending they were our totes besties and we loved having them there. Because obviously enduring their company, however grim, however racist, however keenly believing of everything the *Daily Mail* claimed, was better than the alternative, which was having an arse-clenchingly awkward conversation to revoke our invite. And apart from the shame and embarrassment and general *horror* such a chat would involve to any British person, there was also the consideration that on my part, things were still a little too tender 'down there' to think about the bum-clenching stress of such a thing.

'Well done, Ellen,' Simon said grimly as we walked back to our own lovely functional pool. 'That's our holiday royally fucked then, isn't it?'

Wednesday 10 August

Well, it had only been a few days, but it seemed my rash offer wasn't the disaster we'd feared it would be. Angie and Steve were lovely. They didn't take the piss by coming straight over on Sunday, but rather tentatively popped their heads over the fence on Monday afternoon to ask if it would be a terrible imposition if they came over for a quick swim for an hour. We'd been lying by the pool all day by that point, and I thought the children had probably had enough sun, so I said, no, not at all, we were going in shortly anyway.

Jane, however, who had been whining she was too hot for at least an hour already, suddenly changed her mind and announced a desperate desire to stay beside the pool, begging and pleading that she just wanted to swim a little longer. I found this odd, but felt I should encourage anything that didn't involve her sitting in the dark watching YouTube make-up tutorials, and since I didn't really feel I could abandon her to strangers, I resigned myself to staying at the pool as well.

'You can bloody well stay too, I'm not being left alone with them,' I hissed to a grumpy Simon, who responded with a furious 'Fuck's sake' and sat back down on his sun lounger.

'I hope you don't mind,' I said brightly to Angie. 'The children just wanted to stay out a little longer.'

'Mind you using your own pool?' Angie laughed. 'Of course not! This is beyond kind of you. I finally got through to the maintenance man, and from what I can gather it's some kind of local holiday today, but he'll come out at some point.'

'Oh you poor things,' I sympathised. Meanwhile Steve, clutching his iPad, had sidled up to Simon and murmured something about cricket. Simon nodded enthusiastically and murmured something back to Steve, who nodded equally enthusiastically, and Simon belted back to the house, while Steve and his iPad settled down under a parasol.

Simon returned in double-jig time, bearing Sylvia's cool box, which it transpired he'd filled with beer. 'And I brought some pink sunshine wine for the ladies,' he said proudly. 'Oh, unless, you'd rather have a beer, Angie, I mean,' and he floundered for a moment trying not to be a sexist pig until Angie took pity on him and said, 'I don't want a beer. But thanks, Simon.'

And with that, the two of them huddled under the umbrella engrossed in the iPad.

'What are they doing?' I asked Angie.

'Steve's got some kind of dodgy Firestick thingummy so he can watch the cricket,' Angie sighed.

'Ah. Simon will be in hog's heaven then. Usually he has to go and watch it in his shed because it so's boring and goes on for so long and I can't understand the rules however often he explains them to me, and I get annoyed at him lolling on the sofa for hours. He must regard Steve as a kindred spirit, or some kind of ministering angel, providing him with cricket when he's on holiday and I've no jobs for him to do around the house.'

'Steve will also be delighted. After all, how can I complain about him watching cricket with the people who have so kindly given us pool access? No doubt he'd tell me it would be *rude* not to watch it with Simon.'

Meanwhile Jane, who I'd expected to have a huge tantrum about the UNFAIRNESS of Simon being allowed to watch an iPad by the pool when she wasn't, seemed torn between starstruck adoration of both Imogen and Ben.

'Do you like YouTube make-up videos?' she demanded of Imogen.

Imogen laughed. 'No,' she said. 'What a load of nonsense spending hours and hours rubbing all that stuff over your face, just to make yourself look like a cut-out copy of everyone else. Who can be bothered with that? Not me!'

'Nor me!' said Jane fervently and untruthfully.

'Do you like reading, Jane?' asked Ben.

Jane fluttered her eyelashes in a very un-feminist way. 'Oh *yes*,' she said, equally untruthfully. 'I *love* reading. What's your favourite book?'

Peter and Alex had made fast friends from the moment they arrived, when Alex had informed Peter that he knew a joke about farts.

'I know *loads* of jokes about farts,' Peter countered loftily.

'Go on then, tell me one of your fart jokes and I'll tell you mine,' Alex said.

The 'jokes' seemed mainly to consist of making loud fart noises at each other and laughing uproariously, but they both seemed to be having fun.

I looked hopefully at the cold bottle of rosé Simon had brought out, condensation beading invitingly on it, looking so cool, so refreshing. It was *ages* since I'd had a little glass, well, OK, three glasses with lunch. Surely it was time for a little afternoon pick-me-up? It was practically an *aperitivo*, wasn't it? All right, it was only three o'clock. And they have *aperitivos* in Italy, but well, we weren't far from the border, were we (only about 1,000 km, Simon had informed me scornfully yesterday when I'd come up with this rationale for an afternoon drinky-poo-poo)?

'Would you,' I licked my lips thirstily, 'would you like a glass of wine, Angie?'

I braced myself for cries of 'Medical emergencies', 'Drinking around children and water is so dangerous' and 'What would you say to the coroner?' from Angie, but she just replied, 'Oh God, yes *please*!'

'Mmmm,' Angie said as she took a gulp. 'I know it's silly, but pink wine always reminds me of raspberry cordial.'

I stared at her. 'Raspberry cordial?' I repeated.

'Oh dear, see, I said it was silly. Of course, it's nothing like raspberry cordial, and it wasn't even raspberry cordial they drank in the book I'm thinking of.'

'Are you talking about when Anne gets Diana drunk because she mixes up the raspberry cordial and the currant wine?' I breathed, hardly daring to hope.

'In *Anne of Green Gables*?' we finished together.

'Yes!' said Angie in delight. 'Goodness, have you read them too? Most people nowadays have only seen the TV series.'

'The *proper* one, I hope, with poor lovely Gilbert Blythe,' I sighed. 'I can't believe he's dead. But I *love* the books.'

'Me too!' said Angie. 'Imo is always telling me to stop going on about them, that they're stupid books.'

'Jane too! She said Anne just witters on about imagination all the time, and it's boring! Boring? Anne Shirley's imagination? Sometimes I think she must be a changeling.'

'That's a very Anne thing to say,' Angie said solemnly.

'Oh, but if we're both Anne fans,' I cried, 'that surely means we must be –'

'KINDRED SPIRITS!' we laughed together.

'We must have another glass of wine to celebrate,' I insisted. 'I like your swimming costume, by the way.'

'Oh, thank you,' said Angie, glancing down at it. 'Every year I tell myself I'm going to have the confidence to wear a bikini, and every year I just can't quite bring myself to do it. I love yours, though!'

'This old thing?' I laughed merrily. 'Well, actually it's not old, I got it in the White Company sale for going on holiday last year.'

'Well done,' Angie congratulated me. 'I do love a bargain.'

Angie and Steve live in Aberdeen, where Steve works offshore and Angie works for a bank. By the end of the first bottle of rosé she'd laughingly told me that the only reason they stayed married was because Steve spent three weeks at a stretch away from her. I laughed too, and said, 'Oh God, lucky you! I wish Simon did that, but he just sits in his shed.'

'Steve does a lot of that when he's at home too,' Angie said. 'Cheers to sheds and oil rigs!' and we clinked glasses.

In the end they didn't go home after an hour, but stayed for a barbecue. When they finally tottered back through the garden gate, Simon and I both insisted they must come over as soon as they wanted tomorrow, and not delay for politeness' sake. Angie is clearly going to be my new BFF, and we're all going to live happily ever after in a hazy Utopia of pink sunshine wine and imagination and ginger orphan children!

Friday 12 August

Angie and Steve just got better and better, which was lucky, as when their maintenance man finally turned up, after much head scratching and shrugging, he'd announced the impossibility of getting parts to fix their pool in less than a month (which Simon was very smug about, insisting that was exactly what he'd said), so they've continued to pop over to use ours.

This morning I realised that despite Sylvia leaving enough provisions for an army, we'd rather depleted the stocks, not least of the wine, what with our jolly afternoons with Angie and Steve, though in fairness they'd brought round plenty of drink themselves and we seemed to be taking it in turns to have barbecues. The cupboards were nevertheless bare, and I reluctantly informed Simon we were going to have to brave the *supermarché*.

'Really?' he said. 'But it's so hot. Are you sure you can't manage with what we've got, darling?'

'Yes,' I said firmly. 'Quite sure. Come on, let's just get it over and done with.'

'Arrrgggghhhhhh,' groaned Simon, pretending to headbutt Sylvia's artisan rustic farmhouse table.

'Don't do that,' I snapped. 'Your mother will never forgive me if you get blood on that!'

I sorrowfully texted Angie to say that we wouldn't be at the pool this morning because we needed to go shopping, but we might see them this afternoon, and she replied to say that she needed to do the same, so why didn't we go together and leave the men and children to save themselves instead of dragging everyone along.

Ellen: I can't do foreign driving though?

Angie: I can. No point in taking two cars anyway, is there?

I looked at Simon, still groaning and dramatically banging his head on the table. Honestly, he was worse than the bloody children sometimes. Part of me thought if I had to spend a morning sweating my tits off in a French supermarket, why should he be spared the pain? Another, better, part of me thought how much quicker, easier and more efficient it would be if Angie and I went ourselves instead of forcing grumpy men and obstreperous children along just to prove a point. And *of course* Angie could do foreign driving, because Angie was my Perfect Friend. Hannah couldn't do foreign driving. I suspected Gemma and Fiona couldn't either, but it probably didn't matter because their alpha-dog husbands would never expect the little women to drive, and anyway, they probably had some kind of posh deli service deliver food on holiday instead of having to brave a Carrefour with broken air-conditioning in 27-degree heat.

Ellen: OK. Pick me up in 10?

Angie: Perfect.

'You've got a reprieve,' I announced to Simon. 'Angie needs to go shopping too, so we're going together, and you and Steve can stay here with the kids.'

Simon leapt up and waltzed through the kitchen before giving me a smacking kiss. 'Hurrah,' he cried. 'Hurrah for Angie. I love Angie!' I gave him a look. 'I mean you, darling, my dearest, long-suffering wife. Hurrah for *you*, I love *you*!' he added hastily.

'You still have to look after the children,' I reminded him. 'You can't just sit and watch cricket all morning.'

'I know, I know.' He flapped his hands blithely. I suspected poor Imo would be deputised for lifeguard duties, but oh well. For one morning, it wasn't my circus, nor my monkeys.

'Do put sunscreen on them,' I shouted after him as he skipped out the door.

As we drove out the gates, we only narrowly avoided the thing I'd been dreading happening since Angie and Steve first came over. As we passed Louisa's house, she rushed to the gate and attempted to flag us down. Luckily, Angie was concentrating on pulling out, and I stared straight ahead and pretended not to see her flapping and waving and shouting, 'Ellen! Ellen!' at me.

I'd hoped we wouldn't see too much of Louisa this holiday, as she avoided the pool, because of the killer chlorine, and shunned the tennis court, as competitive sport was against her beliefs, but she had come up to the house last Sunday afternoon 'before my retreat guests arrive. Are you sure you don't want to do any of my workshops? I'll give you a very good price for them since you're family.'

She had hung around, offering to read us her 'poetry', which she seemed to have written with a stick in some sort of vegetable juice on Sylvia's Smythson writing paper, as she couldn't use a laptop because it would enable the Chinese government to spy on her.

With much drama, Louisa had explained to us yet again how she'd also had to abandon the graphic design work – her original career, before she embraced a more 'alternative lifestyle' – that Simon had found her, for exactly the same deluded reason, and said that she'd taken up writing poetry full time.

While I was no expert on poetry, I felt fairly certain she wasn't going to be making her fortune with such works as 'Dripping Vulvas Singing Doom' (which appeared to be heavily influenced by Baldrick's 'war poem' 'Boom Boom Boom' in *Blackadder Goes Forth*) and 'My Aching Nipples Throb for My Lover' (the *Sunday Sport* seemed the most likely contender as the strongest influence on this).

Eventually, Louisa had sorrowfully announced she must go and prepare for her guests' arrival, whom I assumed were now sleeping in the ragged teepees that appeared in her (MY!) garden. But she lingered on, dropping heavy hints that perhaps we'd like to look after her children for her for the week.

Simon had said that was fine, but they'd have to adhere to our rules if they were here, and had then banged around the kitchen aggressively microwaving anything he could find, until Louisa gathered up her brood and scuttled off, muttering about 'death rays' and how she couldn't expose the Children of the Moon to such toxins, so on second thoughts she didn't actually think she could trust us with them. I'd hoped that between the 'retreat' and the chlorine fear, I could avoid Angie having to ever meet Louisa and judge me by association.

Angie had, however, caught sight of Louisa out of the corner of her eye. 'My God, did you see her?' she breathed. 'Apparently

there's a mad woman who lives in that house. Paul, the maintenance man, was telling us all about her. He said she dances about
naked and worships the moon and is a complete loon by all
accounts. They call her "*la sorcière anglaise nue*", he says – "the
naked English witch". Do you know anything about her? Have
Simon's parents said anything?'

'Er, no.' I squirmed 'No, I don't think they've ever mentioned
her.' God, I'm going to end up with arthritis in my hands, the
amount of time I spend crossing my fingers.

The supermarket shop was, as I'd predicted, completed far more
quickly and with far less stress than if I'd been trying to do it with
Simon and the children. We loaded Angie's car to the gunnels and
made our way back home again, and as we drove through the little
village nearest the houses, Angie turned to me with a grin and
said, 'I've had an idea. Shit, I should really watch the road. Look at
the square, and the cafés and bistros. Isn't it all gorgeous? Why
don't we come down and have a drink tonight – it's only about a
ten-minute walk? Just you and me? A girls' night out?'

'What a fucking *fabulous* idea!' I beamed.

Simon and Steve, however, didn't think it was such a fucking
fabulous idea. In fact, they were quite resistant to the entire plan
and came up with a 'better' one of their own.

'Why don't we *all* walk into the village and have dinner?' they
suggested.

Angie and I muttered a little, as we'd been excited about our
'girls' night', but we were eventually worn down by their persis-
tence.

'After all, Ellen,' Simon said smugly. '*You're* the one who's always
telling me this is a *family* holiday, and we should be doing things

as a family. So it's not very fair if you slope off on your own, is it? That's what you always say to me.'

'Fine,' I said ungraciously. 'FINE.'

I felt bad, though, as the children were actually quite excited by the thought of a grown-up outing, in the evening, to a grown-up dinner. Jane would normally have been hanging round my make-up bag, trying to inveigle the gaudiest eyeshadow I owned for herself and pleading for at least a little bit of lip gloss, Mummy, but under the excellent influence of make-up-shunning Imo and sweet, bookish Ben (whom she definitely had a thumping great crush on), she had her nose buried in a book.

'I'm just finishing this, Mummy,' she explained, brandishing *The Colour of Magic* at me. 'Ben lent me it, and he says he wants to hear what I think about it. But I was playing tennis with Imo this afternoon, so I'm a bit behind on the book. Aren't Ben and Imo *great*?' she sighed with shining eyes.

Tennis? Reading? Who was this child, and what had they done with Jane? I wondered if Angie and Steve would let us adopt Imo and Ben, but I also felt I should have a discreet word with Jane about the two of them.

'They're both lovely, darling, but you know, you shouldn't change who you are to make other people like you? You should just be comfortable being yourself.'

'Don't ruin things by being yourself,' I heard my mother say again. I quashed the voice firmly. My mother might not have taught me many positive things about parenting, but she'd given me any number of valuable lessons about what *not* to do.

Jane just looked at me blankly, though. 'I've not changed,' she said sweetly. 'I don't know what you're talking about, Mummy.'

Oh well. Maybe this tennis-playing, reading child *was* the real Jane, and the screen-obsessed, make-up-smeared diva was the illusion she put on for others. One could but hope! If only dear sweet Imo felt the love for *Anne of Green Gables*, but I supposed one couldn't have everything. I was brought abruptly back down to earth from this reverie when Peter started telling me his latest fart joke, so at least one of my children was true to their authentic self.

The walk to the village was actually quite delightful. The oppressive heat of the day had faded to a gentle background warmth, the moon was rising, the stars were out, the hedgerows fragrant with … some sort of nice-smelling French flowers, and best of all, Imo took charge of marching all the young ones along. Well, it was mainly Peter and Alex who needed taking charge of. Ben was never any trouble, and Jane was too busy channelling Imo – her new heroine – and trying to impress Ben to start any nonsense. And Peter, whom I suspected was almost as in love with Imo as Jane was with Ben, was also on his best behaviour, although saddened it would take more to win Imo's heart than his best fart jokes. That just left Alex, who, as the youngest brother, was accustomed to a well-timed clip round the ear from Imo anyway, so decided discretion was the better part of valour.

'How did you get her to *do* that,' I whispered to Angie, as Imo jollied the little ones along, suggesting games and songs when they complained the village was *so far away*, and they were *hot* and *thirsty*.

'I don't really know,' Angie whispered back. 'I don't feel like I can take any credit for it. She's always been better with the boys than me – it's just how Imo *is*, and I don't think it's anything to do with my parenting. Look at Alex. He's not like her at all.'

'Do you know how lucky you are, though?'

'Oh yes! Imo lulled me into a false sense of security. If I'd had Alex first, he'd probably have stayed an only child.'

The village square was quite magical in the dark. There were fairy lights strung round, a golden glow spilled onto the cobbles from the café windows, and red-and-white gingham cloths were even spread out on the tables. People sat around the square, drinking wine, laughing, smoking, strolling around and being so terribly *French* that Mumsnet would probably have short-circuited and crashed with the biggest communal online orgasm ever seen, had it only been there to witness the scene. I certainly thought it would get Fiona more excited than Hugo ever had (not that I wanted to imagine Fiona's sex life, but one simply couldn't conceive of the bloodless Montagues being conceived in any kind of throes of passion)! There was a band playing in one corner, an old accordion player on the other side, and in the third corner – no. Oh no. Nonononono.

'Keep walking,' I hissed to Simon. 'Just keep going. Don't look. Don't make eye contact. Jane, Peter, come on, chop chop, Daddy booked a table and we're going to be late, quick!'

'What are you doing, Ellen?' Simon hissed back, as an all-too familiar voice rang out behind us. 'SIMON, ELLEN, YOOOHOOOO!'

It was Louisa. Louisa and two other women who also looked like they knitted their own tampons. From what I could gather, before Louisa had noticed us and started trying to attract our attention they'd been having some sort of open-air poetry recital. There was a hat on the floor in front of them with a few coins in it, chucked in, I assumed, by traumatised passers-by in the futile hope that they might stop.

'Ellen, she's my sister. We can't ignore her,' Simon snapped, as he slowed and turned back towards Louisa.

'We can,' I said, tugging frantically on his arm. 'We most certainly can ignore her. What will Angie and Steve think? Angie said people call her *la sorcière anglaise nue*, Simon. The naked English witch!'

'I know what it means.'

'They think we're normal. I've made a new friend. She won't want to be friends with me if she knows I'm related to the naked English witch! She'll no longer think we're kindred spirits!'

'You're being ridiculous. She's still my sister. Lou, hi!' and Simon gave Louisa, who had been panting after us, a friendly hug.

I scuttled after Angie, Steve and all the kids, who luckily had been so entranced by the lights, the accordion player and the band that they hadn't noticed anything untoward. Simon joined us at the restaurant a few minutes later, and I gave him my best and brightest smile, but he just scowled at me.

Later, once the children were asleep, we had our customary Holiday Row. We always have one, usually about Simon not pulling his weight or his mother's barbed comments towards me, but this time, obviously, it was about Louisa.

'She lives at the bloody end of the driveway, Ellen, how did you think you were going to keep them from finding out who she is?'

'Well, we've been here a week, and they haven't,' I said defensively.

'She's been busy, running her poetry workshops, and she seems to have set up some sort of commune down here. Hopefully it will all work out for her, or at least enable her to pay her bills herself. Anyway, she's invited us over for lunch tomorrow.'

'What? Why? What will I tell Angie?'

'That we're having lunch with my sister.'

'Your sister is *la sorcière anglaise nue*! What will she think?'

Simon sighed heavily and said, 'Why do you care what she thinks?'

'Angie's my friend. She thinks there's a mad witch living at the end of the driveway, and now she's going to find out that this mad naked witch is my sister-in-law and she'll judge me.'

'Then she's not much of a bloody friend, is she?' Simon shouted. 'We've let them use our fucking pool all week, so if they can't deal with a little thing like Louisa …'

I snorted in disgust at the nightmare that was Louisa being described a 'little thing'.

'Well, then,' Simon continued, 'they can fuck off and find someone else's pool to use. Louisa was really hurt by you tonight, Ellen, and she said you blanked her this morning. All to make a good impression on Angie.'

'I've made a new friend. Is it so wrong I want to make a good impression?'

'It is if you lie and hurt people, and pretend to be something you're not.' Simon sighed. 'I heard you earlier telling Jane not to change to make people like her, but you do exactly the same. I know you lied to Gemma and Fiona about us owning this place. Your mother told me. She was proud of you, but I wasn't. And now you're lying to Angie about Louisa. And she's not even a real friend.'

I gasped in shock. 'How can you say that? She is, she is a real friend. The first real friend I've made in years.'

'No, Ellen. She's someone you've met on holiday. She lives in Aberdeen.'

'Angie is a *kindred spirit*,' I snapped indignantly.

'Ellen, you need to stop this obsession with "kindred spirits". Just because someone likes the same obscure Victorian children's books as you, it doesn't mean that you've got anything else in common with them or that they have to be your lifelong friend.'

'How *dare* you question whether a suitable appreciation of Anne Shirley constitutes a kindred spirit or not!' I spat. Simon knew *nothing*. *Nothing*.

He sighed again. 'Look, Ellen, they're a nice family, but they're still just holiday friends. Think about it. What do you really know about Angie?'

'Loads,' I insisted sulkily. 'Like, she can do foreign driving. And she also thinks Boden is very overpriced.'

'Ah, really deep and meaningful stuff. And do you even know where Aberdeen is?'

'Scotland?' I ventured. 'Quite far north?'

'Better than I thought you'd manage, given your grasp of geography. Which means, realistically, are we ever going to see them again after next week? Probably not. They're just holiday friends. So all the more reason to be yourself with them. Who cares?'

'I care!' I shot back. 'I CARE! Because my mother says I ruin things when I'm myself, and I don't want to ruin things. I want to be the sort of person who makes friends, says the right thing and knows the right thing to do. And is NORMAL. MYSELF isn't someone anyone likes. So I've got to find someone else to be!' and I burst into tears.

Simon came over and gave me a hug and a gentle shake. 'Ellen,' he said. 'Ellen, listen to me. Your mother is a poisonous, bitter old bitch. She's never forgiven you for being your father's favourite. And lots of people like you exactly as you are. Me. Hannah.'

'Hannah doesn't,' I said sulkily. 'She abandoned me.'

'Oh for Christ's sake,' Simon said. 'When Hannah gets back I'm going to knock both your heads together. Seriously, darling. Just be honest with Angie and be yourself. Like I said, what does it matter? You'll probably never see her again.'

Saturday 13 August

Louisa, for all her many faults, doesn't hold a grudge. We duly went to lunch, although despite Simon's insistence on 'honesty', I simply told Angie we had a 'family thing' and hoped they didn't see us trooping down the drive to Louisa's.

Louisa didn't mention anything of the previous day's events, and I tried to make it up to her by looking as enthusiastic as possible about the unidentifiable sludge that's her signature dish and even saying 'yum yum' as I choked it down. I also stopped myself from saying anything about the 'commune' she seemed to be running in the garden of MY HOUSE, and even plastered on an expression of joy when she proposed reading some poetry.

I did wonder if it was a dig at me when she announced she'd be premiering a poem called 'Betrayal. Or St Peter', as an audience of the knit-your-own women from the night before and a couple of others came creeping out of the tents in the garden to sit enraptured at her feet. It did, however, seem to feature errant penises a lot, so I don't think it could have been about me, particularly the lines that went, 'Your hard robbing cock has stabbed my heart, like your hard throbbing cock stabbed my womb, I'm stabbed, stabbed, stabbed by your robbing throbbing cock'?

I was dismayed to find that the effect of Imo and Ben on Peter and Jane only seemed to work when they were around to impress, and, left to their own devices, they reverted to their usual semi-feral selves. I say 'semi-feral', because compared with Louisa's cherubs, they were really quite civilised.

We were finally making our escape when Louisa said, 'Wait a minute, Ellen, I want to talk to you.'

Here we go, I thought, now I get the lecture about what a terrible person I am, and she's even sent Simon away so I've no one to defend me, although in fairness, Simon would probably have been on her side, as he still very much regards me in the wrong for denying knowing her.

'Sit down,' she said, patting the mossy log that did service as a garden bench. I sat down at the far end, and Louisa shuffled up next to me to take my hand and stare at me earnestly.

'I know you think I'm batshit –' she said.

'No, no, no,' I protested.

'You do,' she insisted. 'It doesn't matter. I don't care. I once used to be like you, Ellen. Caring what people thought. Pretending to be someone I wasn't. And I can't tell you how wonderful it felt it when I stopped doing that, when I finally gave myself permission to be free to be who I really am, to let the Goddess sing within me. Try it, Ellen, try it here with me now. Don't be afraid. What are you afraid of? Be your real self!'

To my horror, she leapt to her feet and ripped her blouse open, and tits a-swinging began to dance, chanting, 'I'm Amaris, the child of the Moon Goddess. Join me, Ellen. Join me. Who are you?'

I stood up awkwardly, gave a little hop and said, 'I'm Ellen.' I felt like an idiot.

'Set Ellen free!' cried Louisa. 'Be yourself. Open yourself. Open yourself up to the universe.' She gave her tits a violent jiggle, and Boreas – the youngest – seeing his mother's boobs, trotted up in search of snackerels. Following him came Edith, one of the commune poets, to see what was going on.

'We're having an opening ceremony for Ellen,' Louisa announced.

'Are we?' I said in surprise.

'Everyone join the circle, come on!' Louisa commanded.

A few more women wandered over. Taking the lead from Louisa, they also took their tops off and began to sway around, mumbling.

'Um, the thing is, Louisa, great chat, and actually I do feel very open now, thanks for that, but I do need to go. I've got this … thing … errr … byeeee!'

'Don't forget, Ellen,' Louisa called after me. 'Be yourself – everyone else is taken!'

I frowned at that, as I was pretty sure Louisa had nicked the sentiment off a fridge magnet I'd once seen in Clinton Cards.

Wednesday 17 August

I'd done my best to take Simon and Louisa's advice (at least the advice received before she got her tits out – it always goes pear-shaped once Louisa's bosoms are given an airing) and tried to be myself with Angie. Actually, apart from the Louisa thing, I *was* being myself. But I was determined to prove Simon wrong and show him that Angie *was* a real friend, and that I could do it, I could make new friends.

Our two families spent almost all our time together at the start of that second week. Angie and I cooked together, swam together, played tennis (badly) together, and most importantly we laughed and laughed. I felt free and happy and confident with Angie. I could be myself, and she did like me. She just didn't need to know about Louisa, who was busy hosting another poetry course anyway and so largely left us alone, or about my *EastEnders* addiction, which I may have omitted to mention when Angie declared she couldn't understand why people wasted their time and rotted their brains watching soap operas. She was right, really. I had been meaning to wean myself off it for years, so why not just do it? There were possibly a few other little details that I'd perhaps had differing views on from Angie too, but wasn't that the point of friends – to make you see things differently and challenge your preconceptions about things?

This morning we'd decided that we needed a treat, since to my great sadness Angie was going home tomorrow, and I'd probably be spending the last two days of the holiday packing and scrubbing Sylvia's house from top to bottom so we could return it in the state we found it, despite her insistence that we weren't to do a thing, her wonderful cleaning lady Suzanne would deal with it all after we'd left. I knew I couldn't do that, though, because either Suzanne would sneak, or more likely, Sylvia would interrogate her and she'd find out that we'd left the place a tip. Obviously, it would be me who was responsible for the state of the house, not her beloved and irreproachable son.

So I suggested to Angie, who luckily didn't have to do more than take out the bins and put the dishwasher on before she left, that we should take ourselves off to the village this morning, just the two of us, for *un café et un gâteau* – a bijou moment of joy, really, before the looming reality of life crashed down on us again.

I'd successfully put all thoughts of getting through the rest of the holidays at home without even Gemma and Fiona, of the return to school and worst of all, the soul-crushing return to Cunningham United Nautical Trust, out of my mind and was refusing to think about any of those things until I had to, because until then, I was ON HOLIDAY! So really, I deserved a little treat.

There was also the small matter of there being a jolly French market in the village on a Wednesday morning, and I thought if I could escape there without Simon, there was a good chance of me being able to purchase something *charmant et bijou* from the rather pretty little *brocante* stall I'd spotted there on previous visits, and which Simon had always steered me firmly away from, muttering, 'Tat, Ellen, tat. We've got enough tat, and I'm not spending good money on more!'

The walk to the village was really more of a trudge in the heat of the morning sun than it had been in the cool of the evening a few days before. I'd also taken the foolish decision, in the name of 'being myself', to abandon my Fiona and Gemma uniform, and wear a puffed-sleeve blouse (as a nod to Anne) and some rather natty capri pants, with wedged espadrilles. Fiona and Gemma had declared espadrilles to be *très passé*, and apparently it was all about the Birkenstocks now, but I was defying them.

I'd considered myself the height of chic before I left Sylvia's blissfully air-conditioned bedroom, but alas, neither my outfit nor my shoes were really suitable for traipsing through the heat of the day. The chi-chi little scarf I'd wrapped around my neck was at least coming in handy for soaking up the sweat running down from my hair, and since my espadrilles were somehow rubbing my feet, which I didn't even think it was possible for them to do, I could no doubt use it to mop up the blood too. I tried not think about how comfortable Birkenstocks probably were.

By the time we got to the village, we had one thought and one thought only, and that was a cold drink. We collapsed at a pavement table outside the café, and I was forced to remove my now sodden scarf. I feared I was no longer exuding effortless chic. Coffee – quite apart from the fact I didn't actually like it anyway, but then you could hardly ask for PG Tips in a French café – seemed a hot and disgusting idea.

'Orangina?' I suggested, looking down the menu the handsome young waiter had brought us. When I'd visualised this excursion, he'd looked at us – but especially me – with shy admiration, a beautiful, stylish, urbane, older woman, out of his league, certainly, but nonetheless to be admired from afar. In reality he appeared vaguely horrified, and had given us the menus rather stiffly from an arm's length. In fairness we *were* very sweaty, and I was rather regretting the outside table too, as the sun was beating down relentlessly.

'Ha ha! It's that, or wine,' laughed Angie.

'I mean, we could …' I looked up hopefully.

'I was joking?' Angie said, sounding unconvinced.

'So was I,' I said, even less convinced.

'What time is it?'

'Half past ten. Bit early?'

'We could call it breakfast wine?'

'Breakfast wine …' breathed Angie. 'I like it. Do you think they'll judge us?'

'No, we're in France. They'd probably judge us if we *didn't* have breakfast wine.'

'Well then. It would be rude not to, really. We deserve this.'

'We do, don't we?' I agreed warmly. And so we summoned the unenamoured young waiter and ordered *deux verres de vin blanc*.

It was remarkably restorative and I felt quite perked up within three or four sips. The waiter had insisted on bringing a large jug of water as well, and of course we were very sensible and had a glass of that too.

We were so revived by the hydration and the lil' pick me up, that we were just debating ordering another one when a familiar cry echoed across the square. Stall holders fell back and made the sign of the cross against her, as Louisa, *la sorcière anglaise nue*, shouted and waved as she made her way over to us. I sighed. I'd so nearly made it over the finish line with Angie. Why did Louisa have to ruin everything?

'Is that her?' whispered Angie. 'The naked witch woman? Does she *know* you?'

'Um, sort of,' I mumbled, and before I could say any more, Louisa had plonked herself down at the table.

'Ellen!' she beamed. 'So nice to see you. I only had a two-day workshop this week, so I thought I'd come down and do one of my impromptu recitals in the square, the locals *love* them, seriously they can't get enough – "*s'en aller, s'en aller*", they shout at me, which I think means "go on, go on". Seriously, they never want me to stop.'

I realised the stall holders were probably crossing themselves not in fear of Louisa putting the evil eye on them, but worse, reciting her poetry to them.

'Anyway, where are my manners?' Louisa turned to Angie. 'I'm Amaris, nice to meet you.'

'Um, Angie, Angie Robinson,' said Angie.

'Oh, I don't have a surname,' Louisa airily informed her. 'It's too patriarchal. I reject it.'

'How do you manage, legally?' asked Angie curiously.

'Oh well, *legally* I have to use Russell, which is all very tedious. I *wanted* to it change to Child of the Goddess, but Daddy wouldn't pay for it, which was very unfair, as it's his fault I'm saddled with his patriarchal legacy.'

'Gosh, what a coincidence,' said Angie. 'Ellen's surname is Russell as well.'

Louisa looked at her oddly. 'It's not really a coincidence, is it?' she said. 'Ellen's married to my brother. Golly, have you two got a touch of the sun already?' Luckily she was distracted by the sight of our empty wine glasses. 'Oh!' she cried in delight. 'Are we having wine? How lovely. *Garçon, garçon! Une bouteille de vin blanc, s'il vous plait.* It's much better value to get a bottle than to buy it by the glass! I knew as soon as I saw you sitting here that it was a sign from the Goddess that we were meant to spend some bonding time together, Ellen. Shall we order some snacks?'

Bonding time, indeed, I muttered to myself. More like a sign from the Goddess for Louisa to have a good freeloading session at my expense. She was still talking, though, now quizzing Angie about her aura and the state of her womb, for some reason.

'Of course, if you do have any troubles with that sort of thing, I offer womb healing as one of my treatments,' she was telling Angie, who was looking slightly stunned.

'How … er … how … do you heal wombs? Are you a doctor?' Angie finally managed.

Louisa laughed heartily 'No! Doctors? What do doctors know? My knowledge is far older. I use *crystals*,' she finished proudly. 'Here.' She rummaged in a grubby basket she had slung over one shoulder and produced a greyish-looking rock. 'Any friend of Ellen's is a friend of mine. Pop that in your pocket, and you'll notice a difference almost straight away. You can have that for free!' she added generously. 'Oh good, here's the wine.'

To my astonishment, Louisa and Angie appeared to be bonding, even when Louisa related the scurrilous tale of finding her husband Bardo in bed with a woman whom he suggested became her 'sister wife', and her subsequent indignant departure with the six children. 'I didn't mind so much about him, but he was using my best piece of rose quartz as a butt plug. My chakras would never have been the same again, but at least he must now have a very well-balanced arsehole! I had to throw out all my crystals and start again, because I didn't know where they'd been. Don't worry' – she nodded at Angie's pocket – 'that's one of the new ones, it's not been anywhere near his bum. Ooff, must go for a pee,' and she staggered off into the café.

'God, she's inspirational,' said Angie. 'Not at all what I expected from the nudey witch. I feel terrible, why didn't you tell me she was your sister-in-law?'

'Well, she's not always like this,' I tried to explain, as the waiter very pointedly put another jug of water on the table.

'I'd no idea there was so much going on, so close to hand,' sighed Angie. 'I feel a bit like I've wasted my holiday, lying round and drinking wine, when I could have been at poetry workshops and learning about building up the sisterhood.'

I didn't know what to say to this. Angie had spent those days wining by the pool with *me*. We'd had fun! So much fun. Was she seriously saying she'd rather have spent her time sitting in one of Louisa's goaty tents, learning to write poetry like Louisa's and prance around with no knickers on? How was that more fun than we'd had?

Angie tottered off to the loo when Louisa returned, the café's 'amenities' being of the one-in, one-out variety, and she came back sighing about the trickiness of managing a moon cup in the somewhat primitive facilities provided.

'That's partly why I free-bleed,' Louisa said smugly. 'So liberating, not to mention cleansing. I keep telling Ellen she should try it, but she won't even use a moon cup.'

Angie frowned at me in confusion. 'I thought you'd said you did use moon cups?'

'Um, yes, yes, of course I do,' I lied wildly.

'Really?' Louisa said delightedly. 'Oh Ellen, I'm glad, because when I brought the subject up last Sunday, you were so resistant. What was it you said? You might as well take a sink plunger to your fanny?'

'Ha ha ha, I was joking!' I laughed heartily to demonstrate how much I'd been joking. 'Of course I was open to the idea, and obviously I use one now.'

'That's good,' said Angie. 'They're so much better for you and the environment. I shudder when I think of all those of years of tampons, and the damage it did both to me and the planet! I can't understand why everyone doesn't switch.'

'Oh me too, me too,' I said guiltily, hoping Angie didn't spot the Tampax Super I always kept in my bag in case of emergencies.

After a couple more bottles, and a basket of free bread the waiter had brought – I suspected more to act as blotting paper than as a declaration of his hopeless love for me – I was attempting to entertain Angie and Louisa with the tale of the arse-waxing.

'So then he said, "Why does your arse smell of bacon?"' I gasped, through tears of mirth, as they both stared at me, and then Louisa patted my hand and said I mustn't blame myself for feeling pressured into adhering to the patriarchy's outdated ideas on beauty. I was lost for words again. How had *Angie* not found that funny? She was a kindred spirit, after all. A shadow fell across the table just then, and we looked up to see Simon. I guiltily attempted to hide my wine glass under the table.

''Lo, darling.' I squinted at him and tried to give him a sober smile. 'What are you doing here?'

'Looking for you,' said Simon grimly. 'We were worried. You said you were going for morning coffee, and it's now two o'clock.'

'Is it?' I attempted to focus on the town hall clock. 'Golly, I can't think how that could've happened. How peculiar.'

Simon heaved a great sigh and said, 'No, darling, neither can I. Come on, I'll settle the bill and give you all a lift home!'

Simon dropped Louisa off at the end of the drive, to my relief, so I could finally check with Angie that they were all were all coming over for a last-night barbecue.

'Oh God, Ellen, Amaris has asked me over to hers. She still has some of the women staying from the poetry course and she suggested we had a mini workshop tonight. She said to bring Imo too, and I think it would be a great last-night thing for Imo and me to do together – you know, before she gets into those really stroppy teenage years! Make some happy memories. You don't mind, do you? We've barbecued together every night, after all, and you must be sick of the sight of us.'

'Right. Of course.' Louisa had stolen my friend. MY friend. I'd finally made a friend, and I'd been almost myself with her, and would she ever have found out about the moon cups, really? It's not like we'd do spot fanny checks, after all, like when the teachers at school would decide to do random checks of whether our uniform was labelled or not (I never really understood that, as they always wanted to check the stuff we were wearing, and how could we lose a skirt while we were *wearing* it?). And now, fucking LOUISA, of all people, had swanned in and stolen her. It wasn't *fair*.

I could feel tears pricking at the back of my eyes as I swallowed hard, trying to get rid of both the tears and the dreadful urge to whine, 'She's taking you away from me' – the plaintive cry of small girls in playgrounds everywhere if their best friend showed any interest in another friendship group. I wasn't five, and I wasn't going to show that I cared.

I made one last try. 'That won't go on late though, will it? Steve and the boys could come over to ours, and then you and Imo can just stop in afterwards for something to eat? All very casual.' So casual. LOOK AT MY CASUAL FACE, ALL VERY CASUAL, LOUISA CANNOT HAVE YOU, YOU'RE MY FRIEND! I'm TOTALLY CASUAL about it, though!

'Mmm, well, you know, last night and all that. I'll probably still have a lot of packing to do. And we should probably have our last night just us as a family ...' Angie trailed off.

I'd messed it all up again. But where? Where had I gone wrong? Was this about the moon cups? Had Louisa told her I'd once been so gripped by a storyline in *Home and Away* that I'd blurred the lines between soap opera and reality, and had found myself wondering how Chloe was because I hadn't seen her in a while?

Maybe it was just that I was a dislikeable and terrible person, and no one would ever want to be my friend again and I'd die alone, all alone, friendless and unloved, and my body would be found weeks later by the milkman because no one had even missed me? Or, and I wasn't sure which scenario was worse, Simon was right and Angie was just someone I'd happened to meet, not a real friend at all, and friendship, indeed Kindred Spiritship, was built on a lot more than spending a fortnight in the same place and sharing a hankering to have been a spirited and misunderstood Victorian orphan.

'Look,' said Angie, who must have felt guilty about ditching me, as well she should after shamelessly using my pool all this time (well, Sylvia and Michael's pool), 'why don't you come too? Bring Jane. Amaris won't mind, will she?'

'No, thank you,' I said with as much dignity as I could muster. 'You're right, we should all spend time with our families, on a family holiday. Do have fun with your poetry. And safe trip home.'

'But we'll come and say goodbye before we go in the morning,' Angie protested. 'I know the kids will all want to say goodbye.'

'Yes, of course,' I said politely, with a forced smile. I just wanted to go back in the house, take off these bloody (literally) shoes and have a good cry. I was at the very most depressing stage of drunkenness, where you're sober enough to know you're drunk and to have a headache, but drunk enough that all emotions are heightened and things are starting to become too much to cope with.

Later on, both children did nothing but whine about their friends not coming over that evening. It was very hard to resist shouting that it was all very well for them, they had LOADS of friends at home they'd see soon, not to mention the whole of their lives ahead of them to make other friends, but WHAT ABOUT ME, staring into my lonely, friendless future ('Where am I as your lifeless corpse is found by the milkman?' was all Simon had said when I sorrowfully explained my tragic fate to him. I pointed out women live longer than men so he'd have shuffled off years before, and he muttered something about 'being melodramatic' and 'going on a bit').

Insult was soon added to injury, as we could hear the noise of Louisa's evening drifting up the drive in our direction. We'd never noticed it before, with Angie and Steve and all the kids around. Eventually, curiosity got the better of me, and after we'd eaten I suggested we all went for a little walk. Simon looked doubtful, and said he'd stay and do the dishes. Jane and Peter were equally unwilling, but urged me to go alone. The fresh air, said Jane nobly, would do me good. I suspected they were both counting on Simon being distracted by performatively 'putting things in to soak' (his idea of 'doing the dishes') to snag themselves a good long stretch of screen time, if only they could just get Mean Mummy out of the way. Even my children were rejecting me.

I stumped down the drive and quite coincidentally found my shoelace untied, just in line with a gap in Louisa's hedge that enabled me to see into the garden and the yurt where she was having her 'mini-workshop'.

I peered through, definitely not still hopeful that everyone would be sitting round looking depressed and gloomy, especially Angie, whom I trusted was *not* having such a horrible time that she'd realise the error of her ways, and come rushing back to apologise and beg me to be her friend again, insisting that she'd been addled with drink when she'd agreed to go to Louisa's, and it was all a dreadful mistake and Louisa was HORRIBLE and I was her best friend ever in the whole world.

To my dismay, though, everyone appeared to be having a wonderful time, laughing and joking, and not even drinking Louisa's usual sort of beverage (homemade parsnip wine being her most popular vintage) but rather something that looked suspiciously like a case of Saint-Émilion, which I presumed she'd 'liberated' from her father's wine cellar before we arrived.

I sniffed back tears, turned round and made my way back to the house, where I found another case of Michael's good red wine, and sat on Sylvia's tasteful terrace until one o'clock in the morning, weeping to Simon about the perfidy of kindred spirits, while he made helpful remarks like 'I did try to tell you, darling.' Simon was also unsympathetic to my claims that I had no friends at all, pointing out I had Sam and Gemma and Fiona and lots of other people in my life, to which I simply sobbed, 'But they're only friends with me because the children are! I've no friends that are my friends just for ME!'

Finally, as it was clear that I was not being dramatic enough, and needing Simon to really feel my pain, I repeated the dead milkman scenario several times until he assured me that he'd try his hardest not to die before me and leave me to such an ignominious fate.

Thursday 18 August

After too much wine, too much sun and not nearly enough sleep or water, despite the best attempts of the nice young waiter at the café the day before, I woke up with a thumping headache, a feeling of great gloom at the state of my life and a sense of nagging despair at the thought of spending the next two days scrubbing Sylvia's house into a state she considered worthy of her.

I was touched, though, when Angie kept true to her word and they all came round to say goodbye. Maybe she'd seen the error of her ways last night?

We came out with all the usual platitudes, made all the hollow promises about 'keeping in touch', promises that yesterday I'd have believed wholeheartedly but now was unconvinced that anyone really meant. Steve and Simon said they'd found each other on LinkedIn, which seems as far it as it goes for male bonding, and Angie gave me a hug and said, 'Hopefully I'll see you next year!'

'Really?' I said happily. I'd misjudged her! She *did* want to be proper friends after all.

'Yes!' said Angie brightly. 'I'm coming to one of Amaris's poetry courses, and I hope you'll be here too. It's time for me to do something new. I want to discover the creative side of me and maybe poetry is my calling. I'm so excited to explore more about it!'

I made vague and noncommittal noises about Angie's poetry calling, and dutifully waved them all off before slouching back to my mop and bucket, and surveyed the kitchen in misery. I decided I deserved a break, and a little sit-down. Maybe a glass of wine? Ugh. No. Wine wasn't my friend either. Never drinking again, etc, etc.

I slumped out onto the terrace, collapsed on a chair and stared at my phone aimlessly, scrolling through Facebook and Instagram to make myself feel better. Oh bloody hell – Chloe Watkins had had a secret beach wedding in Bali with 'just twenty-five of my closest friends to make the most special day of my life perfect'. Fuck off, Chloe, with your twenty-five besties. It was probably like that awful party you tricked me into. Or maybe, she really does have twenty-five best friends. No milkman death scenes for Chloe, no sirree Bob!

I decided to look at my emails instead. I'd been trying not to on holiday, because there was nothing of any urgency in them and I was trying to 'switch off', but there had been a lottery draw last night and maybe they might have emailed to say I'd won eleventy fucking billion pounds, and now I'd never have to go back to work and could 'embrace my creativity' like Angie and her bastarding poetry and every other fucker on Instagram that could take a photo of a fucking sunset.

But I hadn't won the lottery. My emails were the usual barrage of promises of 30 per cent off everything (not everything, actually; about six things, and only if you spent £500) and enticements from foreign generals about how they'd share their wealth with me as soon as they got out of prison if only I'd send money to help them access it.

Then my heart sank when I saw one from the HR department at work with the subject heading 'Return to Work interview'. I didn't *want* to think about returning to work. I didn't want to *ever* have to think about it, but I certainly didn't want to think about it a single second before I had to set foot through the doors and sit down in my sticky cubicle, with its faint and disturbing aroma, which I suspected was the previous occupant's jizz. And I *definitely* didn't want to think about it while I was still on *holiday*.

I muttered darkly to myself as I opened it and realised the Return to Work interview was scheduled for 31 August, which was before I was even due back in. That was doubly unfair. I rushed off to Simon and furiously waved my phone at him, demanding to know if they could legally do that. He shrugged and said it probably depended on what had been agreed when the time off was arranged, and how come I didn't know the details?

So, I'd got no friends, I'd got no creativity in my life, and I'd have to give up one of my last precious days of the very summer in which I was supposed to find creativity and make Happy Bastarding Memories with my children, to return to the soul-crushing environs of my soul-crushing office. There I'd doubtless have my soul crushed by Sally in HR, as she asked me, well, whatever you get asked at these things, and I attempted to concentrate on what she was saying and not play BuzzWord Bingo with myself as she spouted her favourite corporate jargon at me. Couldn't they have at least waited till I was back from France?

But maybe I should just jack it all in? Be like Louisa. Announce I was a Free Spirit and couldn't be constrained by society's outdated rules and Down with the Patriarchy, and then I'd just sit back and wait for someone to give *me* a house and prance around with *my* tits out, declaiming terrible poetry and charging people for the privilege of learning how to do the same? I couldn't, of course, because what would people think? I sighed, and returned to my mop and bucket. The water had gone cold and a beetle had drowned in it.

Saturday 20 August

We left France in glorious sunshine and arrived in Dover in glorious sunshine too, which obviously made Simon chunter again about why did we bother going away in the first place. He declared that I could drive the rest of the way home too, since he'd done all the driving for the last fortnight on account of the Foreign Driving Issue.

I wasn't looking forward to getting home to Mum. She'd spent the last two weeks texting me incessantly about things like 'The boiler is making a funny noise' and 'Do you know the cooker clock is five minutes fast?' and 'Have you heard from Jessica? I want to know what she's doing for Christmas, as if Geoffrey hasn't seen sense by then and I'm still here, I think it would be nice if both my daughters were here to support me.'

I didn't even dare tell Simon that Mum was still contemplating staying with us over Christmas. To be perfectly honest, I could barely entertain the thought myself, and I was giving serious consideration to driving up to Yorkshire when we got home and begging, pleading, *threatening* Geoffrey – whatever it took for him to apologise and for Mum to go back to him.

We were all very weary when we got home at last, the children complaining bitterly about the pins and needles in their legs due to having to sit with them on top of the cases of emergency wine I'd bought again in Calais on the way back. The house was in pitch darkness, and hope sparked in my heart that perhaps Mum had gone home and failed to tell me. I knew, of course, that this was highly unlikely. Mum would never consider simply returning to Geoffrey without first staging some sort of high drama in front of us for her to wallow in, for what was the point of drama without an audience?

Far more probable was that she was just off at one of her interminable 'supper parties' with her 'chums', and she'd roll in through the door shortly, pissed up on gin. Hopefully it wouldn't be like the night just before we'd gone on holiday when there had been an incident with the taxi driver returning her back to our house, when Mum claimed she'd simply 'slipped' when getting out the taxi on account of a defective taxi design, and definitely hadn't fallen over, landed in the lavender and had to be assisted up the path by the mortified young taxi driver, before tottering into the sitting room, pouring a large measure of Simon's Glenfarclas and ranting about 'bloody men, darling' at me until 2 a.m. I was too tired for my mother's scorned-woman-fury act.

We staggered into the hall and I felt the pang I always feel when I come into an empty house with no indignant little dog bristling out into the hall to nose at me in OUTRAGE for having had the temerity to leave him, the same level of disgust being shown whether I'd been gone for five minutes or five days. I couldn't wait to get Judgy back from the dog-sitter.

'Right, kids,' I said. 'Upstairs, quick shower, straight to bed. Can you start getting yourselves sorted out while Daddy and I unpack the car?'

I was lugging in a case of wine when Jane shouted down the stairs, 'Mum, there's a funny noise.'

'What sort of funny noise?' I yelled back, thinking oh God, please not the boiler. Mum *had* said it was making a funny noise, but I was so tired, and all I wanted was a hot shower and my bed, and also literally everything that goes wrong with boilers is fuckety expensive, and we'd just come back from a holiday and boiler repairs might finally tip Simon over the edge, and also I'd have to find an emergency plumber tomorrow instead of doing all the laundry.

This would also mean I'd have to endure the embarrassment of Simon suddenly pretending to be the Manliest Man that Ever Manned, like he does whenever there's a tradesman in the house for anything and he suddenly starts talking with a weird Cockney accent and calling the poor chap 'mate' and asking if he wants a 'brewski', and, even worse, him standing watching them while they work and going, 'Yup, yup, that's what I thought it was, mate, yup, need a screwdriver, mate, want me to pass you it, oh, not that sort of screwdriver, sorry, mate, thought that's what you said.'

Worse, he might put on his special trousers that he wears to go to Wickes and B&Q in the hope that someone, anyone, will think that he's In the Trade and mistake him for a plumber or an electrician or a bloke with a Real Man's Job, instead of just being the wanky architect that he is. And, of course, any sort of DIY is a good excuse for him to buy yet another gadget to add to his collection, because he's a Massive Gadget Twat.

'I dunno,' Jane shouted. 'It sounds like a cat. It's coming from Granny's room. Oooh, maybe Granny's got us a cat as a surprise while we were away. I'll go and look.'

'No, Jane, wait.' I thundered up the stairs two at a time, cursing my bloody mother, who was perfectly capable of retrieving her wretched Siamese cats in our and Judgy's absence and installing them here, despite being repeatedly told about Judgy's views on cats setting foot in the house even when he was away. And, of course, he'd be home tomorrow, and if my mother had a bedroom full of cats, he may be only 8 kg of Border terrier, but he was fully capable of battering her door down to get to the bastard things.

At least she'd kept them in her room, I reflected, but my mother's cats were particularly vicious specimens, and if Jane let them out, I didn't relish the thought of trying to capture them and contain them until such time as my dear Mama returned to assist, no doubt simply to lecture me about how I'd traumatised the poor creatures and how sensitive they were.

Last time we went to stay, Portia, the eldest one, bit right through my thumb in the night, when she managed to get the bedroom door open and took umbrage at our presence in HER house. Despite the fact I'd been sound asleep and minding my own business, and needed two stitches in A&E and a course of antibiotics, Mum was insistent that I 'must have done something to upset the poor darling', and was utterly unsympathetic, her pity all being reserved for dear psychopathic Portia. I didn't want to spend the next hour risking the loss of an eye chasing a spitting hell-demon round the house while Simon roared on about what were these bloody creatures doing here anyway and when the fuck was my mother leaving?

I reached Jane on the landing as she was just putting her hand on the door. There was indeed a strange moaning sound coming from my mother's room, though it didn't sound like any cat I'd ever heard. Then again, there was little about my mother's cats that *was* like other cats. Jane was about to open the door, but I hissed, 'Wait!'

'But Mum, I want to see the cat Granny got.'

'It might not be a new cat,' I pointed out. 'It might be Portia or Miranda.'

'Oh.' Jane took a step back. She, too, was acquainted with Portia's delightful nature, and that of her equally dysfunctional but slightly less violent sister Miranda, whose forte was to perch atop curtain poles and shit from a great height on anyone foolish enough to stand underneath. I didn't even know it was possible for a cat to shit like that until I met Miranda, although Mum would always excuse the creature with the claim, 'You must have startled her.'

Despite my loathing of the Siamese thugs, I quickly was very grateful to them for causing poor Jane to take that step away from the door. As I cautiously opened it – VERY cautiously, luckily – I beheld a sight that might finally be the key to me losing my baby weight from Peter, because anytime I think of eating some delicious cake or pizza or anything else carby and lardy and lovely, I can simply summon up this image to my mind and I'll not want to eat anything at all for a week, at the very least.

For there, in my good spare room (well, the box room/office that had a sofa bed crammed in it) spreadeagled on the sofa bed, naked, unless you counted the ball gag in his mouth and the dog collar round his neck, was Malcolm Frobisher, retired vicar and husband of Mum's 'great chum' Judith, with whom she'd stayed on her flight from Yorkshire and Geoffrey's caddish betrayal with Bunty Barnsworth. And sitting astride him, well, doing a little more than just *sitting*, dressed in a latex sexy nun's outfit, was my mother, while the strangulated cat noises were coming from Malcolm, through the gag. Judging from the various *items* I briefly glimpsed strewn around the room, Malcolm and Mum had quite niche tastes, and I appeared to have interrupted them at a key moment. I made a sort of strangulated cat noise of my own and slammed the door.

'Was it Portia and Miranda?' demanded Jane. 'Or is it a new cat?'

I shook my head violently, not trusting myself to actually speak in case I made some unfortunate reference to Granny's pussy.

'No cats, darling,' I managed eventually.

'What was the funny noise, then?'

'Just, errrrr, Granny listening to *The Archers* in bed.'

'Didn't sound like *The Archers*.'

'It was a cow having a problem calving. Now, Peter's out the shower, darling, so go and jump in quick, please. Come on, it's late.'

I staggered downstairs, ashen-faced. Simon was just coming in with the last of the suitcases.

'What happened to you?' he complained. 'I thought you were supposed to be helping me.'

'Something came up,' I whimpered, then flinched at the thought of Malcolm.

'Are the kids OK? Has your mother broken something? Oh God, I know, the boiler's packed in, hasn't it? I was sure it was making a funny noise. An emergency plumber on a Sunday will cost a fortune.'

I could already see him reaching for his Special Trousers in his mind's eye.

'Not the boiler. Worse. Well, different worse. Nothing's broken, except my mother's moral compass.'

I tottered into the sitting room and attempted to pour myself a stiff drink, but the Glenfarclas was gone. I rummaged through the sideboard, found a dubious-looking bottle of brandy, poured myself a large glass and downed it in one.

'Ellen, seriously, you need to tell me what's going on.'

The brandy burned, but it gave me the ability to croak, 'Mum's upstairs dressed in a sexy nun outfit shagging Malcolm Frobisher, and he's got a gag on and is still wearing his dog collar. They had *things*.'

'*Things*?' Simon repeated in confusion as my words sank in.

'You know. *Sex* things.' I reached for the brandy and gave myself another generous measure.

Simon blanched. 'Christ,' he said, 'give me some of that.' He took a large swig straight out the bottle.

'Where's my whisky gone?' he said, looking at the sideboard.

'I think that's the least of our problems right now. But I assume Mum, and possibly Malcolm.'

'Is nothing sacred?' spluttered Simon.

'Not when it comes to sexy nuns and vicars, I guess. Oh my God, they're coming down. What do we *do*?'

'I don't know. Drink more?' Simon took another frantic gulp and handed me the bottle, as we heard the front door close and saw Malcolm skip off down the driveway to his elderly Jag.

Mum sashayed into the sitting room wrapped in her White Company dressing gown. To my immense relief she had removed the latex wimple.

'Really, Ellen,' she said sanctimoniously 'You must learn to knock.'

'I must learn to knock!' I spluttered 'Mum. What do you think you were *doing*?'

'What do you *think* we were doing? For heaven's sake we're consenting adults, you know. It was very rude of you to interrupt like that. If it had been Geoffrey it would have put him right off. Luckily Malcolm is made of sterner stuff.'

'Mum! Stop it! Don't say things like that. I don't want to think about Geoffrey like that. It's bad enough I had to see you and Malcolm like that.'

'Well, if only you'd knocked, you wouldn't have.'

'Stop making out this is my fault.'

'Well, it is.'

'You're madly bonking your old friend's husband on my sofa bed, and the only problem you can see with this is that I should have knocked before I walked in, and not … not … all the *sex stuff …*'

'You shouldn't kink-shame, Ellen,' said Mum primly.

'What?'

'I said, you really shouldn't kink-shame. If two consenting adults want to –'

'How do you even know what that is? I barely know what that is. And how am I the villain here? I'm not *kink-shaming*. I'm just shocked at your lack of morals!'

'Why?'

'Because you were shagging Malcolm. On my sofa bed.'

'Oh that,' Mum waved her hand dismissively. 'There's nothing wrong with that. That sofa bed on the other hand, we need to talk about that, it's really not very comfortable, Malcolm nearly put his back out.'

'Stop it. STOP IT! MY SOFA BED isn't the problem here, YOU AND MALCOLM is the problem.'

'Why?' Mum looked at me with wide-eyed innocence.

'Err, where do I start? Maybe because of Judith, for one thing?'

'But Judith doesn't mind,' said Mum in astonishment. 'She and Malcolm have an open marriage. In fact, she would have joined us tonight, but she had to chair a WI meeting.'

'I'm just going to go and check on the kids,' gulped Simon.

I stared at Mum, as she smiled serenely back at me. 'Well, what about Geoffrey then?' I tried.

'Geoffrey? Well, we have an open marriage as well, darling, obviously.'

'But you don't even *like* sex?' I couldn't get my head around this concept at all.

'Well, I certainly didn't much care for it with your father. He was so very vanilla. But then I found I rather enjoyed a spot of role play, as does Geoffrey.'

'Roleplay.'

'Yes. Well, it's something to do, isn't it? Especially in the winter, when it's too dark and cold for tennis. And the internet is *marvellous* for meeting like-minded people, I discovered. That's where I heard about kink-shaming. Though, of course, you never know quite what *sort* of people you're going to end up with, which is why it's always nice to have old chums to fall back on, isn't it? You don't have to worry about them being common. One chap asked me if I had any "serviettes" to clean up the "couch" with afterwards, which was awfully offputting. Of course, it's different if that kind of language is part of the game.'

I had a sudden terrible image flash into my mind of some sort of twisted and elaborate role play, with my mother thrashing in ecstasy as Geoffrey stood over her, clad in a Burberry tracksuit, shouting, 'Get the serviettes off the couch!' (Mum's objection to the word 'couch' was almost as violent as her aversion to 'serviettes'), and dropping his Hs while *Jeremy Kyle* played in the background and Mum moaned and begged him to keep talking dirty to her. I took another slug of brandy.

'But Mum, if you have an open marriage, why all the fuss about Bunty Barnsworth?' I asked. 'How can you leave Geoffrey over that, if you then just high tail it down here to Malcolm?'

'Because Malcolm and Judith are on the agreed list. Bunty isn't. Bunty,' Mum sniffed disdainfully, 'is a slapper, who is *after* Geoffrey. Open marriages are not about just indiscriminately going off with any Tom, Dick or Harry, you know.' (A poor choice of phrasing from Mum under the circumstances, I reflected.) 'There are *rules* involved. And with Bunty, Geoffrey broke the rules. So he has to be punished. And not in the way he likes, either.'

I shook my head. There were now too many unpleasant images swirling round in it and the brandy was rather causing them to all blur into one. 'But Mum,' I wheedled, not for the first time, 'aren't you worried that if you stay away for too long, Bunty – or someone else – will take your place? After all, it sounds like Geoffrey is quite –' I gagged slightly on the words as I said them, but tonight had convinced me that it was more important than ever that Mum left, as I couldn't have her running Saga Sex Parties in my spare room. '– red blooded. Don't you think if you're not there, he'll just find the next best thing?'

'Not with Bunty,' she said firmly. 'Keith Grimshaw had a thing with her, very briefly. He told me all about it one night, and she won't be able to provide what Geoffrey needs.'

'Keith being on the agreed list?' I said weakly.

Mum nodded smugly. 'Yes, rather a dear chap, though he does insist on referring to champagne as "bubbly". But he got me a *frightfully* good deal on the Land Rover. No, darling, I estimate another two or three days and Geoffrey will realise what he has done. Then he'll be at the door, simply *begging* me to return.'

'Oh good,' I finished the brandy. 'That's nice.'

'Of course,' Mum winked at me conspiratorially. 'I won't let him off that easily. He's been a *very* naughty boy.'

'Stop it! Oh God, how am I going to deal with this? How do I look Geoffrey or Malcolm or anyone else in the eye again? How am I even discussing this with you? What do we do now?'

Mum shrugged. 'I'd say, darling, the best thing is not to discuss it. Just pretend it never happened, wouldn't you say?'

This is Mum's solution to most of my problems. She has been telling me to 'just ignore it and I'm sure it'll go away' for over forty years now, but for once she may have a point.

'So what … we just never mention it again? Ever?'

'Yes, what a good idea!' Mum beamed. 'Just like that. No need to talk about everything, is there?'

'How can you say that? You tell me not to be myself because I'll ruin things, and what will people think, and all the while you're … you're … you're … DOING THIS!' I finished feebly. 'Why can't I be myself?'

'I don't know, it's nothing to do with me?'

'It is. You've always told me not to be.'

'Did I? Oh well, if you say so,' Mum shrugged.

'You did. Even just a couple of weeks ago, you did. You told me not to ruin things with Gemma and Fiona by being myself.'

'Oh yes, I did, didn't I? Well, that was for your own good. Such nice girls. Much better friends than that funny little thing you always used to hang around with.'

'Hannah?'

'Yes, that was her, Fenella's daughter. Such a dull, drab little thing. I always thought you could do much better. But no, always the two of you, together, same clothes, same hair. I dreaded people mistaking you for her. I must say, I was thrilled when I saw you'd got rid of her and got some proper friends.'

'Hannah wasn't dull or drab,' I cried in outrage. 'And Gemma and Fiona aren't proper friends. Not like Hannah. How can you say that? Why do I ever listen to you?'

'I wasn't under the impression you did,' Mum sniffed. 'You might have turned out very differently if you had.'

'Well, I'm glad I didn't listen to you more then!' I shouted, all that brandy making me bold. 'Why do I always try to do things to make you happy when nothing I do is right for you? Do you know what? You're the reason I'm always trying to be someone else, and telling stupid lies to make myself look better and pretending to be better than I am, and I'm not doing it any more. I'm not. Sod off, Mum. Go back to Yorkshire, or go and stay with the Frobishers or something, I don't care.'

'You always were overemotional when you got over tired,' tutted Mum. 'I'm going to go to bed, Ellen, and I suggest you do the same. I'll forget what you said, as I know you didn't mean it. Goodnight, dear.' And she drew her dressing gown around her and swept out of the room without a backwards glance.

'For fuck's sake,' I snarled to myself, then burst into tears.

All that effort, all that time, all the things I'd done to try to be the sort of person Mum wanted me to be, and now I realised that all Mum wanted was for me to be exactly like her. And that was the last thing I wanted to be, even without a naked Malcolm Frobisher and Geoffrey in a sex shell suit thrown into the mix. I'd tried so hard to be the sort of person Mum expected me to be,

I'd spent so long being anyone but myself, because Mum didn't like that person. And for what?

I made so many mistakes with people, because I never felt I was good enough, and I never felt I was good enough because Mum always told me I wasn't, because I wasn't like her. She didn't want me to be strong or independent or feminist. Mum just wanted a mini-her to show off to her friends.

I felt that this should probably be some kind of watershed moment, where I dug deep and found strength and gave some sort of mortifying American fist pump, before I became my own better person and wrote inspirational posts on Instagram about it that didn't really say anything, but accompanied heavily filtered photos of flowers or sunrises. But I was so tired. On top of everything else, finally realising once and for all that any love my mother had for me was only for the glimmers of her own reflection that she saw in me, not for me at all, had drained all the strength and resolution from me. I wanted to go to sleep for a year. And I wanted Hannah.

Sunday 21 August

Somehow, in the dark watches of the night, I'd convinced myself that Mum would come to me in the morning, and apologise for everything that had happened the night before.

I don't know why I thought that might happen, because Mum has never apologised for anything in her life, and certainly not to me. But at four o'clock in the morning I built myself a fantasy world, where Mum flung herself tearfully on me and said she was sorry for every time in the last forty years that she'd put me down, made me question myself and hurt me.

In this wish-fulfilling vision, my mother would tell me she loved me, and that she'd do anything to make it up to me if she'd ever made me feel less than enough, because *of course* I was enough, I was everything to her, and things would be very different going forward. We'd both cry, and maybe spend the day looking at old photos of the two of us and laughing fondly. Or maybe we'd go for a girly lunch and I'd finally properly get to know her. I was so delirious with lack of sleep at this point that I thought we might even become friends. I'd be one of those women who got to say things like 'My mum is my best friend' and 'I talk to my mum every day.'

What Mum actually did, which was what she always did after a row or any situation where she might be considered to be in the wrong, was to behave as if nothing at all had happened. Not me walking in on her and Malcolm, nor me telling her to leave or how sick I was of her sniping at me. And certainly no apologies, heart to hearts, suggestions of quality time together or declarations of her deep, abiding maternal love for me. Instead I got a complaint that there was no skimmed milk, and could I please get some *decent* coffee too when I went to the shop for her milk? Oh, and we were out of whisky too, so could I pick up some more, please.

I stared at her. 'Is that it?' I asked quietly.

'Hmmm?' said Mum, frowning into her substandard coffee. 'Oh, some olives would be nice too. From the deli, darling, not the supermarket.'

'No, I mean, is that it? Is that all you've to say to me? About last night?'

'I was hoping I wouldn't have to say anything and that you would apologise without being prompted,' Mum said tartly.

'ME apologise? For what?'

'You said some very hurtful things.'

'You had sex with a vicar on my sofa bed, having made me feel not good enough for my whole life!'

'You're impossible, you've always been impossible. Everything's always got to be about you, hasn't it? I'm going to take my coffee in the garden. You know where I'll be when you finally decide to be reasonable,' and with that, Mum flounced out of the kitchen door.

I wondered how one goes about having a nervous breakdown, because I really thought I might be on the verge of one. I also wondered whether anyone would even notice. In the absence of being sent to a sanatorium in the Swiss Alps to recover from my 'nerves', though, I decided that neither my mental health nor my drinks cabinet could cope with my mother's presence for much longer and something really must be done. If only I could have asked Hannah for advice. I'd never realised just how much I relied on having her perspective on things, especially where Mum was concerned.

Despite my best efforts at throwing Mum out, she was clearly determined to ignore me, and since I couldn't very well physically chuck her out in the street, there was only one person who could get her to leave, and that was Geoffrey. Loathsome though he was, Mum seemed quite attached to him, or at least to his property and money, so tolerating him was the price she had to pay for them. And while she seemed to have plenty of alternatives to Geoffrey himself for her more *personal* needs, neither Malcolm Frobisher's retired vicar's stipend nor Keith Grimshaw's car salesman credentials were going to provide Mum with both the income and cachet she required. Geoffrey must therefore be got on side. But *how*?

Since Mum had – most fortunately – not gone into specifics about Geoffrey's 'tastes', I wasn't sure if I should play her as the pining heroine, longing for the manly hero to don a pair of tight breeches and stride in wielding his riding crop (ugh) to sweep her off her feet and take her home, or whether I should suggest he had been a very naughty boy and Nanny was going to give him a good spanking (equally ugh).

I came up with quite a number of plans, but discarded them all. I wished there was *someone* I could ask about this. I couldn't even talk to Sam, and I certainly wouldn't have mentioned it to Lucy Atkinson's Mummy or Fiona Montague (though there was something about Fiona that made me suspect she'd probably be quite keen to join in with the sort of shenanigans Mum seemed to get up to, so maybe she'd have been able to proffer some handy tips), even if they hadn't been quinoaing it up in Sardinia. I tried Simon for advice, but he just said he was going to his shed and would be staying there until it was all over.

Eventually, inspiration struck. I was pulling the third load of laundry out of the washing machine when Mum drifted into the kitchen to enquire when I was planning to start cooking lunch, because surely it was time for a little drinkie, but oh Ellen, you've run out of gin again, haven't you been shopping yet? I rummaged through the cupboards and found an ancient bottle of Aldi gin that I thrust at Mum, who looked at it sorrowfully, and said she might just give Nigel and Lavinia Henderson a little tinkle and see what they were up to this afternoon and if they fancied doing something. She took the Aldi gin with her as she went to make her phone call, and it was then that I realised what I needed to do.

I decided I'd better strike while the iron was hot, because if I thought too much about talking to Geoffrey and what I'd have to imply to him, I might not be able to bring myself to do it. I got the Gordon's out from behind the Persil where I'd hidden it from Mum, poured myself a stiff gin and tonic and got on with it.

Geoffrey answered the phone, as delightful as ever.

'Ellen!' he boomed. 'Are you ringing to tell me your mother is missing me and is now ready to come home? She can come back any time she likes, you know, but I'm not apologising about Bunty.'

'Oh Geoffrey.' I tried to sound sweet and girlish and caring, and also a little anxious and pathetic. 'No, I was ringing to see how *you* were. We're so worried about you.'

'Worried? About me? Who's worried? Your mother? She needn't be.'

'No,' I said sadly. 'Not Mum. That's why we're worried. About you. If you're OK, you know, now Mum's having so much *fun*.'

'Fun?' snapped Geoffrey. 'What sort of fun is Yvonne having down there without me?'

As delicately as I could, I implied that Mum, finding herself alone and palely loitering, had wasted no time in finding plenty of both knights at arms and belles dames sans merci with whom to make sweet moan.

'Well, of course, in your sort of …' – I swallowed hard – '*circles*, Geoffrey, for certain things, well, people much prefer an extra woman to an extra man, don't they?'

'You know about that?' Geoffrey spluttered.

'Yes, I'm afraid so. It's impossible not to, really. Malcolm Frobisher's been here quite a bit, and Mum goes over to him and Judith a lot, and then this afternoon she's off to Nigel and Lavinia Henderson's, and I just thought *poor* Geoffrey, I do hope he's all right, and you know, things are going well for him with Bunty, because like I said, people don't really like an extra man on his own so much, do they? Well, unless they're into – you know. Maybe you do like that, it's none of my business, and some people will always find something to do with an extra chap of course, but it's easier for men in a couple, isn't it?'

'I'LL HAVE YOU KNOW I WASN'T BUGGERED AT ETON AND I DON'T INTEND TO START NOW!' roared Geoffrey down the phone, which wasn't quite the response I'd been expecting.

'That's why I'm just so worried about you, because I do think Mum's having so much fun, she might not come back. And then, well …' I said hastily, before Geoffrey overshared any more.

'I'm leaving now, and coming to get her,' Geoffrey said. 'We'll put this whole silly Bunty business behind us. Dammit, I'll even apologise, if that's what it's going to take for her to come back.'

'Well,' I pretended to prevaricate, 'she's going to Nigel and Lavinia's in a bit, and I don't know quite when she'll be back.'

'Nigel and Lavinia's?' bellowed Geoffrey.

'Yes, after lunch. I think she said Malcolm and Judith might pop over too, because now Malcolm's retired, he doesn't have to take evensong anymore.' I trailed off, hoping I hadn't gone too far.

'I'll be there in a couple of hours. Tell her to stay put. Sod it, this is an emergency. I don't even care about the Jag's fuel economy, I'm going to PUT MY FOOT DOWN!' and with that, Geoffrey rang off.

I breathed a sigh of relief. He'd taken the bait, and now I just had to hope Mum also went along with it. Right on cue she wandered back into the kitchen.

'Nigel and Lavinia are going to the garden centre and won't be back till three o'clock. Apparently there's a special offer on hydrangeas,' she complained, 'which is very boring of them. They suggested I pop over about four, once they've had time to get ready.'

'That's nice,' I said, looking at my watch. That should give Geoffrey plenty of time to get here, especially as he wasn't driving for maximum fuel economy. I'd better keep Mum distracted till then anyway, I resolved, and produced the Gordon's from behind the Persil again.

'Look what I found, Mum,' I said brightly.

'Ooooh,' she said in delight. 'I'll get a taxi to Nigel and Lavinia's.'

*   *   *

I'd harboured some hopes that Mum was just putting on a brave face after our row last night and deep down wanted to tell me she loved me, was sorry, etc., and that maybe a couple of stiff gins would loosen her tongue and we could make up before she left, but she just sat leafing through *Country Living* and sniffing at other people's décor choices.

'Are you sure there's nothing you want to say, Mum?' I tried in the end, as I handed her another G&T. 'About last night?'

'I don't think there's anything *to* say.' Mum gave me her best There's Nothing to See Here, Now Don't Make a Scene, Ellen smile.

'Really? There's nothing at all you think we need to discuss?' I wasn't giving in that easily. Not this time.

'Oh yes, darling, now you mention it.'

I brightened. It would all be OK. It would be like the end of 'A Boy Named Sue' when they hug and make up and everything's OK, despite all the pain his father caused Sue.

'Yes, I've been meaning to say this for a while. Can you please buy the good tonic, not the supermarket own brand? I know you say it's the same, but it's really not. Gosh, look at the time! I better take this with me while I go and get ready!'

I sighed. Geoffrey had better get here soon and remove her, if not for the sake of my nerves, then certainly for my grocery bill. Mum was never going to change, though. Why had I ever been foolish enough to think she would?

Mum was just sashaying down the stairs, a fresh coat of Estée Lauder lippy and a dab of Allure (Chanel's version, not a euphemism) behind each ear, when there was a fearful hammering on the door.

'YVONNE!' bellowed Geoffrey. 'Let me in!'

Mum flung open the door and drew herself to her full height to give Geoffrey a stern look.

'Enough of this nonsense,' he shouted. 'I've come to take you home. I need you. The cats need you. Portia has shredded the Laura Ashley Honeysuckle Silk.'

'Not the Laura Ashley?' gasped Mum. Geoffrey nodded dolefully. Oh, he was good, actually. Nothing would move Mum more than the thought of her precious Laura Ashley cushions being in peril.

The fate of the Honeysuckle Silk hung in the balance for a moment, though, as Mum remembered why she'd abandoned him in the first place.

'Isn't there something you want to say to me first, Geoffrey?' she demanded.

Geoffrey looked truculent for a moment, then, perhaps remembering Eton, said, 'I'm very sorry about Bunty, darling. It won't happen again.'

'I should think not,' sniffed Mum. 'Well, I suppose we'd better go home and see what poor darling Portia is up to. Oh dear, only I *did* promise Nigel and Lavinia I'd look in, and I *do* hate to let them down. Unless … I don't suppose you want to come?'

Geoffrey looked wolfish and waggled his eyebrows suggestively. 'Always, my dear,' he purred.

I was a bit sick in my mouth.

'I sorted it,' I thought, as, laundry done, I started heaving our empty suitcases back into the attic, before they ended up just sitting on the landing till Christmas. So maybe I could sort everything else out in my life. I'd ace my Return to Work interview and fix things in my terrible job, or at least be assertive enough to say I'd been with the company long enough that I deserved a better cubicle, one that didn't whiff of jizz on hot days, although I might phrase it a little differently, and I'd come clean with Gemma and Fiona about the house in France.

I shoved the last suitcase into the corner of the attic and knocked over the same bloody box of diaries. I really needed to move that damn thing. I picked everything up and shoved it back in, but the temptation to take a peek in one of the diaries was too much, especially when the alternative was stripping Mum's bed, then deciding if burning John Lewis Egyptian cotton was too much or if a boil wash would suffice. Just one. Just one quick look in one. I opened a random page.

1990. Me and Hannah have decided that we're going to have a farm together when we grow up. We're going to breed dogs on the farm, and we're going to have ducks and goats and horses. We're not going to get married, because boys are stupid, and we've had enough of wasting our time trying to make them like us. We'll have a big pond for the ducks and a white farmhouse, and a paddock for the goats and horses. The dogs can live in the house with us. Probably we'll have chickens too. You have to have chickens on a farm, don't you? I'll ask Hannah about the chickens. And we'll live happily ever after, just me and Hannah and the animals and no stinky boys, especially not Jonathan Baxter, who I hate.

On the page across from this entry was a detailed drawing of our 'farm'. I laughed. The duck pond was the same size as the paddock we were apparently going to keep horses *and* goats in. Perhaps it was as well this youthful dream had never come to fruition, as clearly neither of us had the slightest idea about animal husbandry. I suspect a 'horse/dog/duck/goat farm' wouldn't be economically viable.

Then my laughter turned to tears. Oh God, I missed Hannah so much. I'd been so busy being angry with her, that I hadn't realised that the only reason I *was* so angry with her was because I missed her so achingly. It wasn't until bloody Mum started slagging her off last night, and I was defending her, that it had it hit me how much I wanted to see her, laugh with her, just *talk* to her. Especially since Mum's barbed comments had never had so much of a sting when Hannah was by my side. I turned the page of the diary to read another entry.

Got a new haircut today. Like Winona Ryder's. I thought I looked super cool, but Mum said what had I done and I didn't have the cheekbones for short hair and it made me look fat. I went round to Hannah's and Hannah and her mum both said it looked fab, but maybe Mum's right. Why can't I do anything right? Hannah said not to listen to Mum, and her mum said I should stay for dinner and we had mint Viennetta for pudding as a treat, even though Mum says I should avoid puddings as a moment on the lips is a lifetime on the hips. I wish Hannah's mum was my mum. I wish I lived at Hannah's house. I wish I'd Hannah's life.

Oh God. There it was, in blue biro and loopy teenage handwriting, right in front of me. Hannah had been right, I was jealous of her. I'd always been jealous, deep down. Jealous of her family, of her easy, happy relationship with her mother. And maybe, a tiny, horrible bit of me had been glad when her marriage failed and

Dan turned into such a dick, because now Hannah *wasn't* the one with the perfect family anymore. And maybe, just maybe, if I was brutally, totally honest with myself, that's why I was so angry about the South Africa trip. Because if Hannah and Dan started getting on again, then she'd have a perfect family again, along with her brilliant new job, while I was stuck in my dead-end one. But whose fault was that, if I hated my job? Not Hannah's. Oh God. I was a shit, shit, shit friend and a terrible person. I needed to fix this and I needed to fix it now, before I lost my nerve. I pulled out my phone and pressed Hannah's name, and waited hopefully, full of the apologies and remorse I knew I owed her. Come on, come on, I thought impatiently. But she didn't pick up.

Never mind, never mind. She was probably busy, or driving. Or in the loo. Or her phone was out of charge. There were loads of reasons why she wasn't answering.

Monday 22 August

I rang Hannah another three times yesterday and twice this morning, but again she didn't pick up. I bewailed all this to Simon, sharing my fears that I'd fucked it for good, that I'd gone too far or that something terrible had happened to her. Simon pooh-poohed my worries, saying, 'I expect she's busy. Or there'll be some good reason.'

'But I need to talk to her, Simon,' I whimpered.

'Well, I'm sure you will at some point. Is it that urgent, that you've got to speak to her this minute?'

'Oh God, you sound like my bloody father!'

Next he'd be saying, 'What do you even find to say to each other all the time?' like our parents used to when we were young. After school, the first thing Hannah and I would do when we got home was start coming up with reasons to ring each other to chat more, because there was always more to say. We'd been chatting almost incessantly for thirty years, and we still hadn't even come close to saying everything. How could I have thought that just a few days with Angie would make her a kindred spirit?

Back then, of course, despite plaintive beseeching that we simply *had* to ring each other to ask a Very Important Question about homework, we were forced to wait till after 6 p.m., and the 'cheap rate' for the phone calls. To ring someone before the magical witching hour of six o'clock struck was only permitted in actual life-or-death situations. To have made a phone call at 5.53 p.m. for mere social reasons was, as Dad liked to remind me, practically the same as simply setting fire to a pile of £10 notes.

Generous to a fault in other ways, Dad was astonishingly tight about the telephone bill. He'd insist on a fully itemised bill each quarter, and then scrutinise it, demanding explanations for any calls that had been made at peak-rate times. The greatest crime of all in his eyes was the insane profligacy of dialling Directory Enquiries. If we needed a telephone number that badly, he'd roar in fury, we could go to a telephone box and ring it up for free from there. In vain would we plead inclement weather, or point out it was a ten-minute walk to the nearest phone box. He was quite adamant it was Wasting Money, and no 50p coins would be squandered on HIS watch.

Dad's other big bugbear was first-class stamps. If one was foolish enough to enquire if he was in possession of such a thing as a stamp (back in the distant past when we wrote letters to people and had pen pals and were forced to write thank you notes to Great Aunt Maud for the £1 postal order she sent each birthday from her cosy retirement home in Bognor Regis, decimalisation having entirely passed her by, so she was under the impression she was bestowing great largesse upon us), it would trigger an interrogation as to the letter's purpose, recipient, urgency, etc., before he'd declare with a sigh that he only had first-class stamps, and as he didn't think my correspondence warranted that, I'd have to go and buy a second-class stamp (thus in the case of Great Aunt Maud's thank you letters, using up almost 20 per cent of her gift just to satisfy polite convention).

In other matters, though, his generosity was bordering on legendary. To use a first-class stamp would, according to him, bring us to penury and see us in the workhouse, but he blithely whisked me off to London and bought me a dress from Selfridges for my first dance without blinking an eye. When asked about it, of course, he would explain at length how it was precisely those savings that *meant* he could buy ballgowns from Selfridges, and cocktails for women he'd only just met in the American Bar at the Savoy afterwards. I remained unconvinced that we used that many stamps.

In the matter of the telephone calls, though, Hannah and I were not to be thwarted so easily. We had important things to discuss, like whether the boy in the newsagents next to school, where we faithfully procured our Polo mints and copies of *Smash Hits* and *Just Seventeen* (and later our Marlboro Lites and *Cosmopolitans*) had been eyeing us up, or whether he just had a squint (a squint, it turned out). We needed to talk about how much we hated Lisa and Lindsay and Karen, and whether we should get a fringe when we got our hair cut, and if our mums would *ever* give in to our begging and take us to Toni and Guy for said haircut instead of Hair By Elizabeth Ann in the High Street. It was also vital to decide whether we should squander our precious pocket money on a top from Miss Selfridge or a skirt from Top Shop, and more importantly, which of these garments might achieve the Holy Grail of making *boys* notice us, and the merits of Luke Perry versus Christian Slater, and a million and one other *essential* topics that if we didn't talk about we'd *literally die*.

Once the magical hour of 6 p.m. arrived, one of us would eventually convince our parents that we absolutely HAD to ring the other to ask if we were to do page 13 or 15 for our biology homework, and permission would be granted amid much grumbling about 'writing things down *properly*' in our homework diaries and 'improving our handwriting so we could actually read it' and 'paying attention in class, because I'm not paying all this money in school fees for you stare out the window, you know, Ellen'.

We didn't care, though, because we were already on the phone, upstairs on the innovative and modern invention of the *extension phone* in our parents' bedrooms, chatting happily, and circumventing parental outrage about the phone bill by the simple method whereby I'd phone Hannah, so her parents heard the phone ring, and then we'd hang up after a minute or so and Hannah would call me back, so Mum or Dad heard *our* phone ring, or vice versa, so that when the furious shouts came up the stairs of 'Are you *still* on the phone' and 'Think of the PHONE BILL', we could indignantly remind the outraged parent that their phone bill was *quite* safe, as she'd called ME, remember? Inevitably, there was a reckoning when the phone bill arrived and there would be bellows of 'HOW MUCH?' but our parents never seemed to cotton on to our devious system.

Jessica was the main source of interference in our cunning ploy, as she wanted to use the same trick to spend the evening talking to *her* friends, and she didn't care who had rung whom, she just wanted me to get off the phone so she could have the same conversation with her best friend Claire about the boy in the newsagents with the lazy eye. Hannah was fortunate enough to have a younger brother who didn't need to spend hours on the phone, though, as she often lamented, why couldn't he have been an *older* brother, so he could have introduced us to his friends? An eight-year-old *Sonic the Hedgehog* fanatic was no use to us at all on the boy front. We'd sigh in envy at the American teen films we were obsessed with, not just because of the ease with which the girls met boys and got off with them, or their wonderful clothes, or the fact they all seemed to drive cars from the age of about nine, but mostly because they each and every one *had their own phone lines in their bedrooms* and could talk to their heart's content, with no angry parents or siblings constantly trying to kick them off! What luxury! What bliss!

And then suddenly we grew up, and mobile phones happened, along with the internet, and instead of mobile phones – which really were an updated version of that longed-for personal phone line – enabling us to talk more, they paradoxically made us talk much less. We shopped, we watched videos, we looked up information, we planned travel routes with them, but actually making a phone call now became a strange and exotic thing, something I'd reached the point with where I almost feared it, dreaded it, put it off and avoided.

Not with Hannah, obviously. Talking to Hannah was almost like breathing – something essential to existence. What I mean is ringing insurance companies or plumbers or garages, etc. But apart from Hannah, there was no one else I'd call just for a chat. Not even Sam. And I definitely couldn't see myself phoning Lucy Atkinson's Mummy or Fiona Montague for anything other than some sort of child-related emergency. Phone calls nowadays had become *special*. Once upon a time, I'd even ring up Chloe Watkins, but now, to call for a chat was something you'd only do with those most dear to you. Instead, we'd text, or WhatsApp, send gifs and memes and videos, and I wonder whether we are losing the art of conversation? I once showed Jane and Peter a phone box. They stared into it, baffled by the concept of a life without mobiles and the internet.

'But how did you know what number to call?' Jane had asked, a confused look on her face.

'We just remembered them,' I said. 'I can still remember Hannah's number now from when we were young,' and rattled off 339 1304 without even having to think. I couldn't remember where I'd put my car keys most of the time, and yesterday I forgot the word for 'door' (though that might have been something to do with the Mum/Geoffrey/Malcolm Frobisher/latex nun outfit), but Hannah's phone number was engraved on my heart, even though it had been twenty years since her parents lived in that house and I'd last dialled that number.

So even though we no longer spent every evening on the phone dissecting important topics like 'Do you think it's actually true that in French kissing he *puts his tongue in your mouth* because ewwwww?' we still chatted, in one way or another, every single day. Even when we were in labour with our children, we managed a few messages along the lines of, 'WHY DID I THINK THIS WAS A GOOD IDEA' and 'FUCK THE FUCKING WHALE SONG CD, I WANT THE FUCKING DRUGS NOW, ALL THE DRUGS' and 'I SWEAR TO GOD I'M GOING TO RAM THAT FUCKING WHALE SONG CD UP SIMON'S ARSE AND MAKE HIM SHIT IT OUT AND MAYBE THEN HE'LL STOP WITTERING ON AT ME ABOUT AM I SURE I WANT THE DRUGS AND WHY DON'T I TRY BREATHING FOR A BIT LONGER BECAUSE SHORTLY HE'LL NOT BE BREATHING IF SOMEBODY DOESN'T GIVE ME A FUCKING EPIDURAL!!!!!!'

Given all this, I couldn't believe Simon's casual 'Hannah's probably just busy' line. We were never ever 'too busy' for each other. And we'd never in thirty years gone for so long without any kind of contact, apart from on family holidays in our teens, and even then we'd ring each other from a phone box at the airport and send postcards and buy tourist tat souvenirs for each other (my mother had had a fit of the vapours when Hannah brought me a rather graphic keyring from Crete with movable parts depicting a couple Doing The Sex. Oh, the hypocrisy, Mother Dearest!).

How, *how* had I let it go so long without speaking to her? Before yesterday, I'd simply thought dark thoughts and told myself Hannah was just as much to blame, if not more so – *she* was the one who had buggered off and *she* could just as easily get in touch with me. But now I knew it was all my fault.

'Maybe I should go round there?' I suggested to Simon on his way out the door.

'If she's not answering her phone for whatever reason, it's hardly going to be convenient if you just turn up on the doorstep,' he pointed out in his most annoyingly reasonable tones.

'Well, what if Dan has the kids and she's all alone and she's fallen down the stairs or something, and she's lying there concussed and dying and no one even thought to check on her? What if her decomposing body is found in a month's time when the neighbours complain about the smell, and the children are orphaned and Hannah is DEAD and it's all my fault!' I wailed.

Simon pointed out that it was quite unlikely that this would happen, if only because Dan would try to return the children at some point and even he, useless though he was, would probably notice the lifeless body of the mother of his children at the bottom of the stairs and do something about it. And technically the children wouldn't be orphans, because they would still have their father.

I glared at him. 'You're not helping.'

'I need to go to work, Ellen. I'm sure Hannah's fine, darling, don't worry. I'll see you later. Bye, kids!' and he gave me a brief kiss and departed to his Busy and Important Office Life, where, as far I can work out, he spends at least half the morning occupied with his Morning Poos. Still, better he does these at the office than at home, in the Non-Shitting downstairs loo.

Monday 29 August

Well, the longest dark *week* of the soul was over, at least. Hannah still wasn't picking up her phone, and Simon eventually persuaded me that calling her every twenty minutes was starting to border on stalking. I'd not called her since last Monday, when I left a message apologising profusely for *everything* and begging her forgiveness. At the start of the week, every time my phone buzzed, I grabbed it, spirits soaring, hoping it was Hannah. But it never was.

I started to convince myself I was seeing Hannah everywhere – round the corner in the supermarket, across the park, in a car that didn't looks like hers at the traffic lights. I dragged the children round Sainsbury's in a mad trolley dash, only to find it was a bemused woman who actually looked nothing like Hannah when I finally caught up with her beside the gluten-free pasta. And I wept at Simon for the entire evening at the idea that Hannah might have got a new car and I didn't know.

'But you said it *wasn't* Hannah at the traffic lights?' he said in bemusement.

'Well, no, but it *could* have been, that's my point,' I wailed. 'One day she'll be driving round in a totally different car, one I don't even recognise, and I won't even know.'

'Would you really recognise her car now?' Simon asked me.

'Yes! Of course I would.'

'What sort of car does she drive then?'

'A silver one.'

'Yes, but what *sort*? Make, model?'

'A SILVER SORT!' I shouted crossly. 'Oh, how can I make you understand? It doesn't matter what fucking "make" or "model" it is, I know what it looks like! That's what matters. I know everything about Hannah's life. Or I did. We've always known everything about each other, and now she's going to have a whole new life that I don't know about, and I'm going to do things and have things happen and she won't know about them. How can't she know about Mum and Malcolm? Or Angie? And I don't want that. If I chuck in my job, I want Hannah to know –'

'You're chucking in your job?'

'Maybe. I haven't decided.'

'Were you planning to discuss it with me?'

'Yes, of course, when I've got a clearer idea of what I'm doing. I just think I could do better, you know. I only took that job because it fitted with the school hours, but the kids are getting older now and I hate it there. I've always hated it there. Maybe I could make another game or something, or find a job that's more fulfilling and creative, that stretches me. Something like that. Maybe I'll find my dream job.'

'Dream jobs don't exist, Ellen. They're a myth.'

'Fine, fine, just something that doesn't actively CRUSH MY SOUL EVERY FUCKING SECOND I'M THERE THEN! OK? I'm not going to do anything stupid, don't worry. I'm not about to jack it all in and turn into Louisa, I just want more. But right now, I just want Hannah. I just want to fix it with her. How do I do that, Simon?'

'I don't know, darling. I really don't.'

The only other person I could have turned to for advice, or at least some news of Hannah, was Sam, but he was on holiday. I even considered messaging Angie to pour out my woes, despite her poetic perfidy with Louisa, but now we were all home again, I realised Simon had been right. We really didn't know each other that well, and long, rambling texts trying to explain I was very sad because I'd fallen out with my bestie were probably not going to be appropriate.

I'd even have welcomed Fiona and Gemma as a distraction, and I found without Fiona there to boss me and point us in the direction of wholesome activities, or Hannah to make days out fun, and make me see the funny side even when everything went wrong, it was hard to find the motivation to take the kids out to make those all-important #HappyMemories.

I no longer knew what to do with myself, as I seemed to have used up the very last shreds of my initiative when luring Geoffrey into removing Mum from our house. Now that moment was past, I'd become a sloth-like creature who wanted nothing more than to lie on the sofa watching repeats of *Jeremy Kyle* to make myself feel marginally better about myself. After all, while I may have fucked up my life massively, at least I'd never taken a lie detector test on national TV to see if I'd cheated on one cousin because I was shagging another.

In desperation, I attempted to channel my inner Fiona one day and do crafts with the children, but when I got all the craft stuff out, I remembered how Hannah and I bought it all months ago in

Home Bargains with great plans, and then we brought it home and accidently got drunk on dodgy Home Bargains wine and had terrible hangovers afterwards, and I thought I was going to cry, so I said the children could do whatever craft activity they wanted and they'd had a glitter fight while I was snivelling in the loo. And then I shouted at them, because they're not The Fucking Montagues, and I'm not Fiona, and then *they* cried and I felt even worse.

It didn't help that the heatwave continued apace. A month ago, we'd all donned our shorts and flip-flops and skipped about and said how continental it was, and how nice, and God, just imagine if this weather lasted the whole summer, wouldn't that be *amazing*? But we're British, we're not accustomed to such conditions and we wilt after a few days. Now, everyone drooped about complaining it was 'too hot' and it was 'not natural'. I heard someone in the corner shop gloomily predicting it would be 'plagues of frogs or locusts next', and I'm pretty sure they weren't joking.

The news was all of burning moorlands and The Heatwave. Simon came into the kitchen this morning to find me sadly watching the latest report on Sky News about the wildfires and gesturing at it hopelessly while intoning, 'Everything's burning. It's a metaphor for my life.'

'Pull yourself together, Ellen,' he said briskly. 'You can't sit around here moping for the rest of your life. Go out and do something, you'll feel much better.'

'But what?' I demanded dramatically. 'What can be done? It's so hot. And we've done everything. Everything!'

'That's simply not true. And enjoy the weather while it lasts.'

'That's all right for you to say, with your air-conditioned office.'

'Your phone's binging by the way.'

I picked it unenthusiastically. 'Oh good. It's the Summer Fun WhatsApp Group. Gemma and Fiona are back from Sardinia, and they're summonsing me to Fiona's to plan what to do with the rest of the holidays.'

'Well, that's nice, isn't it? They want to see you. They're including you in their plans.'

'No. They only want to show off about their holiday and lord it over me.'

'Oh for FUCK'S SAKE, ELLEN.' Simon lost it with me. Simon hardly ever loses it with me. In fact, I think I can count on the fingers of one hand all the times he has *properly* lost his temper with me in all the time I've known him. We argue, yes, he gets exasperated by me, certainly, and he often complains about things I do or say and we fall out, but it's vanishingly rare that he gets truly, furiously *angry* with me. Today, however, he was.

'You've done nothing but whine and complain and bitch and FUCKING MOAN like a spoilt brat about how lonely you are. About how you've got no friends. About what are you going to do for the rest of your life without Hannah. And then, then, YOUR FUCKING FRIENDS text and ask you over, and oh no, it's still not good enough for Ellen, is it? She'd rather sit here, in her little pity party, feeling sorry for herself because she's not got her own way and is in a situation that is ENTIRELY OF YOUR OWN FUCKING MAKING, instead of getting off your arse and DOING SOMETHING ABOUT IT!'

'Why are you shouting at me?' I whined. 'Can't you see how horrible this is for me? I've lost Hannah, my mother doesn't love me – and never has, and never will – and now you're angry with me too. Why can't you just be on my side?'

'I AM on your side. Can't you see that? I am. And so are Fiona and Gemma and Angie and Sam and lots of other people. For just one minute, can't you focus on what you do have, not what you don't? Your mother is a narcissistic old witch, so what if she doesn't love you! *I* love you. Your children love you. Lots of people love you, so to hell with her. And to hell with this. You need to sort things out!'

'YOU told me to stop calling Hannah and not to go round there!'

'I MEAN your life. Move on. If Hannah doesn't want to know, what are you going to do? And even if you patch it up, it'll do you no harm to have other friends. What if Hannah dies?'

I burst into tears. 'Why would you say that?'

'Or moves to Australia? If you make it up with her, you're still allowed to have other friends, you know. It might even be better. Take the pressure off you both, things wouldn't be so intense between you. Look,' he said less angrily, 'just go round to Fiona's, OK? I think it would do you good. Do the kids good. Yeah? I'm worried about you.'

I blinked. Simon was worried about me? But *I* was the one who worried about people. No one worried about me. Had I been that awful? In a small voice I asked him this.

'No,' he said gently. 'I'm not worried because you've been awful. I'm worried because you're not yourself. You've not been yourself since Hannah went away.'

'Maybe I'm *not* who I am without Hannah,' I said sadly.

'You are,' Simon said. 'Or you *can* be. You just don't want to be.'

'No,' I agreed, 'I don't.' I didn't know who I did want to be, though, but it definitely wasn't this miserable wreck of a woman. And no one else could make me be who I wanted to be. 'I hate it when you're right,' I added crossly.

'I know. Come on, I'm late for work. Text Fiona, tell her you'll be round shortly, and go and have a shower.' He looked at my red, puffy eyes and added, 'Maybe put some make-up on too.'

'Simon!'

'I'm just trying to help. Right, I really need to go. Love you, bye.'

And with that he was gone. Despite his initial anger, he'd been trying to be kind, so I suppressed the ignoble thought that the main reason he'd dashed off was because otherwise he'd be late for his first work poo of the morning, and as he liked to tell me, 'Nothing goes right once the schedule's thrown off course.'

I did as I was told, and agreed to go to Fiona's. I bullied Jane and Peter out of their pyjamas, and into the respectable shorts and T-shirts I'd bought in the Boden sale for going on holiday – it was astonishing how when I took my eye off the ball for a few days they went completely feral – and went upstairs for a shower.

I did my best with my face. It was really too hot for much make-up, apart from a bit of waterproof mascara, as it would all just melt straight off. But I found a sample tube of something called 'Brightening Vitamin C Serum' in the back of the bathroom cabinet that promised 'Instantly refreshed and glowing skin – like 8 hours sleep in a bottle', and slapped it on hopefully. It made fuck-all difference. I still looked like a puffy, dull-skinned wreck. Oh well.

Maybe someone ought to make 'over-emotional, probably peri-menopausal, under-slept, middle-aged, in-need-of-a-haircut chic' a fashion thing, the way 'heroin chic' was all the rage in the nineties? Perhaps I should write a sternly worded letter to *Vogue*, to remind them of their demographic? But who was I kidding? I wasn't *Vogue*'s demographic. *Heat* magazine, maybe. And anyway, people got very cross nowadays about how inappropriate the whole 'heroin chic' thing was, so maybe it was better not to bring *that* up.

And what about clothes? I rifled through my wardrobe and wondered who I was going to be today. No, I corrected myself. What I was going to wear, not who I was going to be. I realised, as I took out various combinations of clothes and rejected them all, that I never dressed as myself.

I'd spent my whole life dressing up as someone else, whether I was channelling a film character, or someone from a book, or Fiona and Gemma, or just some cool girl I'd seen on Instagram. I had no 'personal style' of my own. Maybe that should be my first step in finding out who I was without Hannah. Develop My Personal Style. Ha! See? Look at me being a functioning adult.

I could go even further with it. If I knew how to use Instagram properly, I could make a video about developing My Personal Style, and then I could do 'Get Ready With Me' videos, and everyone would be so enchanted by my quirky individuality that I'd be famous and my new job would be as a fashion Instagrammer! Go, ELLEN! When I'm a famous fashion Instagrammer, I thought smugly, I'd caption moments like this '#Adulting', even though whenever I saw anyone on social media claim to be 'adulting' it made me want to smash my phone with irrational rage.

My elation faded as I realised that I still needed to find that personal style. How did you do that? How? Maybe Meryl Streep was right in *The Devil Wears Prada* when she tells Anne Hathaway that no one is quirky and individual, and that we all, in one way or another, wear what the fashion industry tells us to?

With no idea of how to get a personal style, I regrouped and decided that dressing as whatever character I was trying to be that day wasn't the worst thing to do, was it? It could be quite empowering really, and surely in one way or another almost all of us were dressing as the character the world imagined us to be. I just took it a bit further and basically played dress-up with a wardrobe full of TKMaxx bargains, in much the same way I'd done with my grandmother's ball gowns and fur coats when I was a child.

Ah ha! I thought excitedly. That was quite philosophical. Maybe I could become a philosopher, and post really wise and meaningful soundbites on Instagram, and everyone would think I was very clever, and then I could make them all into a book called … let's see … *The Little Book of Wiseness*, and it would sell eleventy fucking billion copies and I'd be mega-rich because I was so WISE! The more I thought about it, though, *The Little Book of Wiseness* was a shit title, and the only soundbites of wisdom I could think of had already been put on fridge magnets, like Louisa's 'Be yourself – everyone else is taken.'

BUT, I thought, I'd come up with two possible new careers just while getting dressed. Three, if you counted my 'middle-aged, tired, mummy chic' idea, which could have made me into a beauty guru. All right, they weren't *good* ideas, but I'd come up with them without even trying, so who knows what I could come up with if I *did* try. And technically, I wasn't dressed, I was still sitting on my bed in my bra and pants, and I needed to get a move on if Fiona wasn't going to tip her head to one side and ask me in a caring voice if everything was all right if I was ten minutes late.

I dragged a bright pink linen mini sundress out of the wardrobe and considered it. It did look very cool, in the sense that it wouldn't make me sweat too much, rather than as a fashion statement. I'd bought it in a sale years ago and had never quite possessed the nerve to wear it, it was so very pink. And I wasn't sure who I was trying to be wearing it, but it was very jolly, and God knows I needed jolly. I chucked it on, and was delighted to find that between losing half a stone because I was too sad to eat and topping up my French tan lying in the garden with a bottle of white wine because I was so miserable and it was too hot to drag the children anywhere, it really looked rather good. Maybe I *did* have a personal style. Ooooh! Maybe I could make an app helping other women discover their personal style. Sort of like Cher's wardrobe in *Clueless*. Had anyone done that yet? I could check later.

I flung the children into the car and we headed off to Fiona's. Gemma was already there, and Fiona sent the children off to the playroom to find Lucy and The Montagues, and led me through to her blissfully cool kitchen, thanks to a large and expensive-looking air-con unit in the corner (Fiona's kitchen is very nearly as nice as Gemma's but not quite, but still considerably nicer than mine), where they appeared to be drinking something peculiar, sitting at Fiona's giant kitchen island ('Carrara marble. Expensive, of course, but it will add significantly to the value of the house').

'You look nice, Ellen,' Gemma said. I tried not to look smug. 'I love that dress,' she went on. 'I wish I was brave enough to wear something like that.' Oh. Brave. Everyone knows 'brave' is a polite way of either saying, 'You look batshit' or 'Your tits are falling out that dress.'

My disappointment must have shown on my face, because Gemma quickly added, 'That sounded wrong. But I really love that outfit. Where did you get it?'

'Oh, this old thing? I've had it for years,' I said casually.

'Bone broth, Ellen?' enquired Fiona, proffering a mug of brown liquid at me.

'*What?*'

'We're just having our morning cup of bone broth,' explained Gemma.

'In this heat?'

'Oh yes, it's terribly good for you. Helps support your gut, wonderful for weight loss and it's *packed* with nutrients. Lots of collagen too, so it's marvellous for the joints and hair and skin,' Fiona informed me.

'But what is it?' I asked, sniffing at it suspiciously. It smelled quite nice, I had to admit. Sort of rich and meaty and savoury. It reminded me of something.

'Well, it's marrow bones, simmered with vegetables and herbs,' explained Fiona. 'So healthy. I have a cup every day and I feel *marvellous* for it.'

That was what it reminded me of.

'So it's basically stock?' I said, taking a tentative sip. It was quite tasty, in fairness.

'No,' said Fiona scathingly. 'It's *bone broth.*'

'But it's made exactly the same way as stock,' I protested. 'Bones, herbs, veg, all boiled down together. You could stick in a few dried peas and you'd have a nice soup, actually.'

Fiona and Gemma both gave a squeak of horror. 'Peas are so high in carbs,' Gemma protested.

'Full of sugar! Absolutely loaded with it,' Fiona sighed. 'Sometimes, for a treat, I do add some shredded kale. That's nice in the bone broth.'

'Stock,' I said to myself. They could call it 'bone broth' until they were blue in the face, but whatever wanky name they called it, it was thick stock. And actually, when you came down to it, what was a really thick stock if not gravy? Not that I was necessarily averse to drinking a mug of gravy at ten-thirty in the morning, indeed, I'd often been known to do so the day after a roast dinner, complete with dunking leftover Yorkshire puddings in it. I didn't dare suggest Yorkshire puddings to Gemma and Fiona, though – that would be a carb too far for them.

But was this my life now? Drinking posh Oxo cubes and extolling their health benefits? It was, I told myself firmly, still better than the loneliness of the previous week, although I hoped Sam never got to hear about it. At least now when Simon told me I was disgusting for drinking gravy I could lecture him about how actually I was doing it for the *nutrients* and the *collagen*, so there. Now I just had to come up with a good excuse about why eating leftover cold curry and cold pizza for breakfast also conferred many health benefits.

I pulled up a stool and sipped my bone broth.

'God knows I need to lose weight,' groaned Gemma. 'I'm as fat as a pig after the holiday.'

I stared at her. She looked exactly the same.

'How was your holiday?' I asked politely. I could hardly not ask, but I was braced for the onslaught of how it was the best holiday ever, how they simply adored it, how they were so embraced by the locals and really soaked up the atmosphere and were presented with the freedom of the village by the mayor, and how everyone cried when they left and the villa was just *divine* and Jude Law was staying next door, yes, and Sadie and the kids, they all get on so well, don't they, such a *modern* relationship, and Sadie's so sweet, actually we've kept in touch and she's coming for supper on Saturday, I'm doing Ottolenghi.

'Wonderful!' they both instantly said in unison. 'Great. Really marvellous. Fabulous.'

Neither could quite look me in the eye.

'Well, that's good,' I said, wondering what on earth had happened. Had Hugo had it off with Sadie Frost? Maybe Giles and Jude had had a bunk-up? Or was Gemma now part of an alliterative throuple? I couldn't resist poking the tiger, though, and asked blandly, 'Anything interesting happen?'

'NO!' again in perfect harmony. 'Nothing happened.'

'Nothing at all!' stressed Fiona.

Gemma sighed and put down her bone broth. 'Oh come on, Fiona. Who are we kidding? What's the point in pretending? It was awful if you must know, Ellen.'

'Really? Awful how?'

'Well, the villa for a start,' Fiona said indignantly. 'It was grim. Nothing like the photos, which were clearly taken from very careful angles. It was filthy, the pool was a mess and the stove didn't work. Nothing in the kitchen worked, actually. The gardens were a death trap, there was no hot water, and when I tried to complain about all this to the house manager, he said something about the Mafia, which I think was a threat, so we didn't dare say anything else!'

'Isn't the Mafia in Sicily, not Sardinia?' I asked, fascinated by this litany of woe that had befallen the perfect Yummy Mummies' Perfect Holiday.

'Are they?' said Gemma 'I *told* you he wasn't in the Mafia, Fiona, but you insisted we'd be murdered in our beds if we made a scene. Anyway, because nothing worked in the kitchen, we had to eat out every night, but it was bloody miles from anywhere, and the nearest restaurant gave Hugo and Giles food poisoning. We'd have

come home days ago, but we had to stick it out until they recovered because they were so afraid of shitting themselves on the
flight. Quite frankly, it was *awful*, Ellen, I'm a wreck and I must
have aged a decade, minimum!'

I stared again. Nope, still perfect. Skin as golden and unlined as
ever, and not an ounce appeared to have been gained on that
elegant gazelle-like frame.

Fiona shook her head. 'We should have known. If it's too good
to be true, then it is. There had to be a reason somewhere that
looked so idyllic on paper was available at such short notice. We'll
never make that mistake again. If we're stuck next year, we'll take
you up on the offer to evict Cousin Albertina and Great Aunt
Susan.'

Oh God, why had I told that stupid lie? And why had I made it
worse with the bloody consumptive Victorian relations or whatever I'd said was wrong with them. I was about to launch into a
full-scale explanation about how Cousin Albertina's dying wish
was that Great Aunt Susan should live out her last days in our
French holiday house. Alone. With no one else. Ever. Great Aunt
Susan was a recluse. Jilted in her youth, she now sat in her wedding
dress, mumbling over lost dreams while her wedding feast decayed
around her. For fuck's sake, Ellen. That was Miss Bloody Havisham,
they'd never believe that. Maybe Great Aunt Susan was one of
those nuns that shut themselves up and the nunnery had chucked
her out on account of the consumption, so she'd walled herself up
in our house? Or were they called anchorites?

I gave myself a stern mental shake. Why was I piling lie upon
absurd lie? If Fiona and Gemma were going to be friends beyond
the summer, as I now hoped they would, I couldn't keep pretending I had some kind of fabulous house in France that they were

forbidden from visiting because there was a mad nun barricading the door against us. They'd been honest about their terrible holiday, after all. The first thing they'd done on their return was invite me over for a nice cup of gravy, so the least I could do was come clean. What was the worst that could happen, apart from them shunning me forever more and telling all the other school mums I was a mad fantasist. That probably wouldn't even be news to some of them. Right. Let's do this.

'About that,' I said, 'er, about our place in France. I mean, it's a sort of family place, but it's really Simon's parents' house. We were just staying there while they were on holiday. I mean, *technically* we do have a house in France. But it's not very nice. And Simon's sister lives in it. And she's batshit.'

'But where do Cousin Albertina and Great Aunt Susan stay then?' asked Gemma.

'I was just … being silly?' I said hopefully. 'A sort of … joke?'

'Cholera is no joking matter, Ellen,' said Fiona sternly. Ah yes. Cholera. That was what Cousin Albertina had been so sadly afflicted by. Just as well I'd not tried to keep up the yarn, and trust Fiona to remember all the details.

'So Great Aunt Susan still has both her legs then?' asked Gemma.

'Yes,' I said. It seemed simplest.

'I got a bit carried away as well,' Gemma admitted. 'My Umbrian castle was more a big house with a turret attached. And they didn't cancel it because the Clooneys wanted it. The drains went. But it sounded so *prosaic*. And I panicked. You were going off to your house in France, and then Giles rang about dodgy drains. So I went with the double booking, it sounded less grim, and then Fiona started wittering on about the Clooneys. She was livid when

I filled her in, but because she'd already gone on about the wretched Clooneys so much, I was half expecting to meet them in Sardinia.'

'I'd almost convinced myself of a summer romance with George too,' said Fiona sadly. 'Which made the Casa della Hovella all the more disappointing. It seems we all got a bit carried away with what other people thought. How very silly of us.'

Fiona had never seemed so human as at that moment. It was a fleeting moment, though, as she immediately added, 'I don't know what I was thinking. I always tell The Montagues that it doesn't matter what other people think, because *they're* The Montagues, and that's what's important.'

I was still unable to entirely grasp exactly what it was about being The Montagues that made being The Montagues so wonderful, and why Fiona was so convinced that just by *being* The Montagues they were automatically superior to everyone else. But how lovely, I thought, to have a mother who thought you were so fabulous, so beyond reproach, so eternally *right*. Given the choice, despite the endless *Boggle*, Museum Projects and the truly terrifying quantities of quinoa, I'd have rather grown up with Fiona's no-nonsense, capable and unquestioning love and belief in her children than my own mother's dubious approach to her maternal responsibilities.

It also dawned on me that despite her unshakeable faith in The Montagues, Fiona perhaps suffered from her own insecurities and fears. Gemma too. No one's life was as perfect as Gemma's appeared on the surface, and there had to be a reason she worked so relentlessly to present this beautifully polished façade to the world. I wondered if I could ask their advice about Hannah. I knew Simon's views on it, but I didn't think Simon, or indeed any man, could ever truly understand female friendship. Fuck it, I thought. Just like I couldn't pretend forever that I had a holiday house full of anti-social nuns, I couldn't equally pretend for ever that Hannah didn't exist.

'Can I ask your advice about something?' I said. Fiona immediately looked delighted, as it was rare for anyone to actually *ask* her advice. Usually she gave her opinion of what people should be doing long before they ever got the chance to ask.

I explained about the situation with Hannah. I tried to be as honest as possible, yet I couldn't help but gloss over the worst of my failings. It's one thing admitting these things to yourself, even to your husband; it's quite another saying them out loud to other people.

'Oh!' Fiona clapped her hands in delight. 'There was a Mumsnet thread the other day about how to deal with friends who ghost you. Hang on till I find it … ooohhhh, here we are. Yes, you need to send her a text.'

'I've sent texts.'

'No, you need to send one like this, they give some examples. OK, here is one of the templates they suggest. "Dear X …" well, "Hannah", you'd put "Hannah", I suppose. "Dear Hannah, it has come to my attention that you don't appear to be performing at the optimal level I'd have hoped and expected from you when it comes to our friendship. Please consider this as a written warning that if your performance does not improve, I'll have *no choice* but to take steps to terminate our personal relationship. Yours sincerely, X." I imagine that's meant to be your name, not a kiss. I wouldn't add a kiss.'

'What?' I cried, aghast. 'Are they actually seriously suggesting someone sends that to a friend who isn't answering texts quickly enough? I can't send that to Hannah. I want to *save* our friendship, not destroy it even further. That sounds like something a really bad HR manager would send shortly before they got sacked themselves.'

'You don't think it would work then?' Fiona sounded disappointed. Had Mumsnet let her down?

'It's a bit harsh, Fi,' Gemma said gently. 'I think Ellen was hoping for some more … empathetic advice?'

'Yes,' I said gratefully. 'Really, I just want to know what you think? Simon says I should leave her alone and she'll come round in her own time. But I'm worried that if I do that, she'll think I've given up and just don't care anymore. My feeling is that I should go round and try to talk to her. What do you suggest I should do?'

'You should definitely go round,' Fiona said firmly. 'Definitely.'

'Do you think?' I said doubtfully. I'd lost some faith in Fiona's advice after the text suggestion.

'I agree,' said Gemma. 'Think about it. What have you got to lose? If she never wants to see you again, she'll still never want to see you again. And if she does want to see you, well, it's always better to talk in person than on the phone or by text. You should go. You should go now!'

Gemma looked genuinely concerned for me. It felt nice to have someone actually care about me, apart from Simon, who had to because he was my husband. And maybe not every single friend has to be a Kindred Spirit or a Best Friend, and even people you seem to have nothing in common with can still be good people to have in your life.

'I can't, I've got the kids, and I thought we were supposed to be planning our final week's activities?'

'You can leave your two here,' Fiona offered. 'I've already sorted out today's activities, and Gemma and I can plan the rest ourselves.'

'I can't ask you to do that.'

'Of course you can. We're going to make home-made water microscopes this morning and then we'll gather samples from the garden to examine with the microscopes, so we'll cover physics – teaching them about the magnifying properties of a convex lens – as well as biology – looking at the structures of leaves and flowers.'

'Wow,' I said, feeling very intimidated, in awe of Fiona's organisational skills and dedication to the ongoing education of The Montagues and any other children fortunate enough to ascend into their gilded sphere, but also touched by how much she was putting herself out to help me.

'I know,' laughed Gemma. 'Fiona's awfully good at this, isn't she? I suddenly realised Lucy and Mr Waffles had had over an hour of screen time yesterday because I'd lost track of the time unpacking while Giles was at golf and they'd been watching *Pokémon* the whole time! So this makes up for it a bit. You should have been a teacher, Fiona.'

I'd thought Fiona would bristle at the suggestion, but she suddenly looked a bit wistful. 'I'd have loved to have been one. I really wanted to teach in a primary school,' she said, 'but my mother was horrified at the idea. She said she hadn't spent all that money on St Mary's Ascot for me to slum it teaching other people's children, getting covered in snot and glue, and I'd never meet any suitable men, even though I pointed out that Princess Diana was a nursery assistant and she married Prince Charles, but Mummy said that was different. So I ended up with an accountancy degree, got a job with an investment bank and married Hugo. And here we are! Lucky Giles, though, Gemma, managing a round of golf. Hugo thought about it, but he didn't yet have quite the confidence in his tummy to be out that long.'

Good grief. It seemed once one crack in a perfect life showed up, they all did. Although, now I thought about it, it must be quite lonely for Gemma, rattling round her huge house with just Lucy and Mr Waffles, while Giles is golfing or away on yet another of his mysterious business trips, and Fiona's obsession with educational activities made much more sense in the light of her revelation that she was compensating for her thwarted ambition to be a primary school teacher.

'Go on, go!' said Fiona. 'You can tell us how you got on when you pick the kids up, but there's no rush. We're having lovely broccoli and lentil quiche for lunch, and then if we get everything else done, we might have a bit of fun and make batteries out of potatoes later on!'

I blinked. Sometimes Fiona said words, and I knew each of them individually made sense, but the sentence as a whole was just so random I couldn't quite believe that was what she'd actually said. But her heart was in the right place (naturally – as if a Montague organ would dare be so unruly as to be anywhere else).

'OK,' I said.

I felt physically sick as I walked up Hannah's path. I wanted more than anything to talk to her, but at the same time I quite hoped she wouldn't be in, so I could just run away and I wouldn't have to properly face up to anything. I couldn't see her car, but that didn't mean anything as she often was annoyingly grown up and actually used the garage for parking instead of filling it up with all the random shite you don't want in the house. Simon and I have had quite a few arguments over our differing conceptions of what garages are for.

I rang the bell and waited a while, then I saw someone coming down the hall through the glass in the door. Oh God. I really was going to be sick. Maybe Hugo had infected the bone broth with his gippy tummy and I really wasn't well. I could run away, there was still time. I could bolt down the path, hide behind the hedge and no one would ever know I was here except –

'Dan?' I said in astonishment as the door swung open.

'Ellen,' he smiled politely. 'What a surprise. You look … well.' He paused just a fraction too long before the 'well', as his eyes roamed over me in the short pink dress. I'd forgotten what a sleazy creep he was. He'd never laid a finger on me, but he was one of those men who just made you feel that if you let your guard down for a moment, he'd take it as an invitation and then call you a cock tease when you rebuffed him.

'Is Hannah in?'

'Hannah? No, sorry, she's taken the kids to the park.'

'Oh. Dan, um, what are you doing here then?'

'Me? I live here now. We're back together, Hannah and me.'

'Back together,' I repeated stupidly.

'Yes. The South Africa trip went so well, we thought, "What the hell! Let's give it another go." So here I am.'

'Wow.' I was genuinely lost for words. Of all the things I'd been expecting, this wasn't one of them.

'Uh. Do you know when Hannah will be back?'

'Nope, sorry.'

'Right. Could you tell her I popped by?'

I was so stunned by this revelation that I didn't even know how to process it, and so fell back on trite phrases like 'popped by' instead of what I should be saying, which was something along the lines of 'How bloody dare you try to smarm your way back into

Hannah's life again, you sleazy bastard wanker weasel piss FUCKER!'

'Sure. Nice to see you, Ellen. Hopefully see you again soon.'

Again, that quick flick of his eyes up and down, lingering for an extra beat on my breasts, before a blank smile that didn't reach his eyes.

'OK. Bye, Dan.'

Tuesday 30 August

The weather finally and unexpectedly broke overnight. I never thought I'd be so happy to wake up to the sound of pouring rain, but it was a blessed relief. Well, a relief to everyone except poor Judgy, who had forgotten all about the indignity of being made to go out and pee in the rain. It was most unfair, he told me. He was a proud and noble Border terrier, how dare I suggest he had to piss outside? Why couldn't he just cock his leg against the sofa? It was surely against his canine rights. It was initially a relief not to have to walk him super-early to avoid the heat, but as I dragged Jane and Peter round in the rain with me, both of them seamlessly swapping their complaints about it being Too Hot for it now being Too Wet, suddenly those 6 a.m. walks, just me and Judgy, didn't seem too bad.

Simon had been no help whatsoever about the Dan situation. I didn't tell him that Gemma and Fiona had overruled his advice and that I'd gone round to Hannah's, merely saying vaguely that I'd 'heard' they were back together. I suggested that if he had any bright ideas as to how to break them up, now might be the time to share them. But he told me I was not to interfere.

As the tipping rain and the threats of thunderstorms had somewhat put paid to Fiona's plans for a delightful scavenger hunt in the grounds of a National Trust property (no yellow Joules mac was going to withstand this monsoon; it needed full waders and sou'westers, as we discovered mid-dog walk), I suggested, in the spirit of new experiences for the holidays, etc., that we should go to a soft play instead, as astonishingly, Gemma and Fiona had both managed to avoid this particular circle of hell until now.

It took a bit of persuasion, but in the end I convinced them that it wouldn't be so bad. I convince myself of this every time as well, of course. I think it will be an opportunity to enjoy a cup of tea in peace and quiet, and have a chat, and then take tired children home and have a nice chilled afternoon with them. And every time, I step through the door and wonder what on earth possessed me, as you're hit by the noise and the heat and the faint, lingering smell of faeces that you can only hope was from a child shitting themselves and not one of the adults, although when you look around at some of the people there you really can't be sure.

Although I'd been incredulous when I discovered that neither Gemma nor Fiona had ever been to a soft play before, I was absolutely gobsmacked to discover that neither had Lucy or The Montagues.

'But what about birthday parties?' I asked, and Gemma and Fiona both shook their heads, as it seemed their children didn't get asked to parties by the sort of children whose parents held them at soft plays. Thinking back, I did recall excuses being made by them both for Jane's sixth birthday, which I think was the last one I'd been foolish enough to do at one of these places. The only thing worse than taking your own children to a soft play is taking fifteen other people's children to soft play at the same time, and paying £10.99 a head on top of the usual entry fees for the privilege of a 'bespoke party buffet' in one of the 'individually designed party pods'. This turns out to mean that for your £10.99 you get to choose between mechanically reclaimed chicken nuggets, OR processed hydrocarbons masquerading as sausage rolls, OR limp discs of misery – topped by cheese-flavoured non-dairy fats – that claimed to be pizza. Never fear, though, for these culinary delights were washed down with an unbranded 'Fruit-Flavoured' Fruit Shoot knockoff.

Oh, and you had to provide your own cake, which a member of staff would usually manage to drop on the way to the party pods, which consisted of three alcoves off the main room covered in faded dinosaur decals, with dried red smears on the crumb-strewn table that you could only hope was ketchup from the previous party and not blood. But again, you were never entirely sure. With hindsight, I could hardly blame Gemma and Fiona for avoiding such events.

Being the first wet day in months – and during the summer holidays – the soft play was full of every other family in the surrounding area, who had also tricked themselves into entertaining the same hopes-cum-delusions that I always fell for. We were the last through the door before the bored teenager on the front desk put up the sign reading:

Dear Funky Flamingoe's, Sorry but we are now full of Funky Flamingoe's. Please come back later for your Funky Flamingoe Fun(k)!!!!!!

I had so many questions about that sign, and I could see Fiona on the verge of developing an eye twitch as she read it. For once, I couldn't blame her.

The noise was deafening as we stepped inside, but Fiona still audibly gulped as we looked around, and Gemma whimpered. 'What is that *smell*?' she whispered 'How often do you think they disinfect the ball pit?'

'Oh, every night, I expect.' I lied.

'Every *night*?' gasped Gemma. 'I would have thought hourly was the very minimum needed. Lucy, Lucy, darling, try not to *touch* anything. Oh God, I think that child over there might have ringworm, Ellen! What have we *done*?'

I discreetly gave the wormy child a once over from a safe distance, and assured Gemma it was almost certainly jam, not ringworm. Meanwhile Fiona was dispensing mini bottles of hand sanitiser and Dettol wipes to The Montagues, instructing them to disinfect the play equipment as they went round.

Fiona sighed heavily as the children vanished into the melee, and said, 'I suppose we must look on it as a teachable moment for them. An important cultural experience, if you will. And perhaps we could take swabs from them before we decontaminate them when they get home, then see what we can discover under the microscope!'

'I don't think I want to know ...' shuddered Gemma. 'All I can think looking around is impetigo and slapped cheek syndrome.'

'No, I think one of the other kids *has* just slapped that child,' I reassured her. 'And think of what all this will do for their immunity!'

'I buy very expensive vitamins from Sweden for that!' retorted Gemma.

'Why Sweden?' I couldn't help but ask.

'Well, the Scandinavians are so healthy, aren't they?' she said vaguely, before giving a little scream as Lucy hurtled down an enormous slide headfirst, before running over pink-cheeked and breathless to shout, 'This is BRILLIANT fun' and disappearing again.

There was a small scene at the tea counter when it turned out that there was no oat milk or soy milk, and 'NOT EVEN', as Fiona said in despairing but nonetheless ringing tones, any almond milk. It was probably just as well, as the tea was served in the sort of polystyrene cup that made BPAs look like a safe natural alternative, and she had to be dragged away before she could finish her lecture on single-use plastics to the tired-looking girl behind the counter as I hissed in Fiona's ear, 'I think if you get paid the minimum wage, we can assume you're not personally making the polar-bear-killing decisions!'

Another dicey moment arose when Miles and Cosmo came running over with two little tykes in Baby Burberry shell suits.

'We met some other twins!' they cried in delight.

'How nice,' said Fiona faintly.

'This is Dolce,' said Miles.

'And this is Gabbana,' added Cosmo.

'Ottilie is playing with their big sister Gucci-Dior, and guess what, their big brother has the same name as Daddy!' Miles told Fiona in delight.

'Their brother is called *Hugo*?' Fiona said in astonishment, and you could see her visibly thawing towards to the twins.

'Yeah,' said Dolce. 'Yugo Boss, innit.'

'Oh,' said Fiona, hope quickly ebbing away.

'Can they come back to play?' asked Cosmo.

'Ummmmm, I think we're busy, darlings. We've got that … thing,' Fiona hedged wildly.

'But Mummy, we've told them all about your famous quinoa and courgette cupcakes and told them they can play *Boggle*,' wailed Miles.

'Do you 'ave a PlayStation?' enquired Gabbana casually.

'No, Mummy says they rot your brain,' Miles explained.

'Big telly, then?' Dolce suggested.

'Mummy says big televisions are common,' Cosmo said helpfully. 'She says saying "telly" is common too. You should say "television", Dolce, or if you're trying to be funny like Nigella, you can say "telayvizeeohnay".'

Dolce and Gabbana stared at him blankly.

'You know, like Nigella and the "meeecrowahvey",' Miles tried.

'Doesn't your mummy watch Nigella?' Cosmo asked sorrowfully. 'Our mummy loves Nigella.'

'No. Our mum watches *EastEnders*.'

Fiona gave a small cry of horror, though Gemma remained silent. I suspected she was more of a fan of the antics down Bridge St Market than she'd ever let on to Fiona.

'What do you play this *Boggle* on then?' Dolce wanted to know. 'Is it only for Xbox or something?'

'You … just play it,' Miles said.

'Like *Scrabble*?' Cosmo offered.

Dolce and Gabbana shook their heads. 'What's the *point*?' they wanted to know. Peter arrived at that moment and agreed firmly with Dolce and Gabbana that the best games were played on consoles, not round a table as a merrily laughing family.

'Are you allowed to play *GTA*?' he asked the twins longingly.

'Yeah. We play it every night!' Dolce and Gabbana said firmly. Unfortunately for them, their big sister Gucci-Dior arrived at that moment with Ottilie and blew the boys' street cred by scathingly telling everyone that they most certainly were *not* allowed to play *GTA*, and that the closest they got to *GTA* was *Mario Kart*. Dolce and Gabbana slunk away muttering at that point, as Fiona took a proper look at Ottilie, who appeared to be sporting bright blue glitter on her eyelids, lurid pink gloop smeared over her rosebud lips and was reeking of synthetic strawberries.

'What *happened*?' wailed Fiona.

'Gucci-Dior did a makeover on me!' said Ottilie. 'Do I look pretty, Mummy?'

'Very pretty,' I said quickly, as Gemma applied industrial-strength Rescue Remedy to a fainting Fiona.

Eventually, once Fiona had recovered, and had hissed to The Montagues *not* to reveal their address to any of the other children, lest this hell on earth be a ploy to case out suitable middle-class houses to rob, and I'd assured them that I'd never heard of any soft plays being shut down because of an infectious disease breakout, Gemma asked if I'd heard anything from Hannah yet.

'No,' I said sadly. 'I don't even know if Dan will tell her I came round. I was thinking of texting to wish her congratulations about getting back together, but I was worried that it might just sound sarky in a text. But I do hope he has told her and that she's thinking about getting in touch.'

'She'll come round,' Gemma insisted. 'I know it. How can she not?'

'Or we could all go round?' mused Fiona. 'Like an intervention?'

'Ooooh, we could get Sam to come too when he's back from holiday,' Gemma said hopefully.

'Good idea!' Fiona beamed.

'Noooo!' I put a stop to their dramatic fantasies of us rocking up mob-handed at Hannah's house. Gemma already had her phone in her hand and by craning my neck I could see she was googling 'sexy but classy outfit for intervention', and I suspected Fiona was at this very moment composing an impassioned speech in her head.

They both looked as deflated as Dolce and Gabbana had when they'd been so cruelly denuded of their *GTA* street cred.

'This is Hannah's actual life,' I reminded them, 'not a new interactive Netflix drama.'

'We know, we know,' said Fiona huffily.

'We're just trying to help,' said Gemma, 'but Fiona just gets carried away sometimes.'

'*I* get carried away?' Fiona was indignant at this utterly unfounded and baseless accusation. 'What about you? What about the time you bought an alpaca for the garden because Lucy had expressed a passing liking for them at the zoo?'

'That was simply a misunderstanding. I thought I was just adopting one, like you do with a snow leopard, and then the man turned up on the doorstep with it. Giles was *furious*.'

'Imagine how much more furious he'd have been if she'd taken a notion for a snow leopard!' Fiona snorted.

Gemma bristled, and I feared a falling-out, but just in time we were alerted through piercing shrieks – just before a Tannoy announcement summonsed us – that The Montagues were in peril. As we squinted up far above at the play equipment right up in the rafters of the converted church the soft play was situated in, we could see three terrified little figures stuck in the foam rollers, which had somehow malfunctioned and trapped The Montagues. Lucy, who had cheerfully abandoned her friends to their fate in favour of scooting down the big slide, told us that she thought Dolce and Gabbana may have had something to do with the malfunction, as she'd seen Dolce luring The Montagues in and

Gabbana fiddling with the foam rollers, which were supposed to spin in and out so the children could wriggle through the gap à la Indiana Jones, but were now jammed closed.

'I must go up and rescue my babies!' wailed Fiona.

'No adults on the play equipment,' intoned a bored and spotty youth, who was clearly reconsidering his life choices.

'But how will they get down?' Fiona whimpered. 'Shall I call the fire brigade?'

'Only trained staff can access the equipment,' the youth informed her.

'Well, access it then!' Fiona was near hysterical now.

'Can't.' The Youth didn't even look up from his phone. 'Not trained. Only Allan's trained.'

'Well, where is Allan?' Fiona demanded.

'On a break.'

'Get him back.'

'Can't. Union. Entitled to a break, innit?'

'Somebody must be able to do something.' Fiona was well beyond the aid of Rescue Remedy now.

'Yeah. Allan. But he's –'

'On a break, we know,' I chimed in helpfully, because Fiona was now dangerously close to tearing her hair out. It was like Ross and Rachel all over again, I thought.

Lucy, ever the source of helpful knowledge, then informed us that The Montagues could be rescued from the foam-roller trap by the simple expedient of going back down the way they'd come up.

'But they're too scared to try to climb down the ladders,' Lucy said with relish. 'So they're stuck!'

'What if they fall?' Fiona moaned. 'What if there's a terrible accident while they wait for "Allan" to finish his break? What will

I tell the coroner? How will I explain how my children came to be in such a place? How will I tell Hugo his children died at the hands of creatures called Dolce and Gabbana?'

'Come on, Fiona,' I said soothingly. 'It's really not that bad. Kids get stuck at soft play all the time!'

'Not The Montagues!' Fiona cried dramatically.

'Look!' Gemma pointed. 'Something's happening.'

'Is it Allan?' Fiona quavered.

'No,' Gemma squinted. 'It's Jane and Peter. They've gone up too.'

'Oh, for Christ's sake.' I was really quite cross. 'What on earth are they doing? They're so nosy! They're just going to get even more in the way.'

'No, look, Ellen. I think … I think they're helping.' Gemma pointed again.

'Oh yeah,' Lucy shrugged nonchalantly. 'Jane said they were going to go up and show them how to get down.'

'Didn't you want to go and help?' Gemma asked her.

'Nah,' Lucy shrugged again. 'Ottilie's a pain in the arse, she can stay stuck.'

'LUCY!' Gemma yelled after Lucy's departing back as she raced off to go down the big slide again. Fortunately Fiona had been too engrossed in the drama unfolding above our heads to hear Perfect Lucy Atkinson's less-than-perfect comments about one of The Montagues.

'Oh …' Fiona breathed. 'Oh my God. I think, I think it might be all right. Provided they don't fall. Jane and Peter, look at them!'

Sure enough, Jane and Peter were carefully guiding The Montagues back down the ladder to the next level, then helping them scramble down the climbing wall to the level below. After that it was just a matter of scooting down the big slide after Lucy, and The Montagues were restored to the arms of their doting mama, who was now openly weeping over them.

'Oh my babies,' she sobbed. 'My darlings, I thought you were dead. The coroner's report … oh the shame. My precious ones, Mummy shall never let you encounter such danger again, don't worry.'

'Muuuuuuummmmy! Stop it! Everyone's looking.' The Montagues wriggled free of Fiona's smothering embrace.

'It was fun,' Ottilie said.

'Well, it was a *bit* scary at first,' Cosmo admitted.

'But once Peter and Jane came to help us and show us what to do, it was fun,' Miles insisted. 'We want to do it again.' And The Montagues ran off back into the throng.

Fiona turned to me, tears in her eyes. 'How can I ever thank Jane and Peter for saving my little ones?' she cried. 'How did they know what to do? I could see The Montagues panicking before they got there, but they stayed so calm. How did you teach them that? I see now I must incorporate controlled danger into The Montagues' education, but how do you start? What course did you do to teach Peter and Jane how to think independently and cope with danger?'

'Um. I just sort of allow them to get on with it,' I said. 'I don't think there's a course, Fiona. You just have to let them find their own way sometimes?'

Maybe, I thought, like I'd discovered there was a middle ground in friendship, maybe there was the same middle ground in parenting, somewhere between Mum's cold detachment and Fiona's smothering idealisation. Maybe I didn't need to compare myself to other people all the time and find myself lacking. Sometimes, perhaps, I could compare and find the positives. Or, even better, channel my inner Montague and just not compare myself at all!

Fiona was clearly still struggling to process the notion of 'letting The Montagues find their own way', unguided by her loving maternal hand, when a siren went off, and she whirled round, shrieking, 'Fire! FIRE! EVACUATE!' before I could reassure her it was just signalling that the session time was up, and all the little darlings with red wristbands on, including our own, now had to go home, which was probably just as well, as I feared Dolce and Gabbana may have been laying more booby traps for the unsuspecting Montagues.

We joined the scrum making for the door with some relief. Everyone else seemed to feel the same way, and the jostling to finally escape was akin to trying to board a lifeboat on the *Titanic*. Unfortunately shouting 'Women and children first' would have done no good, as it was all women and children, apart from one solitary, frightened-looking man caught up in the stampede.

I became separated from Fiona and Gemma as the slow process of exiting continued (for safeguarding purposes, you and your children had your hands stamped with matching numbers, and the staff had to check you were only leaving with children sharing your number, so it took forever, despite the fact that the 'checks' were more of a cursory glance, and I doubt they even registered what they were looking at. They just wanted us all to fuck off). And then, as I saw Fiona ahead of me – holding up the line, explaining that it was The Montagues' first time at Funky Flamingoes, and she didn't know what had happened to Miles's number, he'd definitely been stamped and he was *definitely* hers,

could they not tell A MONTAGUE when they saw one? – I noticed
a familiar figure to my left, on the other side of the counter, in the
queue to get into the Funky Flamingoes Hell.

I'd thought I'd seen Hannah so many times now that I couldn't
quite believe it was her. She looked shattered under her Cape
Town tan. Jane and Peter had somehow got up ahead with Fiona,
who was still arguing for possession of Miles while trying not to
gag when he admitted he'd 'licked off' his number. I waved furiously, and shouted 'Hannah, HANNAH!' over the general roar of
whining, fractious children and irritable adults. She turned her
head with a slight frown, as though she wasn't totally sure she'd
heard her name, and looked around her slightly mystified. I waved
and shouted again, and she looked right at me.

'Hannah!'

'Ellen!'

Unfortunately, at that moment the bottleneck of the queue in
both directions suddenly surged forward, just as Fiona had finally
been granted Miles – the soft play staff clearly deciding that they
might as well give him to her as no one else was attempting to
claim him, and so they'd be stuck with him – and the woman with
six children on the way in had finally got all of them stamped, and
now the crowd was carrying Hannah and me in opposite directions. For a brief moment I considered whirling round and chasing
after her, but Jane and Peter were still ahead of me, and the sign
about Funky Flamingoes' Fullness had been slammed back on the
counter already.

The last thing I saw was Hannah turning round and mouthing
something me at as I was pushed out of the door, like we were star-
crossed lovers in a maritime disaster movie. I wanted to yell, 'I'd let
you share my floating door, Hannah, I wouldn't leave you in the

sea to freeze' after her, but I didn't think she'd hear me. Also, people might stare at me and think me a little odd.

Fiona's only comment about the soft play when I caught up with them in the car park, as she forced The Montagues to sit on her bags for life in the car (bags that she was clearly planning on burning just as soon as she'd fumigated the children), was that it had been quite an educational day all round.

Wednesday 31 August

The day of the wretched Return to Work interview dawned. Gemma and Fiona had once again kindly offered to look after Peter and Jane for me, seemingly entranced by the novelty of my having to go to an office. They would be going strawberry picking, they informed me, as a wholesome counterpoint to yesterday's germ, plastic and man-made-fibres death trap. I think the plan was that fresh air and fruit would hopefully cancel out anything nasty the children might have caught at soft play, like Commonness. Fiona brightly suggested I met them at the strawberry farm after my interview.

I was hoping to get the whole Return to Work thing wrapped up sharpish, as really what was there to say?

'Are you looking forward to coming back?'

'No, but I can't afford not to.'

'Have you found your time off to be beneficial to your mental health and well-being?'

'No, because my children are arseholes.'

'So, back to business as usual then?'

'Yes, I can't wait to spend each day staring at a grubby magnolia wall while I'm stuck behind a computer that's always just slightly too old to be fit for purpose, and wondering if that smell really is old jizz, and also pondering what happened to my youthful hope and optimism. Then there are the bright points of every day – well, I say bright points, but I mean less-bleak moments – such as going to make a cup of tea in the kitchen where some hilarious person keeps putting up a printed-out sheet of A4 saying "You don't have to be mad to work here but it helps." It's not even a poster, they're too cheap to buy a poster, which I suppose is fair enough because I'd probably take it down, the way I do with the A4 print-outs. And I'm never entirely convinced that Nigel from Accounts hasn't wanked off into the milk, because the fridge smells a bit like my cubicle, but maybe you'd know more than me about that, Sally – do you remember the time you got off with him at the Christmas party? But anyway, I know, we don't discuss that – so I'll try not think about Nige interfering with himself and instead focus on the fact that every day, hour, minute and second I spend in this benighted place is another slow tick of the second hand on the clock towards DEATH!'

I thought maybe I might need to tweak some of my prospective answers for Sally just a tiny bit.

Sally was actually a very nice woman, if a bit of a liability at Christmas parties, but in fairness, she'd once saved me from making a mistake even more dire than shagging Wanking Nige at an office do when I'd had my head turned by a man called James in Marketing, so I couldn't really hold that against her. She gave me a cup of tea, and filled me in on the office gossip – Nigel had been sacked after being caught doing something unspeakable in his cubicle to a Müller Rice Pudding. Julie Evans had been complaining for weeks that someone was stealing her Müller Rices from her packed lunches when she left them in the fridge, and to everyone's relief, her puddings (not a euphemism) remained safely unmolested in the wake of Nigel's departure.

'He … he didn't put them back, did he?' I asked in horror. 'Julie hadn't been *eating* them?'

'No,' said Sally, and I heaved a sigh of relief. 'I suppose we must be thankful for small mercies. Now, I suppose we should get down to business. How are you feeling about coming back?'

Sally ran through a number of boring, generic corporate questions, and I managed not to reference how every millisecond in Cunningham United Nautical Trust made me contemplate my own mortality and impending death, and then Sally smiled, and said, 'Well, I think that's about it then! We're looking forward to seeing you back, Ellen. But I did want to have a little chat with you off the record. That's really why I asked you to come in today. The rest of this could probably have been done by email, as you're always pointing out.'

Yes! *Someone* had finally taken notice of my impassioned emails about how not every single thing required a lengthy meeting or discussion, and that nine issues out of ten could be solved with a brief email asking 'Should we do X or Y?' Listened, but not put into action – because here I was, still at a meeting – but in ten years' time, perhaps, everything would finally be resolved by email.

I could never understand why people were so keen on in-person meetings and still insisted that a dozen people must be summonsed to a soulless beige room to listen to a middle manager called Brian hold forth for twenty minutes on acceptable levels of paperclip usage.

'The thing is' – bugger, Sally was still talking – 'this is a little delicate, Ellen, and must be strictly between us for now. It's not entirely professional of me to be telling you about it.'

Oh Jesus. Sally got drunk again and did something obscene with Nigel and a strawberry fruit corner in the photocopying room, didn't she, and now she needs me to find and delete the incriminating CCTV. No wonder she said this part of the meeting couldn't have been done by email. My eyes! Maybe I could just delete *all* the CCTV without looking at it? But what if there were other incidents they needed the footage for? I might not like my job, but was I willing to put it on the line for Sally and some dairy-based debauchery? And why was she asking *me*? Was she going to appeal to me for help, woman to woman, because I was the only female in the IT department? Would she sack me anyway if I refused to help? Was that legal? Would I have to go to a tribunal and demand extra damages because the yoghurt aisle in Sainsbury's now gave me PTSD flashbacks?

'You might have heard the rumours,' Sally went on. I fought the desire to stick my fingers in my ears and shriek 'LALALALALA.' I didn't want to hear the rumours. 'About the merger that has been on the cards, with the Taylor Western Associated Trust?'

I relaxed slightly and gave a cautious 'Yeeeessss?'

'Well, strictly *entre nous*, it's going ahead. And, well, obviously there's going to be significant restructuring over the next year or so. You didn't hear this from me, but they're going to be asking for voluntary redundancies, and I've seen the sort of package they're offering – and it's good. More than good. Very generous, in fact. And I just wanted to give you a heads-up, something to think about, before it's officially announced. I know it will be a big decision for you.'

'You want me to go?' I stammered. I'd thought Sally was one of the good ones. I didn't really have any friends at work, but she was as close to a work friend as I had. And now she was basically telling me to get to fuck. Never mind one door closes and another one opens. These last months felt more like one door closes and another slams my fingers in it.

'No,' Sally insisted. 'Quite the opposite. I'll miss you very much. You've always been really nice to me. And you're one of the best people in the IT team. God, Colin can barely even turn a computer on! But, I've felt for a long time that you're really not happy here. That you've been here for so long you've got a bit stuck in a rut. And then we got news of the redundancies, and well, really, I'm telling you this against all the rules – *I* could probably be sacked, I think it's something like insider trading – but I thought if you're thinking of leaving anyway, which I sort of got the sense was part of the reason for the sabbatical, then you might as well hang on for a bit and leave with a decent severance package. And this might be the extra push you need to go and find what it is you do want to do. But seriously, please don't tell anyone.'

'No, no, I promise.'

'It's just something to think about, that's all. Because I really think you're so wasted here, and you could do so much more with your life.'

'Thanks, Sally,' I said, still slightly dazed. It was lovely to hear that someone believed in me. That someone thought I could do more, do better. Simon told me this sometimes, but I'd always dismissed it as the sort of thing husbands have to say to cheer their wives up. But *leaving*? I'd thought about leaving pretty much ever since I started here, so much so that now it was a possibility, I realised that all my talk of leaving and Potential New Careers was really nothing more than a habit.

Now, however, it was a possibility. More than a possibility. And that thinking I could do so much more than this wasn't just hubris on my part, but something other people thought too. But what could I actually do? What would I do if I didn't work at Cunningham? How would I know where the toilets were in a new office? I'd been here so long that I couldn't even remember how I'd found the toilets on my first day.

I decided I was perhaps getting a little ahead of myself. All these things, as Scarlett O'Hara would no doubt say, could be thought about tomorrow. There were so many things to think about, though. And I needed someone to talk to about them. For a fleeting moment, I considered Sally, but then realised that Sally had already stuck her neck out enough for me. She really couldn't discuss things like this any further with me, despite something telling me she'd quite understand my worries about where the toilets were. Sally was still looking at me, though, waiting for me to say something more.

'I appreciate it. You're a mate,' I added, as 'thanks' didn't seem quite enough.

Sally beamed. I recalled the office gossip was that she didn't really have much of a life outside work.

'You'll keep in touch, even if you do leave?' she asked hopefully. 'Maybe we could go for drinks or something sometime?'

'Yes,' I said, and I really meant it. 'Yes, I'd like that.'

Sally's 'little chat' had taken rather longer than I'd anticipated, and by the time I got to the imaginatively named 'Strawberry Fields Pick Your Own Strawberry Farm', the strawberry picking was finished, and everyone was heading back to the car park. Jane and Peter were looking rather green under a liberal, sticky layer of strawberries, and even Lucy was lightly smeared with pink.

Only The Montagues were as spanking clean as when they'd set out that morning. Fiona explained that of course The Montagues had not eaten any strawberries while they picked – what a thought, the strawberries were *unwashed*! Gemma was looking rather anxious about Lucy's blatant disregard of her instructions not to eat the filthy strawberries, and now seemed convinced Lucy would meet Cousin Albertina's choleraic fate.

I was thanking them profusely for looking after my cherubs, and trying to give them a contribution towards the strawberries, when Peter bellowed, 'Mum! I need the toilet! I really need the toilet!'

'Oh God,' I said. 'Can't you just wee behind the car?'

'Don't need a wee.'

'Of course not. That would be too easy. Well, can't you hold it in till you get home?'

'Nooooo.' Peter was groaning now and clutching his stomach. He'd eaten, I suspected, a *lot* of strawberries.

'Ooooooh,' Gemma wailed. 'Is this how it begins? Lucy, darling, how is your tummy? Let me feel your temperature? Fiona, do you have a thermometer in your first aid kit? Do you think Lucy looks flushed and feverish?'

'I think she's just covered in strawberries,' Fiona said reassuringly, before adding, 'Though I do wonder what they used as fertiliser.'

Gemma gave another wail and Peter was still clamouring for the lavatory.

'I'll take Jane back to the cars, if you want to pop to the loo with Peter?' Fiona offered, as Gemma googled homeopathic cholera and typhoid remedies.

'Thanks! Come on then!' and I scuttled off with a still-groaning Peter, back towards the long double line of Portaloos outside the Strawberry Fields Café, hoping desperately that there wasn't a queue.

I stood staring hopelessly at the Portaloos, trying to assess from the outside which was likely to be the least fetid, not that it really mattered as its condition would probably be a great deal worse once it had been visited by a strawberried-out Peter. But given that his attitude to handwashing was even more lax than my own, I thought it was my maternal duty to reduce any further risk of cholera as much as possible. After all, *what* would I say to the coroner? I'd just decided that the loo at the far end was probably the best bet as fewer people would bother to walk that far, when Peter, who had been hopping from foot to foot as I surveyed his doom, gave a joyful shriek and dashed over to a group just exiting the café.

'Lucas!' he howled in delight, and I realised it was Hannah, with Emily and Lucas, and Dan bringing up the rear with a face like thunder.

Lucas and Peter were showing each other the contents of their pockets and whispering conspiratorially by the time I reached them.

'Hannah!' I said awkwardly. 'Fancy seeing you here!'

'Um, yeah. We thought it would be a nice day out. Wholesome.'

'We've had a wonderful day, actually,' put in Dan, lest we forgot he was there. 'So important for fathers to bond with their children, isn't it? Has Simon done much with the kids these holidays?'

'Oh, you know. This and that,' I smiled through gritted teeth. Dan knew perfectly well how Simon felt about wholesome days out with his children in the summer holiday, his typical reaction being to physically recoil and whimper. 'But it will be *hot* and there will be *people*,' he'd say every time I suggested a fun family activity at the weekend. 'I'd love to, but it will be MUCH too busy at the weekend, it would really make more sense for you to take them during the week when it's quiet instead, and also I've that Thing I need to do in my shed, you know, that Important Shed Thing that must be done.'

I gave Dan my best 'everything is wonderful, nothing to see here' smile and turned back to Hannah.

'Did you have fun? I heard this place is quite expensive?'

Hannah started to reply but Dan butted in first.

'You can't put a price on memories,' he said smugly. 'I really regret the time I missed with the kids while Hannah and I were apart. We're thinking about me becoming a stay-at-home dad so I can make up for all that lost time and really support Hannah in her new job.'

He slung his arm possessively round Hannah's shoulders and beamed at me again. My jaw dropped, as Hannah nodded vaguely. How had Dan managed this? His feet under Hannah's table, and now deciding to be a stay-at-home dad, so she was supporting him financially too! Why did Lucas and Emily even need a stay-at-home dad now they were at school full time? And Emily would be going to high school in a couple of years. Where was this grand plan when Hannah was drowning in toddlers and nappies and juggling a job, and Dan was blithely swanning off to the gym at every opportunity, the lazy fucker?

Luckily Emily intervened before I said anything I regretted, asking where Jane was.

'Um, we came with some other people. She's gone back to the car park with them. We just came back because Peter needs the loo.'

I didn't want Hannah to feel like Gemma and Fiona had just slotted in as her replacements.

Unfortunately, mentioning the loo reminded Peter why we were here, as his stomach gave an ominous gurgle. Fortunately, although he had inherited his father's profligacy in pooping, he was rather less precious about it, and he yelped, 'Mum, I need to go NOW, come on, but can Lucas come for a sleepover, please Mum, please?'

'Please, Mum, please, Ellen!' Lucas put in, as Peter dragged me away.

'Hang on, I need to talk to Hannah about it. Peter, wait! Hannah, two minutes, just let me take him to the loo, and I'll be back.'

But by the time I emerged from the end of the long line of Portaloos with an embarrassingly satisfied-looking Peter in tow, Hannah and Dan had vanished. And all I could think of was all the things I could have said – should have said. Like, I love you. I miss you. I'm not myself without you. I need you. Please be my friend again. And most of all – I'm sorry.

Thursday 1 September

There comes a point in the summer holidays when time seems to grind almost to a standstill. People sometimes describe things trickling along slowly as 'moving like treacle', but as part of my attempts earlier in the holidays to entertain the children one day without going out and spending eleventy fucking billion pounds, I'd attempted to bake a delicious ginger cake with them, and Jane upset the tin of treacle on the end of the counter, and I discovered – counter to the simile – that treacle pours out a tin faster than you might think when you're frantically trying to contain it and stop both a small hairy dog and a small sticky boy from covering themselves in it.

Sadly, time warps and stretches and changes again at the end of the holidays. One day you wake up, and those slow, endless weeks suddenly transform into a moment of 'OH FUCK!' because you realise that somehow, all those boundless months of time have vanished and now school is going back, and you've done nothing at all about school shoes, or uniform, or new lunchboxes to replace the receptacles full of rotting cheese sandwiches that you've just realised must still be festering in your cherubs' school bags, as you haven't seen them since July, and so you'll need to get new schoolbags too, because the safest thing from a biohazard point of view is probably just to incinerate the whole thing without investigating the potentially sentient new life forms now growing in there. Unfortunately, that day was today.

I spent a grim afternoon at the shops with the children. There were lengthy and soul-crushing rows over Jane's pernicketiness regarding the exact style of uniform she will and won't wear, and futile attempts to bridge the chasm between what I consider suitable shoes for school and what she does. And at the other end of the spectrum, there were equally hideous arguments with Peter, as he's so unconcerned about what he wears that it takes a huge fight to get him to try anything on to make sure it fits. I finally staggered home laden with full shopping bags and an empty bank account.

Looking at all the bags, though, filled with the sparkling-clean new uniforms and the shiny new shoes, all ready for another new and exciting adventure in my children's lives, really brought it home to me that the Best Summer Ever is nearly over, and so far it has been the Worst Summer Ever. All my plans came to nothing, all my resolve to be the best mummy in the world, creating the happiest of memories, crumbled to dust. Any japes and frolics my darlings have enjoyed were largely the result of Fiona's organisation or Angie's daughter Imo. And now they were going back to school and I was going back to work, and I'd missed my chance.

Just as bad, seeing Hannah made me realise all over again how much I missed her. It was almost like a physical pain, and like a child picking a scab I had a strange desire to poke at the pain, make it sharper, more acute, so that when it faded back to its usual dull throbbing ache, it wouldn't seem so bad. I went back up to the attic, and got down my old teenage diaries. Every single entry started with 'Me and Hannah', or very occasionally I'd remember the grammar my poor English teachers tried so hard to instil in me and would start a page 'Hannah and I'.

We did everything together then. After Chris Bennett, every boy we kissed could only be considered if he had a sidekick for the other. Everywhere we went, every dance, every visit to the pictures, every shopping trip, it was always me and Hannah.

And then I found the entry that made me saddest of all:

3rd October 1995. Me and Hannah are in Edinburgh! Edinburgh! Just me and Hannah! Well, not just us, obviously. There's about a million other freshers too. But it's just us, with no parents, or brothers and sisters, no popular people (there probably are, but we won't be trapped in a fishbowl with them like at school, they can just go off and do their popular thing themselves somewhere else). We're finally going to be grown-ups, but we'll always be best friends, for ever. We've promised after all. We're going on a pub crawl tonight, which is super exciting, and also scary, because we don't know where anything is, and we don't know anybody else, but it doesn't really matter because we've got each other.

We did have each other. And the pub crawl had turned out to be very scary, because it was led by two insane and very drunk final-year girls, who declared themselves appalled that none of the freshers on the pub crawl knew the words to Kevin 'Bloody' Wilson's song 'Do You Fuck on First Dates?', which they declared was a *must* for freshers to know, and then announced we were all very boring and simply abandoned us all to our fate in Whistle Binkies pub. Of course, we didn't know that was where we were at the time, because it was our first night in Edinburgh, but together we got back to our halls of residence. We never did see the mad drunk girls again either. But we were together. That was all that had mattered. I wondered if we'd ever be together again?

I didn't know what else to do, so I found the other diary, where we swore off boys and planned our economically disastrous farm, and I took a photo of the plan of the farm and sent it to Hannah, just saying, 'Good luck with the new job next week. I know you'll smash it, which is just as well, as I don't think we totally thought through our plan B. Still like the idea of a farmhouse full of dogs though xxxx.'

I desperately hoped that she'd remember, and understand what I meant. Assuming, of course, that she hadn't blocked my number and taken out a restraining order on me, given that I seemed to keep turning up in the same places she was. I'd explained to Simon that it was coincidence, nothing more. At this stage in the holidays, we were all running out of things to do, so it was hardly unusual for everyone to be going to the same places. He'd merely said it would look more coincidental if I hadn't rung Hannah multiple times in a twenty-four-hour period the previous week LIKE A MAD STALKER. I found this unhelpful.

My phone pinged with a text a couple of minutes after I'd sent Hannah the farm photos and I grabbed it in excitement. But it wasn't Hannah, it was Angie. I nearly didn't even bother to open it, thinking it would probably be details of her bloody trip to Louisa's or more waxing lyrical about how great Louisa was. But curiosity got the better of me. If nothing else, I could make a note of when she was going to be poetryised, and feel smug about the fact she'd probably get bed bugs and have to eat Louisa's grim lentil and parsnip-based meals of slop.

Angie: Hi Ellen. I've needed get in touch for a while. I've been doing a lot of thinking since I got back from holiday, and I owe you an apology. You were so kind to us all the time we were in France, and I was very rude on our last night, abandoning you for Amaris. It's no excuse, and I'm not trying to pretend it is, but I hate my job. My children are growing up, and I've been really starting to wonder who I am, what I'm doing with my life. Amaris's life, running away to France, getting back to a 'simple' life, writing poetry, suddenly seemed terribly appealing, especially in the sunshine, after a few glasses of wine. I got this crazy idea that I could do all that. That poetry was the answer. Now we're home, and reality has bitten, I realise that all that was just some sort of holiday fantasy, and not the answer to my problems. Also, I've written some poetry since I got home, and I'm really bad at it. But I got so caught up in the idea, and I didn't realise till I got home that I might have hurt you by going off the way I did, by only saying I'd see you if I came to Amaris's. And I feel terrible. I know we haven't known each other very long, but I so enjoyed the time we spent together, and felt we could had been really good friends if we'd had longer together. I'm sorry I wasn't honest with you then, and told you how I was feeling – it's hard sometimes when you try to look like you've got your life together to admit it's not – especially to someone who seems like they really do have it together. I hope we can still be friends, though I don't think we can go back to that house, because how will I explain to Amaris why I never went to the poetry workshop? But even if it's just some kind of modern techy version of pen pals, I'd like that. Love Angie xxx

I was astonished. For a start, did *anyone* actually have it together? I knew I didn't, of course, and now it turned out that Fiona and Gemma's lives weren't as perfect as they made out, and even Angie, with her lovely children, and her proper grown-up job and nice husband, was lost and not really sure who she was.

I could see how, to an outsider who only saw a brief glimpse of it, Louisa's life *might* seem very appealing, drifting about in the

French sunshine, writing poetry, drinking wine, unconstrained by timetables or term dates or annual leave allowances or anyone's agenda but her own.

If you really knew Louisa, though, it was obvious her life was very far from perfect. Financially, she was dependent on her father, and to some extent on Simon and me, for handouts. Her children were demanding, and I suspected all the poetry workshops and the clearly illegal 'commune' in the garden (both of which would probably vanish on her, come the winter) stemmed from her being quite lonely and desperate for adult company. I also suspected her utter refusal to acknowledge the part Simon and I'd played in providing her with a home stemmed from an underlying resentment that she was supposed to be grateful for everything her family had given her. It must be very wearing to be constantly expected to be brimming with gratitude, and I knew enough of Sylvia's attitudes to be aware that she probably insisted on reminding Louisa at every possible opportunity about how much they'd done for her.

Louisa was a master of spin, however, even better than Gemma and Fiona, and could be very convincing about how utterly blissful she found her life. I was never entirely sure how much even Louisa believed this – she was very good at burying her head in the sand and refusing to face reality, but even she couldn't escape it forever, and one day, probably quite soon, she'd have to address the many flaws in her apparently idyllic life plan. Like the urgent need to have a wash.

But I was thrilled by Angie's text as well. She and I *had* enjoyed a real connection. I hadn't dreamt it, and I hadn't ruined it. And she *did* want to be friends. Proper friends. Apart from anything else, I relished any opportunity to say 'I told you so' to Simon. I let half an hour pass, so I didn't look totally desperate, and messaged her back.

Ellen: Hi, It's nice to hear from you. I'm sorry you hate your job. I do too. I understand how Louisa/Amaris can draw people in at first. You've had a lucky escape, though. Her cooking tends to undo that initial effect she has on people. I'd like us to be friends too – after all, we're KINDRED SPIRITS!

Friday 2 September

I'd had this day marked on the calendar and been looking forward to it ever since Jane had seen a notice a few weeks ago outside the local church advertising a summer day camp today. I don't usually darken the doors of our local religious establishments, being if not fully atheistic, then certainly firmly in the agnostic camp. I tried to be open-minded with the children, though, and allow them to make up their own minds, as is the wont of good middle-class mummies everywhere, and so I'd gone along with Jane's sudden desire aged five-ish to attend Sunday School.

She'd been quite fervent about it all, insisting every Sunday that she must go, and asking me why Simon and I were not regular worshippers. After about three months of devotion, though, she suddenly announced she wouldn't be going to Sunday School anymore. When questioned why not, she said she'd mainly been going for the biscuits, and they'd stopped doing good biscuits. I felt this was a very valid reason to give up on the possibility of eternal salvation.

She had, however, recently become fascinated by the sort of American films where children are sent off to camp for the summer – oh what bliss. Cunning Americans, why don't we do that here? – and so nothing would do until she went to 'camp', despite my repeated attempts to explain that a day in the church hall wouldn't be quite the same.

I must also confess that earlier in the summer the prospect of FREE CHILDCARE for a day – after the long weeks when I felt as though there would never be another day when I'd awake without truculent demands about 'What are we doing today?' and 'Why can't I have a snack?' or lengthy arguments about whether or not fruit was a snack (I said it most certainly was, the children disagreed) – was a glorious prospect. That was enough for me to convince myself that surely the point of agnosticism was to keep an open mind?

And how could the children keep an open mind and learn how to extrapolate information and form reasoned opinions, if they were not exposed to both sides of an argument? I explained all this to Simon, when I told him I'd signed the children up – Peter slightly against his will – for the church summer camp. It sounded better than saying, 'While I love my children dearly, after several weeks of their unremitting company, I'm fighting the urge to repeatedly smack my head off a brick wall just in an attempt to gain some blissful silence, and this window of joy is currently the only thing stopping me from starting drinking at 8 a.m. for the duration of the holidays, which are going to LAST FOREVER!'

Jane should have been on commission from the Church of England too, because she then talked it up so much to Lucy and The Montagues that they insisted on going too.

Then Gemma, whether out of the kindness of her heart or to satisfy some sort of blackhearted urge for revenge for the church camp, had in turn suggested that the adults should take advantage of the child-free time today to go and enjoy something she referred

to as a 'forest bathing session'. Initially, I'd had visions of a woodland glade, dappled green light, a cool, mysterious pool, smooth,
golden, sun-kissed limbs sliding into silken water, possibly some
dryads and definitely an enchanted picnic afterwards, and I was
quite on board with this. It turned out that this was not what
'forest bathing' involved.

'So we just sit in a wood?' I said, gobsmacked.

'Yes,' said Gemma. 'It's very therapeutic.'

'Why?'

'Well, studies have shown that spending time in nature –'

'I get being outdoors, in nature, etc., are all excellent for the old
mental health, but what I'm not quite getting is the subtle difference between a walk in the woods with a sit-down for a bit to
think "Isn't this nice?" that's completely free, and paying someone
twenty-five quid to walk in the woods and sit down for a bit and
think "Isn't this nice?"?'

Gemma looked annoyed and said, 'Yes, but it's *guided*, Ellen?'

'They're the dogshit-filled woods I walk Judgy in every day.
What do I need a guide for? Apart from possibly to point out
where somebody keeps letting their fucking Newfoundland shit
on the path so we can avoid standing in it, because if you step in
one of those, believe me, you're up to your *knees*! They must need
rubble sacks, not poo bags to pick up after those beasts!'

Gemma blanched slightly at this image and read out the
description on her phone:

Forest bathing is spiritually, physically and emotionally
healing. Your guide, Arwen, will walk with you through
the unmatchable peace of the ancient woodland, the
Wyldewood of legend, inviting you regularly to stop, stand

and listen, and by doing so, connect with your past, present and future through your heightened sensory awareness and connection with the earth and trees.

'The only thing "wylde" in that wood is Ricky the delinquent cockapoo,' I pointed out. 'It's not even an ancient woodland. The council planted it in 1974 and there's a plaque on the gate that says so.'

I couldn't help but think Louisa was missing out on a trick here, as this was exactly the sort of bollocks she loved to spout. She could be making a fortune fleecing the sort of people who need to be told how to go for a walk in the woods.

I regretfully declined the forest bathing, making a polite excuse about needing to put labels in the new uniforms. I felt that saying no to the 'forest' and 'Arwen's' guided tour (of course she was called Arwen, though I suspected she'd no more been christened that than Louisa had been Amaris) was a step towards being more myself. A few weeks ago I'd have felt obliged to go along and pretend I was loving it, just to fit in with Gemma and Fiona. But if we were going to be friends, I couldn't spend my whole life wasting money on things I hated just to make them like me. They'd have to take me as they found me, or not at all. Despite this brave new Ellen, I'd still definitely implied my morning would be spent 'labelling uniforms', by actually sewing in tasteful Cash's name tapes, rather than just scrawling their names in with a Sharpie.

We dropped the children off, and I waved Fiona and Gemma off to the tender mercies of Arwen, suggesting they could pop by for a cup of tea afterwards, and went home to survey the piles of polo shirts and try to locate my trusty Sharpie. I should probably tidy up a bit too, I thought, since I'd rashly invited people round and the house looked like a bomb had hit it. But first a little cup of tea.

I'd just put the kettle on when the doorbell rang. I panicked, as I hadn't expected Gemma and Fiona for ages. Surely they couldn't be adequately bathed yet? I scuttled up the hall, Judgy barking furiously as I flung armfuls of matter into the cupboard under the stairs as I went, and kicked Moshi Monsters and *Pokémon* cards under the hall table, before plastering on my best hostess-with-the-mostest smile and flinging open the door, suddenly hoping as I did so that it wasn't the DPD man, who would think me even more deranged than usual.

To my astonishment and joy, Hannah stood on the doorstep, looking awkward and defiant and somehow apprehensive all at the same time.

'Hannah!' I had no idea what to say, or how to approach the situation. I wanted to fling my arms around her, babble wildly with joy that she was here, drag her in the house and lock the door to keep her safe from the horrible goblin bastard Dan. But equally I was aware that doing so might further inflame the situation, that maybe she was only here to request the return of a book or a dress or something, or, even worse, to tell me to stop sending her random drawings from my nineties ramblings. But why not just message me or block my number in that case?

Hannah bit her lip and swallowed hard.

'Can … er … can I come in?' she asked quietly.

'Of course, you don't have to ask. Come on.' I stood aside to let her through. 'Sorry about the mess.'

Hannah burst into tears. 'Oh God, is this where we're at? I'm now someone you've got to say "Sorry about the mess" to, instead of someone you know doesn't care if your house is messy?'

'No! No! It's just … it's quite messy.'

'It's fine. Your house always looks fine. Oh God, I'm sorry, I don't even know why I'm here after everything I said,' Hannah sniffed.

'Everything *you* said? What about everything I said. Everything you said was right, I deserved it,' I babbled wildly, determined that this time, however brief a window I might have with Hannah, I'd say *all* the things I needed to say, and fast if need be.

'No, you didn't. I was a total bitch. And then I was angry, and when I stopped being angry I didn't know what to say, and then you started ringing me and I still didn't know what to say, and I thought next time you ring I'll have worked it out and answer, and then you stopped ringing –'

'Because Simon said it was stalkery!'

'And then I saw you, and it was so busy, and I was so glad to see you, but then I realised you were with the Yummy Mummies, and I thought, well, she's moved on, and then I saw you again, and then you sent me the farm, I didn't know you remembered the farm, I wish we'd never bothered with stinky boys and we'd just had our farm together.'

Hannah dissolved into sobs. Judgy, as unsympathetic and disgusted as ever by tears, got off the sofa and went and hid in his own bed, lest anyone cry on him or expect him to offer any sort of sympathy.

'I'm sorry,' she wept.

'No, I'm sorry,' I wailed. 'I'm just glad you're here. I'm so happy to see you, Hannah. You're my best friend, you'll always be my best friend. I've missed you so much.'

'I'm so happy to see you too. I've missed you too.'

Eventually we both stopped crying and Hannah said, 'Do you mean it? That we're still best friends?'

'Yes, you know I do. How can you even ask that?'

'Because I need your help. Even though I've no right to ask for it anymore, I really need your help, Ellen. And I feel terrible that this is what's finally brought me round here, but you're the only one I can ask.'

I hugged Hannah as hard as I could, and said, 'You know I'll do anything for you. Always. What do you need me to do? Are we burying a body? Is it Dan's?' (I just managed to stop myself from adding, 'Please let it be Dan's.' Not until I knew for sure what was going on, anyway.)

Hannah burst into tears again, as she gulped, 'You've always been obsessed with burying bodies. No, I don't need your help to bury a body, although it's nice to know you're still willing to help me do that should the need arise. But I've made such a stupid mistake and I don't know how to put it right on my own.'

The doorbell rang again, 'Hang on,' I said, 'it's probably just the DPD man this time,' but it was Fiona and Gemma.

They were both somewhat indignant that their 'Wyldewood Forest Bathing' had indeed been the somewhat dog-shitty munic-ipal experience I'd predicted, and also that despite charging £25 for the privilege, Arwen had only droned on at them for half an hour, then buggered off to let them make their own way out the woods. To add insult to injury, Ricky the Delinquent Cockapoo had appeared and pissed on Fiona's limited-edition Birkenstocks. I made vague noises that I hoped they might interpret as being less than welcoming, but by this stage we'd moved deep into the hall and Fiona was having a panic attack about what you could catch from dog pee before I could say, 'At least it's not cholera.'

Hannah appeared just as I was ushering Fiona into the down-stairs loo with some Dettol and my Asda-finest flip-flops to wear

home, her pissy Birkenstocks now being declared only fit for the
bin.

'Er, you remember Hannah, don't you?' I said. 'Hannah, you've
met Gemma and Fiona before?'

'Yes, of course,' Hannah mumbled. 'I ... I should go.'

'No,' I yelped, 'you can't. You've only just got here.'

'Are you OK?' said Gemma, suddenly noticing amid all
the confusion that we were both rather red-eyed. 'Are we intrud-
ing?'

'No, not at all,' I lied in that stupid British way, but Hannah had
her hand on the door and looked like she was about to disappear
again.

'No!' I cried again, flinging myself against the door to barricade
it and stop her leaving. At that moment Fiona emerged from the
loo into the hall.

'Whatever is going on?' she said.

'I think we should go, Fiona,' said Gemma tactfully.

'Why?' said Fiona, for whom tact is very much a stranger.

'Because I think Ellen and Hannah have something going on ...'
murmured Gemma, nodding towards the door, though leaving
would have been tricky as I was still barring the way.

'What sort of thing?' Fiona demanded bossily. 'Perhaps we can
help? And I really, really need a cup of tea after this morning,
Gemma. It's been awful.'

I was torn. Hannah needed me. But so, it seemed, did Fiona.
Although life with Judgy meant being peed on by a dog was a
fairly routine event in our house, Fiona appeared genuinely shaken
up by it, and it occurred to me that maybe her hygiene issues
around The Montagues ran rather deeper than I'd thought. And
they'd both been so kind to me all summer that I felt terrible

throwing them out, on the one occasion Fiona had admitted any kind of weakness.

'Maybe we could all go and have a cup of tea?' I suggested feebly.

Of course, Fiona and Gemma's idea of 'tea' was more along the lines of oat milk turmeric chai, not Tetley. I rifled through the back of the cupboard for the many packets of herbal tea I'd bought at various points when I'd decided I was becoming a better person. Since I always felt buying them was enough to make me a better person, I'd never felt the need to actually drink them, so there were plenty to choose from, and finally everyone had some form of hot beverage that was vaguely to their liking. This had taken so long that Hannah and Fiona and Gemma were chatting away quite happily, to my relief, as I'd been worried that Hannah would say something about them being the 'Yummy Mummies' that she'd heard so much about from me (not much of it good before this summer, to my shame), or that they would blurt out something I'd told them about my falling out with Hannah.

I was also surprised and delighted that I was glad to see them all getting on, instead of being jealous that Hannah seemed to have fitted in with them so easily or annoyed that they were stealing valuable time with Hannah from me. My God, maybe I *was* becoming a better person. Maybe before you knew it I'd actually drink a cup of this two-years-out-of-date turmeric and ginger tea (I'd hidden the packet from Fiona). And enjoy it!

I sat down and moved the biscuits out of Judgy's reach. Fiona didn't say anything, but she twitched slightly every time he came near her, so I lured him out with promises of cheese and shut him in the kitchen. Another – nicer – dog, I'd have left Fiona to cope with, but Judgy was a master at detecting people's weak spots, and

I couldn't guarantee he wouldn't pee on Fiona purely for his own amusement, which might just tip her over the edge.

'So!' said Fiona, when I was *finally* settled with my own, by now rather cold, cup of tea. 'What *is* going on?'

Hannah sighed.

'I've got myself into a bit of situation,' she admitted.

'Oh dear,' Fiona sympathised. 'Are you in a pickle?'

'You could say that, I suppose. It's … Dan.'

'What's he done?' I demanded. 'Are you quite sure we don't need to bury a body?'

'Ellen!' Gemma looked horrified. 'What's happened, Hannah?'

'Where do I start? Did Ellen tell you about South Africa, and him wanting us to try again?' Hannah asked. Fiona and Gemma nodded.

'Well, it all started nicely. We really did have a great time in South Africa. He was funny, charming, helpful, kind – the man I'd fallen in love with all those years ago. But mostly, it was the kids,' she explained. 'I didn't realise that he'd been working up to this for ages, asking them, "Wouldn't it be nice if Mummy and Daddy lived together again, wouldn't everyone be so happy?"'

'Oh, this is CLASSIC,' exclaimed Fiona. 'There are threads with literally hundreds of pages about men doing this on Mumsnet *and* Reddit!'

'You know what Reddit is?' I said in surprise. Somehow I'd never envisaged Fiona googling anything much beyond 'Mumsnet', 'Boden' and 'Educational Activities Befitting Gifted and Talented Children'.

Fiona just looked at me, then said, 'Go on, Hannah.'

'Well, he convinced them, and then they convinced me, that I needed to at least consider the idea. For their sake, I couldn't dismiss it out of hand. I thought they'd just come up with this plan, seeing us getting on so well in Cape Town, but I now know that he'd been laying the groundwork for months, probably ever since things got rocky with Michelle.'

'Honestly,' snorted Fiona, 'do they run courses for these bastards in how to do this? I *know* you all laugh at my obsession with Mumsnet' – we immediately demurred politely – 'but in between the mad posts about penis beakers and parking, there are a lot of insights into human nature and relationships and how men manipulate women. And a lot of very useful ideas for using up a chicken, of course,' she added randomly.

Hannah nodded miserably. 'Manipulation sounds about right. I can see it now, and I feel so stupid.'

Gemma patted her hand. 'Oh Hannah. It's always easy to see it *afterwards*. So what happened then?'

I felt awful. Fiona and Gemma were handling this so well, saying all the right things, and all I could think of to say was to call Dan names and make insincere threats to murder him.

'He had his trump card too, of course,' Hannah continued. 'He'd been made redundant, Michelle had chucked him out, so how could he see the kids properly if he was reduced to sofa-surfing at his mates'? Did I want them to have the sort of relationship with their dad that consisted of an hour over a Big Mac, fries and a shake on a Saturday afternoon? Of course I didn't. I wanted more for them, what mother wouldn't? I wanted them to have a proper father, and that's what he was finally promising to be.'

'It's *literally* a playbook!' Fiona chuntered. 'It's almost insulting, the lack of imagination they put into it.'

Hannah was crying again now. 'So I agreed to let him stay, on the sofa, until he got back on his feet, and we'd see how things went. But almost immediately he started telling the kids he was back for good, that we were all going to live together again.'

'I honestly can't understand people who use their children like pawns,' Gemma said angrily, and we all nodded our heads. In all our different parenting ways, the one thing we had in common was, for better or for worse, that we all put the children first, we all wanted more than anything for them to have happy lives, to not make the mistakes we'd made. But so many people, like Dan, didn't feel the same.

'And the kids were so happy about that at first. And I was so tired, of doing everything for them myself every day, every night, every teatime, bathtime, bedtime. And he was so adamant he'd changed, that this could be a fresh start.'

'Where *are* the kids?' I asked, suddenly registering their absence.

'I took them over to Mum's. I've arranged for them to stay the night. I needed them not to be here while I went through all this. Because I can't do this, not with him. It's all wrong. So wrong.'

The first red flag had been that, having assured her they would 'take things slow' and that he understood why she needed him to sleep on the sofa for now, Dan was fed up with that and wanted to move back into Hannah's room, Hannah's bed, Hannah herself. He wanted sex, and Hannah most certainly wasn't ready for that.

'It made me feel sick. My stomach turns whenever he touches me and I literally can't stomach the idea of being in bed with him, naked, having sex with him. I can't even bear the thought of it. And then that comment about not getting another job and being a stay-at-home dad. He's not bought so much as a pint of milk since he moved in, and if I ask him to go to the shops for anything he says he can't afford it because he's got to be careful with his redundancy money. But he's not even looking for another job. It wouldn't be so bad if he at least helped round the house, but he just sits around gaming all day and half the night, and if I say anything, he makes snide comments about what else is he supposed to do all night since I make him sleep on the sofa.'

'What an ... an ... absolute *twatbungle*,' Fiona exclaimed. I was unsure what exactly a twatbungle was, but it was clearly a strong term for Fiona. I wondered if I should tell her of my favourite name for Dan, of the useless streak of weasel piss, or if that might be *too* strong for her, even under the circumstances. Hannah wasn't finished yet, though.

'He's not even done a single load of laundry. I asked him to fold and put away some stuff the other day and he made excuses about working on his CV, then he said he didn't see why I couldn't do it, I wasn't working right now either. And then on Wednesday night ...'

On Wednesday night, after the visit to the strawberry farm, which had not been the successful happy family outing it had appeared from our brief encounter by the Portaloos, Dan had been out with his five-a-side football team. Hannah had wanted to come round and see me, after the kids were in bed, so we could talk, properly. But Dan had insisted it was his football night, and he was going out. 'It was the way he just walked out the door, like he'd no responsibilities at all. Like the kids were my problem and nothing to do with him, just like he always had. I realised he hadn't changed, that he had no intention whatsoever of changing, and all the talk of being a stay-at-home dad was just an excuse to sponge off me even more. I'd still be doing everything myself but also supporting him, while he did exactly as he liked!

By now Hannah was sobbing, but she soldiered on. 'And then that night, Emily and Lucas – they never get on, they never do anything together, but they'd obviously been talking about things – they both came to me to ask when Daddy would be going back home.'

'Oh Jesus, no,' I said. 'Oh Hannah!'

All the time I'd been feeling so sorry for myself without Hannah, and meanwhile *she'd* been dealing with all this. On her own. I felt deeply ashamed of myself, and was determined to make it up to her. I couldn't help but think that all of this was largely my fault. If I hadn't overreacted at the start of the summer, if we hadn't had that stupid row, she'd have been able to talk to me about it before things got this far.

Hannah gulped. 'The one thing I thought would make all of this worthwhile, the children's happiness – it didn't exist. He didn't like their noise disturbing him, and expected them to be quiet all day. If I didn't take them out, he plugged them into iPads and headphones. He liked the house tidy, to the point that it didn't look like any children lived there at all, and he shouted at them for leaving anything lying round. He didn't want to eat at 6 p.m., when they had their dinner, but he also didn't want to eat alone, so he insisted I ate later with him. And the worst thing of all? They said, "Daddy being here is making you sad, Mum, and that makes us sad." They told me all the things Dan had said to them about how great it would be if we got back together. I didn't know until then how much pressure he'd put on them, but they just wanted everything to go back to how it was.'

'Wanker!' said Gemma furiously.

'Wow,' I said. 'Hannah, that's really insightful for kids that age.'

'Too insightful,' Hannah said sadly. 'How long must they have been thinking about this for? How miserable must they really have been to have got to this point? All I wanted was the best for them, and I've fucked up massively. And yesterday I tried to discreetly tell him over the course of the whole day that I don't want this, I want him to go. And he just laughed and changed the subject, or told me that this *was* what I wanted, and he's not going anywhere, and then walked away from me, or said I'm being silly, or that I must be hormonal and am I getting my period? Or he went and deliberately sat with the kids, and then said, "What was it you wanted to say to me?" and smirked at me, because he knows we can't possibly have this conversation in front of them.

'So they've gone to Mum's while I try to sort this out. And I thought maybe you could come with me, Ellen, so we're both there when he gets home from the gym this afternoon – he can't afford milk, but he can still afford his gym membership – then I can tell him he needs to pack up all his gear and move out, and you'll be there for moral support if he starts bloody gaslighting me again, and we can just get him to get his stuff and go. Would you do that for me? Please?'

'Hannah, you don't even have to ask!'

'No,' said Fiona, who'd produced a clipboard from thin air. Where? How? 'No, Hannah, I don't think that's the best idea. I wouldn't give him any access to the house at all.' Fiona was now at her firmest and bossiest. 'It sounds like he's determined to be diffi-cult, and as you've discovered, once he's in, it's a bloody nightmare to get him out. You must get your ducks in a row!'

'She's right,' said Gemma. 'My mother didn't get her ducks in a row when she left my father, and it was quite hard for us all for a long while. He didn't behave very well, and Mum really struggled financially.' She shook her head. 'I said I'd never end up in a position like that.'

Somehow I'd never thought of Gemma as having divorced parents – let alone ones who'd had a messy divorce – or her coming from anything than a less than perfect family and upbringing. But it made sense now, why she was so determined to give Lucy the perfect childhood with all the material things she could, and why she stayed with the mysterious and ever-absent Giles.

'But it's *my* house,' Hannah repeated. 'He can't just stay there! It's not like it's the marital home.'

'I'm not saying you *won't* be able to get him out. Just why make things more complicated? That's why Mumsnet always says you must get your ducks in a row. Your ducks are not in a row, Hannah, they are decidedly muddled. Muddled ducks get no one anywhere!'

Hannah gave me a confused look, clearly as baffled by the duck chat as I was, but Fiona was swinging into action.

'Right, come on, let's go. There's a lot to be done. We're going for a clean break here, with no excuses for him to weasel his way into the house and refuse to leave. We need to pack his stuff, get it out, change the locks, and *then* tell him where to go. It'll be much easier with four of us. I'll start by finding an emergency locksmith to come out as quickly as possible.'

'But why?' said Hannah.

'Hannah, if you've made your mind up, as you said, it's your house. If you let him back in, he's going to delay, try to change your mind, ask to stay another night because he's got nowhere to go. Then he'll be there when the kids get back from your mum's, and it all just becomes more difficult. And you need a locksmith in case he's made copies of the keys, and can let himself in and out of *your* home at will.'

'No, I mean why would you help me? It's very kind, and I appreciate it, but why are you going to so much trouble for me, when you barely know me?' Hannah said anxiously.

'Because women need to stick together, Hannah. Especially when it comes to men! And also, because Ellen is our friend, which makes *you* our friend,' Fiona added. That nearly made me cry. I'd somehow gone from feeling entirely alone, to having the sort of friends who probably *would* help me bury a body, as long as one had made a *proper* plan about how to do it and got one's ducks in a row.

'Yes,' said Gemma. 'Fiona's right. One for all and all for one! All hands to the deck. But you don't need a locksmith, Fiona. I can change the locks.'

'You can change locks?' I said, not meaning to sound quite so incredulous.

'I've many hidden talents,' said Gemma. 'I haven't always been Perfect Lucy Atkinson's Perfect Mummy, you know.' Oh God! How did she know we called her that? Did she mind? She seemed to think it was funny, luckily. 'Come on, let's go,' Gemma chivvied us. 'You three go to Hannah's, I'll swing by Screwfix and get some new locks, if you send me photos of what's there. We haven't got much time.'

Fiona and Gemma were brilliant in the end. Fiona's innate bossiness and desire to organise everyone, coupled with Gemma's righteous indignation, turned Hannah's ejection of Dan from her house into a perfectly executed military operation.

None of us had really believed Gemma's claims that she could change a lock, let alone know what to buy from Screwfix – Fiona had googled a locksmith and saved the number as a back-up –

but she astonished us all by screeching up in her Range Rover fifteen minutes after Hannah had sent her photos of the locks, with not only all the right parts, but also the right tools to fit them with.

'It was quicker than going home and getting mine,' she said airily. 'And anyway, I put it all on Giles's Amex, so fuck it!'

While Gemma got on with the locks (she'd been surprisingly evasive about how she'd learned this hidden skill, simply saying, 'Ask me no questions, and I'll tell you no lies'), Fiona dispensed black bin bags and the rest of us got on with packing up Dan's stuff.

Hannah had said he didn't have that much with him – all the furniture, etc., that he'd insisted on taking in the divorce having been put into storage, because Michelle already had a fully furnished flat (proving he'd just taken it out of spite, forcing Hannah to buy replacements) – but it was surprising how long it took to make sure that every pair of socks was out the laundry basket, every game ejected from the PS4 and every last tedious biography of Internet billionaires packed up, so he would have no excuse to ever cross the threshold again.

We'd never have done it in time without the extra help, and as it was, we'd just piled everything in the outside porch, locked Gemma's splendid new locks and were sitting down for a well-deserved cup of tea when we heard a furious banging on the door.

'HANNAH!' Dan roared. 'Hannah, what the fuck do you think you're doing? Hannah, OPEN THIS DOOR NOW!'

Hannah looked round at us all, and we nodded encouragingly. I gave her hand a squeeze.

'Come with me, Ellen?' she asked hopefully.

'Always.'

The encounter with Dan went as well as you might have expected. But Hannah and I were together, and together we could do anything and no one was a match for us. Certainly not Weasel Piss Dan.

'Why aren't my keys working and what are all these bags doing here?' he demanded.

'I've packed up your stuff and changed the locks,' Hannah said calmly.

'What the FUCK, Hannah?' he yelled.

Hannah clutched my hand, and took a deep breath. 'Dan, I don't want this. I need you to go. You rushed me into this, and I think you need to find somewhere else to live. Now. This isn't working.'

Hannah and I stood shoulder to shoulder, my arm around her when she needed it, just holding her hand when she didn't, as Dan cycled through disbelief, anger, pleading, threats, insults, abuse and emotional blackmail. No doubt he had far more in his repertoire that he'd have hit us with as Hannah sobbed at him to please just leave, and I reiterated what she'd just said, and tried very, very hard not to descend to his level when he called us things like 'evil fucking witches', 'a pair of spiteful old hags', 'probably fucking dykes anyway, because what man would want the pair of you', and various other charming names.

But Fiona and Gemma eventually had had enough. They marched into the hallway, and Fiona drew herself up to her full height of five foot six and three-quarters. I was surprised when she told me afterwards that was how tall she was, because she'd certainly LOOMED in a very impressive fashion. Having been on the receiving end of Fiona's Looming Trick when I'd committed crimes like failing to volunteer fast enough for the PTA Coffee Morning, I was excited to see it deployed on someone else.

'You've been asked to leave the premises several times now!' thundered Fiona. 'If you don't immediately take your possessions and go, I'll be calling the police on 999 to report your threatening and disturbing behaviour. As it is, I must inform you I'll be calling them anyway on 101 to log the incident.'

'Who the fuck are you?' demanded Dan.

'I … am FIONA MONTAGUE!' declared Fiona, with the indignant air of the Queen of England forced to identify herself to some disgusting peasant type. She did look slightly disappointed that Dan had not shrunk back in terror at learning whom he'd crossed.

'And I,' announced Gemma, appearing behind Fiona, her impeccable blonde blow-dry and icy blue eyes suddenly giving her the appearance more of a Valkyrie than the yummiest mummy in the playground, 'am Gemma Atkinson. My husband is Giles Atkinson, of Atkinson Solutions Ltd. Now, first, if you don't leave immediately, I have a very good lawyer, with his number cued up and ready to go, and in three minutes he'll have started the process of getting a restraining order on you. And second, you're some sort of unemployed web designer, yes? Well, my husband knows a *lot* of people, in a *lot* of industries, and one word from him, and the only work you'll be able to get is designing websites for the sort of businesses that still consider Comic Sans to be a professional-looking font!'

I wasn't sure which impressed me more: Fiona's unshakable confidence that people would do as she told them, or the fact that Gemma, who famously claimed she couldn't work a computer apart from internet shopping, even knew what Comic Sans was!

Dan wasn't giving up yet, though.

'This is *my* home,' he blustered. 'I live here with *my* children. You can't turn me out in the street, I have *rights*.'

'No, you don't,' Fiona snapped. 'You're divorced from Hannah. You've been here for less than a month. Just because out of the kindness of her heart, Hannah let you stay on the sofa for a few weeks while you found somewhere to live, doesn't give you any rights over this house. And I've been recording this whole conversation, by the way, including the disgusting sexist and homophobic comments you made to Hannah and Ellen. I'm quite happy to send it to anyone who may be interested. I might post it on Twitter.'

Nice one, Fiona. Why hadn't we thought to record him? And she was on Twitter as well? Where did she find the time for all the educational activities while enjoying such an extensive and secret internet life?

Dan had one last try. 'Hannah,' he whined, 'you can't do this to me. If you don't want to be with me, fair enough. I understand. Maybe I did push it too fast, and you're feeling rushed and a bit spooked. I get it, babes, and it's OK.'

'But it's not OK,' shouted Hannah. 'It's not. I want you to GO, so just GO!'

'Babes …' That wheedling tone again.

'Seriously, Dan,' I put in, having had quite enough of this, 'will you listen to Hannah for once and just FUCK OFF!' I'd been wanting to say that for years.

'You!' he turned on me. 'You did this. I knew she would, I knew she would poison you and turn you against me and ruin our family, because she's jealous!'

'Ellen is the best friend I'll ever have, that anyone could ever have,' Hannah said protectively (and I glowed. I hadn't truly believed until that moment that Hannah had forgiven me). 'She's not trying to ruin anything. *You* ruined our family when you FUCKED OFF with FUCKING MICHELLE. Did you even want *me* back, or did you just want somewhere free to live, and someone to cook your dinners and wash your socks? And you didn't care what damage your selfish behaviour caused to the kids or me in the meantime as long you were all right, Jack?'

'Me? *My* selfish behaviour damaging the kids? You're the one throwing their father out on the streets.'

'I'd have never had you back in the first place if you hadn't emotionally blackmailed me into it,' Hannah cried. 'I certainly wouldn't have let you move in, and it was you telling the kids we were a family and you were here to stay, not me! You didn't give a flying fuck what I wanted, so now I don't see why I should give a fuck about you!'

'Go Hannah!' I shouted. I couldn't believe how well she was doing, standing up to the streak of weasel piss like this.

'But I'm their father.'

'And you can still see them, as per the terms of our custody agreement,' said Hannah coldly.

'Hello, 101, I'd like to log an incident,' said Fiona loudly in the background.

'Julius? Darling, it's Gemma Atkinson,' purred Gemma, also rather louder than was necessary for a normal phone call. 'A chum's having a spot of bother with an ex, and I wondered if you could do a rush on a restraining order. Giles and I would consider it a *personal favour.*'

'Go. Now,' said Hannah and I in unison.

'But where? What am I to do?'

'Quite frankly, my dear, I don't GIVE A FUCK!' Hannah yelled, and slammed the door in his face.

Five minutes later, we saw him attempting to cram the bin bags into his car and then reversing down the driveway with a thunderous expression.

'Where do you think he'll go?' I asked her.

'His mother's, I expect. All that fuss about being thrown out on the street, but his mother will be waiting to welcome her darling boy with open arms. She changes the bed in his old room every week, has done since we got married, so it's fresh for her special soldier in the case of such an eventuality. Did you notice through all that, that he never once asked where the kids were or how they are? Prick.'

'Are you OK?' I asked her.

Hannah nodded. 'Yeah. Better for you all being here. Thank you.'

'I don't think you should be on your own tonight. Come and stay at mine.'

'Thanks, I'd like that.'

'Well,' Fiona beamed at us all in satisfaction. 'I think we can call that one in the eye for the fudging patriarchy! I shall be reiterating to Mumsnet tonight the importance of getting those ducks in a row!'

Alas, poor Fiona, the smugness was immediately wiped off her face when her phone beeped with a reminder.

'Oh good lord! It's half past two! We're going to be late to collect them from the church hall!'

Panic ensued, as Fiona and Gemma had never been late for a pick-up before, and they were anxious about the psychological scars it might cause Lucy and The Montagues. Jane and Peter, to my shame, were rather more accustomed to the fun game of 'late or abandoned', and so far seemed unscarred by it, though I was always wracked with guilt about the staff and/or volunteers if I was a few minutes late. It turned out that Fiona and Gemma's idea of being late wasn't to be there waiting twenty minutes before the children came out anyway, so they beetled off while I stayed to say goodbye to Hannah.

'Actually,' I said, 'I have a very good idea. Why don't you go and get the children from your mum's and bring them over tonight too? Peter and Jane would adore to see them.'

'Are you sure? They'd adore that.'

'Yes! In fact, bring your mother too, I haven't seen her in ages.'

When I picked up the kids, it seemed rude not to ask Fiona and Gemma and Lucy and The Montagues too, after they'd been so helpful today, with the result that Simon was rather nonplussed to come home from work to find five drunk women – Hannah's mum did come along, declaring she could easily get a taxi home, and even Fiona had let her hair down and knocked back four glasses of pink sunshine wine, so I was starting to fear a repeat of the 'Patricia the Stripper' routine she'd done at our New Year party a couple of years ago, which we'd all been forbidden to mention ever again – and eight children rampaging around his garden.

I'd decided to try a barbecue, as I thought that might traumatise Fiona and Gemma less than the alternative of processed pizza or beige freezer food, but Simon was incensed that a mere woman should be trying to take over the Manly Man's task of Burning Raw Meat and ordered me to stand aside, which actually suited me fine, as it gave me greater leeway to get pissed. He attempted to co-op me into helping by doing his usual thing of barking at me to get things out of the fridge and put other things in the oven, because he had to Guard the Fire, for he was the Manliest of Men and the fire couldn't manage without him, but I explained that we were having an important debrief and he'd have to do it himself. Strangely, the barbecue didn't instantly turn to ashes when he stepped more than two feet away from it, as he'd always claimed it would. He couldn't even ask me to fetch another beer, as I'd volunteered him to take Mrs P, Hannah's mum, home.

'Ha ha ha, another blow struck against the patriarchy,' I cackled to the other women. 'He's always made me run back and forth like his barbecue bitch, and then he takes all the credit, but no more! Maybe next time I'll do the barbecuing myself! How hard can it be? Oh look, look, my friend Angie has sent me a ver' funny meme, look, 'bout the bastarding patriarchy!'

'Down with the patriarchy!' roared Fiona.

'Fuck 'em!' cried Gemma.

'Mummy!' said Lucy Atkinson in shock.

Much later, when it had been established that all the children would be staying and Fiona hadn't enquired about what I'd say to social services in the event of a medical emergency, and after they were all asleep, and Fiona and Gemma had gone home, even more pissed because they'd mainly just toyed with salad so were basically drinking on empty stomachs, and Simon was driving Mrs P home, there was just Hannah and me left in the garden, attempting to light a couple of cigarettes from the remains of a very old and stale packet I'd found, using only the barbecue as I couldn't find any matches.

'I wish I'd talked to you sooner,' said Hannah.

'It was my fault,' I said.

'No, it was both our faults. I can't believe I was so stupid.'

'You were just trying to do your best for your children.'

'Do you think they'll be OK?'

'They've got an arsehole father, but an amazing mum who'd do anything for them. I think that counts for an awful lot, and I know they'll be fine.'

'Oh God, what would I do without you? Do you know what made me saddest? That I'd have to go my whole life without ever meeting you at the airport again.'

I laughed. 'I remember how shocked Simon was when you left that message telling me to meet you at the airport, and he thought I was flying off somewhere and hadn't told him. He was furious.'

I hadn't been meeting Hannah at the airport, of course. When we said airport, we actually meant the train station. This private joke had started years ago, when our local station had put in a snazzy travelator like in airports – although more often than not it didn't work – and somehow the joke had developed over the years to mean all train stations. It was such a little thing, but Hannah was right, the thought of spending the rest of my life with no one else understanding about the airport thing was a sobering thought that hadn't occurred to me until then.

'I want us to promise each other something,' Hannah said.

'Anything. I'll promise you anything, as long as we can grow old together meeting each other at the airport!'

'OK. We must promise that we'll never, ever let anyone come between us again. Especially a man. And that whatever we do, we'll always have each other's back, and also, we'll always trust that we only ever have each other's best interests at heart. And that we'll never fall out again. Do you swear?'

'I swear.'

'On Judgy's life?'

'On the life of Judgy and any other dogs I may ever have in the future,' I promised her most solemnly.

'I swear too. And I swear that I'll always be your best friend too, no matter what.'

We had a very drunken hug, and then Hannah said, 'Not that there's much chance of anyone coming between us on my side. Charlie was the best thing that ever happened to me, relation-ship-wise, and I let Dan wreck it. He's cost me so much, I'm just glad I still have you after all this.'

'I'm not that easy to get rid of. And you'll meet someone else. Maybe even someone better than Charlie.'

Hannah shook her head sadly. 'I don't think there's anyone better. He was one of the really good ones. The best one, in fact, and I don't want anyone else. I really loved him, but I didn't realise how much till Dan had convinced me to finish it with him.'

'You could phone him, ask to meet, explain? If he loves you too …?'

'I wouldn't want to see me again if I was him. I should just leave him alone to get on with his life and accept that I'll spend the rest of my life by myself. And when the children leave me and I'm old and grey, I'll come and live in your basement.'

'I haven't got a basement.'

'Well, you better build one then, so we can grow old together.'

'That doesn't sound so bad. But seriously, Hannah. Call him. Text him. Do something. Just be honest with him. Honesty is important.'

'What's happened to you, and what have you done with Ellen?' said Hannah suspiciously.

'I've learned a lot this summer. I'm going to make an app to help people discover their personal style.'

'How?'

'With a computer.'

'Ha ha! I mean, how will you find their style? You're not a stylist.'

'There's bound to be an algorithm or something for style,' I said airily. 'I'll work it out. And then we'll buy a farm, and when we're old and grey you won't have to live in the basement. We'll live together with the dogs and the ducks and the horses!'

Saturday 3 September

I was a little bit broken today, but to my astonishment, Simon was a great deal less censorious than he usually was about my occasional bouts of being 'tired and emotional'.

'Now listen, darling,' he said generously when he came in from his shed. 'Don't worry about doing anything too fancy for dinner. Just keep it really simple. Why don't you do something nice and easy like a lasagne or something?'

Twenty minutes later, I'd finished explaining to Simon for the eleventy fucking billionth time why A LASAGNE ISN'T NICE AND SIMPLE, and exactly where he could insert his bastarding Kango hammer if he ever suggested that it was again.

'Or,' said Simon nervously, 'I've had a better idea. Why don't *I* make the lasagne, and you could see if Hannah and Sam are free for a quick drink?'

'They won't have babysitters.'

'They might. Ask!'

Serendipitously, although Hannah was staying over at her mum's, Sam's parents were visiting him, and they thought a quick trip to the pub was just what he needed. Alas, it turned out to not be that quick a trip, partly because Sam and I came up with a very good idea for Hannah, which had required the sending of many texts, followed by some shots to celebrate when we got the reply to our texts we'd hoped for. When I finally staggered in the door many hours later, I found Simon lying on the sofa looking traumatised. We both surveyed the wreckage of my kitchen in dismay.

'So how was making a nice, simple lasagne?'

'Piece of piss,' he insisted. 'Have you been doing shots?'

'Only a ver' little Tequila Rose,' I said happily. 'Jus' to, you know, celebrate me and Hannah being friends! An' Sam. An' the goats.'

'What goats? Ellen? Did you buy a goat from a man in the pub? I was going to say it's nice to see you back to being yourself, but not if you're going to start buying goats!'

'No goats. But I might have sent a lil' text to Charlie!'

'Hannah's Charlie?'

'Mmmhhmmm,' I nodded happily. 'Aren't I clever? Maybe I'll make a dating app. Oh fuck, Simon. I've not told anyone about this, I've been trying not think about it, but Sally has been talking to me about taking voluntary redundancy. She thinks I can do better than I am now. But I can't tell anybody because nobody knows it's on the cards and she shouldn't have said anything. What should I do?'

'You never mentioned that when I asked you how the Return to Work interview went? I've been telling you for years you were wasted there.'

'So you think I should do it? I got some very good ideas for dating apps and style apps an' ... an' a PHILIOSHOPHY app. Yeah! Imma gonna do it!'

'Do you mean philosophy? I think you should be a grown-up and make an informed, adult decision, based on what you want and need, not what other people think. And you should probably make that decision when you're sober.'

'Fuck, that's boring. Shall we have some shots? I gotta bottle Kahlua somewhere!'

Monday 5 September

Well. Here we are, the last day of the holidays. Once again, it hasn't been quite the Best Summer Ever that we'd hoped for, full of japes and frolics. But hopefully there were some Happy Memories made, and we're all still here, and we're all still talking to each other. Well, all except Weasel Piss Dan, obviously, who's still licking his wounds at his mother's house, but fuck him. It's his loss if he decides to revert to his previous levels of contact with the children, which means either not bothering to arrange to see them at all or cancelling at the last moment. Hopefully, Hannah and I can make up for him, and Emily and Lucas won't notice too much, though we're all sad for them that their father is such a dick and is missing out on so many wonderful experiences with them.

I didn't initially think today would be classed as one of those wonderful experiences, though it seems I may be wrong. We decided that obviously we had to mark the end of the holidays in some suitable way, and what better way than one final day of japes and frolics? Sam took the day off as well, and after the summer we'd just had, Hannah and I persuaded him it would be rude not to invite Fiona and Gemma along too.

Fiona, obviously, took over managing the arrangements at once, declaring there was a castle nearby holding a jousting day and why we didn't we go to that? Despite the complaints from various children that castles were 'boring' and 'lame', and from one child who shall remain nameless (Jane) that they'd been 'overcastled' last summer and never wanted to go to a castle again, we prevailed. I had visions of dashing knights with pennants flying and palely elegant ladies tossing their favours to them, and a romantically ruined castle, with secret passages and forgotten rooms where star-crossed lovers had once pined.

Simon asked me at breakfast what I was thinking about. I fear he knows me too well, because when I looked guilty and said, 'Nothing', he said, 'You're thinking about what would happen if you sustained some sort of accident, possibly involving a light blow to the head and lost consciousness, and when you woke up you'd travelled back through time and were at a real joust, and some dashing knight fell in love with you but it wasn't cheating if you bonk some handsome bloke who died before I was even born, weren't you?'

'No,' I said, blushing.

'You've read *Outlander* too many times,' he said. 'Also, I suspect you're hoping that a spot of time travel would mean you didn't have to go back to work tomorrow. Bit extreme, darling, no?'

'I don't know what you're talking about,' I protested, as he kissed me goodbye and I set about the lengthy business of persuading my children that they did in fact own shoes, and they did know where they were, and what was more they knew how to put them on too, so just get the bloody hell on with it. I was also trying not to think that tomorrow I'd have to get them both out the door by 8.30 a.m., dressed and shod and teeth brushed, with book bags and packed lunches and PE kits sorted, as well as getting myself out and leaving the house in a fit state so that the nice dog walker didn't judge me when she came to let Judgy out at lunchtime. Maybe the summer holidays weren't so bad, I reflected.

I suspect Fiona disagreed, as prolonged exposure to Jane and Peter seemed to have rubbed off on The Montagues. When we all finally sallied forth to the castle, they rejected their mother's quiz sheet on medieval architecture out of hand, and also seemed strangely unenthusiastic at her suggestion of the famous scavenger hunt with the much-vaunted courgette and quinoa cupcake prizes. Ottilie demanded a Twix, and Miles and Cosmo were found with Peter peering down a chute, loudly wondering if the discoloured streaks inside were antiquated poo.

'At least they're taking an interest in history?' I offered, trying to cheer her up.

There was also a minor kerfuffle when Lucy Atkinson pushed Jane down the steps into a dungeon on account of Jane claiming that Lucy would have been imprisoned there as a witch in the olden days. Jane was unhurt, as she was fairly used to being pushed off things by Peter, though Gemma was mortified. Hannah and I secretly agreed it was nice to see Lucy having a bit of gumption and occasionally being less than perfect.

The jousting was quite marvellous, though, and everything I'd hoped for, minus the blow to the head and the time travel, obviously. Even the children watched entranced and were actually heard to declare it was 'really cool' as we walked away.

Hannah's phone pinged as we headed off towards the exit, routed inevitably through the gift shop. She stopped to read it as I went on after the children.

'Oh!'

I heard a gasp from behind me and whirled round to find Hannah staring at her phone, her eyes suddenly bright and her cheeks flushed.

'Ellen,' she held out her phone to me. 'Ellen, read that and tell me it says what I think it says, and I didn't get concussed at the jousting and am hallucinating?'

> Charlie: Hi. I miss you. I wondered if you'd like to go for a drink sometime? Maybe Friday, if you can get a babysitter?

'Oh my GOD! Hannah!'

'It's real, then? He's really asking me for a drink? He said he missed me? I didn't imagine it?' Hannah asked anxiously.

'No, no, it's real. Don't leave him on read. Quick, answer!'

'I'll need to call Mum, see if she can babysit?'

'Just say yes. If she can't, I'll babysit. JUST SAY YES!'

'OK, OK. I can't believe this. I'm so happy. How do you think he heard about Dan?'

I shrugged and tried to look innocent, but I was thrilled my and Sam's drunken gamble with a round of text roulette had paid off. I felt like I was finally making some amends to Hannah, and hopefully, between us, we could get her life back on track.

'It was you, wasn't it?'

'Maybe?'

'Thank you. I love you.'

'If Simon dies before me, can I come and live in the basement with you and Charlie?'

'Of course. Unless we're all living on your farm by then.'

＊　　＊　　＊

'How's your personal style app going?' Hannah asked me outside the gift shop.

'I'm still sort of planning it,' I said vaguely.

'So you're going back to Cunningham?'

'I don't know what to do. There's a possibility of voluntary redundancy. I thought I'd decided to leave when I was pissed the other night, but in the cold light of day I'm just not sure.'

'But this could be such a great chance for you,' said Hannah. 'You hate it there, and although I think you feel both too safe and too scared to leave, it could be exactly what you need.'

'But what will I do?' I said hopelessly. 'It's all very well making noises about style apps and stuff, but what will I actually do?'

'This is your chance to find out. You'll think of something, I've got faith in you,' Hannah said, squeezing my hand. 'And even if things don't go according to plan, you'll make it work. You always do, you know you do.'

Maybe, I thought, I could do this. Hannah believed in me; Hannah had always believed in me. Even in our worst moments she'd trusted me to help her fix things. I'd always envied people like Fiona who appeared to have such effortless self-belief, but maybe what they really had was people who believed in them? And yet so did I. Not only Hannah – there were lots of other people who weren't even kindred spirits but still believed in me.

We entered the gift shop to discover something of an impasse. The children, inspired by the jousting demonstration, were clamouring to be allowed the plastic swords and lances the gift shop sold for ridiculously overinflated prices.

Sam, not realising his faux pas, had bought Sophie and Toby each a lance and a sword, which had added fuel to the furious argument now going on between Fiona and The Montagues, and Gemma and Lucy.

'But we're a weapon-free household. Not to mention the plastic nightmare!' implored Fiona in the face of The Montagues arguing that they just wanted a souvenir of an interesting historical day because they were so very interested in history. In vain did Fiona offer trips to both the Tower of London and the Royal Armouries in Leeds to see lots of *real* weapons.

'We just want a souvenir of the history,' Miles insisted.

'Do you want to spoil history for us, Mummy?' asked Ottilie sorrowfully.

'How can I compare the modern idea of a lance with a real one if you won't buy me one, Mummy?' Cosmo demanded.

Lucy was equally adamant that she wanted a sword, despite Gemma's suggestions of something nicer, like this lovely dolly in a Tudor dress or even this bar of chocolate that cost £9.99 because it had a bad artist's impression of Anne Boleyn on the wrapper. But Lucy too stood firm.

'But why do you want a sword, darling?' asked Gemma.

'To slay the patriarchy,' said Lucy.

Our own cherubs merely brandished their arsenal at us and made menacing noises until we gave in.

Outside the gift shop we wandered onto the lush greensward in front of the castle, where ladies in wimples would once have strolled, casting saucy glances at strapping knights at arms, or perhaps waiting for a herald or messenger to bring news of their love from afar. Fiona crushingly informed me, however, that it was probably where the bakeries and piggeries and blacksmiths and other mundanities of castle life were situated.

And then, on some secret and clearly prearranged signal, all hell broke loose among the children, as they suddenly waged a battle with the weaponry they'd wrung from us with various blandishments, promises and threats.

Lucy charged at Toby with a bloodcurdling roar, and as Gemma gave out a scream of dismay, we realised Lucy had pinched Gemma's Dior lipstick from her bag and daubed it over her face as war paint. All the girls, in fact, were similarly adorned, and as far as we could make out the battle was boys vs girls, so perhaps Lucy had been the only one telling the truth when she said her sword was for slaying the patriarchy, though we hadn't realised she meant she was going to do so by *actually* slaying our sons as a pre-emptive strike, before they'd even had a chance to join the patriarchy.

'What do we do?' wailed Gemma above the war cries.

My newfound belief that I could do anything if I put my mind to it was almost immediately proved wrong, because I was completely unable to break up this almost cartoonish fight scene.

'I'll sort it out!' shouted Fiona, as she waded into the fray with firm commands to 'Stop this now. That's enough. This isn't how The Montagues behave! OW!'

Fiona received a lance blow to the shin and withdrew from the fray. This made me feel slightly better. After all, if Fiona couldn't deal with The Montagues, what hope did mere mortal parents have?

'This is terrible,' she moaned, 'worse even than the day Ottilie only got a merit for her Grade 4 piano. How do we stop them?'

'I don't think we can,' I said. 'At least I've never found a way when they become like this. Hannah, Sam, any suggestions?'

'Nope,' said Sam. 'Ellen's right, the bloodlust is up. We'll just have to let them fight it out.'

'But what if they get hurt?' whimpered Gemma.

'Someone could lose an eye,' Fiona said. 'How will I explain that to Social Services? Or Hugo?'

'No one's ever got hurt before,' I consoled them. 'Well, not really hurt. Not Social Services hurt.'

'Do they do this a lot then?' quavered Gemma.

'Not for a while, actually,' I said cheerfully. 'I sort of forgot this was why we stopped taking them to castles. Oh fuck!'

'What? What's happened?' implored Gemma. 'I can't even tell who's who in that scrum. Is Lucy OK?'

'It's those Germans again,' I groaned.

'What Germans? Where? Oh God, no. The ones from the beach. What are *they* doing here? What must they think? They'll go back to Germany and tell everyone British children are savages and we'll never be allowed back in the EU,' mourned Fiona.

Sure enough, as luck would have it, the same party of Germans who seemed to appear whenever my precious moppets were at their worst, were now standing watching the children fighting, inscrutable looks on their faces, occasionally pointing to the children and muttering among themselves. After another five minutes or so of battering the ever-lasting fuck out of each other, the children started to run out of steam, and the Germans lost interest and started walking up to the castle. One of the older women broke off from the group and came towards us.

'Oh God,' said Fiona, 'she's coming over. Why can't I speak German? Why didn't we concentrate on languages these holidays? What should I say? How can I explain this isn't normal behaviour for The Montagues?'

The German lady broke into a smile as she got closer. Was it a trap? Was she lulling us into a false sense of security? Maybe they'd been running a book on the children and she'd won, and was now coming to thank us? Or maybe she'd bet the farm and was left penniless and was coming to chastise us? But surely she wouldn't be smiling then?

'Hallo,' she beamed, 'I just wanted to come and say to you, my friends and I, we have seen you this summer a few times, yes?'

We shuffled our feet and made noncommittal noises.

'I think, yes? We saw you at the beach, and we saw you and you,' she pointed at Hannah and me, 'in the forest, ja?'

'Maybe …' I muttered.

'Ja, we did,' she said firmly. 'And I wanted just to say to you, we were talking about how much we are enjoying seeing you all out with your children, having fun. The children are obviously very happy, and we are thinking you are good mothers. And I remember, it is hard sometimes, being a mother. Everyone tells you if they think you are doing a bad job, but no one ever tells you if they think you are doing a good job. So I am telling you, you are doing a good job. You are good mothers. And you,' she nodded to Sam, 'you are a good father. Well done. They are going to have happy memories of days like these.'

'Thank you so much,' said Fiona graciously. 'I do try to create happy memories for the children, although I'm not sure this will be one.' She shuddered as Cosmo shouted something unrepeatable at Miles. 'I also take them to museums,' she added desperately to the nice German lady, 'and stately homes. Last summer we went to see the *Mary Rose* and built a scale model replica!'

The lady looked slightly perplexed by Fiona recounting her various parenting triumphs. She nodded kindly, though, and smiled at us all again. 'Just remember, we can make happy memories every day,' she said. 'Not just in the vacation. Not just on the special days. Happy memories can be in the small things too.' And she turned around and trotted after her friends, leaving a stunned silence behind her.

I finally managed to recover myself to shout after her one of the few German words I know.

'*Danke*,' I called. '*Danke* … errr very much!' She waved a hand behind her in acknowledgement.

In the small things. Like a drawing of an impossible farm. A mint Viennetta cancelling out someone's hurtful words. A stupid song. The airport. A squeeze of a hand and an 'I believe in you' when you need them most. The joy in the moments you were least expecting. The memories that were made without you even realising. All these little things that you couldn't force, that you couldn't plan for, that just *happened*, that added up to an unbreakable friendship and a shared past that would last forever.

The children all came rushing up at that point, flushed and glowing, filthy and sweaty, but all of them laughing and grinning.

'That was *brilliant*,' said Lucy, the sweat making no tracks at all in the Dior lipstick, though I'm not sure that was the sort of testimonial to its staying power the fashion house would have wanted.

'Yeah,' said Jane. 'This has been a really good summer, Mum. Thank you. I've had a lot of fun.'

'Do you think,' I asked the children, as we walked back to the car, hardly daring to imagine the answer, 'do you think, darlings, you've made some happy memories this summer?'

The children thought for a minute.

'Yes,' said Jane. 'Yes, I have. This might have been the best summer ever.'

'Same as her,' agreed Peter. 'Happy memories, Mum. Loads of happy memories.'

'Really?' I said in astonishment. 'What was your best memory of this summer?'

'Ummm, the day you let us watch *SpongeBob* all day.'

'The time we had ice cream for dinner.'

Their best memories were obviously going to be about the two things I'd hoped they'd never mention publicly. But, I reminded myself, it's about the little things.

'And will you at least treasure those memories for ever?' I asked hopefully.

'Why?'

THE END

Acknowledgements

As always, there are so many people who deserve the most heart-felt thanks for making this book happen, but chief among them is my wonderful editor Katya Shipster, who always knows when to provide cocktails, strong tea and dogs, as well as the best editorial advice. The book would not be what it is, or even legible either, without the skill and wisdom of Jenny Hutton and Mark Bolland, who have the tricky jobs of reining in both Louisa's wilder flights of fancy, and my ongoing and seemingly incurable addiction to exclamation marks! Sarah Hammond has perhaps the hardest job of all – trying to plan publishing schedules and get authors to stick to them. The hugest of huge thanks to all of you, for everything. The wider team at HarperCollins also always do such a brilliant job, including Tom Dunstan and his amazing sales team, Hetty Touquet, my lovely publicist, and Claire Ward – thank you all so much. And a special thank you to Tom Gauld, for creating yet another stunning and perfect cover.

My wonderful agent Paul Baker, another person who also understands the importance of applying cocktails and dogs at strategic moments to stressed authors – thank you.

To all my divine friends and family, you know who you are, and thank you for putting up with me. But especial thanks are due to

Erica Morton, for her ability not only to see the funny side of everything, but also for giving me permission to use one of her mishaps in this book, and to Victoria Judge, for being my partner in crime the night we abandoned the freshers in Whistle Binkies (also, if anyone reading this was a fresher at Edinburgh University in 1997 and you found yourself abandoned in Whistle Binkies by two mad and very drunk fourth-year girls, please accept my apologies for that). And most of all, thank you to Katie, for being my Hannah.

Finally, of course, no book would be complete without acknowledging my undying gratitude to Buddy and Billy, the Proud and Noble Border terriers, who helped not one little bit, but still expect everything to be all about them!